Marius' Mules II:
The Belgae

by S. J. A. Turney

2nd Edition

"Marius' Mules: nickname acquired by the legions after the general Marius made it standard practice for the soldier to carry all of his kit about his person."

For my parents Tony & Jenny, who have supported my family and I through good times and bad with grace and kindness.

Also for Rupert and Charlene, best of friends and Godparents extraordinaire to our son Marcus.

I would like to thank those people instrumental in bringing Marius' Mules 2 to fruition and making it the success it has been, and those who have contributed to the production of the Second Edition, in particular Leni, Jules, Barry, Robin, Kate, Alun, Nick, two Daves, a Garry and a Paul. Also a special thanks to Ben Kane and Anthony Riches, who have greatly encouraged me towards the improvements in this edition.

Cover photos courtesy of Paul and Garry of the Deva Victrix Legio XX. Visit http://www.romantoursuk.com/ to see their excellent work.

Cover design by Dave Slaney.

Many thanks to all three for their skill and generosity.

Published in this format 2013 by Victrix Books

Second Edition

Also by S. J. A. Turney:

Continuing the Marius' Mules Series

Marius Mules I: The Invasion of Gaul (2009)
Marius Mules III: Gallia Invicta (2011)
Marius Mules IV: Conspiracy of Eagles (2012)
Marius Mules V: Hades Gate (2013)

The Ottoman Cycle

The Thief's Tale (2013)
The Priest's Tale (due Autumn 2013)

Tales of the Empire

Interregnum (2009)
Ironroot (2010)
Dark Empress (2011)

Short story compilations & contributions:

Tales of Ancient Rome vol. 1 - S.J.A. Turney (2011)
Tortured Hearts vol 1 - Various (2012)
Tortured Hearts vol 2 - Various (2012)
Temporal Tales - Various (2013)

For more information visit http://www.sjaturney.co.uk/
or http://www.facebook.com/SJATurney
or follow Simon on Twitter @SJATurney

Dramatis personae (list of principal characters)

The Staff:

Gaius Julius Caesar: Politician, general, governor of two provinces and conqueror of Gaul.
Aulus Ingenuus: Commander of Caesar's Praetorian Cohort.
Cita: Chief quartermaster of the army.
Decimus Brutus: Staff officer and favourite of Caesar's family.
Gaius Valerius Procillus: Staff officer and ambassador for Caesar.
Marcus Mettius: Staff officer and ambassador for Caesar.
Paetus: Camp Prefect, in command of all temporary camp functions.
Pedius: Staff Officer.
Plancus: Staff Officer.
Quintus Atius Varus: Commander of the Cavalry.
Quintus Titurius Sabinus: Senior staff officer and lieutenant of Caesar.
Quintus Tullius Cicero: Staff officer and brother of the great orator.
Titus Atius Labienus: Senior staff officer and lieutenant of Caesar.

Seventh Legion:

Crassus: Commander of the Seventh and high ranking statesman.

Eighth Legion:

Quintus Balbus: Ageing commander of the Eighth Legion.
Titus Balventius: Chief centurion of the Eighth Legion, veteran having served several terms of service.
Titus Decius Quadratus: Prefect of one of the Eighth's auxiliary detachments.
Septimius: Romanised Aedui nobleman serving as a prefect in command of the Eighth's cavalry wing.

Ninth Legion:

Publius Sulpicius Rufus: Young commander of the Ninth.
Grattius: Chief centurion of the Ninth, previously in sole command for some time.
Salonius: Tribune of the Ninth accused of sewing rebellion among the army at Vesontio the previous year; now fled to Rome.
Casco: Cavalry prefect.

Tenth Legion:

Marcus Falerius Fronto: Commander of the Tenth Legion, Veteran of the Spanish Wars, confidante of Caesar and native of Puteoli in Italy.
Gaius Tetricus: Military Tribune attached to the Tenth Legion and expert in military defences and earthworks.
Gnaeus Vinicius Priscus: Chief centurion, or 'Primus Pilus', of the Tenth Legion.
Petrosidius: Chief Signifer of the First Cohort.
Lucius Velius: Senior centurion training officer of the Tenth Legion.
Lucretius: Chief centurion of the Sixth Cohort.
Gaius Pomponius: Chief engineer of the Tenth and lesser centurion.
Lucilius: Prefect of the Tenth's cavalry wing.
Florus: Capsarius in the Tenth Legion.

Eleventh Legion:
Aulus Crispus: Commander of the Eleventh Legion, ex. Civil servant in Rome.
Felix: Primus Pilus, or chief centurion of the Eleventh.
Galeo: Auxiliary prefect attached to the Eleventh.

Twelfth Legion:
Servius Galba: Commander of the Twelfth Legion
Publius Sextius Baculus: Primus pilus of the Twelfth. Long-serving and distinguished veteran.
Vibius Pansa: Auxiliary prefect attached to the Twelfth.

The maps of Marius' Mules II

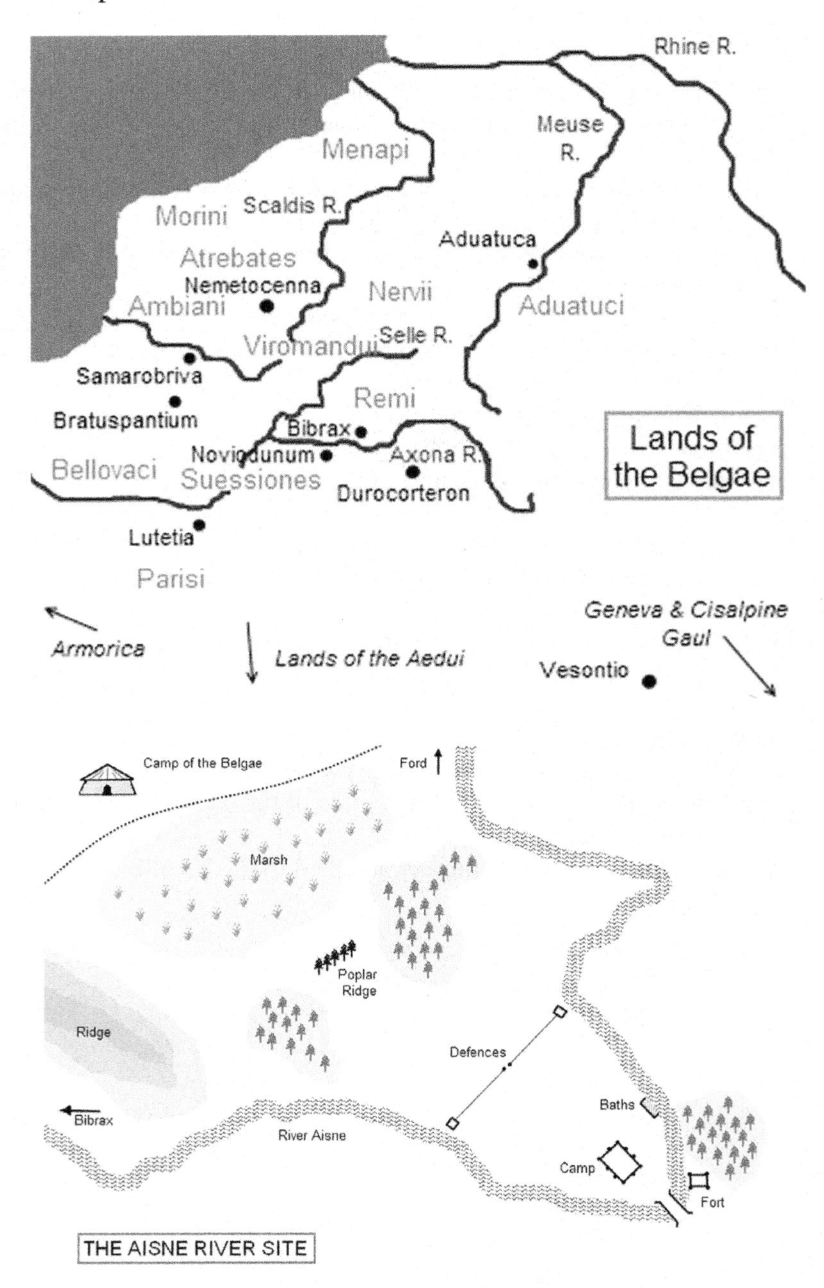

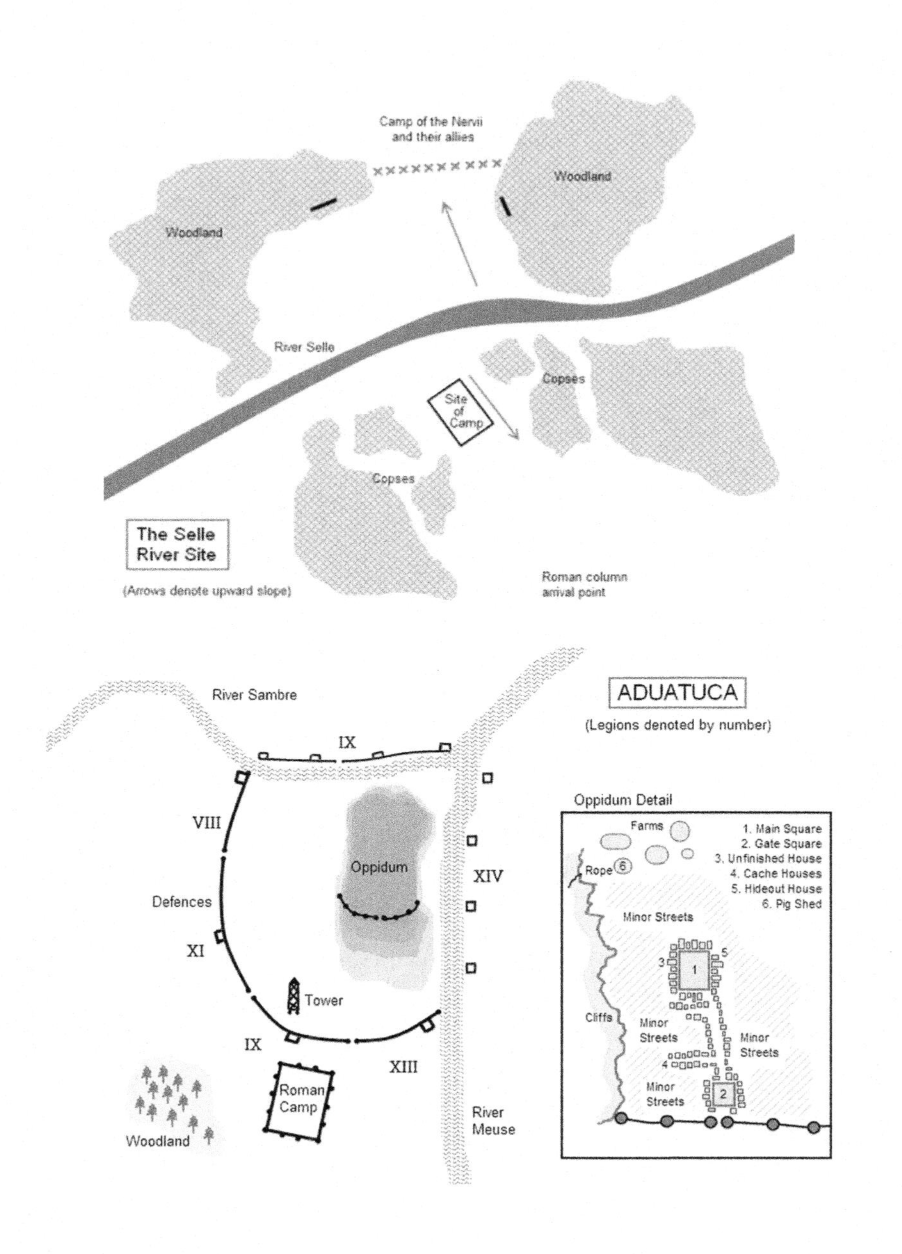

Camp of the Nervii
and their allies
Woodland
Woodland
River Selle
Site of Camp
Copses
Copses
The Selle River Site
(Arrows denote upward slope)
Roman column arrival point
River Sambre
ADUATUCA
(Legions denoted by number)
IX
VIII
Oppidum
XIV
Defences
XI
Tower
IX
XIII
Roman Camp
River Meuse
Woodland
Oppidum Detail
Farms
1. Main Square
2. Gate Square
3. Unfinished House
4. Cache Houses
5. Hideout House
6. Pig Shed
Rope
Minor Streets
Cliffs
Minor Streets
Minor Streets
Minor Streets

PART ONE: THE GATHERING STORM

Chapter 1

(Roman military installation outside Vesontio)

"Quadriga: a chariot drawn by four horses, such as seen at the great races in the circus of Rome."

"Foederati: non-Roman states who held treaties with Rome and gained some rights under Roman law."

"Where the hell have you been?"

Gnaeus Vinicius Priscus gestured angrily with his vine staff from his position on top of a supply wagon as he ground his teeth irritably.

Fronto looked up at his 'subordinate', though the word hardly seemed appropriate. A quick glance around confirmed no one was listening within earshot.

The legate of the Tenth Legion looked tired and haggard. Dark circles beneath his eyes spoke of late nights and long days. Behind him, Aulus Crispus, legate of the Eleventh shook his head, a faint smile lurking somewhere beneath the dust of travel. Fronto growled gently.

"And hello to you too, Priscus. We've come as fast as we could."

To illustrate, he gestured up and down himself, bringing attention to the dust and wear. There was a low muttering behind him.

"What was that?" he barked, rounding on his younger companion.

Crispus laughed lightly.

"I said: 'via every bar between the Pyrenees and Vesontio...'"

He took one look at Fronto's face and wisely turned away to tighten a strap on his horse. Fronto continued to glare at him for a moment and then turned back to the primus pilus of the Tenth.

"I'd say we've done well, myself. We didn't even get the message 'til a fortnight ago in Tarraco. All that way in less than two weeks? And with the horses laden with all our gear? Just be bloody grateful we left the cart behind!"

Crispus smiled benignly.

"Good afternoon, centurion. Forgive my companion. We made the most of our last night of freedom yesterday at a Gaulish tavern in a village around twenty miles from here. My head is troubling me a little, and I suspect Fronto's is a great deal worse."

Fronto grumbled again.

"The wine they serve in some of these local places tastes like feet and feels like being hit over the head with a brick!"

"You should try their beer, Marcus. They may make poor wine, my friend, but they excel at the brewing process" Crispus smiled.

Fronto shot his companion another grim glance and then turned back to his subordinate.

"What's all this about, Priscus? We weren't due to return for almost a month, and here we are, back in camp on the kalends of Aprilis?"

"Let's talk as we walk."

The primus pilus dropped lightly from the wagon to land on the springy turf, his hob-nailed boots leaving a deep impression. He gestured toward the fortifications, and the three men walked onward, Fronto and Crispus wearily leading their horses.

The camp had changed since Fronto was last here. During the previous season, the legions had spent a while encamped at Vesontio and had fortified their position with a palisade and ditch, their tents raised in orderly rows. Some time early in the autumn, Labienus, who had been assigned to command the six legions and their auxiliary support in the off-season, had decided that a more permanent installation was required.

Three large forts had been constructed of timber in an arc around the city, on the far bank of the river. The leather campaigning tents had been packed away for next season, and the army had settled to ride out the winter in relative comfort. With a large Roman army on the doorstep, Fronto could imagine how well the entertainment industry in Vesontio had done.

"How are the legions disposed?" young Crispus enquired. "There is insufficient room here for the full army."

Priscus nodded.

"Yessir. Yours and ours are here, along with the Eighth. The Seventh, Ninth and Twelfth are spread out, one entrenched towards the Rhine, one about twenty miles north and the other off to the west. Commander Labienus thought we ought to maintain a presence in the surroundings just in case. The legions have been rotating through the picket camps on a two-weekly basis. It's all worked quite well, I'd say; Labienus has kept his headquarters in Vesontio, and Crassus has been moving between the three camps keeping the men on their toes and irritable."

Fronto nodded.

"I can quite believe that; so, why the early muster?"

"Wish I could answer that, but I'm in the dark myself. Caesar sent a courier to Vesontio about a month ago, telling Labienus that the legates would be returning during Martius and that the general himself would be here at the start of Aprilis. Looks like you've beaten him here, but only just."

Crispus scratched his unshaven chin.

"So the other legates are all here then?"

Priscus nodded.

"Balbus arrived early last week and has been in and out of the headquarters ever since. Rufus got here three days ago and went straight out to his men to the north. Not seen him since. And Galba came back in the middle of winter. Apparently he felt the Twelfth needed some winter training. Crassus has been lauding him up to Labienus, and I have to admit he's really worked his men this winter."

Fronto grumbled.

"I expect that means the rest of us look lazy! Crassus'll think we wasted winter, but Labienus is bright. I expect he'll know otherwise."

Priscus sighed.

"I am capable of running things here. I did your job quite a lot last year, remember? Balventius, Felix and I kept up regular training and sorties throughout the winter. With all due respect, you're legates… no one expects you to keep your men fit. That's our job. You just make occasional decisions and look pretty."

Crispus laughed.

"He has us there, Marcus."

As they approached the gate of the first camp, a small knot of guards by the strong palisade came sharply to attention. The three officers returned their salute and drew to a halt. Fronto turned to Crispus and raised an eyebrow.

"You got a moment before you head to the Eleventh?"

The young legate nodded.

"They've managed months without me. I doubt that another few moments will cause consternation."

Grasping the reins of his companion's horse, Fronto handed them and his own to a legionary.

"Have them both fed and watered and brush them down. When you've finished with Bucephalus, have him stabled. The legate here will need his horse shortly to head back to the Eleventh, so make sure it's ready."

The soldier nodded, bowed hurriedly, and led the two beasts off in the direction of the Tenth's cavalry section. As the rest of the legionaries stood aside, Fronto and his companions strode into camp and made for the praetorium at the centre. The men of the Tenth saluted as the three officers passed, and then immediately returned to their tasks. As they reached the command building at the centre, Fronto glanced sidelong at his chief centurion.

"Alright, Priscus. You always know more about what's going on than anyone else. Give us the lowdown. I want to be prepared when Caesar arrives."

The primus pilus nodded at the guards by the door and gestured inside to his companions. Fronto and Crispus strolled into the main room and behind them Priscus addressed the various clerks in the headquarters.

"Go about your work elsewhere and take the guards with you. Make sure we're not disturbed."

The actuarii gathered together their wax tablets and scrolls and hurried out, their arms full, bowing awkwardly as they left. Once they were alone, Priscus dropped his helmet and vine staff onto the low table near the door.

"I can certainly make a healthy guess as to why the general sent for you all."

Fronto dropped heavily onto a bench and reached out for a jug of water and a goblet, directing a questioning look to Crispus. The young man joined him on the bench, nodding, and, as Fronto poured two goblets of icy water, Priscus sighed.

"We're not popular out here."

"Nothing new there," muttered Fronto. "We spent last year fighting one bunch of Celts on behalf of another bunch of Celts and from their point of view I can see how they might think it's none of our business."

"It's not just that, Marcus" the primus pilus continued. "If we'd stopped at that, I think there'd be peace now. But the Gauls all thought the legions would be going home. I think we've pissed a lot of people off by not just staying in Gaul, but so far outside our own territory. They think we're here to stay."

He reached out for the jar and a goblet.

"And I think they're right."

Fronto nodded.

"There's no doubt in my mind that Caesar already sees an eagle planted in the middle of Gaul with all the tribes in its shadow."

Crispus nodded sadly.

"I do believe that the general intends to climb the cursus honorum until he can reach the very Gods themselves. And the first step to that is to attain a great conquest."

A chorus of nods greeted that comment.

"So what you're saying," Fronto glanced at Priscus, "is that trouble's brewing among the tribes?"

The centurion nodded.

"You remember that assembly of the Gaulish chiefs we had at Bibracte last year?"

A nod.

"Well that's some great big annual event. And it's happened twice this year already. And the worrying thing is, from what I hear, that none of the tribes allied to Rome were invited to either of them. But the word is that it wasn't just Gauls either; some German chiefs and the leaders of the Belgae were included."

Crispus frowned.

"Sounds awfully like the northern tribes are gearing up to protest the Roman presence, doesn't it?"

Priscus nodded.

"We've had a rash of desertions among the Gaulish levies too. Then there's the native scouts. They've been riding in and out of the city for months, and they all have Labienus' permission to go anywhere they like. They disappear into the headquarters in Vesontio for a few hours, then resupply and ride out again. Then the next day another one arrives. It's even got me a bit jumpy, truth be told..."

"Spies and scouts everywhere… that's Caesar's doing. He'll have had Labienus keeping an extremely close eye on things while he was away."

He frowned.

"But the immediate question is: how prepared do we need to be? Has Caesar called us all back early in case the Gauls collectively decide its time to kick some Roman backside, or does he know something we don't?"

Crispus shook his head.

"It's a problem, for certain. Perhaps we should enquire of Labienus?"

"Shortly," Fronto agreed. "First you have to go show your face to your men. Then, I'd suggest we meet up in a couple of hours and go visit Balbus in his tent before we head into the city. Besides, I'm absolutely shattered. I think a half hour with my boots off and maybe a 'hair of the dog' is in order before I start running around and panicking about agitated Gauls."

Crispus nodded.

"You make a fair point, Marcus my good friend. I shall go and renew my acquaintance with my officers."

Fronto smiled.

"Your horse won't be ready for you for quarter of an hour or so. Might as well join me for a 'hair' eh?"

Crispus grinned and reached across to the chest on which stood a small jar of wine, while Fronto removed his boots with a deep sigh.

Priscus rolled his eyes and picked up his vine staff.

"If you don't mind, I'll go and find something useful to do. Nice to see you both again, but if I spend quarter of an hour in the company of those feet I'll never breathe clear again."

Wafting his hand across his face, Priscus gripped his helmet and left the building, his eyes screwed up tightly.

"What?" demanded Fronto irritably as Crispus breathed in deep ragged gasps between bursts of laughter.

* * * * *

Crispus burst into a fresh bout of laughter. It had been over an hour since he had left Fronto's camp, leading his freshly fed and groomed horse back to his own unit. Though he had not had time to visit the temporary bathhouse, he had taken a quick dip in a tub of cold water, shaved, and raked his hair straight. Dressed in clean clothes from his pack, he once more felt human, though there was an insistent, if gentle, thumping deep in his brain.

Which is why the sight of Fronto, still dishevelled and covered in dust with a hairstyle that... well 'style' was being excessively kind. Crispus covered his mouth and sniggered gently. His peer from the Tenth Legion smelled faintly like a dead bear.

"I shall leap to the assumption that you do not really care what Labienus thinks of you, Marcus? You look like you've had an accident with a quadriga and a midden."

"Shut up."

Raking his fingers through his unruly hair, where they caught in a tangle, Fronto strode across to the gate of the Eighth Legion's temporary fortress. Despite his travel-worn state, he still wore his cuirass and plumed helmet, along with the almost-red military cloak, clearly marking him out as an officer. The guards at the gate stood at attention and saluted, totally straight faced.

"Shut up" he said again, this time to the legionaries whose faces were so sombre that it was clear they were deliberately forcing themselves not to smile.

Accompanied by the grinning Crispus, Fronto strode up the decumana towards Balbus' headquarters. As with his own camp, soldiers saluted as they passed and then went quickly about their business. He was starting to feel a little better-humoured, despite the horrible pounding behind his left eye, when a voice like a saw through marble called out from a side street.

"You look like shit!"

As his head snapped angrily round, Titus Balventius, primus pilus of the Eighth Legion, fell into step alongside him. Fronto opened his mouth and then quickly bit back his acerbic retort. Getting into a battle of insults with Balventius would be a perilous thing indeed.

"Balventius. Did you leave at all during the winter? Did you go and check out your new estate?"

The grizzled veteran rolled his one good eye, the milky white one fixed firmly, if disconcertingly, ahead.

"I went back for a month or so. It's nice, I suppose. Lots of room. Spent a couple of weeks building a fence, bought some horses and put 'em in there. Then a bear came bumbling out of the woods and the horses smashed my fence to pieces and bolted. I wrote half of the property over to my brother and left him to sort out the mess while I came back here."

Crispus smiled uncertainly.

"I have no idea know why, Titus, but I'm having a little difficulty picturing your brother."

Balventius glanced across at him and then turned to Fronto.

"He sounds less posh? I'm not having to concentrate so hard to follow him."

Fronto nodded.

"I've been trying to drive out the orator in him and lower his brow a bit, but I don't think it worked. I think it's all that Gaulish beer that's rotting his brain. That's what's done it!"

Balventius smiled. The effect was fairly frightening through his crisscrossed network of scars.

"My brother's a lot like me," he said, turning to Crispus. "But less handsome. He'd still be serving under Pompey's legions, but he got hamstrung about five years ago. He's been living off his honesta missio, but Pompey's not as generous as Caesar. Half my grant's more than all of his."

Fronto was mulling over the difference between his own patron general and the great Pompey as they arrived at the praetorium. Balventius nodded to the guards outside, and one of them knocked on the wooden door before entering to announce their arrival. As the man returned and stepped to one side, the ageing legate of the Eighth appeared in the doorway, a broad grin splitting his face.

"It's about time!"

The bald, round-faced commander disappeared back into the gloom of the building, and the three men looked at each other, shrugged, and followed him in.

It took a few moments to become accustomed to the dim interior, but slowly their eyes adjusted. Balbus took his seat behind a desk covered in unit strength assessments, supply requests and training reports. With a sigh of satisfaction, he leaned back in his chair and reached for the glass of water nearby.

"So what news of Hispania? Is it still standing?"

"Ha, bloody ha!" Fronto grumbled, rubbing his temple.

"I do not think it was the campaign break that Marcus anticipated," Crispus smiled. "He had planned to visit Longinus' estate to deliver the ashes and his goods and then move on to Tarraco and spend the winter carousing. Severa had different ideas, though."

"Severa?"

Fronto looked at Balbus' questioning expression, glared at Crispus and then sighed.

"Longinus' wife. She... erm... took to me."

"She wouldn't let him stay in Tarraco," Crispus laughed. "Insisted on looking after us personally. Sometimes frightfully personally, I suspect, eh Marcus?"

"Anyway!" Fronto barked irritably, "Let's get to the matter at hand. I gather there've been stirrings among the Gauls."

The humour slid gently from Balbus' face.

"I rather think something's in the wind. The Belgae are getting themselves involved in Gaulish politics and, given their fearsome reputation, that can't be a good thing. I just hope this discontent is limited. If it spreads among all the non-allied Gauls and Belgae, we could be in trouble. Six legions is a lot, but not when faced with a million angry Celts."

"Then the staff's going to have its work cut out."

The other two looked questioningly at Fronto.

"Well... you know Caesar. He's got something up his sleeve. He sent for us for a reason. Something's about to happen, but it's going to have to involve people like us stamping a heavy Roman boot on anyone who openly declares against us while people like Labienus and Procillus trying to persuade the rest of Gaul that we're doing it for them. It's that good old fine political line again."

Crispus nodded.

"And I cannot help but wonder whether Caesar uncovered anything concerning that tribune Salonius and the conspiracies against him at Vesontio, too?"

"Indeed." Everything went quiet for a moment as the four officers looked at each other.

"Jove, it's good to see you boys again" beamed Balbus with a sigh of relief.

Fronto leaned back and ran his hands through his tangled hair once again.

"How are Corvinia and the girls? Good I hope?"

Balbus laughed.

"Disappointed. I'm sure they all expected you to come and visit."

Balventius let out a low whistle.

"What is it with you and women, Fronto? It seems like they all want some of you."

"I think it's a mothering thing," the scruffy legate replied. "They all want to look after me, 'cause they think I can't look after myself. I think they think I'm nicer than I am, too!"

Balventius chuckled and the tent fell quiet once more.

"So," Crispus interjected tentatively, "what is the situation here? Fronto's primus pilus intimated there were stirrings of unrest among the Gauls?"

Fronto nodded.

"We're going to see Labienus after this to get the complete picture. I like to be well prepared for all eventualities before the general shows up. In fact, I'd like to know everything I can."

Balbus nodded. "I've only just returned myself." He gestured to Balventius, and the scarred veteran turned his good eye towards Fronto.

"It's been happening for months. Labienus received a message by courier one day from Caesar. A few hours later he sent out a half dozen scouts; Gaulish auxiliaries, they were. I don't know how many people noticed, but I was a bit surprised. None of them went out with their Roman auxiliary equipment. Just dressed up like plain old Gauls, they were."

Fronto frowned.

"Think I can guess why, but go on…"

"Well," Balventius continued, "since then they've been coming and going regularly. I stopped a few in the early days to find out what they were doing, and they refused to tell me; directed me to general Labienus, telling me they were under orders of silence. I went to see the commander and he basically told me to mind my own business."

He sighed.

"Since then, though, word's started to leak out. No matter how much they're told it's a secret… well…" he smiled at Fronto. "Drink loosens tongues. A few beers and these Gaulish scouts are telling all their friends. They've been scouting out the Belgae and various other tribes."

"I already knew that," replied Fronto, leaning forward. "What don't I know?"

"Well, I think you can safely say this isn't just a bit of unrest. Not like a few Numidians shaking their spears and grumbling. It looks like this is getting organised."

"Go on?"

"The Belgae are violent sons of whores, Fronto."

"Yes…" snapped the dishevelled legate irritably. "And?"

"We've never really concerned ourselves with the Belgae because they just spend all their time kicking, biting and carving each other. I spoke to some of the native levies, and they all agree that you've never seen any people eternally at war with themselves like the Belgae. The only time they've ever been know to stop it and actually turn their energy outwards was the odd time when the German tribes tried to cross the Rhine and have a go with them. Even the Germans are frightened of them!"

Fronto laughed.

"But?"

"But they've stopped fighting each other, Fronto. They've been swapping hostages and making blood pacts and all that other crap. They're one people right now, and that's a bit disturbing. That's a whole new thing. They've banded together, and it's not for defence this time."

The legate of the Tenth nodded.

"So they're getting ready to face us."

"But," Crispus interrupted, "the crucial question is: have they done this because they have decided that Rome is a perilous neighbour, which would mean we have to face them, or have they done this because they've been begged or bribed by other tribes? If the latter's the case, we may be facing half of Gaul shortly."

Fronto sighed.

"I think you're missing the third option there."

"Pardon?" Crispus glanced across at him. Balventius and Balbus also leaned forward, their brows knitted.

"Well," he continued, "it seems pretty obvious to me, but then I've known the general a long time; know how his mind works."

A chorus of nonplussed looks. Fronto sighed.

"Caesar had to engineer a way to get us into Gaul last year. He needs conquest and booty. We're not here because the Helvetii threatened Rome. We could have let them past, but no… they were just the excuse we needed to begin campaigning in Gaul. But it's no use stopping there. We'd gained nothing except perhaps a little stronger alliance with the Aedui and instilled fear in our northern neighbour."

Scanning the interior of the tent, Fronto's eyes fell on a jug of wine. Without asking permission, he rose as he talked, crossed the tent, and poured himself a goblet.

"So… when that was over, Caesar had already spent time putting the idea into the heads of important Gauls that we were the people they needed to sort Ariovistus out. In fact, I wouldn't be surprised if he hadn't pushed the Helvetii all the way to Bibracte just so he was close enough to the Council of Chiefs to be beseeched for help."

Balbus shook his head sadly.

"You mean you really think that Caesar engineered every move last year to get his legions into the heart of Gaul? Somewhere from where it'd be very hard to shift us?"

Fronto nodded.

"Be very careful what you say, Marcus. You're among friends here, but those are the kind of comments that cause officers to become quietly deceased!"

"I know," the scruffy legate agreed, swigging wine. "Don't repeat any of this, for your own sake. Not even to your closest."

Another swig.

"I don't think he's stopped there, though. If Caesar was sending out these scouts and spies as a reaction to news of the Belgae, Labienus would have been the first man to know about it. But no... Caesar sends a message to him, and he starts sending out men who are dressed to look as un-Roman as possible?"

Crispus slapped his head.

"He's doing it again?"

"Yes."

"He's actually fomented discord and rebellion among the Belgae just to provide us with an excuse to put down more of Gaul?"

Balbus glared at his young companion. Balventius stood and crossed the room, opening the door and peering outside.

"It's alright. Nobody's listening."

Balbus sighed.

"A little care, Crispus!"

"He's correct, though," the young man replied quietly. "Caesar has pushed the Belgae until they snapped. Now he's preparing to take them to task. And, of course, the Belgae are the fiercest of all the tribes, or so they say. If Caesar can defeat the Belgae, all of Gaul should fall and cower before him. It's a bold move!"

"It's a stupid move!"

The other three turned to Fronto in surprise. The tired legate took a last swig and grounded his goblet.

"He's riled the Belgae so that he can fight them and beat them and show all of Gaul who's the master. But he's done it *too* well. The Belgae have decided it's time to piss on Rome. But they're not stupid. They know how big Rome is; how powerful. So they, in turn, foment discord among the Gaulish tribes, and the next thing we know is that the Council of Chiefs has been called without any of our allies. So half of Gaul looks like their siding with the Belgae; and they've even thrown out hooks into Germania. There's nothing so sure as most of the German tribes would love nothing more after last summer than to kick six shades of shit out of us!"

Balventius whistled through his teeth.

"Looks like we're wading in it shortly, then?"

Balbus sighed.

"Then I hope Caesar's the tactician everyone thinks he is. We've got to have something up our sleeve, or we're facing odds of at least ten to one!"

He leaned forward and gestured at Fronto.

"Pass me that wine…"

* * * * *

The four men emerged blinking, into the light. Fronto had meant to ask why Balbus had drapes over the windows but, in the end, they had proved useful both for maintaining privacy and for preventing sunlight from worsening his headache. The thumping came back like the weaponsmiths of the Tenth at work.

The other three strolled ahead, chatting, while Fronto plodded along unhappily at the back. They were still set on going to see Labienus, despite the fact that Fronto was sure they would learn nothing new of value. He was filled now with a cold conviction that Caesar had put his men in the worst possible danger for his own vainglorious expedition and, regardless of Balbus' fervent hopes that the general had a surprise up his sleeve, Fronto also knew with leaden certainty that it would be left to men like himself to make the general's grand plans work out.

He spat on the ground with irritation and looked up once more.

As they strolled down the hill toward the river and the bridge that linked the military garrison with the Gaulish city of Vesontio, he noticed the guards at the riverbank pointing and gesturing excitedly to each other. Squinting, for they were still some distance away yet, he tried to focus on the small figures and tracked back from them in the direction they were pointing.

A vast array of armoured legionaries was stomping up the valley in the direction of the bridge and the camps. He stopped for a moment, drawing a tense breath while his companions, unaware, continued on down the path.

No amount of squinting would allow him to focus enough to identify the flags they bore, but his initial fears were easily brushed aside: these could not be the retreating survivors of the first wave of Gaulish counter-invasions. The army in front of him was fresh and tidy. Perhaps Labienus had called the outer legions back to Vesontio before the general arrived.

"Yes… that'll be it" he muttered to himself and then hurried along to catch up with his companions.

As the four officers reached the gate of the camp, the duty guards snapped to attention with consummate professionalism. As always, Fronto studied them carefully. He found the Eighth a great yardstick for measuring the performance of his own legion; the two were the closest among the army in both age and command style.

The spring bees hummed around the grass and scrub outside the gate as the men trod heavily on the dirt track that had formed from months of soldiers tracking to and fro between the camp and city across the river. From here the path ran down a gentle grassy slope to the bridge, where it converged with similar tracks that had been worn from the camps of the Eleventh and Tenth Legions. At the meeting point by the bridge two posts had been erected; one bore direction signs to the city and the three camps, presumably erected so that merchants and teamsters knew where to sell and to deliver; the other post held a banner with the eagle of Rome.

"What is Labienus thinking?" snapped Fronto, as he pointed down at the flag.

"Hmm?" Balbus looked closely and frowned.

"I suppose it's just there to denote the presence of the legions and the headquarters at the citadel in town?"

Fronto grumbled. "Labienus is bright enough to know that you don't plant the flag of Rome in territory we don't own. It essentially tells anyone who sees it that we either think we do own it or that we intend to own it shortly."

Crispus shrugged.

"And yet it remains. I cannot help but wonder why the indigenous people have not requested it be taken down. I'm sure that if they had, Labienus would have done so."

Fronto growled again. "Stupid. Arrogant and stupid."

Balventius rolled his eye around and laughed.

"I think you're crediting them with a little too much intelligence there, Fronto. Six legions bring a lot of money into an area. Even the lowest vagrant in Vesontio is dining out and wearing silk now. After this winter, it's probably the richest city in Gaul. Most of them would let you plant a flag in their back if you jingled your purse!"

"Well..." Fronto pointed up the valley, "it looks like their customer base is about to increase again. Can't see which legion that is, but they're coming from roughly south west. Which legion's camped out west?"

Balventius frowned.

"That would be Crassus' Seventh. Why the hell are they coming in?"

"That's not the Seventh." Crispus shaded his eyes and squinted. "In fact, I have no idea who they are."

He became aware that Fronto was looking at him expectantly, but with a hint of irritation.

"Well I cannot see the legion number on the flags, but all of Caesar's legions bear the Taurus emblem. Those flags seem to have horses."

Fronto boggled at him. "You can't see how many 'I's are on the flag, but at that distance you can distinguish between quadrupeds?"

"It's a simple matter of shape, Fronto. In fact, those symbols look a lot more like Gaulish ones than Roman."

"Let's get to the bottom of this!"

Without waiting for the other three, Fronto started striding purposefully out from the path in the direction of the approaching legionaries. After a moment, he became aware that the others had caught up, Crispus coming alongside in a vaguely undignified scurry, Balbus lagging a little, and Balventius striding calmly along.

The insignia became gradually clearer as the four approached and, once he finally picked out the detail, Fronto came to a sudden halt, as did his companions.

The legionaries in front of him were marching not in one column, as it appeared at a distance, but in two, each column with a width of six men and trailing off like a glinting armoured ophidian. The arms and armour they bore were shiny and new, the shields devoid of any marks, and the banners…

Two new insignia, both with some kind of Celtic-style horse, fluttered below the numbers XIII and XIIII.

“New legions?” Crispus’ tone echoed Fronto’s own surprise.

The column was not being led, as was customary, by the officers, but by the signifers, the eagle standards, and the musicians. The officers were riding alongside in a small knot, with the cavalry stretched out behind them.

Fronto stepped to one side so as not to impede the army, but rather to stand in the way of the command unit. As he placed his fists on his hips in a haughty gesture, he was further surprised at the commands being barked at the men by the lower officers. There was no doubt at all about what he heard. Those commands were issued in fluent Latin, but with a pronounced Gaulish accent. He was still staring in disbelief at the passing legions when he became aware that his three companions had joined him, and the command staff had reined in before them. He looked up.

“Fronto! You look bloody disgraceful!”

Quintus Pedius, one of Caesar’s senior staff stared down at him and a slow smile began to creep across his face.

“Not that that’s anything new, of course!”

“Ha, bloody ha! What the hell’s going on? Why are you dressing up the auxilia as legionaries?”

Pedius gave him a sharp glance.

“You’d be well advised to sheath that mouth of yours, Marcus.”

The staff officer turned to the tribunes behind him.

“Menenius? Hortius? Get the legions to the nearest appropriate flat ground, preferably between these other encampments and have a temporary camp set up for each. Once they’re settling and underway, I want the two of you at the headquarters. Report to me there!"

The two men saluted and rode off to find the primus pilus of each legion. As they went about their business, Pedius dismounted and gestured toward the bridge. As the four officers walked steadily back along their track and the distance between the five men and the legions increased, the staff officer handed his reins to Crispus and removed his helmet with a sigh of relief.

"I need a bath and a shave. And a jug of wine, but that can wait until I've had the bath and the shave. But sadly, both of those will have to wait until I visit the headquarters. Are you gentlemen accompanying me?"

Balbus nodded. "We were on our way there anyway."

"Good. Now, Fronto, what's irritated you?"

The dishevelled legate scratched his bristly chin.

"They're Gauls. They're not Romans, Quintus... they're Gauls! What are they doing in legionary equipment? When the ordinary soldiers find out about this, there'll be riots. It demeans the whole purpose of the legion. That's what the auxilia is for!"

Pedius sighed. "Calm down Fronto. You're going to have a fit if you go on like this."

"Well?"

Balventius nodded. "It's true sir. This is the citizen army. It's against the rules to enlist foreigners into it. There'll be hell!"

Pedius shook his head.

"It's all above board, gentlemen. I can tell you some of it, but not all. Present company, you see?"

He indicated Balventius, though respectfully.

Balbus shook his head.

"My primus pilus is as solid as they come. Caesar tried to make him camp prefect, remember? Anything you can say in front of us, you can say in front of him!"

Pedius regarded Balventius for a long moment and then nodded his head.

"Very well. This is in strictest confidence. I expect the general will put some spin on it for the public, but some of you will know there's more anyway. You remember that tribune who stirred things up in Vesontio last summer?"

"Salonius? Yes. He scurried off back to Rome with his tail between his legs as I remember."

"He did." Pedius lowered his voice fractionally.

"But Caesar thinks the man's been carrying on his campaign of disruption in political circles back in Rome. The general has been blocked with almost every political move he makes. Finally, we managed to find out where we could get to Salonius in private to 'have a little word' and before we turned up someone knifed him and tipped him in the Tiber. Pickpockets was the official line, but that's unlikely."

Crispus bore a shocked look. Pedius sighed.

"A man called Clodius, who seems to have a network of spies and an almost unlimited chest of gold, is stirring things up in Rome like a madman. And not just against Caesar, but against Crassus and Pompey too. The general thinks Salonius was an agent of this Clodius."

They began the descent toward the bridge and Pedius took a deep breath.

"Caesar needs some serious victories and a lot of money. He owes important men, but more critically, he's losing political ground. He requested permission of the senate to raised new legions in Cisalpine Gaul. The senate actually refused him. I'm sure you can imagine how that went down!"

Fronto winced, glad he had not been there for that meeting, and Pedius continued. "So Caesar did what he does best. He found a way around the rules."

Fronto issued a small half-smile.

"I think I can see where this is going…"

Pedius nodded. "Caesar managed to have the Helvetii, the Aedui and a few of the smaller allied tribes classed as foederati. If they're treaty-bound with Rome, their men can theoretically be enlisted into the legions. It's not common and not popular, and it's an extremely grey area legally, but it can certainly be done. They wouldn't let Caesar raise citizen troops from Cisalpine Gaul, so he used his own authority to raise two new legions from our allies; mainly the ones who speak Latin, though. They're now Roman citizens. There's been a shit storm over it in Rome and Caesar's just dealing with the aftermath before he joins us."

Fronto nodded.

"We think we know what the general's planning; if it's true he might well need those two new legions."

Pedius nodded.

"Best go see Labienus and inform him of events then."

Fronto nodded as he watched the new 'Gaulish' legions marching across the hill toward the camps. There was no doubt that the Gauls fought fiercely, but should they be enlisted in the legions? He could not shake the feeling there was trouble in his near future.

Chapter 2

(Vesontio)

"Praetor: a title granted to the commander of an army. cf the Praetorian Guard."

As the party of officers strode across the square to the main building that had been commandeered by Caesar for his headquarters almost a year ago, Fronto became acutely aware of how scruffy he must look compared with the others. Pedius had just arrived from over two hundred miles of travel with his legions, and he was parade-smart. Fronto had been here for hours and still looked like he had been dragged behind a horse. And his sister wondered why he failed in politics!

The guards by the doorway were already at attention, in their prominent position among the senior staff of the army. Pedius, at the head of the group, acknowledged them with a slight nod of the head and they went inside. The headquarters building was in what could only reasonably be described as 'organised chaos'. Fronto knew from experience that the headquarters of a legion ran smoothly and with the minimum of fuss, since there was a hierarchy that worked with machine-like precision. The headquarters of a large army was different, though. There were six legions based around Vesontio, all with the same hierarchy and, while the general's command had its own clerical staff, they spent most of their time trying to respond to the legionary clerks and filter, prioritise and just plain argue with them. The net result was that the higher one went in the military, the messier the administration became.

The three men entered the main room to find Labienus at a wide desk covered in parchment and wax tablets with the chief quartermaster, Cita, and the camp prefect, Paetus, opposite him. As he rattled out answers to their quick-fire questions, they made marks and, without turning, held out the tablets behind them where a junior clerk would grasp them and run off to deal with the issue, only to be replaced by another haggard-looking legionary clerk.

Pedius stopped in the doorway, his companions behind him, and waited for a moment, blocking the entrance and exit of various clerks, before clearing his throat.

Labienus looked up in surprise.

"Pedius? Good grief. I wasn't expecting to see you for a while yet. Does that mean Caesar's with you?"

That last question had a note of desperate hope in it, Fronto noted with a smile.

"Not with, I'm afraid; though I doubt he'll be far behind. Can we interrupt your burdensome tasks?"

Labienus nodded; a little too quickly, Fronto thought again.

"Thank you, gentlemen," he addressed Cita and Paetus. "We'll resume tomorrow morning. I think I need some time to rest anyway."

The two officers stood and bowed to the interim commander. Turning, they saluted the officers in the doorway, who shuffled out of their way with some difficulty. Once the others had left, Balventius closed the door and the other four men walked across to the desk, while he remained standing by the door like a guard.

Labienus gave a long-suffering sigh.

"Almost my entire day now consists of two things: military bureaucracy like 'which legion has to produce the engineering detail to maintain the command section', and politics, like the local farmers complaining that the latrines of the Tenth are emptying into a tributary stream that their wives use to wash clothes. I just don't understand how Caesar gets anything done!"

Pedius grinned.

"Because he delegates the irritating parts to us, you know that."

"Ha!"

Labienus leaned back and gestured to the seats opposite him. As the officers sat, he looked up at Balventius.

"Centurion? If you're here on business, I suggest you sit. No one will interrupt us with my door shut."

Balventius nodded respectfully.

"Thank you sir, but I'm comfortable standing."

"Very well," Labienus said, stretching, "nice to see we've got all the staff and legates assembled again. Once Caesar arrives, I very much think we'll be on the move quickly. There are troubles stirring."

"We're all aware of that" said Fronto flatly. "And I think Caesar's already prepared. Ask Pedius who escorted him back from Cremona."

Labienus turned to his peer and raised an eyebrow inquisitively.

"I had the honour of escorting the newly-raised Thirteenth and Fourteenth legions to camp."

Labienus sank miserably back into his chair, visions of a new cartload of documents rolling inexorably toward his desk.

"And that's not all..."

Fronto smiled broadly.

"They're vaguely Romanised Gauls, not citizen troops!"

Labienus face slipped into bleak misery.

"There'll be fights. Complaints... possibly even fatalities. We'll have to keep them apart."

Pedius shook his head.

"No. Integration is the key. I've sent them to set up between the existing legions. They may have a funny accent, but Caesar levied them months ago. They've been well trained by veterans at Cremona. They've all taken the oath. Hell, they think of themselves as Roman. So does Caesar apparently, so we'd better shift our perspective a little."

Such news apparently did little to raise Labienus' spirits. Pedius smiled sadly.

"There's two more things yet."

"Oh good."

"Two letters; orders in fact, from the general himself. One for you, and one for Crassus."

Labienus sighed.

"I can't be bothered to read them right now. Just give me the highlights."

Pedius laughed.

"Well Crassus' letter orders him and his Seventh Legion out to the north west. He's to fortify up at the Gaulish Oppidum they call Cenabum and monitor the activity of the tribes between there and the sea. We've had word that there's anti-Roman sentiment growing in the area.

Fronto frowned.

"If we're going to be fighting a million Belgae shortly," he muttered, "I'm glad Caesar's given some thought to the danger of allied attacks on the flank, but if there's real trouble stirring out there among several tribes, sending one man with one legion could be a death sentence."

The others nodded their agreement.

"And the one for me?"

Pedius shrugged.

"Crassus' orders were standard military orders; yours come sealed with wax. I'm intrigued, myself."

He leaned forward and let placed a tightly rolled parchment of finest Egyptian import quality on the desk. It rolled toward Labienus a little until it hit the wax seal and stopped.

Labienus raised an eyebrow again.

"I expect I'm supposed to open this when I'm alone then?"

Fronto made a 'tsk' noise and tapped on the table.

"For Mars' sake, Labienus, we're all senior officers. Just open the bloody thing and tell us what to expect."

Labienus retrieved the scroll and leaned back in his chair again. With a slowness and a thoroughness that irritated Fronto intensely, the interim commander cracked the seal and unrolled the parchment. Fronto watched as the man scanned down the text, noting with interest the various expressions that crossed his face. A long, silent moment passed and then Labienus let go of the lower end, allowing the scroll to roll up once more before he dropped it onto the desk.

He whistled quietly through his teeth.

"I can see why that was sealed."

"Come on, man" barked Fronto irritably. "What is it?"

"It's an arrest warrant."

Crispus, a look comprised of equal parts excitement and worry, leaned forward.

"An arrest warrant for whom?"

The commander stared at him in silence.

"Labienus!" barked Fronto, and the man jumped slightly and shook his head as if to clear it.

"I'm to arrest Paetus, the camp prefect." He sat in silence for a moment, staring at the scroll. "Paetus! I've known the man for years!"

Fronto reached out irritably and grabbed the orders, unrolling the parchment and reading for himself.

"Looks like Paetus has been playing a few games. His family are clients of Caesar, but it appears he also belongs to Publius Clodius Pulcher, and that man's already a serious thorn in Caesar's side."

Crispus turned to the older legate.

"But we cannot arrest a member of the patrician class just because he might be playing dubious political games with multiple patrons. We'd need senatorial approval."

Fronto sighed.

"Not for a trial in the field. If the man is found guilty of treason against the army, the general can do whatever he likes with him. Oh, there might be ripples to deal with later in Rome, but nothing will stick to Caesar or us. See, if Paetus is linked to Clodius, then that means he's linked to Salonius, and that bastard tried to turn the army against us. I think Paetus has made some careless choices."

He turned back to the parchment.

"We're to detain him and 'extract' a confession from him. Caesar authorises us to do whatever we must to get any useful information about other saboteurs and 'problem individuals'."

Balventius stepped forward from the door and gestured at Labienus.

"Sorry to have to point this out, sir but, with you and Paetus being longstanding friends, then you really need to delegate this to someone, and quickly."

Labienus nodded and gestured to Fronto.

"What do you think, Marcus?"

Fronto let the scroll roll up once more and turned to the one-eyed veteran centurion.

"Well, Balventius. If you're willing to do this, I would feel confident in passing it to you." He held out the scroll. "Also, Paetus is the camp prefect, and since Caesar wanted you to consider the position, you may have to fill in for a while in the role. Besides, if Labienus appoints you to the role of interim camp prefect, you'll have enough of a level of authority to arrest Paetus without having a senior officer present."

Balventius sighed and nodded.

"I can handle it. Do I assume none of you gentlemen want in on the details?"

Labienus shook his head.

"Just get results. That's what Caesar cares about."

Balventius nodded and turned to the three legates.

"I'll draw a few of the less reputable men from my legion."

"Be very careful," Balbus cautioned him. "If this goes wrong or Caesar changes his mind, there could be accusations of all sorts.

Make sure you cover your own back and those of your associates. I don't like this."

Balventius nodded.

"Don't you worry, sir; I can scare the shit out of a man without even touching him. I'll bet he drops his traitor friends in it before I get within a foot of him."

* * * * *

Paetus stood with his back to a hut wall and three centurions before him like disobedient children being disciplined. Balventius stopped at the entrance to the compound to where he had tracked the man and leaned casually against a gate post. This had to be done professionally, but also subtly, since it could cause ripples as far as Rome.

The camp prefect jabbed in the direction of one of the junior centurions with his vine staff in the manner of a disciplinarian. Balventius was only half-listening, planning, as he was, how to approach the problem. Behind him, out in the road, were half a dozen men, hand-picked from three legions for their loyalty, their discretion and, above all, their willingness to overlook certain proprieties.

What was being said was something to do with use of the training ground that had been levelled out in the area beyond the camps; something about efficient booking of facilities. Once again, Balventius smiled at the very idea of anyone suggesting that he would have been any good in that job. Too much bureaucracy and not enough exercise. Indeed, Paetus was becoming slightly expansive around the middle, despite having been on campaign for a year.

The grizzled centurion waved a hand behind him at his men, gesturing that they should maintain their position and stay out of sight. As he mused on what sort of a man would actually want the job of camp prefect, he realised something. For all the lack of respect he felt towards men like Paetus who ate and slept well and stayed out of the fighting, getting slowly more rotund, he would rather poke his remaining eye out than try that job. That anyone had the patience, let alone the desire, to solve problems in camp logistics boggled the mind.

And whether Paetus had been involved in conspiracy at any level or not, he had to admit that, under the man's careful observance, life in the camps of six legions had run pretty damn smoothly.

He shook his head irritably. He was spending too much time these days hanging around with the officer class. He was starting to analyse his orders before carrying them out.

Blinking away a bead of sweat in the height of the afternoon sun, he focused on the scene before him again. Paetus had finished dressing down the three centurions who, thoroughly chastised, saluted and turned to march away.

Balventius watched the camp prefect open a wax tablet and scribble a few notes. With a quick gesture to the men behind him, he strode forward purposely across the compound, grinding his teeth. Paetus looked up as the shadow of the frightening veteran loomed over him.

“Centurion Balventius? Can I do something for you?”

The primus pilus adjusted his thinking at the last moment and came to a halt, standing easily in front of his prey.

“Prefect. May I request we adjourn to your office?”

Paetus raised an eyebrow.

“This a private matter, centurion?”

“Somewhat delicate” agreed Balventius with a nod.

“Very well.”

Closing his hinged wax tablet and putting away his stylus, Paetus turned and walked calmly across the dusty ground toward his office. This compound in the corner of Vesontio’s citadel had been allocated as quarters for the camp prefect and his staff and was surrounded by a new Roman stockade of its own. The low building in the centre that held half a dozen offices was obviously an original Gaulish structure of stone and rough hewn timber. The largest office was that of Paetus, while the others belonged to three tribunes assigned to assist him and the two chief clerks under his command.

The door to the room lay open, and Paetus strolled into the cool interior, lit by two windows in opposite walls that also allowed for a breeze to pass through; a feature the lesser offices almost certainly would not have, Balventius would be willing to bet.

The grizzled centurion stopped at the door and made a number of gestures at his men. Efficiently, the group split up; two men following Balventius into the office while, immediately behind them, two more pushed the door closed and stood outside it.

Paetus looked up uncertainly.

"It's a warm week, Balventius" he said with a slight smile. "I'm generally leaving the door open for the breeze."

Balventius remained silent but gestured at the two men with him, who lit the oil lamps that stood on shelves at points round the room. As the camp prefect watched them with confusion and a sinking feeling, the window shutters were pushed closed from outside with a gentle thud, plunging the room into a deep gloom.

"What is the meaning of this, centurion?"

Balventius allowed himself a sad sigh.

"Actually, Paetus, I'm not currently holding the rank of centurion. Today I hold the temporary rank of prefect."

Confusion forced Paetus' face to change repeatedly. The room was dark and warming by the moment with the cloying smell of the burning oil.

"What's going on, Balventius?" he said, earnestly, and with a slight tremor of fear.

"I'm afraid, Paetus, that I have been asked to assume your duties for the time being."

He let that sink in for a moment, and as Paetus opened his mouth to speak, the primus pilus rode roughshod over him.

"On the authority of Titus Labienus, commander of the forces of Rome in Gaul and of Gaius Julius Caesar, praetor, governor of Cisalpine and Transalpine Gaul, and of Illyricum, I arrest you on suspicion of complicity in conspiring against the army and its commander, and in the causing of unrest among the legions last summer."

Paetus was staring at him, open-mouthed.

"I have no particular desire to see you suffer, prefect, so there are different ways we can proceed here. It's all up to you."

The two soldiers, having finished lighting the lamps, returned to the doorway at Balventius' shoulders, where they lurked, menacingly. Paetus clamped his mouth shut, and Balventius had to grudgingly admire the steadfast look that appeared on the prefect's face.

"Go on, before I speak."

Balventius nodded respectfully.

"Very well. Firstly, you can tell me everything you know that's relevant and resign your commission and step down. That offer is mine alone, and I will answer myself to Labienus and Caesar if you accept it... and you should. I will take your oath on the eagle that you have told me everything and allow you to officially tender you resignation of the position to Labienus and return to Rome. I'm not even sure why you're still here. I know you planned to step down last year. That was why they approached me."

Paetus nodded soberly.

"And?"

"Option two is less pleasant. Let's just leave it at that. Take my offer."

Paetus sighed.

"I'm going to make a huge leap in logic and assume that Caesar has taken exception to something I've done, since I'm damn certain I've never been involved in treachery or causing unrest and have always given my complete loyalty to the Julii. Care to give me a clue, Balventius?"

Balventius folded his arms.

"The general is aware of your other patron. You remember Clodius, I presume, since you're on his client list?"

Paetus nodded, frowning.

"And?"

Balventius grumbled.

"They say no man can serve two masters. It's certainly true in this case. Clodius and Caesar are not the closest of friends."

Paetus shrugged.

"I'm aware that Clodius has some unsavoury practices, but surely…"

Balventius cut him off mid flow.

"Publius Clodius Pulcher has been undermining Caesar in the senate, along with other high profile patricians. He is the patron of Salonius, who you will remember tried to turn the army against the general last year. Anyone who is on that list is no friend of Caesar. You know that!"

Paetus wandered across to the desk and took a seat.

"Do you really need your escort?" Paetus enquired, gesturing at the legionaries behind the centurion.

Balventius stood silent for a moment, and then gave a curt nod before turning to the two men by the door.

"Go back to the gate and take the others with you."

One of the legionaries stepped forward slightly.

"Sir?" he said, gesturing at the camp prefect.

Balventius turned his baleful glare on the man.

"Go!"

Hurriedly, the two men left the room, shutting the door behind them. Balventius waited a moment, listening to the brief flutter of conversation and then the soldiers leaving, and then allowed his shoulders to sag slightly.

"Alright, we're alone now. Go on…"

Paetus placed the flats of his palms on the table and fixed Balventius with a steady gaze.

"I'm Caesar's man, not Clodius'. I'm no traitor and, truth be told, I would rather stay a thousand miles from Clodius, given the choice."

The scarred centurion frowned.

"Then why are you on that list?"

Paetus sighed.

"My father-in-law owed him a lot of money; and I mean a *lot* of money. He was an idiot and ran up a gambling debt like the loot of the Cilician pirates. He couldn't pay anything back, and when Clodius' thugs started threatening my wife as well, I stepped in. Problem is: things just sort of spiralled out of control. Clodius is a monster, and he's not above casual violence. One of his other clients went broke and flatly refused to pay him. They burned his house down with his children inside."

Balventius shrugged.

"Not that I don't sympathise, Paetus, but that's not really our concern. You deal with your personal issues, and you keep them away from the rest of us. You need to sever your ties either with Clodius or Caesar. If you denounce Clodius, I'll support you, and I'm pretty sure most of the staff will too. If not, I'll have to carry out Caesar's wishes, and I suspect it'll go badly for you."

Paetus sighed.

"As I said, Clodius is a monster. I am under no illusion that Caesar is anything other than a political opportunist, but Clodius is in a different class. I would happily walk away from the man, but I can't tell Caesar anything useful to him, because I simply don't know anything."

Balventius frowned, and the prefect continued.

"And Clodius isn't interested in me paying him back now. He wants to have his hooks into people. I tried to pay off my father-in-law's debts a few months ago, but he wouldn't have it. I suspect I'm too useful to him as I am. And if I renounce him as a patron,

Calida and her family will turn up skewered in a ditch, and I've no intention of allowing that to happen."

He shrugged.

"You see my problem, centurion?"

Balventius nodded. It was a problem, for certain. Paetus was in trouble whichever way he turned. Unless…

A slow smile began to crawl across his face.

"You find this funny, Balventius?"

"No," the scarred centurion replied, fixing him with that one good eye. "But I have an idea. There's a way we could turn this to our advantage, Paetus."

"Whose advantage?" the man asked suspiciously.

"Largely Caesar's... and yours."

He leaned on the table and faced the prefect.

"I need to speak to the staff and then to Caesar when he arrives. In the meantime, I trust you're happy glossing over this as though it never happened?"

Paetus nodded.

"Then you get back to your work, and I'll get back to mine."

Turning, he pulled the door open and strode, blinking, out into the sunlight, leaving a dazed prefect sitting in the dark and pondering an uncertain future.

* * * * *

Labienus leaned forward across the desk, his eyes blazing.

"You did what?"

"I let him go" repeated Balventius.

Balbus wandered across and stood next to his primus pilus.

"He's got good instincts, Labienus. I might have done the same."

"Oh, very noble" Labienus spat. "All well and good, but Caesar might not see it that way. He gave us specific instructions!"

"If I might interject?" Crispus spoke up from his seat.

"What?"

"The actual instructions Caesar sent were to detain him, which is exactly how the centurion proceeded; to extract a confession, which Balventius did; and to do whatever was necessary to get information. Although it might take a moment for the general to calm down and accept it, we have, in fact, followed his instructions precisely."

Labienus glared at the young legate.

"Great. Just wonderful. Alright, Balventius. What are you proposing?"

The primus pilus shrugged.

"This could be turned to the general's advantage, but someone will need to persuade him of that. This Clodius, from what I understand, is trying to undermine Caesar with the senate?"

"Yes."

"And he believes he has Paetus by the balls."

"Yes" replied Labienus again, impatiently.

"Then he has no reason to doubt anything Paetus tells him."

Fronto, freshly bathed and shaved, gave a brief, thoughtful chuckle.

"That could work out particularly nicely for Caesar. He could send all sorts of misinformation to the man; make him look like an idiot. The general should see the appeal of that."

He turned to Balventius.

"Has Paetus agreed to this, then? It could put his family in a lot of danger."

Balventius nodded.

"He hasn't agreed yet, 'cause I haven't asked him yet, sir. But what choice has he got? He's pretty much got to agree. We ought to work out something to make sure his family are safe first, though, if what I hear about this Clodius is true."

The room fell into a thoughtful silence.

After a long pause, Crispus sat up with a deep frown.

"I..."

He was interrupted by a hammering at the door.

Labienus turned, irritably.

"Enter!"

The door swung open to reveal a legionary standing in the doorway at an approximation of attention, his face a plum colour and sweat pouring down from his hairline. The man had clearly run fast and hard.

"What is it?" Labienus asked the exhausted soldier.

"Sir..." the man managed, his breathing laboured. "The general is at the gate..." wheeze... "with his praetorians." Another ragged breath. "He's on his way now, sir."

Labienus nodded.

"Thank you, soldier."

As the legionary closed the door and disappeared, the interim commander pushed his seat back and stood with a sigh.

"Well, gentlemen. It appears things are about to start moving."

The officers in the room shuffled as they stood, brushing the creases out of their tunics and cloaks and straightening their belts.

Out in the corridor, they heard heavy booted footsteps and soldiers crashing to attention. They stood smartly and waited. Moments later the door opened, and the young moon face of Aulus Ingenuus, commander of the general's guards, appeared with a broad smile. Fronto stared. Ingenuus was still little more than two years under the eagles, yet he had, though bravery and a little luck, secured one of the most prestigious positions in the army. The change in him over a single winter was noticeable, though. While he still had his air of youthful innocence, his face had taken on a hard edge, defined slightly by an unfashionable but neatly-trimmed beard. Moreover, he had acquired a thin scar that ran down his cheek to his jaw; the reason, Fronto suspected, for his new beard.

Ingenuus' grin widened as he took in the faces round the room. They had no time to exchange pleasantries, however, as he immediately stepped aside and jammed his plumed helmet under his arm, to make room for the general.

Caesar strode purposefully into the room, waving an arm in a vague fashion of greeting without letting his gaze settle on the men. Fronto eyed his commander as Labienus stood aside and vacated the chair and the general approached the desk. Caesar looked older somehow. His hair had receded a little further and thinned noticeably, and his face looked slightly pale and drawn, as though sleep, never easy for the great man, was now coming rarely and sporadically. Politics was clearly causing the general a great deal more grief than Fronto had realised.

Without a word of greeting to any of them, Caesar dropped his helmet unceremoniously on the desk and appeared to pay attention to the miscellaneous records on the table, leaning over them with his palms flat down.

"Is Crassus gone?"

Labienus straightened.

"The instructions have been delivered, Caesar, but only just. Pedius only arrived today with the new legions. I expect Crassus is making preparations to get underway. With respect, general, we weren't expecting you yet?"

Caesar grunted.

"So we have seven legions at our disposal here, and Crassus will be leaving today. That's acceptable. What of Paetus?"

There was a pause.

"Come on!" barked the general.

Balbus cleared his throat.

"The prefect was detained and questioned, Caesar."

"And?"

Balventius took a deep breath.

"And it is clear to me that he knows nothing of any conspiracy, Caesar. He is…"

The general's arm shot out accusingly in the direction of the primus pilus of the Eighth.

"Tell me you have him under arrest."

"With respect general, I allowed him to retain his position while we…"

He was interrupted as Caesar swept his arm across the table, wiping his helmet onto the floor where it landed with a dull thud and rolled slowly back and forth.

"His head, or your head, centurion. It's your choice!"

Fronto cleared his throat and deliberately stepped forward between Balventius and the general's accusing finger.

"Caesar, he's right. I agreed with him; we all did."

The general fell quiet for a moment, and his head dropped forward so that he faced the surface of the table. Fronto held his breath; this could go either way. He swallowed nervously as the general looked up. The remaining colour had drained from his face and his eyes burned with cold fury.

"Get out!"

Crispus reached the door first and almost threw himself out of it, closely followed by Balbus and then Labienus. Pedius and Balventius followed quickly, avoiding looking back at the furious commander. Fronto, however, remained perfectly still, his arms folded. From the doorway, Balbus beckoned to him. Fronto shook his head and motioned for his peer to close the door. As Balbus, bearing a worried frown, pulled the portal to with a click, Fronto cleared his throat. Caesar had not taken his eyes off the legate before him; moreover, he had not even blinked.

"Caesar, you need to hear me out."

The general glared at him.

"You push me too far, Fronto. I am the commander of this army; the governor. We're a long way from Rome and a long way from the senate. Out here, I am imperator. I gave out orders, and they've been disobeyed by the entire cadre of my senior staff."

Fronto shrugged and held the general's stare, calmly.

"That's not what's bothering you, Caesar. You know we always act in your best interest. What's happened?"

Caesar's glare remained but, as Fronto watched the heat slowly went out of it.

"The senate. A group of bickering old women, the lot of them. None of them will give me any room to manoeuvre. Clodius spins in the centre like an enraged bear; ripping at anyone he can get his paws near, seemingly at random. He's trying to undo almost anything I try, but it's not just me; he rakes at all the others. Then there's Cato, who seems to want nothing more than to plunge a knife into my back. Even Cicero! A few years ago I invited the man to partner with Pompey, Crassus and myself, even though Crassus disapproved! I even gave his brother a position on my staff, and how does he repay me? By denouncing my every move to the senate as nothing more than self-promotion."

He growled and hammered his index finger down onto the surface of the table so hard that he almost broke it.

"Mark my words: the days of the senate are slowly coming to an end."

Fronto grimaced.

"I mean it, Marcus. We threw the kings out of Rome because they were corrupt and useless. But what are these meddling morons if not corrupt and useless. Rome will never accept a king again, but it has to find something better than this!"

He sighed and sank back into the chair.

"I apologise, Fronto. My whole winter has been spent fending off political attacks, and I tire of it. I returned to Vesontio early because there's an honesty in soldiering that the senate lacks."

Fronto nodded earnestly. Caesar and he could disagree on many things, but with that point, he could find no room to argue.

Caesar reached down and collected his helmet, brushing the dust from the plume.

"Very well. Tell me about Paetus."

Fronto nodded and finally took the seat opposite the general.

"Paetus took on his father-in-law's debt to Clodius. Now that arsehole thinks he owns the man. The problem is that while Paetus' family are half a mile from Clodius, but he's here with us, the bastard pretty much does own him. Balventius is convinced of Paetus' innocence, and I tend to agree."

Caesar nodded soberly.

"So?"

"Well," Fronto went on, "that leaves us in an unusual and useful position."

"Do tell" the general replied, steepling his fingers.

"I'm not sure what you'd want to do to cause Clodius trouble, but Paetus is your pipeline to doing it. If we can persuade the prefect to deliver information back to Clodius, you could feed him a line of whatever rubbish you felt like. I'd bet you could make him look like a complete tit in front of the senate, if you thought about it."

A slow smile spread across Caesar's face.

"I can see you've thought this through, Marcus."

Fronto shook his head.

"Actually, this was all Balventius' idea, but there's a small hitch."

"What?"

"Well Paetus is unlikely to want to help us if it's putting his family in danger. We need to think of a way to protect them from Clodius."

Caesar smiled. Fronto shuddered. It was not a nice smile at all.

"I think I can sort that out, Fronto. When we're done here, go find Balventius and Paetus and bring them here. I'll…"

He suddenly frowned and reached across towards Fronto.

"Is there a smell like tin?"

Fronto frowned.

"Caesar?"

"And it's not got a little darker?"

"Erm… no, Caesar."

The general stood, slightly stiffly.

"I think we're done for the moment, Marcus. Best get to your duties."

Fronto stared.

"Caesar?"

"Go, Fronto. Get to work. Come back tomorrow with the others."

Fronto stared for a moment longer and then bowed and strode for the door, opened it and, exiting, pulled it shut behind him. As he stood alone in the corridor, staring at the wood, he wondered what the hell had got into the general. After a moment, he shrugged and, turning, made his way from the building.

Out in the courtyard area, the other officers stood in a small knot, arguing in low voices. The sound died out sharply when Crispus drew their attention to the puzzled legate as strode from the headquarters building.

"Marcus? What happened?"

Fronto shook his head.

"I wish I knew." For a moment, he stared into nowhere and then realised they were speaking of the argument.

"Politics. Bad moods. He's alright now."

Gesturing at Balventius, he smiled.

"He wants you, me and Paetus to come back and see him in the morning, but I think we're off the hook for the rest of the day."

He grinned.

"All of a sudden I find myself immensely thirsty. Anyone care to join me? We have to walk past the taverns on the way out of town, after all…"

Chapter 3

(Tavern on the main street of Vesontio)

"Mansio and mutatio: stopping places on the Roman road network for officials, military staff and couriers to stay or exchange horses if necessary."

Balbus grinned unevenly.

"Problem is..."

He sat for a moment, pointing a shaky finger at Fronto as his face went blank.

"Problem is that I can't remember what the problem is!"

Fronto burst out laughing as the older legate stared down forlornly into his mug. Next to him, Crispus made snorting sounds, and on the other side of the table, Labienus grinned.

"I swear the Gauls put something in this wine that rots the brain."

"It's what you're putting the wine into that's doing that!"

As Balbus turned to stare at Labienus, the other collapsed in fresh waves of laughter.

"So..." Fronto pulled himself upright and rubbed his face with his hand. "The general's been here two weeks. We're rushed back from the blue shores of the Mare Nostrum in such an awful hurry because the Belgae are stomping around getting twitchy, and then we sit in camp waiting for something to happen. Come on, Titus. You've spent the most time with Caesar. What's he told you? Why are we still sat here?"

Labienus shrugged.

"He's waiting on a few things; that I know for certain."

He tapped his mug on the table rhythmically as he spoke.

"I've been told to watch for a report from Crassus on the situation with the tribes up in Armorica. It's possible Crassus managed to get his legion to Cenabum in a week, since it's just men and kit with no baggage or artillery, though that's a tall order in itself, being best part of two hundred miles away. Let's say he can get a courier back to us in, what... five days? I mean there's no mansios or staging posts out here in Gaul; nowhere to change horses, so he would have to let the beast rest. That means that even at breakneck speed, he would only have had a couple of days to check up on the tribes. I'd say we've at the very least another week or two before we look like moving."

He quickly glanced around to make sure no one else was listening.

"And those riders he sent back to Rome too." He tapped the side of his nose conspiratorially. "You know… the Paetus thing? He's waiting for a reply from them too."

He sat back, letting his mug sit still long enough for Balbus to refill it.

"And there's still almost a dozen native scouts out there among the tribes near the Belgae. He'll be waiting for those to come in with their information."

Fronto grumbled.

"So basically, he's waiting for his mail to arrive!"

Balbus laughed.

"What's up, Marcus? Are you so desperate to get stuck into the Belgae? From what I remember, the last few fights you've been in, you've ended up wounded and convalescing. You do look a bit too healthy at the moment."

Fronto glared at him.

"You can go off people really quickly, you know that, Quintus?"

"Ahem…"

The four of them turned at the sound of the throat clearing. The yard was attached to the side of the tavern itself, surrounded by a low stone wall and sheltered by a wooden structure covered with ivy. Apart from the other two tables and the benches that served them, the yard was empty. Over the wall, however, life and business went on as always on the steeply-sloping main street.

Titus Sabinus, senior staff officer and currently one of the general's busiest aides, stood in the road with folded arms and a false frown. As the four stared up at him like vacant fish, he slipped into a smile.

"Thought I'd find you lot in one of the bars. This is the third one I've tried though."

"Us too!" Balbus grinned.

"I've brought some weary travellers to join you" the staff officer announced.

Turning, he beckoned down the street and, moments later, the travel-worn faces of Rufus and Galba, legates of the Ninth and

Twelfth Legions, appeared around the corner. Galba, a short, stocky and swarthy man, looked tired to the point of exhaustion. Rufus, younger than Galba by several years, looked equally weary, yet walked with a straight-backed professionalism. The two men looked across at the men in the tavern yard and gave a faint smile.

Sabinus pointed at Fronto while addressing the two latecomers.

"This man knows how to relax. You've been training solidly for weeks. Take a rest. You'll need it, because you won't be here long."

He turned to the others.

"Look after them."

Crispus frowned.

"Caesar's pulled all the legions back to Vesontio?"

Sabinus nodded.

"All but the Seventh, of course. Things are in motion, Marcus. Won't be long now. "He gestured at the mug in front of the legate." Make the most of that. I doubt the Belgae will be as hospitable!"

Fronto mumbled something and then took a deep pull from his mug.

Galba and Rufus entered the yard as Sabinus gave a nod and wandered on up the street to report to the general. After a brief discussion, they collected a table between them and, carrying it over, butted it up against the one at which their companions sat. Retrieving the benches, they sank gratefully to the oak seats. Balbus grinned and banged heavily on the table.

The Gaulish innkeeper came scurrying out of the doorway. As soon as he saw his two new customers, he rushed back inside and returned with two more jars of wine and two more goblets, which he distributed appropriately round the table.

Galba sighed with relief and poured a drink for himself and his companion.

Labienus regarded them with a raised eyebrow.

"You two been overworked? You look exhausted."

Rufus shrugged lightly.

"Crassus set a pretty heavy training schedule for the forward camps this last month." He glanced at his companion. "And Galba here is determined not to be outdone, so he's driven his men to work twice as hard as that!"

Galba nodded.

"We're still a new legion, and when we get into the thick of it this year, I'm determined the Twelfth are going to weather it with the best of them. Most importantly, I'm bloody damned if that humourless dick is going to prove a better legate than me, just because he was born with a golden rod up his arse."

Rufus gave a tired chuckle.

"And of course, if Crassus is pushing his men to the edge to prove they're best, and then Galba starts doing the same on the other side, what am I supposed to do in the middle?"

He let out a small laugh.

"Actually, I gave my men an easy run of it compared with these other two, but then the Ninth has always had a good reputation anyway." He raised his goblet to Fronto. "You'll remember that, I guess, since you're responsible for a lot of it."

Fronto smiled. There was something vaguely sad about Rufus. He could not define exactly what it was, but even when the young man was smiling and passing on a compliment, it felt like he was delivering cheerless news. There was a permanently haunting look about that young face that made him turn away, back to his drink.

Clearing his throat, he looked back up, this time at Galba.

"Far be it from me to question another commander's methods..."

He paused for a moment as he noticed the scathing look in Labienus' eyes and ignored it as best he could.

"You should be careful about taking your cue from Crassus. That man's bad news. For us; for you; but most of all for his own men!"

"Fronto..."

He flicked his eyes across to Labienus, who was giving him a warning look.

"No. I'm right. Crassus is a dangerous man. He's got the drive, the ambition and the ruthlessness of Caesar..." he ignored Labienus' frantic motions to shut up. "But he doesn't have Caesar's redeeming features. Caesar's a showman and tactically sound. He knows what to do and when to do it, and he knows how to make his men love him. Crassus is just making his legion resent him, and that's never a good thing."

Irritably, he pushed Labienus' waving hand down to the table.

"Mark my words: Crassus is going to find himself in trouble out there in the west. He's got one legion. They're a good legion, and he's had them training like mad, but still, even with his auxiliaries and support, there can't be more than seven or eight thousand of them."

He waved his arm in a sweeping motion to indicate the whole of northwest Gaul, knocking Crispus' mug in the process so that the young legate had to grab it quickly to prevent spillage.

"But there's hundreds of thousands of Gauls out there."

He waited for that to sink in during the silence that followed.

"Eight thousand versus more than a hundred thousand. That's the odds if it comes down to a fight against all the tribes up there. And, let's face it: Crassus is going to push something until it breaks. He's as diplomatic as a turd stew."

Labienus grasped his waving hand and forced it down.

"Fronto, there are soldiers out in the street who can hear all this. For Jupiter's sake shut the hell up!"

Fronto growled at him.

"Shan't!"

He pulled his wrist free.

"And even if he manages to maintain peace, I wouldn't trust his men not to revolt against their commander. He treats them like slaves."

"For Gods' sake Fronto, shut up!"

Fronto pushed Labienus' arm aside.

"And the worst thing? Absolutely the worst thing that could come of any of this? What if Crassus somehow pulls this round and makes himself look good? You know as well as me that there's only one possible reason Caesar sent him out to be surrounded by those odds with only one legion? It's a bloody death sentence; that's what it is!"

He became aware that Galba and Rufus were staring at him in disbelief and that Crispus had joined in the arm motions encouraging him to calm down. For a moment, he wondered whether he'd had too much to drink, but the drink-fuelled courage told him that was stupid, and he had an important point to make. Can't back down now…

"A waste though, don't you think? Sacrificing a veteran legion just to get an inconvenience out of the way?"

There was a crunch and Fronto's world went black.

Balbus rubbed his balled fist and sank back down to his seat as the unconscious form of his best friend slid gracelessly from the bench. Crispus stared, his head snapping back and forth between the equally startled Galba and Rufus, the heap that was Fronto, and finally to the silent crowd in the street who had, to a man, stopped whatever they were doing to stare into the tavern yard. Sighing, Crispus stood and turned to look over the wall.

"I am going to count to three!" he shouted. "And any man I can still see when I get there is on latrine duty until they get pensioned out!"

The street burst into life as men ran this way and that to clear out of the furious young legate's gaze. Balbus looked up at him.

"Thank you."

Labienus stared at Balbus and slowly began to smile.

"No, Quintus. Thank you!"

"He's just had a little too much. No harm done, eh?"

Labienus gave a pointed look to everyone round the table.

"No... no harm done. Just jesting, eh?"

With a sigh, Balbus stood and gestured toward the heap of legate opposite him.

"Crispus? Give me a hand getting him to his quarters would you? I think I may have damaged my fist."

As the two men collected Fronto and dragged him up, draping him between them, Balbus clenched and released his fist several times. Each time he did, there was an unpleasant crunching sound and he winced with pain.

"Damn, that man has a hard jaw!"

Crispus tried not to laugh.

"I think you must have a pretty hard hand, Quintus. I hope you haven't broken him. His nose is a funny shape."

Balbus shrugged.

"You know Fronto. I can't believe this is the first broken nose he's ever had."

Quietly they lifted Fronto and, with a wave of acknowledgement to their companions, left the tavern yard and walked out and down the street toward the bridge and the military compounds beyond.

* * * * *

Fronto was still unconscious as the two legates dumped him unceremoniously on his bed, though whether through his injury or substantial consumption of alcohol was a matter for debate. They had collared a legionary at the entrance to the camp of the Tenth, telling the guards that their legate had had an accident and to call for a capsarius.

Crispus looked up at Balbus from where he sat on the edge of the cot, his face filled with concern.

"Do you think he's alright? I thought he would have woken by now."

Balbus shrugged.

"He's still breathing. You can hear that from the nasty bubbling sound!"

The younger legate tried, unsuccessfully, not to smirk. They'd had to shut Fronto up, clearly. His mouth had seriously run away with him in a public place, but when it came right down to it, Crispus was convinced the man was right. Moreover, he was sure the same was true of Balbus and the others and, indeed, every legionary that had been in the street. Still, casting aspersions about the morals and the ability of some of the highest members of the patrician class was a career breaking move, guaranteed.

And Fronto, while his rank indicated he was from a patrician family, from everything else, it was just as clear that they were one of the less noble and haughty families and even that Fronto held most of his own class in particularly low esteem. That was one of the things that truly fascinated Crispus about the unconscious bloody mess snoring noisily next to him. Until he had been appointed to the Eleventh, he was ashamed to admit, he had hardly ever even spared a thought for anyone of a rank lower than equites. And now, a year of friendship with this man had changed him so much that often he found himself considering the results of any potential action on the common people before his own. Such an un-Roman viewpoint, it constantly amazed him.

His attention was brought sharply back into focus by a knocking on the door. Balbus, leaning against the tall cabinet by one wall and wiping his forehead with his scarf, turned and called out.

"Come!"

The door opened. Crispus was surprised to see not a medicus, but a legionary in his armour, without weapon, shield or helmet.

The young capsarius bowed curtly.

"Sirs."

Balbus smiled benignly at the young man.

"Florus, yes? I remember you. I take it the medicus was otherwise occupied?"

Florus smiled weakly.

"Errr… Sort of, sir."

A raised eyebrow.

"He said he wasn't going to treat the legate for another drink-related injury and that I could handle it, sir!"

Balbus' grin widened.

"What does he do to get this kind of reputation with the medical service?"

Florus gabbled hurriedly "It's alright though, sir. I'm well trained. I almost certainly can handle it, sir."

"I'm sure you can."

Crispus had been sitting frowning as he looked the young soldier up and down. Young? Ha. There was probably only a couple of years between the two of them. With a flash of memory, he suddenly remembered where they'd met. After the battle against Ariovistus last year, when Fronto'd had that bite wound on his heel. He joined Balbus in the smiling.

"I suspect your legate has a broken nose. Apart from that, he should be fine, other than a nasty bump from where the bench hit him in the back of the head…"

Florus wandered over to the cot and knelt to examine his commander. The nose was, indeed, distinctly misaligned.

His tongue poking gently from the corner of his mouth, Florus reached down to his belt and unfastened his small medical pack, which he dropped to the floor beside him. Professionalism taking over, he looked across to the young legate sitting next to him.

"Could I ask that you hold the patient very steady?"

Crispus nodded and reached across, holding Fronto down by the shoulders.

"I think you will find that he's fairly anaesthetised anyway; in fact, he's been anaesthetising himself for around five hours now. You could probably amputate his leg without waking him."

Florus gave a curious little half-smile.

"I've been looking forward to this for a long time."

Crispus glanced sharply at the young man, who smiled widely.

"Sorry, sir. I just mean that the legate's nose has actually been misaligned for years. A decade or more probably. Must have had a nasty break some time. I've been dying for an excuse to straighten it."

Behind him, Balbus gave a deep belly-laugh.

"Most of Fronto's charm comes from his oddities, medicus."

"On three?" said Florus. Crispus nodded.

"One." The young man settled over the legate and reached down to his face.

"Two." Gritting his teeth, he grasped Fronto's nose carefully but firmly.

"Three!"

As Crispus held Fronto tightly down, and Balbus looked on expectantly, the legate's nose returned to a perfectly straight position with a crack and a small spatter of blood that caught Crispus across the upper arm. Fronto never even flinched, though the pitch of his snore changed instantly.

"Apologies, sir."

Crispus laughed.

"I've been covered in more than that in my time with the Eleventh. And there's more coming yet, soldier."

Florus smile faded slightly.

"Of course, sir."

As silence fell, Florus carefully wiped up the blood from around the break.

"Is that it?" Crispus asked in surprise.

"That's it, sir. Set it back and wait."

"But do you not have to apply splints or pack the nose or anything?"

Florus smiled again.

"It'll heal on its own sir, in good time. Tomorrow it'll swell and the bruising will come. I'll only start to worry about complications if it's not back to almost normal in a week. It'll be tender for a while though. And..." He looked up at the two legates in the room. "And it'll be obvious that he's got a broken nose, sirs. No one will believe he had an accident."

He frowned as he looked carefully at Balbus.

"If it's not an impertinent question, sir..."

Balbus smiled.

"Go on..."

"Is it vaguely possible that during the legate's... erm... difficulty, he accidentally fell nose-first onto your hand?"

Behind him, it was Crispus' turn to laugh out loud.

Balbus frowned.

"Only," the capsarius added quickly, "it looks like that was a very heavy blow and if that was the case, I really ought to check your hand over for fractures, sir?"

Balbus sighed.

"I'd rather it didn't go racing round the camps that one of their commanders had to break the nose of another, Florus, if you get my drift?"

The young man nodded.

"Of course, sir. I am the very soul of discretion."

Before he let go of Fronto, however, he gently rolled him to one side and examined the back of the legate's head. There was a bloody patch but, as he gently probed the wound, he found no sign of a break or anything more serious than cuts and bruises.

"Legate Fronto will be fine," the young man said as he gently lowered his patient back to the bed. "I'll check on him from time to time, though I suspect he'll be out for a while yet."

He walked over to Balbus and gestured to the campaign chair nearby. The older legate sat with a sigh of relief and held his hand out open, palm down. Florus took it gently and started manipulating it, lifting the fingers gently one by one and folding them back toward the palm. As he reached the middle finger, he heard a gasp from his patient and looked up to see Balbus' eyes watering.

"Sorry sir."

"Don't be. I take it that's broken."

Florus nodded.

"Not badly, though, sir. I could bind and bandage your fingers or your entire hand, but it would be fairly obvious to everyone how the injuries had occurred."

As Balbus frowned, Florus smiled.

"Or you could just be very, very careful sir and let it heal as is. Without binding it to another finger, you run certain risks of later troubles or diminished movement."

Balbus grunted unhappily.

"How long will it take to mend?"

Florus shrugged.

"A week or two and it should be strong enough to use for ordinary everyday purposes. There will be a little bruising, sir, but with it being that finger, it shouldn't be too bad. The medicus has a paste, sir that seriously decreases bruising and dramatically reduces healing time, but he doesn't dole it out unless it's critical. It comes from some kind of tree and gets imported through Arabia or Egypt from past the Parthian Empire, so it's very hard to get hold of and extremely expensive."

Balbus' jaw took on a firm set.

"I think I can persuade him to part with some of it. We may be back in action in a couple of weeks and both Fronto and I need to be at full fighting fitness before then."

Florus stepped back and stood up.

"I had heard we were marching north, sir. Against someone called the Belgae?"

Balbus nodded.

"I think so. Possibly even all of the Belgae."

Florus frowned.

"Are they worse than the other Gaulish tribes, sir? People seem to be frightened of them."

Crispus cleared his throat. In his mind he pictured the map of the tribes.

"Actually, they're not Gauls at all, Florus. They're separate, like the Germans. And they're split into their own tribes like the Gauls and the Germans are. The Geographies I read always refer to the Gauls, the Belgae, the Germans and the Aquitanii as 'peoples' and then the subdivisions as 'tribes'.

He thought for a moment.

"Though I rather fancy that these are names that were given them by our own geographers many years ago and that they use their own names. The Gauls, for instance, call themselves 'Celts'. It's all a little complex and jumbled really."

Florus nodded soberly.

"But they are the worst of all, though, sir?"

"That's what they say, soldier. Whether they can withstand the advance of Roman iron remains to be seen, I suppose."

The young capsarius nodded again.

"Then I'd better make sure my kit is well prepared. Is there anything else I can do, sirs?"

Crispus looked up questioningly at Balbus, who shook his head.

"I think that's all, Florus, thank you. Please inform your medicus that the legates of the Eighth and Eleventh will be dropping by shortly to requisition a little of his expensive oriental paste, if you would?"

Florus nodded with a smile and, bowing, turned and left the building.

Crispus looked down at the unconscious patient and then up at Balbus with a smile.

"He's not going to be able to do much about that but admit to it."

Balbus nodded.

"But the soldiers wouldn't dare mention it, and those of us that are close enough to do so know him well enough we know exactly what to expect. He'll just have to come up with some convincing and exciting lie."

He sighed and stood.

"Come on. We need to go get some of that stuff from the medicus before my hand starts to blossom."

"What about him?"

Balbus smiled like an indulgent father.

"He'll sleep for hours yet."

* * * * *

"Enter!"

The three men at the door to Caesar's office looked at one another. Fronto entered first, followed by Balbus, with Balventius bringing up the rear and closing the door. The general sat behind his desk scribbling on a tablet. Without looking up, he swept his arm, indicating the three seats across the table from him.

Wordlessly, the men took their seats and waited patiently for Caesar to finish his administrative tasks. After a moment, the tablet snapped shut, and the general placed his stylus neatly alongside it, pushed them off to his left and then, in a moment of obsession, lined them up neatly with the edge of the table. After that, he sat back, raised his head, took a deep breath, laid his hands on the table before him and tapped rhythmically.

"Your face is a mess, Fronto."

"Yeth, thir."

"Any point in me asking?"

Fronto swallowed noisily.

"Twipped on a wabbit hole, thir."

Caesar stared at him.

"Stop that. You sound like an idiot."

"Thir?"

"People always resort to slurring and impedimented speech when they have a nasal injury or a heavy cold. It's all psychosomatic, just like limping. Force yourself to talk properly, man."

"Yes, general."

The look of startled realisation on Fronto's face threatened to make Balbus laugh. Caesar pulled himself straighter.

"Alright, gentlemen. Time for action."

The three men blinked, and Caesar nodded, as if in answer to an internal question.

"Firstly, tell me about my two new legions."

"Well…" Balventius leaned forward. "I think we're narrowly avoiding serious trouble, particularly with the Fourteenth. It's ridiculous, general. They're encamped between all the other legions, but none of them will even exchange a greeting with the new men. Everyone looks down on them. And it's not helped by the fact that the new legions are staying firmly in their own camp and not even trying to interact. Hell, sir… they don't even speak Latin when they're amongst their own."

Caesar frowned.

"That's not good at all. I'll have to do something about this. Or rather, perhaps I should say 'I'll have to have something done about it.'"

The other officers' turn to frown.

"Caesar?"

"First let me explain the two legions to you. I know you're aware of their origin. However, you won't have the details. Neither of them currently has a legate assigned. I was, unfortunately, a little tied with potential recruits. I would have preferred all Latin-speaking recruits and to have filled every centurion and optio role with a veteran from Aquileia or Cremona."

He sighed.

"Unfortunately, I couldn't find enough suitable men. So, what I have done is given preference to one of them: the Thirteenth has all Latin-speaking legionaries, and each officer is a Roman veteran. I don't want to assign any of my current staff to them, as most would take the assignment as a demotion, given the Gaulish nature of the Thirteenth."

He smiled and shifted his gaze between the two legates.

"So, for the time being, I want you two, Balbus and Fronto, to maintain command of the Thirteenth between you, as well as your own. You have the patience to work with them. I want them fully Romanised, integrated into my army and proud of their eagle. You two can give them that. Once they're settled and proved, I'll look at assigning them a legate of their own."

Fronto and Balbus looked at one another. The older legate raised an eyebrow and Fronto shrugged, immediately wincing at a number of bruises and pulled muscles from his 'fall'.

"We can do that, Caesar," Balbus nodded. "And what of the Fourteenth, then?"

The general's expression shifted almost imperceptibly.

"Sadly, the Fourteenth will take considerably more effort. Only around a half of them speak Latin with more than a few words. Less than a quarter of the centurionate are Roman veterans; the rest are minor chieftains among the Aedui. In all, while they're trained as legionaries, they still think and act like Gauls. The chief trainer at Cremona says he'd trust them to keep formation in battle, but that's about as far as it goes."

"So…" Fronto grunted, "basically they're useless?"

"I wouldn't say that." Caesar smiled. "They shall be kept in reserve. I'm going to give standing orders that they remain as camp guards or take rearguard in battles to protect the artillery and baggage trains… that sort of thing."

Fronto nodded.

"I suppose it's possible that that way they'll learn gradually."

Balventius laughed; a harsh bark.

"And they can't get themselves or the rest of us into too much trouble that way."

Fronto nodded again.

"So what poor sod are you going to put in charge of them? If none of your staff will lower themselves to lead your top-notch Gaulish legion, who's going to agree to command the dregs?"

Caesar's smile widened.

"Lucius Munatius Plancus."

"Plancus?" Fronto almost spat out the name. "But he's a prat! He..." Light dawned on him slowly.

Caesar nodded.

"Yes. A legion of unintelligible Gauls in the hands of an unimaginative and inexperienced commander. Sounds perfect for guarding the engineers and baggage. And another problem I'd had was that I owe Plancus' father a favour, and I've been wondering what to do with him. Now I can make him a legate. His father will be pleased and, after a while I can send him back to Rome where he can climb the ladder and be a burden to the senate instead."

Fronto smiled.

"Very nice, though I'd warn you, Caesar, that we may have to call on the Fourteenth along with everyone else if we land in deep shit up north, especially without Crassus' Seventh here."

"I'm aware of that."

The general sighed and stood, wandering over to a large map of Gaul and its surroundings.

"I don't know whether you're aware... I expect you are, since Fronto always seems to know about things before even I do... that the scouts have now all returned?"

The three men before him nodded.

"We're going to be moving very soon. I intend to call a general staff meeting shortly and pass out the orders to my officers, but, to assuage your curiosity, this is the situation in a nutshell..."

He jabbed his finger into the centre of Belgic lands on the map, where the legend 'NERVII' was just visible in the low interior light.

"Deep in their territory, most of the Belgae have combined to create one large army. And when I say large, I do mean large. I have been unable to ascertain numbers no matter how many spies and scouts I send out, but I have heard words like 'sea' and 'carpet' used to describe the assembled mass, so I'm going to assume we're talking about a very large group. And some of them are Germans who've crossed the Rhine to join in. Most of my other legates are young and lack the experience that you two have. I'm going to rely more and more in the coming weeks on the pair of you, along with Labienus and Sabinus."

Fronto rubbed his nose reflectively without thinking and gave a slight yelp.

"I assume then, Caesar, that you fully intend to take us against the Belgae, whatever their strength?"

The general nodded.

"Frankly, Fronto, I cannot back down now. I'm sure you understand. The Belgae have the greatest reputation of the northern barbarians. If we can defeat them, our allies will be safe; no other tribe will dare move against us. If we run back to Narbonensis with our tail tucked between our legs, however, we will lose the respect of the tribes, our allies will likely desert us and side with the Belgae; we will lose our foothold in Gaul and with it any hope of loot for the men and a triumphal return to Rome. The officers will be ridiculed by the senate and the men will be pensioned with little booty to show for the two years of activity."

He smiled a horrible smile.

"And then one day the Belgae, who will no longer have any reason to fear us, will take their cue from the Gauls long ago, and will cross the border and sack Italia."

He waited for any objection from the three in front of him, but no one spoke.

"No. We must prove ourselves now. We must claim our stake in Gaul. However, I would prefer to even the odds."

His finger moved down the map toward the more southerly Belgae lands.

"Here, in their nearest territory, is a Belgic tribe called the Remi. My scouts tell me that, while the Remi are far from the strongest of the Belgae, they are actually open to Roman negotiations; and if the *Remi* are, then it is possible that other tribes may follow suit. Basically I cannot formulate a full plan until after we have met with the Remi."

The general, his face showing some signs of stress, slapped the area of the Belgae on the map with the flat of his palm.

"And herein lies my problem. I need to plan. I don't like being unprepared for eventualities, but until I have seen for myself, I have to rely on my gut feelings and the usual couple of tricks I have up my sleeve."

Balbus shrugged.

"Then why not delay, Caesar? Send ambassadors to the Remi and stay here until you're fully apprised of the situation? The Belgae won't get any bigger in the meantime."

The general shook his head.

"True: the Belgae will not increase, but there are two other potential problems. Given extra time it's quite possible that more and more Germans will cross the Rhine and sign up to the Belgic cause. Even if not, it is possible they will decide they are strong enough, march over or through the Remi and come after us. That way we lose a potential ally, the incentive, and any hope of choosing the ground when we do meet."

He sighed.

"No, we have to go now. Strike, as the smith says, while the iron is hot."

Balventius nodded professionally, and Fronto cleared his throat.

"I was given to believe, Caesar, that you were waiting on other things yet too? Crassus for one thing."

A dark look crossed the general's face.

"With Crassus, what will be, will be. I had expected to have heard from him by now. It is entirely possible that the Belgae already have allies in the west; that they have successfully stirred up trouble against us there and that Crassus is already hanging from a tree with his eyes pecked out by the crows."

He gave Fronto a particularly searching look.

"A possibility, I might add, about which I have somewhat mixed feelings…"

The legate had the grace to look down and avoid his gaze.

"But I have put a safeguard in place in case of Crassus' failure and demise."

He straightened and squared his shoulders.

"I cannot tarry for news of Crassus."

Fronto narrowed his eyes.

"What safeguard?"

The general sighed again.

"Fronto, you're one of my senior staff, but you really don't need to know everything!"

Balventius cleared his throat.

"Caesar?"

"Yes?"

"Why am I present, sir? I'm not involved at a command level."

The general returned to his seat and sank gratefully into it.

"You, however, are the man my senior staff saw fit to land with the task of arresting and questioning Paetus. And in that role, I have further use of you."

Balventius merely sat straight and raised his eyebrow.

"My courier returned from Rome this morning."

Fronto leaned forward.

"Slip of the tongue, Caesar? Courier's', surely? You sent a half dozen riders."

The general flashed an irritated look at the legate.

"I know what I mean, Fronto. Shut up."

Turning back to Balventius, he pointed at him.

"Paetus' family are now under my protection, though I cannot be seen to coddle them or Paetus becomes useless as a source of misinformation. Do you remember my niece Atia and her husband, Octavius?"

Fronto nodded.

"I met them in Rome at a party a few years ago. Nice, I remember."

"Octavius passed on to the Elysian Fields a couple of years ago but, with the way things are in Rome, Atia maintained his bodyguards to protect her and the children. They number quite a few, and Octavius chose able men. They have Paetus' family under observation. The moment anything turns against them, they will be whisked away to the safety of Atia's villa."

He smiled.

"So. Balventius, I need you to start paving the way with Paetus. I want him thoroughly with us. I want him to be ready to sell his father to protect his wife if needed."

He ignored the disapproving looks Fronto was throwing at him.

"And you, Fronto? I want you to start thinking of how we can use this. Bear in mind that the stronger I become and the weaker my enemies, the better position I am in to protect and advance your sister and yourself. Think hard."

He stood again, scraping the feet of the chair across the floor.

"I think that's it, gentlemen. Get yourself an hour's rest or food. Fronto? Balbus? We reconvene with the rest of the officers in an hour. Time to start preparing. We march on the Belgae tomorrow."

Chapter 4

(Durocorteron, in the lands of the Remi)

"Curia: the meeting place of the senate in the forum of Rome."

"Pilum: the army's standard javelin, with a wooden stock and a long, heavy, lead point (plural 'pila')."

Caesar's sudden decision to move had caused a stir among the legions. They had been encamped around Vesontio for months and had become settled in their ways. Though everyone knew they would be moving off on campaign soon, the legions' officers had been assuming they would wait for word of Crassus, and then suddenly Caesar had given the entire army one night's notice. Every man had been short on sleep when they were called to attention by the cornicens and subsequently packed their gear, stowed their baggage in the wagons, secured the artillery for transport and systematically took down the defences, demolishing the palisades and infilling the ditch as was the tradition with a departing army.

Then had begun the interminable journey. In actual fact, the army had only been on the road for two weeks, but it felt like so much longer. A legion could travel fast, but out here with only native dirt tracks instead of good Roman paving, in unknown territory that had to be scouted in advance of the column, and with the ancillary wagons, staff, artillery and other clutter of seven legions and the command section, travel was painfully slow; sometimes as little as ten miles in a day.

But then, that was the price you paid for having your entire support system with you. This was no small punitive expedition, but a show of Roman power with a fully supported army. The merchants and tavern keepers in Vesontio had been sad to see such a rich source of revenue leaving their land, though they would live fat and wealthy for the next year at least; Caesar had ordered the quartermasters to stock up for the campaign and, with a great deal of foresight, Cita had purchased every last spare grain of corn available in a twenty mile radius around Vesontio. Back in that city, men would be rubbing their hands with glee while stacking their denarii.

And finally, three days ago, they had reached the lands of the Remi. The scouts had returned to inform the staff that the 'capital' of that tribe was just over twenty miles distant.

Since arriving in the territory of the Belgae, the pace of the army had almost halved again as they moved forward with considerable caution, the outriders constantly circling the huge mass of troops. Caesar had called the officers to him that night and stated his intention to camp at the centre of Remi lands. It served a threefold purpose: firstly, it was the safest place within the Belgae's territory; secondly it was a hub for trade, politics and information; and thirdly, a show of such strength amidst the Remi would serve to remind them of the power of Rome and the wisdom of alliance.

And so, last night, they had made camp four miles from the town and prepared.

This morning, a fresh and gleaming Roman army numbering some thirty thousand regular troops, along with thousands of cavalry, mostly of Gallic auxiliary status, slowly tramped and stomped their way over the hill and toward the river and the wooden bridge that gave access to the Remi's oppidum of Durocorteron. The sight must have been overwhelming for the ordinary folk of the tribe.

Without sending a single man across the river to the Remi, the legions, as prearranged, began to set up huge temporary camps; three in all, each large enough to accommodate fifteen thousand and the necessary gear. The men had worked hard and, within two hours, camp had been established, even before the last of the immense military column had arrived on the scene. A wide ditch and rampart surrounded each camp, and once the baggage arrived, a defensive palisade was formed of the sharpened stakes that were carried in the wagons and could later be undone and stowed for reuse.

The show must have been mind-boggling for the locals. Certainly, by the time the camps were complete, in the late morning, the number of native men, women and children watching them intently from across the river had grown to number in the hundreds. Caesar had deliberately kept the army from interacting with them; every centurion and optio had their orders. Whether these Belgic folk shouted disparaging things at the men, or even enticing ones, the soldiers barely glanced at, let alone acknowledged, them.

The afternoon had set in with the legions setting watches and passwords, creating their temporary workshops, mucking out the horses and all the regular daily camp duties. Everything the general did here was designed to both worry and impress the leaders of the Remi.

And it must be working. For now, as the sun began to sink from the sky and afternoon began to give way to evening, many of their civilian observers had become bored and left, but a number of well-dressed and armed warriors had taken up stations on the far bank and the bridge. Fronto stood on the rampart of his camp and watched them with interest. With the quality of their armour, they were likely the chieftain's own men. He was just wondering how long they would watch before trying to force some sort of interaction, when a commotion began up the hill in the centre of the town.

From here, Fronto could see up the main road between heavy, low buildings and scattered oak trees. Up there must be some kind of centre; perhaps a marketplace even? And something was happening there. Between the branches and trunks of the trees, he could see light; the flickering light of many torches. The legate dithered for a moment as to whether to alert the command, when a noise like a bull being castrated sprang up on the hill.

Fronto jumped slightly at the sudden cacophony, before realising it was supposed to be music; a fanfare presumably. And there was movement high on the hill.

He reached across to the legionary next to him on the bank.

"Leave your weapons here. Get to the principia as fast as you can and inform the general and his staff that we're about to have guests."

The soldier saluted and turned, dropping his shield and pilum, and ran as fast as he could toward the rear of the huge camp. The three fortifications had been carefully placed in a horseshoe around the near end of the bridge, such that each rampart was the same distance from it. The central camp, that of the Ninth and the Tenth, also accommodated the senior staff.

Fronto watched with fascination from the rampart as a procession of sorts began to make its way down the main road of the oppidum toward the Romans. The group numbered around a hundred and at first glance appeared to be some sort of strange parody of a Roman military column. As they got closer, Fronto gradually picked out more detail, though the awful noise was setting his teeth on edge and forming the beginning of a headache.

First came four men blaring out 'dying goose' sounds through tall bronze horns with flared ends shaped into the likeness of wolves. Behind them came four more with a horrifying instrument that involved the squeezing of some sort of bag. The resulting noise sounded like a deflating ox. Fronto stared at them with a strange mixture of horror and amusement. Behind the 'musicians' came the standard bearers. No flags here, just poles with bronze animals on them; boars, wolves and bears. And behind that was a crowd of warriors in what Fronto presumed to be their ceremonial gear, surrounding two well-dressed tribesmen on white horses. The warriors on either side of the column lit the way in the dusk with burning torches.

The Remi probably thought it was impressive. Indeed, it might have been impressive if it were not for the deflating animal sounds. Fronto, trying to keep his men in position with a straight face, had to bite his lip gently to refrain from sniggering.

Suddenly the worst of the noise stopped. Fronto breathed deeply in relief and then realised with horror that it was only a moment's grace. The airbags were now empty, and the musicians reinflated them with a sound like a hundred men farting in a cave.

No amount of lip biting could prevent the laugh that came then and, even as the players began the full blare of the awful noise once again, all around Fronto on the rampart men burst out laughing. Indeed, as he listened carefully over the cacophony, he was sure he could even hear men laughing at the other camps.

He gave them a few moments of laughter, but this sort of thing looked bad, even if it was his own fault.

"Silence!" he bellowed along the line, and the men of the Ninth and Tenth Legions fell quiet and straightened themselves.

By the time the Belgae had reached the bridge, the staff were approaching Fronto's position inside the camp. Caesar, Sabinus and Labienus climbed the slope with long strides and stopped next to the legate of the Tenth.

"What is the name of Charon's teeth is that noise?" asked Sabinus, a horrified look on his face.

Caesar smiled at him.

"Ceremonial music. I've heard those pipes before at Celtic gatherings. Aren't they awful?"

He turned to Fronto.

"Pass the word along here and to the other camps as quickly and quietly as you can. I want silence from the men. Not a word or movement. In fact, tell the other legions that their officers are to remain in their camps."

Fronto frowned.

"Are we not going out to meet them? I thought they wanted to be our allies?"

Caesar shook his head.

"I don't know how trustworthy they are, and this is our first show to the Belgae. We want to be as powerful and impressive as Rome can possibly be. I want word to spread from here. If we can make the Remi tremble and fall in line, then it's possible other tribes of the Belgae will follow suit. Every tribe we can frighten into submission means fewer warriors that the leaders can call on against us. This is the time for a show of strength, not diplomacy."

Fronto shrugged and gave the word to two of his tribunes who began to make their way along the wall, passing on the details.

The noise was becoming unbearable now that the chieftains' party had reached the near bank. There was a brief pause then; trying to decide where they should go, Fronto guessed. The two men on horseback consulted for a moment and then the column moved on, heading for the central camp. As they approached, finally reaching a position where the men, their night vision blinded by the guttering torches, could make out the Roman installations, Caesar stepped back from the wall, gesturing for the other officers to do so.

As Fronto dropped back down the slope, he raised a questioning eyebrow.

"Let them be challenged by the guards as though they were nobodies," the general smiled.

"Do we open the gate?"

"Most certainly not."

Fronto frowned. As the officers waited behind the stockade, they heard someone address the legionaries on guard in the strange language of the Celts.

The guard, drawn tonight from the Ninth, answered in clear Latin.

"Approach and be recognised."

There was a long pause and some heated discussion in that odd language again. The centurion at the gate took a deep breath.

"For the last time, advance and be recognised!"

As the squabble among the visitors intensified, the centurion called along the walls: "make ready!"

Two dozen men on the embankment turned sideways and raised their pila into the discharge position. The argument among the Remi intensified, and finally a voice called out in intelligible Latin.

"Friends. Remi are friends of Rome. We must see your commander. Bring your commander."

The centurion turned to look at Fronto and the officers nearby. Caesar made smoothing motions with his hand and put a finger to his lips. The centurion and his men stood silently.

"Roman?"

Caesar tapped Fronto on the shoulder and leaned close to whisper.

"Go tell him we're too busy to see him tonight. We'll visit him tomorrow when we have more time."

Fronto stared, unsure whether to smile or not. It all seemed so childish, somehow.

Taking a deep breath, he climbed the embankment slowly. When he reached the top, he looked down at the assembled warriors and tried not to laugh. They looked decidedly uncertain and, having lost the impetus of the parade, were now milling around aimlessly below the stockade.

"Greetings to the Remi" he called. "Unfortunately, we do not have time to consult with you at the moment. Please return to your village and we will call on you as and when the opportunity arises."

The speaker on horseback seemed to inflate as though he would explode. Fronto couldn't quite see in the bad light, but would be willing to bet the man's face had gone red with rage. The man raised his hand and pointed at Fronto, opening his mouth to speak, but the legate had already left the wall without waiting for a reply.

As he returned to the staff, Sabinus was rocking with silent laughter. Labienus bore a wide grin and even Caesar greeted him with an uncharacteristically genuine smile.

Patting Fronto on the shoulder, Caesar chuckled.

"Well I wanted to make them feel inferior, but that surpassed all my expectations. I hope you haven't pushed them so far they get angry instead of frightened!"

Sabinus grinned, taking a deep breath.

"Village?"

Fronto shrugged.

"It hasn't even got a stockade."

"But village?" Sabinus laughed again. "It's the capital city of their tribe, and you just called it a village. And turning your back on his answer? Good grief, man!"

Fronto shrugged again.

"To hell with them."

Leaving the baffled and irritated Remi outside the gate, Caesar and his staff strode off toward the principia. Fronto smiled at the centurion.

"Let's not be too mean. If they're still there in an hour, take them out some cheese and bread."

As he walked off to catch up with the general, he could hear the centurion chuckling behind him.

* * * * *

It was after lunch the next day when the messenger arrived at Fronto's tent.

"Caesar calls his staff to the main gate, sir."

Fronto nodded and grabbed his helmet and sword before striding out of his tent. He had been dressed and equipped now for two hours in order to be ready when the general called. He strode outside to find Priscus standing irritably nearby, tapping his vine staff on his greaves.

"What's up with you?"

The primus pilus grumbled.

"I'm getting sick of all this camp building and diplomacy crap. If our lads don't get to kick some Gauls soon, they're going to have forgotten which end of a sword goes into the enemy. They're getting soft!"

Fronto laughed lightly and patted Priscus on the shoulder as he walked past.

"Only you, Gnaeus. Only you could stand in unknown territory, facing possibly ten to one odds in our very near future and be bored."

"Pah!"

The centurion watched Fronto irritably as he walked off toward the camp's north gate. The legate of the Tenth was hardly recognisable. Knowing the general's desire to make an impression, Fronto had not only bathed, combed and shaved, but his armour was buffed to brilliance and his clothes freshly laundered. He looked every inch the Roman officer, an effect only slightly muted by the faint waft of stale wine that followed him.

Caesar was already at the gate as Fronto and Rufus converged from different directions. Most of the staff officers were present.

"Good afternoon, general," Rufus addressed Caesar, nodding respectfully to Fronto.

"Good afternoon, gentlemen. Are you prepared?"

Fronto grumbled.

"Depends what for."

"Are we not to be mounted, Caesar?" enquired the young legate.

The general shook his head.

"Firstly, I don't want them to think we're soft; secondly, I want to approach at a steady marching pace; and thirdly…" he gave a sly smile in the direction of the Tenth's legate. "Thirdly, after Fronto's performance last night, I don't want to present too easy a target for any irritated assassin!"

The staff officers chuckled quietly, which caused Fronto to grind his teeth.

"Let's just get this over with so we can go and kick someone" he grumbled. "Priscus is bloody right."

Ignoring a number of questioning looks, he strode out of the gate. In front of the fort, Aulus Ingenuus had formed up Caesar's bodyguard without their horses. In the distance, he could see Balbus and Plancus striding from one camp and Crispus, Galba and Varus from the other. So; all the senior commanders in the army in one place. He frowned and addressed Ingenuus as he reached the honour guard.

"I hope your men are alert! Caesar's got every senior officer walking blindly into that place. If the Belgae really wanted, they could end this campaign in one fell swoop. It'd probably only take a couple of dozen men if they planned it right!"

Ingenuus laughed and held up his hand in salute, the remaining three fingers on his right hand spread wide.

"I'm very careful these days, Fronto!"

Fronto stood watching with his customary sour face and grumbles as the officers assembled. As usual, when he cast his eyes around his companions, he felt like the badly-dressed poor relation.

Caesar arrived next to him, clapped his hands together and rubbed them vigorously.

"Bear in mind, everyone, that we have a fine line to walk today. I don't want to actually insult the Remi any more after Fronto's excellent display, but I do want to appear powerful enough that they feel as though we'd be doing a favour by letting them join us."

He smiled benignly at them.

"Which, of course, we are."

There was a chorus of laughs.

"Alright, Ingenuus. I think we're all here. Lead us out."

The young officer saluted and formed up his dismounted cavalry. The guard fell into a heavy step as they marched towards the bridge, the commanders striding along roughly in time in the centre of their protective unit.

At the bridge, the locals hurried out of the way of the iron, bronze and red linen column of men that shone and impressed in the early afternoon sun. Fishermen at the far end grabbed their lines and moved off the wide bridge and down to the adjacent river bank. Indeed, as the Roman party, some hundred strong with their guard, arrived on the far side, the road cleared ahead of them all the way up the oak-lined avenue to the centre.

Fronto examined the Remi and their town of Durocorteron. While Caesar and most of his staff officers marched on, their eyes straight ahead and their sight locked on a future of Roman domination with their own backsides firmly planted in the curia in Rome, Fronto could see past his own career progression. For Caesar and his cronies to secure their future, all they required was a conquest, but Fronto's thoughts went deeper than that.

He doubted the general had devoted a moment's thought to what would happen to Gaul once he'd had his triumph and climbed to the top of the ladder. If Caesar could actually pacify Gaul, would he set about its Romanisation? Would he care? And, of course, would it work? Cisalpine Gaul has been a province of Rome for a century and a half and was, in truth, as Roman as his homeland around Puteoli. Africa, on the other hand, had never truly settled since the days of Carthage, with occasional uprisings that kept the governor on his toes.

No matter how much the Belgae might think of themselves as a separate people to the Gauls, Fronto could see just how similar they were as he met the defiant gazes of the men and women in the gardens and doorways of the houses they passed.

Their clothing and armour appeared to be the same, their hair braided the same way; the language in which they exchanged comments about their visitors was, to Fronto's ear, identical to those of the Helvetii and the Aedui, and very similar even to the Ariovistus' Germans, if less guttural. As his gaze swept across Durocorteron itself, he realised that even their towns were the same; their oppida. The houses were constructed in the same fashion, the lower courses of heavy local stone, with a timber upper. The towns were organised in much the same layout.

He smiled to himself. If there was one thing that Rome could learn from the Gauls, it was trees. Roman cities were well organised and efficient. Everything was built to a pattern that kept the streets clean and clear of traffic. Paved roads and gutters; side streets, kerbs and rings for tying horses; the front doors of blocks of housing opening onto the roads. But there were no trees. Flowers and trees were planned in Roman cities, but restricted to parks and gardens in set and usually private enclosures.

But there was something about striding up this packed-earth street. It was probably horrible in rainy winter time, but the houses were all set back with a well maintained garden fronting the road and a small path. Trees gave the road shelter and kept him cool.

If Gaul could be Romanised, he mused, it might be a nice province to retire to one day.

He became aware that Crispus was staring at him with his eyebrow raised.

"Just taking it all in. Know your enemy, eh?"

The young legate gave him a light, unconvinced, smile.

"Whatever you say, Marcus. Pretty gardens though, aren't they?"

Fronto rolled his eyes and shifted his gaze to the front once more. They were almost at the top of the hill; the long, sloping road stretching back behind them to the bridge and the Roman camps, now obscured by the branches of the trees.

As Caesar's guard reached the open space at the centre of the oppidum, Ingenuus gave orders, and they fanned out into a protective cordon. Caesar and the staff strode into the centre and came to a halt. Clearly, the arrival of the Roman party at the bridge and their march up the street had been enough to draw the leaders of the Remi from their houses. Two men, whom Fronto would be willing to bet were the two riders from last night, stood with their arms folded opposite the Romans, their warriors armed and armoured behind and beside them. For a moment, Fronto wondered whether he had gone too far last night and turned the Remi against them. He briefly considered trying to become less visible in case of reprisals, but quickly chastised himself. These people had no idea who he was, and they certainly would not recognise him, given the low torch light last night.

His fears were allayed as the two men bowed deeply and Caesar nodded respectfully in return.

"My apologies for being unable to find time to greet you yesterday. I'm sure you understand that an army this size requires a considerable amount of control and administration."

Masterful, Fronto smiled to himself. In one stroke he just made a conciliatory gesture, while reminding them of the enormous power of Rome and the very present danger of a huge Roman army across the river.

The two men exchanged words briefly before one of them stepped to the side and gestured to a large building. Essentially a long single-floored hall, constructed in the same manner as the other structures with a thatched roof and several windows, the building was clearly important. Perhaps the house of a chieftain, or some Belgic version of the curia?

Caesar nodded. Before he could step forward and enter, however, Ingenuus and two of his men strode ahead and walked in, giving the interior a quick check before the general arrived. The other senior officers followed on.

The interior of the hall was quite dim, though the windows let in enough light that the eyes would soon adjust. In the centre, a sizeable fire burned in a carefully-constructed stone-lined pit, while the column of smoke rose up and disappeared through a small round hole in the roof. At one end of the hall stood a large and impressive chair, carved from oak with dragons and wolves and boars. Behind it, the wall was covered with cured animal pelts, weapons and shields. Warriors stood around the periphery, armed, but with weapons sheathed. Fronto experienced a moment of doubt. Even with Ingenuus' men at the ready, it would be reasonably easy to murder the entire Roman command here.

Fronto found that he had his jaw clamped tightly shut and was carefully examining every warrior. He forced himself to relax. The truth was that they could have been killed just as easily in the main square. Caesar was sure of the Remi; if he had not been, they would not have come and, whatever misgivings he might have about the general, lack of forethought was not one of his greater flaws.

Ignoring the chieftain's seat, the two Belgae leaders walked across to the fire and warmed their hands over the flames while servants brought benches in and placed them centrally in the hall around the fire pit. Fronto nodded to himself. The Remi chieftains were being extremely careful to show their deference to Caesar, even abandoning the symbol of their tribal power, the throne, in order to meet the general on a level. Without a word, the two men sat on one of the benches and gestured to Caesar, who nodded and turned to his companions.

"Gentlemen? Let's sit and get on with this."

As the Roman officers joined them by the fire and took their seat, Ingenuus and his men filed around behind them, echoing the stance of the warriors at the far side.

"My name is Antebrogius" announced the shorter of the two men. "This is Iccius. We are two of the eleven Remi chiefs. Iccius does not speak Latin, but he is the chief of an oppidum on the border close to the Nervii and has brought me the latest and best information about the gathering army. I rule here in Durocorteron and am the only Remi chief who can speak your language."

Caesar nodded.

"Indeed, you speak it exceedingly well. May I ask where you learned?"

The chief shrugged.

"I make it my business to learn about the more dangerous peoples in the world. I also speak the language of the Germanic tribes and that of the Greeks."

Caesar smiled, clearly genuinely impressed. Fronto sat and grumbled under his breath. He spoke Latin well enough, of course, but his tutor had despaired of his deplorable Greek.

"Very well," Antebrogius continued, "I have been authorised to speak on behalf of all the chiefs of the Remi in this matter. All of the Belgic peoples have been concerned since last year that the armies of Rome are coming close to our lands. Our druids rally the tribes in defiance of you, general. They call on all of the Belgae and of the Gauls, the Germans and the Britons to come to their aid in opposing you and everything you stand for."

Caesar frowned.

"I see. They are not aware that we are here only in response to requests from our allies."

Antebrogius shook his head.

"They are aware of that. They do not believe it, Caesar."

He sighed and gestured around him.

"Forgive my bluntness, general, but it is clear to all of our peoples that Rome means to take these lands and to make them her own. There is little point in denying it. We are all convinced."

There was an uncomfortable moment of silence.

"However," the man went on, "a man of vision looks into the future and takes the path scented with lilies, not the one the cows have shat on."

He smiled.

"We are in a dangerous position, quite frankly. We are the border people of the Belgae. If we listen to our druids, I am under no illusion that Rome will beat and enslave the Remi first and use our oppida as staging posts to deal with our brethren."

The smile turned vaguely sad.

"And those with vision can see that Rome will win. Rome will always win."

Caesar raised an eyebrow, and Antebrogius shrugged.

"As I said, I study these things. I have read of your wars with Carthage and in Hispania. Of your friend Pompey and his pirates. Rome will always win because Rome does not believe it can lose, and a Roman never gives up. One day we will all speak Latin and no one will remember the language of the Belgae."

He slapped his hand on his chest.

"I can see this, and my people can see it too, even if the druids and the rest of the Belgae cannot."

He stood.

"So… on behalf of the Remi, I offer our people and our lands to you, general. We have refused the call to stand against you and have made enemies of our brothers. Thus, I entreat you to deal with us as allies. We will provide you with information, supplies, food, shelter and even men. In return, we ask only that Rome promises to grant its protection to the Remi. What is your answer, Caesar?"

The general smiled.

"Antebrogius, you are a wise man indeed. Though I myself intend to stay in Gaul only to protect our friends and our interests, I would say that you are correct. One day these lands will know the benefits of Roman law and engineering, of that I am sure. And when those days draw closer, it is those who embrace them that will gain the most. I would ask whether you are alone among the Belgae in seeking peace with Rome?"

Antebrogius nodded sadly.

"We tried in council to persuade our neighbours, the Suessiones, to join us. They are part of the same people as the Remi, but there was little support for us among them, and in the end, pride won out and they have sent their warriors to the gathering Belgae. It pains me, but yes; we are alone."

Caesar's brow furrowed. "What can you tell us about this army?"

"The force will be vast, general. Not only all of the other tribes of the Belgae gather, but also many of the Germanic tribes from near the Rhine and even some from across it. Much of the blood of the Belgae is descended from those Germans who settled here generations ago. It is said that it is the fierceness of the German blood, mixed with the cleverness of the Gauls, which makes the Belgae so dangerous."

"We need more detail, Antebrogius. Numbers, even, if you have them."

The two chieftains exchanged looks and words quickly in their own language and then Antebrogius turned back to the visitors.

"Our information is a little vague, of course, since we have not been present at the war council. However, we have a slight advantage. Those same Suessiones who we failed to convince of our wisdom have been made the leaders of the gathering host and, through estimates from familial connections, we are able to estimate their numbers at around three hundred thousand men."

Fronto realised he had just whistled through his teeth and clamped his mouth shut. Unprofessional idiot! But still… three hundred thousand warriors. Not a long way from ten to one odds. He found himself wondering about the wisdom of the Remi's decision.

Caesar, however, seemed to have been unfazed by this revelation. He nodded thoughtfully.

"Any details on how that is comprised? Anything we can use?"

Antebrogius nodded.

"The Bellovaci are known as the bravest of all the Belgae, and they have given the most men. Probably around sixty thousand. The Nervii are by far the most warlike. It is they who called for war in the first place. Between them and the Suessiones, they will field around a hundred thousand. Perhaps forty thousand will be Germanic allies. Other than that, smaller numbers from the other tribes."

Caesar sighed.

"Are any of those smaller tribes likely to be open to persuasion?"

Antebrogius shook his head. "Not with the Bellovaci, the Nervii and the Suessiones in control."

Caesar nodded.

"Very well. Here is my offer."

He leaned forward in a businesslike manner.

"You will supply us with food out of only the excess your tribe can spare. Your chieftains will each levy a number of men to be assigned to our cavalry. It is the custom of Celtic allies to give hostages to one another to promote loyalty. As such, I will require the eldest heir of each chief to be delivered to me. That man will act as our hostage, but will also be assigned to lead his own tribesmen."

Antebrogius frowned. "This is a great deal to ask, Caesar."

"But I am not finished, Antebrogius. Those men will serve with us for this year. After that, we will renegotiate. However, bear in mind that those men will be taught everything we have to teach about war and the army. They will become more powerful than ever before; more powerful than other Belgae war chiefs."

He smiled. "Also: In return, we will provide a small garrison to protect each of your settlements during this campaign. These men will be a mixture of professional legionaries and auxiliaries and can teach your people Latin, how to build roads, create aqueducts, and the rudiments of civic defences, as well as providing protection. Think what this could do for the Remi."

Antebrogius sat back and nodded slowly to himself.

"I see the wisdom in your words, Caesar and, since I speak for the Remi, consider our word given. It may take a little time to explain this to my peers and to gain their agreement. I will visit your camp tomorrow morning, if that is acceptable?"

The general nodded.

"Most acceptable, Antebrogius. I look forward to it."

He stood and nodded to the officers. "Gentlemen? I believe we're done here. Let us return to camp."

Wordlessly, the Roman commanders followed Caesar's lead, standing, bowing to the chieftains, and then leaving the hall in single file.

Once they were safely out of audible distance, and half way across the square, Fronto caught up with Caesar, checked that none of the other officers were too close, and cleared his throat.

"At the risk of irritating you," he said quietly, "that was uncharacteristically generous of you?"

A look of surprise passed across Caesar's face before he settled once more into an unreadable expression.

"Marcus, we are in extremely dangerous territory, facing very heavy odds. What do you expect?"

"But to offer to train them and their leaders? You could be teaching a future enemy how to beat us."

Caesar shook his head.

"If they help us win this war it'll be worth it, and we'll have a staunch ally. If we lose, it won't make any difference to us. We have a massive force arrayed against us, but it's made up of lots of smaller groups with age-old internecine feuds. We have to widen the cracks until the Belgae shatter. It's all a matter of playing the odds, Fronto. You're a gambler. You should know that."

Fronto fixed his gaze on the road ahead and grunted.

"I think at this point, I'd pick up my dice and my remaining denarii and go home!"

* * * * *

Antebrogius the Remi chieftain bowed deeply to Fronto in the bright morning light as the man left Caesar's tent. The legate of the Tenth nodded back absently, stepping aside to let him return to his town with his accompanying warriors. Waiting only a moment, tapping his foot on the springy turf, he entered without knocking.

Caesar looked up in surprise from the documents on his desk.

"Fronto? I didn't send for you?"

The legate nodded.

"I know, general, but I need to go through a few things."

Caesar pushed aside the lists he had been examining and sat back, folding his arms. "Go ahead, then. This can wait."

"I've been looking at the campaign maps of the Belgae lands, and there's just no way we can move on the army while protecting the lands of the Remi, and those defensive garrisons you were talking about will be adequate for the look of things, but they'd be slaughtered to a man if the main host of Belgae suddenly hove into view."

Caesar nodded quietly and thoughtfully.

"Give me specifics, Fronto."

"Well..." the legate said, wandering across to Caesar's map, hanging on the wall of the command tent, and illustrating his points with a finger.

"We're here in the south, where the Remi are." He pointed further up. "The Belgae are massing to the north. That's where we'll have to go to fight them."

He waved his arm vaguely to the left.

"Yet there's a lot of Remi land over here, away from the area the two armies will meet, but with a lot of borders with the enemy. We cannot be sure the entire force is massing in the one place. If we march north and find only three quarters of the enemy, it's possible the other quarter will sweep west and south and extinguish the Remi and our garrisons and sever our supply lines."

Caesar smiled. "And you think I've not planned for this?"

"Well unless Crassus is really hiding just over those hills out there, or you've got two more magic new legions hidden outside, then that would mean splitting the army. And the odds are already bad enough."

The general's smile was starting to irk him as it always did at times like this. It seemed vaguely smug.

"What!"

Caesar sighed. "We have a secret ally. I'm trying not to reveal too many of the tricks I have hidden up my sleeve, Marcus. It's a surprise, and I want it to stay like that. The more people know about it, the more chance there is of word reaching the Belgae and of them being prepared."

Fronto grumbled.

"I'm not going to run and tell the bloody Belgae, am I?"

"I suppose not. You remember the half dozen riders I sent out from Vesontio?"

Fronto nodded. "To your niece in Rome, yes."

For a moment, Caesar looked nonplussed. Just in the blink of an eye, before an ophidian smile slithered across his face again.

"Yes. Not all to Atia, though. Two to Rome. Three to Bibracte."

"Bibracte?"

Fronto's mind rushed ahead. "You called on the Aedui for help. You've got Divitiacus' Gauls coming up as a second army?"

The smile widened on the general's face. Fronto could understand that, but couldn't quite lose the image of that moment of blankness just now regarding the couriers. It nagged at him.

"They should already be encamped perhaps ten miles from the edge of Remi territory in the lands of the Parisii, just north of Lutetia."

Fronto frowned. "And if there isn't another army out there? What's Divitiacus to do then?"

Caesar smiled unpleasantly. "Then he has orders to burn the enemy lands to a cinder until there is. He's got to attract their attention. We need to split the enemy up and even the odds a little. Cracks widening, remember?"

Fronto nodded slowly. "I can see that, yes."

In the privacy of his own head, he added 'but I wouldn't approve of scorching the land to attract their attention. One day we might need these people.'

There was a moment's silence and then Caesar stretched.

"I've been thinking about Paetus and I've decided what we should do. I can't be certain whether Clodius is the hub of all my troubles, or merely a piece in the game of someone more dangerous. Clodius is certainly disrupting things for myself and many of my allies, but two things nag at me about it."

Fronto raised an eyebrow.

"Firstly," the general said quietly, "I wouldn't have credited him with enough intelligence to create a network of men, even in provincial armies, stirring up trouble. Clodius always struck me as a thug; a blunt tool. He's ambitious, but I can't believe he's shrewd enough to work out how to play men like Crassus, Pompey and myself off to achieve his goals. That sounds to me like someone else pulling his strings."

Fronto nodded slowly.

"That would mean someone more powerful than Clodius too."

"And richer," added the general. "That's the other thing. Clodius isn't from a great line like Crassus. His family were of middling importance like mine, and I had to borrow to the point of bankruptcy to get where I am. So where does Clodius' money come from?"

Fronto sighed.

"So it looks like Clodius is himself being used."

"Yes. So we need to employ Paetus, not for disinformation, but to try and discern more about what's happening in Rome. I can get a strong sense of what's going on when I'm there, but I can only get to Rome in the winter. For the summer, I have to be here. We need to somehow flush Clodius' patron, if he has one, out into the open."

Fronto nodded.

"So what do we know about Clodius that we can use?"

Caesar sighed. "It's not something I try to advertise, but the man seduced my wife."

Fronto blinked. "He seduced Calpurnia?"

Caesar rolled his eyes.

"Gods, Fronto, no! My former wife, Pompeia. Don't you pay any attention to what goes on in Rome? Didn't you even wonder why I divorced her?"

In the privacy of his own head, Fronto trotted through several exceptionally unkind responses while deliberately keeping his expression blank.

"I try not to pry, Caesar."

He frowned. "So the question is: did he do that to get to you, in which case he was already conspiring against you years ago, or is what he's doing now is some sort of weird revenge?"

"It was the reason for our divorce four years ago, as I said. I divested myself of her, but actually helped Clodius avoid prosecution to keep the scandal as detached from me as possible." Caesar frowned. "He can't want revenge... I saved him from trial. At the time I blamed Pompeia but, in retrospect, with what has been happening this past year in Rome, I'm starting to wonder whether perhaps it was all down to Clodius."

Fronto tapped his finger on the table.

"Perhaps Pompeia is the key? She's not remarried, has she? Perhaps she's still in league with the man? Or at least perhaps he is interested in her? We need to know more before you decide what to do. Could you ask her about him?"

Caesar laughed a laugh with no humour. "Pompeia will not exchange a single word with me. I'm afraid I was quite unkind when we parted. Besides, Calpurnia and I have only been married two years. She may take exception if I communicate with Pompeia."

"Hmm." Fronto drew a deep breath, once again thanking Nemesis, his unusual patron Goddess, that he had managed to remain blissfully single for so long. "You need to find out more about Clodius. Pompeia might have the information you seek, but won't speak to you. I do believe the answer's staring you in the face, Caesar."

A frown.

"Paetus…" Fronto said, tapping his finger on the table.

"Paetus can send a message to Pompeia, imploring her to speak to Clodius and intervene with the matter of his debt."

Caesar shrugged.

"It's highly likely Pompeia has no connection at all with Clodius now. If she does, she'll certainly have no leverage."

Fronto slapped his hand flat on the table.

"But you'll know. You'll know whether any of this involves Pompeia."

Another unpleasant feral smile crossed the general's face.

"I think we can go one step better than that."

Fronto raised a suspicious eyebrow.

"We can have Paetus send that message, but imploring her to speak to Clodius' patron and intervene instead! We can discover in one move what connections the man has."

Fronto nodded, but his frown deepened.

"That's true, but I have to point out, given what I've heard about Clodius, the amount of danger that will put Pompeia in."

"Yes, yes," Caesar said dismissively, waving an arm, "but think of what we could learn. Go and find Paetus. Speak to him about…"

His voice tailed off as there was a knock at the doorframe.

"Yes?"

The duty guard centurion stepped inside and saluted.

"Apologies for interrupting, Caesar, but some of our scouts have just returned at high speed."

Fronto turned, interested.

"They report a large force of Belgae moving south through the lands of the Nervii towards us."

Caesar smiled. "Sounds like it's time to move, Fronto. Time to put away all this intrigue and deal with plain old war. We'll speak to Paetus later."

He turned back to the centurion. "Sound the general muster. I want officers to me, and all the legions to begin decamping. And send me three riders."

He stood and squared his shoulders.

"Time to get the Aedui advancing too."

Fronto smiled with relief. Thank the Gods for that. His head was getting tied up in all this political crap. The more he delved, the more he remembered why he stayed away from Rome. Life was so much more simple when it came down to just putting the boot into a few barbarians.

Chapter 5

(By the Aisne River, around fifteen miles from Durocorteron)

"Groma: the chief surveying instrument of a Roman military engineer, used for marking out straight lines and calculating angles."

Fronto strode forward to the command party. Caesar and half a dozen of his staff officers were standing at the head of the halted column, gazing down the slope and across the river to the far bank. Here, the grassy hill dipped down to a small copse by the water. The river was perhaps thirty or forty feet across and deep by the look of it. On the other side, a little off to the side a small hillock rose with an impressive command of the valley.

Caesar smiled.

"We cannot be more than ten miles at most from the Belgae here and, given their numbers, I want a well protected position to work from."

There were nods of assent around him.

"Clearly that's the place for the camp" said Labienus, pointing at the hill opposite."

Fronto cleared his throat.

"Absolutely. But you're going to have to leave a force on this side too."

The officers all turned to look at him.

"Why?" enquired the general, his brow knitted.

"Well if we're going to spend more than a day or so here, then you can't rely on rafts for crossing. You're going to have to build a bridge. The supply line to feed an army this size is just too big and busy to rely on boats. The engineers can have a solid bridge here by nightfall. I'd suggest directly below the camp for protection. And then, because you can't leave such a vital crossing unguarded, you're going to have to put some sort of garrison at this end."

He shrugged.

"Unless you're intending to move on in the morning, of course."

Caesar smiled.

"There are times I'm extremely grateful for your pragmatism, Fronto. Good thinking."

He turned back to the other officers, who were all nodding their approval.

"Sabinus? Take one cohort from each legion and start constructing a camp on this side of the river."

Turning once more to Fronto, he frowned.

"Who's that tribune in the Tenth? You remember? The one who fortified Geneva for us?"

Fronto smiled.

"Tetricus, Caesar."

"He's a good engineer, yes?"

Fronto nodded.

"Probably the best in the army, general, yes."

"Good. I shall take the rest of the legions across and start the construction of the fortress. Get Tetricus to gather whoever he needs and set him to building the bridge. There should be plenty of timber for him here in this copse."

Fronto shook his head.

"With respect, Caesar, you want Tetricus with you constructing the camp. If we end up fighting off a few million barbarians, I'd like Tetricus' talents behind the defences. He's a tactical engineering genius."

He gestured at the river.

"Pomponius is my chief engineer. He's the man who built that impressive bridge overnight last year when we were chasing the Helvetii. He's the one you want for this."

Caesar waved an arm dismissively.

"Whatever you think, Fronto. Just get me my bridge."

Fronto nodded and turned to head back to the Tenth.

Tetricus was with the other tribunes at the head of the legion, chatting to Priscus, who wore his usual disgruntled look. The officers all turned as their legate approached.

"Tetricus? I need you to go see Caesar. He's building a camp for the entire army on that bluff across the river. I want you to make sure he does it well enough to withstand an attack by the Belgae."

Tetricus nodded and squinted across the river.

"The location's a decent start. But we'll want at least a triple ditch."

Fronto patted him on the shoulder as he stood marking out lines in the air with his fingers and muttering under his breath.

"That's the sort of thing, yes. Go on."

Tetricus looked up as though he had forgotten momentarily where he was.

"Mmph? Oh yes."

He turned to the nearest group of soldiers, the legionaries of the First Cohort, standing at attention behind Priscus.

"You!" he pointed at a random legionary. "Find a groma and follow me."

Fronto smiled. Engineers were all the same; they drifted along in a daze until you prodded them and gave them a project, and then nothing short of an earthquake would distract them. His smile widened as he turned and wandered down the line of men.

"Pomponius?" He called out as he reached the Third Cohort.

One of the centurions, a young, fresh faced man, stepped out of the column and saluted.

"Sir?"

"How'd you like a task?"

"A fun one, sir?"

Fronto let out a light laugh.

"Only an engineer would get to the end of a long march and look forward to building something!"

"With respect, sir, marching doesn't exactly tax the brain. I like to keep mentally limber too."

Another laugh.

"Good. Get your kit together and get down to the waterline. Caesar wants a bridge built below that hill, wide enough and strong enough to carry the entire supply column. You can draw what men you need from any of the legions."

Pomponius shrugged.

"Got everyone we need in the Tenth, sir. Happier if we keep this party in our own house, eh?"

Fronto shook his head in amusement.

"You engineers are weird, you know that?"

Leaving the centurion, he strode back to the head of the column to find Priscus tapping his foot impatiently.

"Gnaeus, we'll be moving out any moment now. Pomponius is taking whatever he needs to build a bridge and Sabinus will be back in a moment to second a cohort. I'll leave which one up to you.

Oh, and Tetricus will require quite a few men to help with constructing a fort. Once they've separated off, take the rest of the legion with the others across the river and get into a defensive position. It's going to be dark before all this is done and I don't want any nasty Belgic surprises in the meantime."

The primus pilus grunted.

"I'm sure with the dozen men I'll have left in quarter of an hour we'll be able to do a great deal!"

Fronto laughed.

"You wanted a fight, and there's one coming, so stop grumbling."

Priscus gave him a sour glare and then started passing word down the line.

Fronto smiled and strode off back towards the command party, meeting Sabinus striding fast in his direction en route. The staff officer looked concerned.

"What's up?"

Sabinus stopped and pointed back down the slope to the staff officers gathered around the general.

"Think we've got trouble, Marcus. Three scouts coming hell for leather on the other side of the river, but one of them's wounded."

The gentle comedy of dealing with determined engineers quickly forgotten, the seasoned campaigner in Fronto took over instantly.

"Get those cohorts sorted and fortify here. We need to get moving. Priscus knows you're coming. When you see him, tell him to get across that river now."

Sabinus nodded and jogged on toward the Tenth.

Heading in the other direction, Fronto picked up speed and sprinted down the slope towards Caesar and his men. Twice, on the uneven ground, he almost lost his footing as his leg threatened to buckle beneath him. Ever since that German bitch had bitten into his heel last summer, his running had been impaired.

As he slewed to a halt before the general, breathing heavily, he looked up and across the water.

The scouts had now reached the far bank. The three auxiliary riders ploughed into the water, the middle one supported in his saddle by the arms of his comrades as he wavered around and slumped periodically.

Fronto turned to Caesar.

"With respect general, whatever the news is, you need to get the army moving across and fortifying. We can't afford to waste time."

Caesar shook his head as if to shift a daze.

"You're absolutely right, Fronto."

He turned to Labienus.

"Get the army moving."

As the staff officer marched off toward the group of tribunes gathered nearby to distribute the orders, Fronto looked down at the river. Pomponius and a few of his men were already at the waterline just downstream, taking measurements. The riders finally waded ashore on the near bank and two of them dismounted and led their horses up the slope to the officers, while the third remained in his saddle, clutching his neck, drenched in blood.

"Report!" commanded Caesar.

The two scouts saluted.

"Ave, Caesar."

The general waved aside the niceties dismissively and with a little irritation.

"What happened?"

The smaller of the two men looked up at the general.

"The Belgae are close, sir. They seem to have split into two groups. The larger part is camped about twenty miles away, but a sizeable part of their army is besieging the Remi oppidum at Bibrax just downstream. The town won't hold for long."

"Damn it!" the general barked. "Bibrax is too far north, right on the Remi's border. They haven't been sent a garrison unit yet, have they?"

One of the officers in the crowd shook his head.

"No sir. The garrison's still with us. They were supposed to be heading to Bibrax when we're finished here."

Fronto growled.

"Got to do something, Caesar. Break a promise of protection to the Remi and you risk losing the alliance."

The general shook his head.

"The Remi can't expect us to have supplied troops to somewhere we haven't even reached yet. And in the grand scheme of things, it's just one barbarian town."

Fronto started to open his mouth and wave his hand angrily, but Caesar raised his voice and rode over the top of him.

"I can't send anyone. We need the legions here to get these camps constructed, else we'll be in the same state as Bibrax when the enemy get here. They're only eight miles away, Fronto. We've barely got time to get sorted even with our full complement!"

Fronto growled dangerously.

"We have to help them. Spare me one cohort and I'll go help them."

"No."

"One cohort" shouted Fronto jabbing a finger toward Caesar, spittle landing on the general's cuirass. The rest of the senior officers melted away from the two of them, hardly appearing to move. Caesar's face had gone purple. Behind him, Fronto could see Labienus making subtle, yet frantic motions to Fronto to stop.

"Alright, just two centuries" he bellowed. "For Juno's sake, that's less than a hundredth of your men. For just that, we might be able to save Bibrax, our alliance, and even your reputation!"

Caesar had begun to tremble slightly.

"Fronto, your mouth runs like a thoroughbred horse. One more word from you and you can take your vine staff, your reputation and any hope of Julii patronage, and run off home with it."

The legate began to open his mouth again. He was clearly as angry as the general.

"Fronto, I put up with your breathtaking disobedience and insolence because you may very well be the best commander that Rome has to offer, but this is my army and I will not risk it. If you wish to go help the Remi and risk your own life, by all means do so, but you will not take my legions with you."

Caesar had gone very pale now, and the legate recognised the signs. The general had been pushed as far as he would go before he snapped, and Fronto had seen the results of that before in Hispania. He shivered involuntarily and forced himself to calm down.

"Very well, Caesar. You cannot spare your legionaries. What about the auxiliaries? Will you allow me to take auxiliary units and try?"

The general glared at him for a long moment.

"The Gallic cavalry will be no use in a siege, Fronto."

"We have other units, Caesar…"

There was a long, tense silence.

"Very well. Inform your primus pilus that he is in command of the Tenth in your absence and draw whatever non-legionary staff you require. I sincerely hope you succeed, though I still consider you foolish for trying."

Fronto locked the general with his gaze for a moment and then nodded and turned to run off toward the legions. As he passed the silent and shocked gathering of staff officers, Labienus stepped out and grasped him by the arm.

"For the sake of Nemesis, Fronto, be very careful. We would miss you!"

The commander of the Tenth gave him a lopsided grin.

"Nemesis herself can't shift me, Labienus. You know that!"

With a laugh he turned and ran on. The Eighth Legion was now in the lead, marching down to the water's edge ready to cross. He grinned at Balbus.

"I'm going off on a little errand. Look after things here. Don't let Caesar cock it up for the rest of us."

Balbus raised an eyebrow.

"I know that look. Whatever you're up to, do it carefully."

Fronto gave a mad laugh and ran on.

* * * * *

The oppidum of Bibrax was considerably smaller than the one they had seen recently at Durocorteron. The population of this place could not be higher than a thousand or fifteen hundred folk at most. Situated on a wooded plateau rising above the Aisne River, it was in a reasonably defensive position, but could not surely muster more than seven or eight hundred warriors at most. For a moment, Fronto wondered whether Caesar had been right and considered turning with his force and heading back to camp.

Shaking his head, he once more cast his eyes over the panorama. There must be thirty thousand Belgae here at the very least. That was a very small portion of the Belgic army, but still enough to make the odds more than ten to one. He shook his head again and turned to look at his relief force, which threatened to make him laugh.

He had been denied the regulars, and the Gaulish cavalry would be of little or no use. Following half an hour's consultation with his fellow legates, he had selected the units he could and formed what must be the most bizarre military force ever commanded by a Roman patrician.

His army, which numbered just under a thousand in total, was formed entirely of missile troops attached to the various legions. Slingers from the Hispanic islands drawn from the Ninth and Tenth marched alongside Cretan archers from the Eighth, Eleventh and Twelfth with their short, flexible bows. And from the Thirteenth and Fourteenth: yet more archers, though these were dark as night, mustered from the Numidian peoples of northern Africa and freshly drawn from the training centre at Cremona for those newly-raised legions. Almost a thousand non-Roman soldiers, of whom half at most would be able to speak Latin with any real aptitude. The Roman prefects in charge of these irregular units all bore tired and resigned expressions, sure that the path of their career had reached a dead end. Indeed, on their eight mile hike from the bridge site, only one of the prefects had displayed any enthusiasm at all; a man called Decius, in charge of a unit of Cretans.

Now, Decius lay next to his commander on the brow of the hill, looking down at the scene with trepidation.

"How in the name of Bellona do you intend to get past them, sir?"

'How, indeed?' Fronto thought to himself as he once more examined the situation.

The oppidum rose amidst a carpet of Belgic warriors, who surrounded the town, keeping currently at a safe distance from the walls. The only way that stood remotely clear for access was to the south, where a steep slope of the hill came down straight to the waters of the Aisne. The Belgic leader had thought to cover every conceivable escape route, though, and had stationed a group of several hundred warriors on the far bank.

"Only one way in, Decius. Just the one. And it's wet."

The middle aged prefect, badly-shaven and vaguely dishevelled, blinked.

"Swim? Are you mad, sir?"

Fronto grinned. He liked Decius. Being scruffy and unshaven was frowned on among officers and often meant that man was more concerned about doing the job than pleasing his commander.

"It has been said, yes."

He pointed down at the water.

"Clearly there's no way we can fight through them, so the only way is to sneak in. And the only way to sneak is to get into the water down here, wade along the bank to the slope and then climb up to the oppidum. There's just no alternative I can see."

Decius frowned.

"I suppose you're right, but we'll be right under the gaze of those warriors on the far side."

"True," Fronto nodded, "but the water's fast and noisy and will cover our sound. And if we go at night, we can probably get right up to the walls without being seen.

The prefect spluttered.

"You seriously want to make a thousand men wade downstream in a strong current silently in the dark?"

He whistled gently though his teeth.

"People are right. You are mad!"

Fronto laughed quietly.

"Don't panic. We won't be swimming; just wading in the shallows. The bank's high enough that we should be covered from view."

Shading his eyes, Decius focused on the oppidum. "They're holding back from the walls because they're busy undermining them. They must have picked off most of the missile-bearing defenders, but there'll still be a few. The Remi are screwed when that wall collapses though, so we'd best hope it lasts until dark."

Fronto nodded.

"If you look really carefully, you can see there's no big piles of earth, so they can't be very deep yet. We've got time. And I've got an idea, but we need to get in there first."

Decius grinned.

"Fair enough. I'd better warn the others."

Fronto grabbed him by the wrist as he moved away.

"Make sure they all know how quiet they're going to have to be. I've seen Hispanic warriors in bars. They sing like they've got delicate parts of them caught in a door."

Decius grinned.

"Got it. Everyone very quiet; especially the Hispanics."

The wait for darkness had been tense. Throughout the afternoon and evening, a four hour wait, the veteran commanders had become more and more twitchy, waiting for the off. It was anyone's guess how the Hispanics, Greeks and Africans felt, but they were certainly fidgety and their officers had been forced to quieten them more than once.

Up high on their viewpoint with a constant watch on the action below, they were far enough away from the Belgae that conversation should have gone unheard, but Fronto knew better than to risk it. All afternoon and into the evening the Belgae had worked at digging their three undermining tunnels beneath the walls of Bibrax. Now, heaps of earth outside showed how far they'd got, though they'd disappeared from view in the failing light around half an hour ago.

And now, in traditional Celtic fashion, the Belgae had abandoned their assault for the night, safe in the knowledge they had Bibrax cut off and that it would fall tomorrow, and moved instead onto celebratory singing and drinking. Fronto smiled. It was not unlike the legions in a way. Still, a loud and drunken army would be considerably easier to sneak past. With a last glance toward the oppidum to be sure of his bearings, he wished them all a pleasant feast, offered up a quick prayer to Bacchus, and dropped down below the hill to issue the orders to move out.

He had entertained himself throughout his four hour vigil by conversing with Decius and had been surprised to learn that the man had served in many of the same places in Hispania as Fronto had during that campaign. Given the risk of what they were about to try, he found himself exceedingly grateful to have an experienced veteran of that calibre with him.

He crouched and made his way across to Decius and his archers. The Cretans looked so underdressed for war, in Fronto's opinion. Plain linen tunics and sandals, with a helm, shield and bow. But he had to admit, they moved fast, light and quiet. In retrospect, given what they would have to do, he could not have chosen better units for the job, though he would have preferred a colour that stood out less than plain linen. At least they were not bright white. One of the prefects had come up with an idea that the men roll around in the dirt to darken their clothes, and it had worked to some extent. Black tunics would still have been better, though.

His jaw clamped tight, he gestured to his men and the various prefects began moving their units down the slope as slowly and quietly as they could. As always, Fronto led the column, Decius directly behind him, and the large, mismatched force slipped down the grass and into the reeds at the water's edge like ghosts.

Fronto stepped carefully amid the treacherous plant life and sucking mud as he slowly made his way along the bank, watching for the occasional tree root that snaked out of the soil to his right and threatened to catch or trip him. Insects whined around his ears and repeatedly bit him on the arms and scalp while his feet slowly numbed in the cold water.

He smiled as he imagined what this would look like from the far side. Ghosts is what they'd seem, pale and silent in the darkness. It was going to be a long trek. They would have to travel the better part of a mile at this slow and difficult pace before they could even think of climbing the bank unnoticed. Somewhere behind him he heard a splash and he glanced irritably over his shoulder before stepping on.

The last purple shimmer of evening lay ahead and to the right on the skyline, outlining the bulk of the oppidum on its plateau and the shallow v of the river in its dip. Fronto kept glancing nervously ahead and to the left, trying to make out the details of the Belgic guards on the far bank.

He could see the flicker of camp fires, but could not tell whether they were singing and drinking due to the increasing noise from close by on this bank. They were approaching the host of Belgae now. Fortunately, the enemy had had the sense to encamp some distance from the river to avoid the midges and other winged nuisances that continued to bother Fronto and his men. Still, an insect bite was less worrisome than a sword blow, as he kept telling himself.

As least, even with plain linen tunics, they would be unlikely to be spotted from the far side. The temperature was dropping rapidly, as it seemed to do in Gaul during the late spring and early summer, and that had resulted in the Belgae huddling around their campfires. And the beautiful thing about fires was how thoroughly they destroyed a man's natural night vision.

Fronto grinned at the twinkling lights slowly drawing level opposite.

They must be half way there now. Not as bad as he thought.

Suddenly the sound of splashing stopped him in his tracks. For a moment he could not discern from which direction the noise had come, and glanced back angrily, but the sound was coming from somewhere ahead.

Squinting into the ever deepening darkness, he finally spotted the man standing on the ground above them and ahead, noisily urinating down into the river while whistling some native tune. As Fronto watched with the growing relief that they were still upstream, he noticed that the man had a sack of wine in one hand. As he watched, the man let go of himself in mid stream in order to tilt his head back and use both hands to squeeze the last of the wine out of the skin. With a guttural laugh, he began to shake his hips left and right, spraying a wide arc out onto the water.

Were it not for his situation, Fronto would have laughed, it was so comical.

As he watched, he crouched silently in the shallows and waited tensely as the man finished, slung the bag over his shoulder, tucked himself away, spat down into the water, and finally strode away to rejoin his fellow revellers.

With a frown of distaste, Fronto waited a while, partially to give the man time to get out of earshot, and partially so that the water ahead would have cleared. A moment passed and then the column began to move again.

With interminable slowness they made their way along the shore, the sounds of the Belgae revels rolling down on them from above. Regularly on the unpleasant journey, Fronto found himself offering up fervent prayers to Bacchus that they would not suddenly find themselves under the aim of ten thousand emptying Belgic bladders.

It was with an immense sigh of relief that he noted the sounds of the drunken warriors next to them beginning to fade. Though it was now very dark down here in the river valley, shaded by trees and tall plants, the looming bulk of Bibrax was quite close and quite clear. That, combined with the decreasing volume, put them in the no-man's land of the slope between the Belgae and the oppidum.

A quick glance across the rippling surface of the water placed the camp fires of the waiting Belgae almost opposite now. Fronto stopped and, turning, made a motion to Decius. The command went down the line into the distance. It was ridiculous, really. Much like a marching column of multiple legions, this line of almost a thousand men must stretch almost half way back to where they'd started. There could be Hispanics back there being urinated on by drunken Belgae, and he would never know until it turned into a brawl.

He clicked his tongue, irritated at his own distraction, and made further gestures to be passed on as he climbed slowly and as quietly as possible out of the water and began to clamber up the steep slope at a crouch toward the walls of Bibrax.

He was finding his breathing more ragged and laboured the higher he climbed and set his gaze resolutely on the nearest area of the walls. Bibrax was clearly packed tightly within its perimeter and limited by the geography. A sizeable building of typical stone and timber construction rose up amid the occasional trunks of oak and beech trees.

He examined the surrounding wall as he climbed closer. Strangely, despite having spent time around the walls of Bibracte, Vesontio and Durocorteron, he had never examined their defences. Of course, he had always been off-duty with no likelihood of having to utilise those walls. These ones might mean the difference between life and death for him and his army.

He tutted with irritation. The defences of Bibrax were clearly, even at first glance, nowhere near as strong as those of the larger oppida he had visited. Vesontio had had defensive towers, for a start. This wall had no towers, though at least, he noted with relief as moonlight put in a brief appearance, they were faced with stone. They had been constructed by creating a strong wooden framework and then packing the intervening space with tamped earth. Very good against men and they'd be superb against rams or onagers, but flimsy when it came to undermining the structure. Fronto frowned. His plan might still work, but now it carried more danger.

With a sigh, he finally reached the base of the wall and gestured to the men following him to form up on the riverward side. As the auxiliaries began to join him at the summit, Fronto gazed down the slope at the myriad fires twinkling out across the ground below like a mirrored image of the stars. With a deep breath, he called on Nemesis, his favourite deity, to protect them all tonight and tomorrow. That was a lot of Belgae. He'd have to play it smart, as a straight fight would be suicide.

Another few gestures and his men began to climb the side of the wall. Stretching, Fronto turned his gaze back the way they'd come. The last hundred or so of his men were just reaching the slope and climbing out of the water now.

Simultaneously, the world around him exploded into activity. Behind and above him, one of the Remi guards above the rampart had finally spotted the men climbing and had thrust out with his spear, catching a Cretan auxiliary with a nasty stab in the shoulder and hurling him from the wall. The shout went up on the rampart, and Bibrax burst into noisy life. Men appeared above them with spears and the Cretans climbing the wall paused in their ascent, afraid to climb further.

Fronto did not have time to worry whether he could call out to the Remi and claim friendship without drawing attention from the rest of the Belgae below and endangering the last of the troops in his column. Something had happened at the back; perhaps another urinating warrior had seen them? He could not tell from this distance, but clearly something had gone wrong.

Trying to block out the noises above him for a moment, he concentrated and could finally hear the faint sounds of combat down by the water.

"Shit!"

He turned and looked up.

"We're Romans!" he yelled. "Roman relief force, get it?"

There was no reply, so he bellowed out again.

"Roman!"

Somewhere on the wall, a guttural voice said "Romani?"

"Yes, bloody Roman! Roman!" he shouted again, as the call was taken up by the prefects and other Roman officers.

Moments later, ropes were fetched and lowered down the wall for the Romans to climb. Fronto shook his head. Why the hell, now that it was clear who they were, didn't they just direct them to a gate and open it? Grumbling, he turned to look back down the hill. There was now quite a clash going on in the narrow difficult triangle where the hill rose by the waterside. A small party of Belgae had risked the advance in the darkness and were engaging the rear of Fronto's army. He barked his annoyance at Nemesis for her lack of care. The poor bastards at the back were a unit of Hispanic slingers, whose grand concessions to armour and weaponry were a linen tunic, a sling and a dagger. Caught up with fierce armoured Belgae wielding large blades, they would be cut to pieces in short order, and there was not much Fronto could do about it from up here.

"Decius! Galeo! Get your archers gathered together here and start loosing down into that crowd."

As Decius relayed the commands, Galeo stared at Fronto.

"You'll hit your own men!"

Fronto shook his head irritably.

"Those men are already dead. The Belgae are cutting through them like a grain harvest. At least if we shoot down we might drive the Belgae back and save some of our men! Now get to work!"

As the two units of archers rained their arrows down over the small group of warriors laying waste to the slingers, the remaining troops, now running up the hill to get out of the line of missile attack, climbed the ropes and made their way to the relative safety of Bibrax. Fronto waited a moment, watching the carnage below, before turning back to the two officers overseeing the covering shots.

"Keep going until the Belgae leave and the last survivors are on their way up, and then get yourselves up and over the walls. I'm going ahead to find the chief."

Decius nodded and turned back to his work as Fronto grasped one of the ropes and began to climb.

* * * * *

Inside the walls was a state of chaos. Many of the dirty and bedraggled archers and slingers who had arrived were in position on the walls, ready to give cover to their compatriots still clambering up closer. Warriors of the Remi were in position with heavy swords and long spears. Fronto gazed around the town itself. It looked surprisingly peaceful, with torches burning here and there, lighting the house fronts.

A figure strode forward out of the press of Remi warriors. He was only of average height, and armed like the rest, but wearing a heavy gold and bronze torc and expensive wristbands. He looked vaguely familiar for some reason.

"You Roman… Durocorteron."

Fronto frowned.

"Yes, I was there… I… Wait a moment? You're the other chieftain who was there with Antebrogius. Iccus or something?"

"I Iccius. Bad Roman."

Fronto stared.

"I beg your pardon?"

"Bad Roman" repeated Iccius, and tapped himself repeatedly on the chest. Fronto laughed.

"Ah, you can't speak Latin! Of course." He frowned. "Then this is going to get extremely difficult. I'm assuming none of your people can, and I sure as shit can't speak yours!"

"Eh?"

Iccius' face was a mask of incomprehension.

"Oh for Gods' sake, this is ridiculous. Thank you, Nemesis... I must remember to piss on an altar some time!"

"What was that?" asked Decius as he arrived.

"Oh, nothing. Communication issues. Our men are all Hispanic, Greek or Numidian apart from the Roman officers. His are all Belgae. No one speaks anyone else's language here. If it weren't so bloody frustrating and inconvenient, it'd be comical!"

Decius frowned.

"We should have brought a few Gaulish auxiliaries, I suppose. Still, afterthought is no better than no thought, eh?"

Fronto glared at him.

"Very helpful."

He sighed and turned back to the blank and confused face of the Remi chieftain.

"This is going to involve a lot of sign language."

"Eh?"

"Oh, Nemesis!"

He turned back to Decius.

"If I were someone like Crassus or Caesar, I'd be delegating this shit to you."

Decius grinned.

"If you were someone like Crassus or Caesar, sir, you wouldn't be here without seven legions!"

Fronto laughed and squared his shoulders.

"Right. Let's try and explain to these Remi what needs to be done."

"You've not told us yet, sir…"

Fronto nodded.

"I'm not sure how feasible my ideas are yet. Wish I'd brought a good engineer with me."

Decius opened his mouth, but Fronto cut him off.

"Yes, I know: afterthought is no better than no thought!"

He gestured to the growing crowd of damp and uncomfortable auxiliaries.

"First thing's first: get them in position right the way round the walls, two archers and a slinger every so many paces apart. I'm guessing the Remi defenders didn't have many missile weapons before. That's how the Belgae got in close enough to undermine. They could only throw rocks down. Well when they come back in the morning, I want to be able to pick off every other man who sets foot on this hill. Let's thin 'em out before they get anywhere near the walls. We can't fight them off, but with enough attrition from missiles we might be able to make them give up and move on."

He frowned as he rubbed the slimy wet linen of his red tunic between his fingers.

"And once they're in position, gather a small group. Get them to collect any loose or dead wood. I want fires at regular intervals. The men can rotate positions every half hour so that everyone gets a chance to dry off and keep warm."

"And rest, sir?"

"Sorry?"

Decius smiled wearily.

"The men need some sleep. I would suggest every group of three organises one to stay on watch in shifts."

Fronto nodded.

"Sounds good. Get to it. I'll be somewhere around with 'Eh?', teaching him about siege warfare."

He turned to Iccius.

"Isn't that right."

"Eh?"

With a sigh, Fronto grasped Decius' shoulder and then turned away to the chieftain.

"Come with me."

To illustrate his point to Iccius, he beckoned. The chief nodded and followed him, three warriors at his back. Fronto took a deep breath as he approached a clear section of wall and pointed at it.

"Romans." He held up three fingers.

Iccius nodded so Fronto mimed two archers and a slinger to him. Another nod. With a relieved sigh, the legate pointed behind him and held up three fingers again.

"More Romans."

Another nod, so he turned and pointed ahead, repeating the process. As comprehension sank into Iccius, Fronto mapped out regular positions with his fingers.

"Here comes the first tough one."

With another deep breath, he mimed two lots of three Romans again and indicated the space between them.

"Remi" he announced, miming spears and swords.

"Eh?"

"You have to be joking! I'm doing my best, man."

Waving his arms frantically and interspersing three fingers here and there, he walked back and forth along the wall, announcing:

"Roman, Roman, Roman.... Remi... Roman, Roman, Roman.... Remi..."

A slow smile crept around Iccius' face. He turned and talked to his companions, and they all made affirmative noises.

"Alright," Fronto said with relief. "I'm going to assume that means you understand. Let's move on."

He beckoned and climbed onto the wide wall. His plan might work, or might end in disaster. It was all a gamble but, as Caesar had said back at Durocorteron, Fronto was a gambling man. Of course, this gamble was made more perilous when translated from Latin by hand gestures and carried out by a motley force drawn from all over the world. As Iccius joined him, he pointed down at the Belgae.

Iccius nodded.

"So far, so good."

Reaching down, he mimed digging.

Another nod.

He repeated the gesture and pointed up and down the walls, shrugging.

"Eh?"

"Nemesis, give me some bloody help here!"

He repeated the process and added wandering along the wall, looking down. There was a long pause and finally Iccius laughed. Beckoning, he strode fast along the wall. Fronto followed him until he reached a spot that looked like any other and stopped with a smile, pointing at the floor beneath him. Fronto glanced over the parapet and squinted. Sure enough, just below him and to one side was a pile of earth.

"Thank you. Finally, we have some understanding. Alright, there's three of them."

Looking around urgently for a marker, he reached out to the warrior at the chief's shoulder and grasped his spear. The man gave him a growl. Without a word, Fronto irritably ripped the spear from his grasp and, walking back to the parapet, he carefully examined the ground and located the entrance to the tunnel outside. Tracing it across the wall with his finger, he jumped down the inside and jammed the spear in the ground there, point-first.

"Listen, Iccy. We're going to mark out the three tunnels, and then I'm going to send you on a little scavenger hunt. We're going to arrange a little surprise for your countrymen in the morning."

"Eh?"

Chapter 6

(The Remi Oppidum of Bibrax)

"Testudo: Lit- Tortoise. Military formation in which a century of men closes up in a rectangle and creates four walls and a roof for the unit with their shields."

"Miles: the Roman name for a soldier, from which we derive the words military and militia among others."

The early morning light was eerie. Fronto stood on the wall of Bibrax under the shade of a particularly bushy beech tree and tried to make out details of the Belgae on the plain below. The majority of the Belgic army lay encamped to the east of the oppidum, and it was on that side that their main siege works were being carried out. With the sun about to climb, watery and pale, above that horizon, the mass of enemy warriors below was hard to make out in the shadowy gloom.

Clicking his tongue in irritation, he reminded himself that the longer his own men got to rest before the inevitable, the better, so long as it was not more than an hour. Then the timing would be extremely tight. He turned and looked down inside the walls. Here, shade cast by the buildings and trees left the defenders still sitting in virtual darkness, lit by burning torches spaced periodically around the circumference of the oppidum.

"Enjoying breakfast?"

A number of blank uncomprehending faces looked up at him from the gathering behind the wall. While one man in each section remained on watch, the rest of the defenders, whether they be Belgae, Cretan, Hispanic, African or Roman, were all gathered in small groups around fires tucking into boars that had been roasting since not long after midnight. An army always fought better with a full belly than an empty one, so long as there was time for it to settle… and Fronto knew how this morning would begin.

There would be a few forays and tests of the new defences but no serious fighting until later, once the Belgae were sure there was no better way and that they could win. Likely, though, the first move would be the continuation of the undermining that had been begun the night before. He smiled.

As soon as things had settled last night, with the Belgae back in their camps and drinking, the defenders dry and warm and in position, Fronto had climbed down outside the wall and examined the three tunnels. At first it had struck him as strange that they should have left the tunnels so open to investigation, but then any warriors they had left behind would have been in danger overnight and would have been easily picked off from the walls. The defenders could hardly collapse the tunnels, as they would likely finish the enemy's job for them that way. Briefly, he had given thought to filling them in from the spoil heaps the Belgae had left nearby, but in truth it would not have taken them long to clear it back out with such loose earth. No; he had his idea and it should work. He had looked carefully at the tunnels and nodded appreciatively at the effort that had gone into them.

Groups of warriors had dug the three tunnels and transported the dirt out to the mounds. A long line of warriors protected by wicker shields had carried timbers up the slope, probably under enemy arrow shot in the early stages of the siege, and these had been used to bolster the mine. The tunnels were well worked. Currently, the Belgae had actually reached the level of the wall itself, the tunnel sloping gradually upward so as to avoid the need to dig into the bedrock of the hill.

Without a great deal of knowledge of Belgic siege tactics, Fronto had assumed that they followed much the same system as the civilised peoples to the south. Certainly they had no intention of merely digging tunnels for ingress to the oppidum. Any warriors emerging from the tunnel would be in single file and would be cut to pieces; so the tunnels were there to collapse the wall. The tunnel would have to go another three or four feet beneath the wall itself and then open out slightly to either side. Then, during the first assault of the day, grapple lines would be thrown over the defences. A hefty tug from the Belgae and the wood and dirt-packed walls would crumble and collapse into the holes.

With a grin, Fronto dropped down the inner face of the wall and walked over to the spot where he had marked the location of a tunnel with a spear. Since late last night, teams of auxiliary soldiers and Remi locals had worked under the directions of Roman officers, throughout the hours of darkness, to complete the tunnels from within the walls. Now there were three clear passageways under the walls, shored up with strong timber. Mounds of spoil sat next to the tunnel entrances both inside and outside the walls.

He smiled again and, wandering over to the fire, gathered a plate full of meat cuts and a few chunks of fresh bread. Returning to the wall, he settled down to wait, watching the enemy below while eating the tasty meal.

The Belgae finally came once the sun was fully above the horizon. At first they came with great care, some warriors holding large screens constructed of several layers of woven wicker backed by leather and light wooden spars to protect their companions from arrow shots, the rest gathered into three groups, heading for the tunnels.

Fronto heaved a sigh of relief as missiles began to drop down towards the attackers, but only occasional potshots as the opportunity presented itself. Satisfying. It had taken quite some time last night to explain through his officers to the multinational assembly that was his army, that they needed to take enough shots at the enemy so that the Belgae would be lulled into a false sense of security, but not enough to actually stop them reaching the tunnels or frighten them off. An arrow whizzed past him and landed one of the wicker shields below with a dull thud.

Fronto tapped his finger on his lower lip as he watched the approach. It was slow going. His men would have to show serious restraint, as he was sure that they could easily have picked most of them off before they reached the tunnel entrances. Finally, the Belgae reached the spoil heaps and the screen-bearers peeled off, running around the entrance and planting the wicker shields heavily into the ground, supporting them with beams and creating an effective missile screen.

As the first warriors reached the tunnel mouth, Fronto raised his arm and dropped it.

"First team!"

Despite the communication difficulties, plans had been drawn up during the night and set with appropriate groups. At his command, by the entrance to all three tunnels, a group of four Remi overturned a barrel into the entrance. The top of each barrel had been punctured with a hole around a hand width across. Liquid glugged and gurgled from the holes, pouring into a carefully-angled drainage channel the Roman defenders had excavated in the floor of the tunnel.

With another satisfied smile, Fronto watched the barbarians below enter the tunnel. He could hear them talking in their strange language and hoped against hope that they had not realised their error. He took a deep breath. There was laughter. Likely the barbarians had smelled the roasted hog drifting down the long passageway. Hopefully it would not occur to them that the smells should not permeate a half-dug tunnel.

Once more he raised and dropped his arm.

"Second Team!"

As the first groups of defenders rolled the barrels away to the side of the tunnel entrance, where they continued to issue a steady stream while remaining clear of any further activity, another group arrived, split into two groups of two men each. One group carried the remnants of the smouldering hog on a sharp wooden pole; the others bore torches.

Without the need for further orders, the pig was dropped into the stream of oil in the tunnel entrance. The fat hissed and popped as the two men with torches leaned gingerly forward and ignited the bubbling carcasses. The charred remains burst into flame with fresh vigour and, working furiously in the face of searing heat and splashes of hot fat, the men heaved the pointed wooden poles out of the burning hogs and used them to set the flaming bundle rolling.

By now shouts had gone up inside the tunnel. The lead warriors of the mining party had discovered that their passage had been completed. They were probably now aware of the small river of oil flowing beneath them and gathering in a small pool around the lower entrance to the tunnel. If they were bright, they might have connected that with the smell of roasted hog. If they were really clever, they had turned and were already running, but they had no hope. The tunnel was still fairly narrow, and there were more than a dozen men in there. There would be chaos in the darkness as they tried to push back through their friends.

Fronto chewed on his lower lip in vague irritation. He did not like doing something like this to people; even to enemies. A man could die in battle with a blade in his guts and go proud and happy, but this was horrible. There was an explosive, incendiary noise somewhere below him, and he thought for a moment that he felt the ground shake.

Then silence for a single heartbeat…

And then screams; screams that issued from inside and outside of the walls, from the entrances of the tunnels. Those attackers that had not been ignited by the flow of burning oil that ran down the special gutter had found themselves face with a huge flaming carcass rolling down the slope in the enclosed space. There was no escape.

Black roiling smoke rose from the tunnel entrance, carrying the scent of burned meat. The men among the wicker shields below were in a panic, unsure of what to do, when the first blazing figure emerged from the dark maw, screaming and running in a blind panic until he tripped and tumbled down the slope toward the rest of the Belgae. Behind him, the half dozen men that had lived long enough to reach the exit burst out into the light, shrieking in agony and falling at the tunnel mouth, rolling down the hill. The slope failed to extinguish all of the flames, as the oil and fat had thoroughly soaked them now, and the figures, long dead by the time they rolled to a halt in front of their comrades, were still licked by flames.

Glancing back and forth along the hill, Fronto nodded sadly as he saw the same sequence of events unfolding at each tunnel. Raising and lowering his arm once more, he shouted “Third Team!”

Behind him, four more men lifted the oil barrel back upright and poured two open topped barrels of water into the passage to extinguish the flames and prevent the wooden supports from collapsing and bringing the wall down with them. Then a group of ten men grasped shovels, both manufactured and makeshift, and began to backfill the tunnels with earth, carrying them down into the passageway and starting below the wall itself to make sure the fire was no longer a threat to the defences.

Fronto nodded with cold satisfaction. It would take several hours for the men to fill those tunnels enough to prevent them being of further use to the Belgae but, judging by the chaos below, his demonstration had had the desired effect. The wicker shieldbearers had dropped their screens and fled, only to fall to the archers on the walls, who were no longer restricted in their shots.

He could imagine the conversations that were going on between the tribal leaders of the enemy below. Certainly plans were being redrafted. No one was going to be in a hurry to run up the hill again, so his men should have time to finish their work and be prepared for the next move.

With one last look down the slope, he turned and walked away to the left along the wall, to the far tunnel, where Decius was ordering his men around.

"Well that's given them something to think about eh?"

Decius grinned.

"Did you see those bastards run? If we'd not shot 'em down they'd have kept going 'til they drowned in the Rhine!"

Fronto laughed.

"It's certainly bought us some time. I'd say we're safe at least until the afternoon now. What I expect for the rest of the day is a few small pushes to test our defences. They knew they'd cleared most of the Remi's original missile defences from the walls, but now they also know there's a new threat. I don't think they'll send more than a hundred at a time, and probably not even that. And they'll come from a different direction each time."

He sighed wearily.

"I'm just hoping they stick to that and don't come en-masse. If they do, we're done for wherever they come from. No matter how clever we are, we just can't withstand those kind of odds."

Decius nodded and smiled.

"If they do it probably won't be until tomorrow."

"Don't be too sure. They won't want to give us another night here, having seen what we managed with the first one. I think they'll keep testing us all day until late afternoon. Then they'll just 'all-in' to get rid of us before nightfall."

Fronto dropped to a crouch and started to tap the wall top absently with a stick.

"What we need to do is to get every man here with a brain thinking of ways to take down large groups of them and bolster our defences."

Decius nodded.

"I've a few ideas, particularly for the northern sector. You haven't been round there yet, have you?"

Fronto shook his head.

"That's going to be the weak spot for missiles. The slope is covered with woods. The only bonus is it's going to be a bastard of an ascent for the enemy too."

Fronto frowned.

"But you've got ideas?"

"Sort of. Need to work on them a bit and perhaps try and speak to Iccius about it. Mostly I don't want to do anything about it while we're only expecting little forays. It'd be a shame to waste a good surprise on a few men."

Fronto nodded.

"Try and get everything ready so you can put any plans into action quickly. When they start to gather for a big assault, we might not get more than half an hour's warning."

Decius laughed.

"I must say that serving with you is certainly an adventure, sir."

"Indeed. Go to it, Decius. I'm going to go speak to the others and see what ideas we can rustle up."

Just as he had expected, there was little activity from the Belgae for some time. It was later morning before the first assaults began. Small pockets of Belgic warriors bravely tried the ascent from all sides, not a single man managing to survive within forty feet of the wall.

The fourth such attempt, as the sun rose high, involved what appeared to be a testudo formed of those wicker shields they had used to protect the miners. For a moment, the defenders were nonplussed and shot a few random stones and arrows at the approaching block, which bounced harmlessly from the protective surround.

Then, irritably, Decius had appeared on the scene and accosted one of his archers. Grumbling, he had snatched an arrow from the man's quiver, dipped the head in the oil barrel stationed at the rear of the wall, lit it with one of the torches that had been kept burning throughout the day, and then passed the flaming missile back to the man. The Cretan smiled with comprehension and, aiming, sent the burning arrow in a tight arc, where it landed in the wicker with a thud. The dry screen caught light instantly, and the warrior was forced to discard it hurriedly to one side. Barely had he let go of it before two arrows plunged into his chest and a heavy lead sling bullet broke his temple.

The plan had quickly passed down the line of archers, and the wicker assault screen was left a flaming mass, surrounded by the bodies of the warriors that had borne it.

The morning wore on with regular small attempts to scale the hill. Those coming up the southern slope above the river found themselves easy targets for the defenders, who saved their missiles and dropped rocks down the steep escarpment. The brave few who took either east or west slope in full view of the walls on open ground learned quickly what Rome already knew about the quality of the slingers bred on the Balearic islands, and those who picked their way carefully through the wooded northern slope struggled as they reached the top only to be met with arrows.

As the sun began its lazy arc down toward the rear of the oppidum, Fronto once again found Decius, standing at the edge of the woods on the northern slope, where he could still make out the hordes of Belgae on the eastern plain.

"Afternoon, Decius."

"Sir."

"I think it might be time to start putting together your surprise. We've not had an assault from any side in an hour, and there's a lot of movement and organisation going on down below."

"You think the big push is coming?"

Fronto nodded.

"I don't know how big, but as big as we're likely to see. That's only a tenth of the whole Belgic army down there but, when you think about it, Bibrax is a relatively small target. I don't think it can be that important to the Belgae or they'd have come here in all their glory. If it was only worth a small vexillation of their army, then I doubt their leaders will commit all thirty thousand or so. We'll probably see half of them at most. If the cost of this place is too steep, they won't buy."

Decius nodded.

"Still… that's going to be about five to one. We'll have to work to make the price too high."

"It's all about keeping them at arm's length. Up close these auxilia will be pretty useless. It'll be down to the Remi to save the day then. Right!"

He took a deep breath.

"Let's get to work."

* * * * *

In retrospect, Fronto had to express admiration for the timing of the Belgae's attacks. They had estimated the time taken to assault all four slopes of the oppidum and had adjusted accordingly, so that the defenders could not draw men from one sector to help defend another. The first assault to be launched was the northern offensive, hampered by the thick woods and undergrowth of that slope. The second, perhaps a quarter of an hour later, was the steep incline above the river. Finally, the east and west assaults, the easiest terrain, began simultaneously a couple of hundred heartbeats later.

Fronto, commanding the main gate and the eastern sector above the camp of the Belgic army, gritted his teeth and hoped that these often-overlooked and unsung auxiliary prefects were worth their pay grade, and more besides.

A quick glance back down the slope and he shook his head. The main block of the assault was coming at him; somewhere around seven or eight thousand men, all told. He had seen a legion with its auxiliary contingent many times and that was roughly what he was looking at here: the Belgic equivalent of a standard Roman field army. If the Belgae had been innovative thinkers, Fronto and his men would not have stood a chance. If what people said about the Belgae's fierceness was true, only their own ingenuity would save them.

He turned to look at his small groups of defenders in position along the walls, shading his eyes from the sun that sank over his left shoulder toward the now thinning treetops of the oppidum. Perhaps six hundred men, including the Remi sword and spear bearers that stood interspersed with his auxiliaries.

Shit.

Odds of more than ten to one were enough to put the wind up even the most seasoned commander. He smiled a grim smile.

Still, large numbers was no offset for monumental stupidity. They may be brave, but they were also foolhardy.

He watched the front line of the Belgae. Like most barbarian armies he'd had to deal with, the Hispanics included, the Belgae gathered in large crowds, excited themselves into a frenzy of bloodlust and a need for personal glory, and then poured towards the enemy like a burst dam in no semblance of order and with no real plan of attack.

Seven thousand men or more in a heaving sea of violent lust pouring up the hill.

With a weary smile, Fronto turned to the Remi warrior nearby and made throat-slashing motions.

The man nodded and gabbled off in his own dialect with other warriors. Fronto turned back to the massed charge on the slope and watched with interest.

There was a crunch to his left and a bang, followed quickly by similar noises to his right. More noises sprang up from both sides, and he nodded sadly.

It had taken a little over an hour for his men, along with the Remi, to saw down six of the beech trees at the far side of the oppidum; the southwest, out of sight of the main force. They had been stripped of branches and cut down to lengths of around twenty feet before being transported across the village and raised up onto the walls. There they had stood for the last quarter of an hour, just out of sight of the attackers below, until the signal was given.

The Remi warriors along the walls braced themselves on the stonework and heaved at the logs until they began to rock. A little more leverage and they tipped from the wall and began their lethal descent down the slope.

The Belgae experienced instant panic. Those at the front turned and tried to push their way back into their own ranks. Some men at the edge of the assault manage to get clear, leaping to the left or right to avoid the horrifying assault from above.

The first tree trunk hit the front line of warriors, already in chaos and trying to push in half a dozen different directions. The momentum after thirty feet of slope carried the trunk over and through the army with an almost unstoppable force. Some men were broken in half while others were crushed or driven into the ground, their limbs torn from them by the force. They had no chance to deal with the carnage before the second, third and fourth logs hit the mass.

By now, the assault had failed utterly. The charge had died in the opening moments as the remaining tree trunks hit each other and bounced around like some sort of toy, creating an unpredictable rolling hell than flattened all before it. One of the last few logs pitched as it struck something and leapt into the air, carried by its downward motion, plummeting down into the centre of the fleeing mass.

It was possible the remaining warriors might form up and try once more but, given the phenomenal losses they'd just suffered,

Fronto doubted the warriors would charge again, even if their chieftains ordered it.

Prefect Galeo rubbed his chin thoughtfully as he watched the Belgae at the base of the slope on their way up, howling like wild dogs. Galeo had been in the service all his adult life and had, he believed, reached as high as he was likely to reach. The only promotion an auxiliary prefect could look forward to was perhaps as a tribune among the legions, but most auxiliary units were commanded by their native leaders. Only the longstanding units like his had reached such a point of permanency that they attracted a Roman officer. And they were then pretty much forgotten. In the field, Caesar's staff only noticed the job done by the auxiliary cavalry.

He grunted. Look at that young ponce Ingenuus! Barely out of children's clothes and now commanding Caesar's bodyguard. But nobody even saw the Numidian archers or their commander.

Another grunt. Today was a chance. Make or break, as they say. A good job here and he might get commended and tagged for higher things.

And yet, despite the fact that he had been given the western slope - the best position to defend - his damned poor stagnant brain could not come up with anything useful to help him. His wits had atrophied from so long babysitting these Africans that when legate Fronto had asked the officers for suggestions to even the odds, while the others had been coming up with clever little ideas, Galeo had just stayed quiet, flapping his lips worriedly like a stunned fish. Fronto had even frowned at him.

"Damn it!"

"Mmm?" enquired the dark skinned archer next to him.

"Oh, nothing! It's not like you understand a damn word I say anyway. If it weren't for your centurions, I might as well not even be here."

He looked back at the line of men slowly advancing on his position.

Very well. If he could not find some clever way of gaining an edge, he could do what he had always tried to: fight a decent and solid action in the best traditions of the legions, even saddled as he was with a load of illiterate Numidians.

He carefully scanned the crowd below. Couldn't be more than a couple of thousand there. This place was the furthest from the main force of Belgae and one of the most easily defensible positions with a good field of missile shot. The odds would be about six or seven to one. Really, there was not much chance to show off but, on the other hand, he should be able to safely hold his position. Each of his men would have time to let off over a dozen shots before the Belgae got anywhere near closing with them.

He smiled.

They may be strange and have precious little Latin among them, but the one thing he did know was that his centurions were confident, and they'd had the archers practicing on a daily basis, even over winter. In theory, even if his men missed with every other shot, they should be able to deal with the situation before there was hope of close combat. He turned to the centurion nearby, a Romanised Numidian with reasonable Latin.

"Get ready. Every man marks his target and makes each shot count. I want every single one of them dead before they get anywhere near this wall. Caesar wants the Remi, so we'll save 'em eh?"

Above the slope, looking down at the river below, prefect Pansa smiled at the Belgae. There would be perhaps four thousand or so down there. They could so easily overwhelm his position, should they get within reach… but Pansa had plans. He had almost laughed when he explained to the legate what he wanted to do. In fact, Fronto had chuckled a little himself, which must be unusual, given the legate's dour reputation.

Four thousand, or possibly five, against his less than four hundred men, including the Remi natives with their Celtic blades. Something like ten to one odds. Frightening, he supposed, but there was just something comic about watching these heavily armed barbarians floundering on the slope as they tried to climb the steep ascent while keeping their eyes on the defenders above. More than once he saw a figure slip and slide, toppling backwards and taking a few of his fellows.

Pansa had served in Caesar's legions since the early days in Hispania, and he had seen some of the most horrifying sights a man could ever hope to on a battlefield. He was aware of how little regard

Caesar held for human life. Pansa was different and had been relieved to discover that legate Fronto was, too.

To Pansa, it was far more important to save his men than to win some kind of glory. He had seen the look in Galeo's eye at the briefing. Hopefully the fool would stick to his defence and not go trying to win points.

He smiled. The leaders of the Belgae were now two thirds of the way up the slope and almost in missile range for the slingers and the few archers he had with him.

"Right lads…"

He gestured with an overarm swing down to the advancing barbarians below.

As he shaded his eyes and peered down at the eagerly-advancing defenders, he chuckled. Behind him were several dull thuds. He stepped back from the edge of the wall for the sake of his own safety and watched as two dozen large barrels, much of the stored drinking water of the Remi, were tipped over the wall, and the liquid began to pour down the slope in rivulets.

There was no tide that threatened to wash away the attackers; that was not what Pansa wanted. His objective was to make the ascent here so difficult and unpleasant that the Belgae would give up in disgust. Gallon after gallon of water tipped over the wall and flowed down relentlessly, softening up the earth and making the grass slick and slippery. The effect as the rivulets finally reached the advancing warriors was almost too funny for words.

Pansa looked back at his men and cleared his throat. He could not be seen laughing at this. People would think he was an idiot… but it really was quite funny.

He turned once more to gaze down the hill. The barbarians were slipping and sliding around like something out of a Plautus play. Where the water had made the lower slope wet, the longer Pansa watched, the more hilarious the comedy ascent became. Men trying desperately to keep their feet and climb were making the ground worse, churning the mud and creating slides. Some of the mid section, as they slipped, took a dozen or so warriors with them, and the whole group collapsed in a flurry of arms and legs as they slid gracelessly into the river.

Off to the right, one of the men laughed. He opened his mouth to discipline the man, but changed his mind. Let them laugh.

It was funny and, after all, being laughed at might demoralise the enemy. Turning, he addressed the centurions.

"Save ammunition. I don't want anyone to waste a shot until they get up to the level of that pile of rocks."

He smiled. If they get that far, he thought to himself, and found that he was laughing along with his men.

To the north, Decius peered down into the woods. Though he could not speak a word of this local language, he could make an educated guess as to what was being shouted by the Belgae as they climbed through the woods. That was swearing and cursing if he had ever heard it. They were having fun with all the tripwires, ankle-breaking covered pits and hidden sharpened stake points that his men had been placing in the woods for the last hour. Their advance had initially been at a good pace and presented a reasonable front, or so Decius' scouts had reported as they returned from their observation points in the woods. But now they had slowed to little more than a crawl as the first few men fell foul to the Romans' hidden defences and the attackers began to carefully scour the forest floor for traps as they moved.

He smiled at the thought of so many eager warriors milling about in the trees, getting sore feet, tripped up, broken bones, lacerations and general irritations. In all likelihood the rest of the siege would be over for the day before these Belgae reached the top.

He kicked an errant pebble from the wall down into the trees and eyed, once again, the piles of heavy boulders lining the walls. This was his second surprise for when the Belgae finally reached the higher slope. These piles of stones, each boulder almost a foot across and weighing the same as a small cart, would bounce several times on the forest floor and would rip through even the toughest of undergrowth. He certainly would not like to be climbing that hill when the piles were levered off the walls.

He sighed and sat down to take a long swig of water from his flask.

Somewhere down below there was a shriek and a great deal more swearing.

Time drifted slowly on for Decius, listening to the sounds of slowly advancing soldiers.

"Need a hand?"

He looked around in surprise to see Fronto.

"Legate? Not seen a sign of them yet. I think they're getting a bit pissed off with my woods, to be honest."

Fronto laughed.

"You must have led them a merry dance, man. The main frontal assault dispersed in agony just now. I'm on my way to see what's happening at the other sectors, but I've left a skeleton crew watching the main gate area. I'll leave you a couple of hundred more men."

"Why thank you, sir. And it's not even my birthday!"

He grinned at Fronto and the legate strode off, laughing, toward the western slopes, hundreds of men following him.

Three of the centurions led their units across to Decius, who smiled and examined his reinforcements. Two were Cretans and the other a Hispanic; probably not a word of Latin between them.

"Get into positions," he told them, waving his hand and pointing vaguely up and down the line of the wall.

He kicked his heels absently on the defences and smiled down into the forest. It was looking increasingly like reinforcements would be unnecessary. Suddenly, he saw a movement in the trees. He strained his eyes peering ahead. Was that the Belgae?

Standing, he shaded his eyes and peered into the canopy of gloom.

No, that was another of his scouts. He sighed and sat down again. Slowly, the scout clambered up through the undergrowth and then climbed the wall close to his commander.

"Are we expecting them any time soon?"

The Cretan looked at him quizzically.

"Gods, I'll be pleased to get back to camp where at least the occasional person understands a single word I say!"

Pointing down into the woods, he tried to mime Belgae warriors climbing the hill. The scout shook his head and said something unintelligible. Decius had never bothered mastering Greek. It was the language of thinkers, not doers; but even if he had, the strange dialect these Cretans spoke was an entirely different entity. He listened with an uncomprehending smile as he realised what the accompanying hand gestures meant.

The way he was waving his hand flat and gesturing to the plain…

"They've given up?"

He laughed.

"We loaded all these boulders on the wall, and they never even got halfway up?"

Grinning, he slapped his thigh.

"Wait 'til Fronto hears that!"

* * * * *

Fronto passed his wine skin to Decius, who took it gratefully and drank deep. Down on the plain, the last of Belgae tribal bands were striking camp and moving away to join the massive force leaving the valley.

"I'd say we have to call that a rousing success, wouldn't you, gentlemen?"

Decius nodded wearily. To the other side Pansa and Galeo smiled.

"Think Caesar will give us any kind of reward, sir?"

The other three turned to stare at Galeo.

"Reward?" Fronto said in surprise. "The fact that the Remi have our back now is a pretty bloody good reward as far as I can see. Iccius over there…"

He pointed at the chieftain, who was grinning like an idiot. His reputation would be growing among the Remi now. Regardless of the help of Rome, his small oppidum with its few warriors had fought off a huge army of their countrymen and had lived, intact, to tell the tale. The role of Rome would, of course, be downplayed in the tales of the Remi, but Fronto couldn't blame them for that. Whatever anyone could say, the Remi would now recognise their ally, Rome, and honour them. For the cost of remarkably few men, Fronto had given Caesar what he needed most. Not because of the general, but rather in spite of him.

Fronto sighed. He was in danger of getting extremely angry and bitter once again over Caesar's lack of concern. One day he would snap. Admittedly, it would be Fronto who ended up being sent back to his sister in an urn if that was the case, but there were days when…

Decius nudged him.

"I don't know what you're thinking, but you're making people nervous with that grimace. And you didn't finish your sentence."

The legate shook his head.

"Sorry. Where was I? Ah yes, Iccius. Lack of sleep, you see."

He sighed and squared his shoulders.

"Iccius will pass the word of what we've done for him among his people. And it might put a bit of fear into the enemy too. All in all, I think the benefits of what we did here today are tangible. And of course, most important of all, we lived to tell the tale!"

He sighed again.

"By rights we should get our gear stowed now and get underway back to camp."

He noted with humour the tired and crestfallen expressions of his officers.

"But we can move a lot faster than an army that size. Besides, they've got to meet up with the rest of their people before they move on Caesar. We've got time, and I, personally, need a rest."

He smiled at Iccius and mimed drinking from a mug. The chieftain laughed and shouted something to one of his spear bearers.

"Besides… I believe Pansa spilled all their drinking water, so we'll have to rely on their beer instead."

He noted with genuine humour the look of distaste that crossed Pansa's face.

"Yes," Fronto smiled, "I've never acquired a taste for the stuff myself either, but Crispus, the legate of the Eleventh, is quite a fan. He can even work out where it's been brewed by the taste, or so he says. To me, it always tastes like it's been brewed in a sock."

Next to him, Decius laughed.

"Frankly, I don't care," added Galeo. "If it's alcoholic, I'll drink it."

"Well said."

The four Romans walked towards the beckoning leader of the oppidum.

The moon rose high over Bibrax, now partially denuded of trees, and over the plain below, littered with the refuse of an army long gone. Everything looked so peaceful, particularly through the thin veil of drunkenness. The other Roman officers had long since collapsed into a stupor and would regret their activity in the morning. Fronto had, for better or worse, a cast-iron stomach and the alcohol tolerance of a marble quarry, and was now nicely hazy after a solid six hours of celebrating. The only Roman who had stayed with him was Decius, something of a prodigious drinker himself, it appeared. The prefect yawned and dangled his bare feet off the wall's edge.

"It might sound a bit weird, sir, but I think I might be a bit sorry to go back to the army."

Fronto laughed drunkenly.

"For the sake of all that's good, stop calling me sir. Even Galeo stopped eventually. We're both officers and patricians. When there are no enlisted men around, you can safely use my name."

A pause ensued.

"Anyway," he said suddenly, startling his companion, "how come you ended up as a prefect of a minor auxiliary unit? Your family's got to be better off than mine, and probably more popular, given that I'm as popular in political circles as a turd in a city bathhouse."

Decius laughed.

"I have a nasty habit of speaking my mind. Get's you in trouble, that kind of thing."

Fronto's turn to laugh.

"You have no idea..."

"Well the problem is that I served in the Seventh from the outset. It was good in the early days. But then early last year before all this started we got assigned Crassus as a legate. Now I know he's one of the leading lights of Rome and all that, and I suppose I don't really want to talk out of turn, but..."

"But the man is an arsehole of the highest order. Yes, I've noticed. But if you're in the Seventh, why aren't you out west with him getting massacred by angry Gauls?"

Decius chuckled.

"Well I inadvertently mentioned something about his ancestors having evolved from goats. He demanded I resign my commission in his legion and return to Rome. But legate Balbus was looking for men to take on his auxiliary units at the time. So I accepted a demotion. I left the Seventh and all my glory and honour to come live with a bunch of Greek hunters in the Eighth."

Fronto frowned.

"That's a hell of a pay cut."

"As you mentioned, my family's not poor. I just need to stay away from home at the moment. My wife's just had her third baby and her mother's living with us."

Fronto laughed.

"Shouldn't you be back bringing up your child, though?"

"I don't think you heard me, Fronto. I've been in Gaul for a year and a half, and my wife's having her third baby..."

"Oh."

Fronto looked down at his feet.

"Sorry."

"Don't be. When I do one day get back to Rome, I shall make it a very messy and public divorce and I shall get rid of her and her harpy of a mother in one fell swoop."

Fronto tried not to laugh as Decius mimed a swoop with his hand, and the effort and momentum caused him to topple over sideways. He failed.

"I think I should have a word with Balbus. You need to be in a more commanding position than this. I imagine he can find room for another tribune."

"Thanks. Now where's that beer. I need to drink 'til I've forgotten about Vespilla and her harpy mother again."

Chapter 7

(Caesar's camp by the Aisne River.)

"Laconicum: the steam room or sauna in a Roman bath house."

A cheer went up among the men of the Tenth as their legate, dirty, limping and dishevelled, plodded through the wooden gate of the enormous camp. Behind him came the various auxiliary units, elated by their victory at Bibrax, but weary and largely suffering on account of bad heads. The linen tunics of the archers and slingers were stained brown and grey, and the Roman prefects who led them marched in traditional fashion, but with a stiffness and tiredness to their gait.

Fronto smiled at the men at the gate and returned their salute. He wondered how these auxiliary missile troops felt about being cheered by professional, well trained legionaries. It must be odd for them. He smiled again to himself. As far as most of the army would be concerned, Fronto and his officers had pulled off an impossible task.

Standing by an armaments cache on the main via, Priscus, the primus pilus of the Tenth, laughed and folded his arms.

"Fortuna certainly kisses your arse, sir."

Fronto grinned.

"Priscus, you have no idea. I am Fortuna's servant. I make her luck!"

He threw up his arm to halt the advance of his column.

"I'm going to take the prefects to headquarters. Can you have somewhere set aside for these units to relax and stand down?" He smiled wearily. "Oh, and send someone to Cita and requisition some decent wine for them all. They bloody well deserve it, and it'll wash the taste of Bibrax's nasty beer out of their mouths."

Priscus raised an eyebrow.

"Could cause resentment in the legions, sir, if you show such favour to noncitizens? No one's giving our lads any wine."

Fronto shrugged.

"They may not be citizens, but they just fought hard and well for Rome. Get the wine. If anyone complains, I'll deal with it personally."

Priscus nodded and beckoned to a couple of legionaries standing at attention nearby. While he relayed the appropriate orders, Fronto turned to look back along his column, formed up four abreast.

"Decius, Galeo and Pansa. Follow me."

He stepped out ahead of the column and turned as the three officers made their way from the bulk of their men and converged on the legate.

"Sir?"

Fronto smiled wearily.

"I'm going for debriefing with the general. You three gentlemen were instrumental in our success yesterday, and I want to make sure Caesar knows that, so I want you all to accompany me."

The three men shared surprised glances but nodded respectfully.

"Shouldn't we clean up a bit before seeing Caesar?" asked Pansa, indicating his drab and dirty red tunic, torn in several places and with stains that may now be permanent.

Behind him, Priscus laughed.

"Caesar's used to seeing the legate looking like that. It'll come as no surprise, I'm sure."

Fronto shot an irritated glance at his second in command and then turned back to the three prefects.

"Right now, you look like you've just fought a nasty action. You look like victorious soldiers. If you get smartened up, you'll not stand out quite so much."

Without waiting further, he turned and started marching up toward the command block in the centre of the camp. The legions had done a tremendous job in his absence. The bridge across the Aisne was strong and wide enough for two carts; a camp protected the far side with a palisaded annexe that contained all the supplies and supply wagons that constantly rolled across the countryside back and forth to keep the legions fed. Very efficient, but nothing quite as impressive as this fort.

Tetricus had constructed on this hill above the river a camp of traditional rectangular shape, but the dimensions and the fortifications were breathtaking. Once or twice in his career, Fronto had come across a camp big enough to accommodate two, or even three, legions, but this was on another scale entirely. A single camp large enough to hold the bulk of seven legions, plus all their auxiliary units, cavalry and artillery. It was almost mind-blowing to see. The four men had walked fully quarter of an hour from the gate before they came to the edge of the principia: more than a dozen campaign tents, with Caesar's imposing headquarters at the centre.

The general's guard maintained their perimeter and stepped forward to challenge the four scruffy men approaching.

"State your name and purpose!"

"Gods," Fronto laughed, "Ingenuus has you lot on form, doesn't he? Legate Marcus Falerius Fronto of the Tenth Legion, accompanied by three auxiliary prefects, to see the general."

The two men before him saluted, and one turned and ran off into the principia. The other remained at attention.

"If you would just bear with us while we inform the general?"

Fronto nodded and the four men stood, kicking idly at the dried mud and few surviving tufts of grass on the ground. After half a hundred heartbeats, the guard returned and beckoned, escorting them into the general's tent.

As they entered, pausing to allow their eyes to become accustomed to the gloom, Caesar rose from his seat behind the table.

"It is good to see you alive, Fronto. I was starting to worry. Last night I poured a libation on the altar of Mars and asked him to bring you back unharmed."

Fronto sighed wearily.

"With respect, general, it wasn't Mars that did it. It was us; myself, the three officers behind me and their men."

Caesar blinked.

"Did it? Did what?"

Fronto smiled.

"Brought you the Remi, safe and sound. Bibrax stands firm. In fact yesterday it stood firm amid a sea of Belgae around thirty thousand strong."

The general was clearly astonished.

"You succeeded? I had assumed you harried the enemy and pulled out? You actually succeeded?"

Fronto nodded.

"Not only that, but you remember those chieftains we met back at Durocorteron? Iccius and Antebogus or something?"

"Antebrogius" corrected the general absently.

"Yes, well it turns out that Bibrax was Iccius' village. Good job we did go, eh?"

The general's eyes flashed momentarily at the barely-veiled note of accusation in the legate's tone.

"Then you gentlemen did me a great service."

Fronto nodded.

"At the very least I'd say these three need seriously looking at for decoration and promotion."

Caesar nodded thoughtfully.

"Identify yourselves, gentlemen."

"Titus Decius Quadratus, auxiliary prefect of the Eighth."

Decius saluted wearily. As he stepped back into line, the next man stepped forward.

"Servius Galeo, auxiliary prefect of the Eleventh."

Another step forward.

"Vibius Pansa, auxiliary prefect of the Twelfth."

Caesar smiled benignly. Fronto knew that smile and how the general had perfected it such that it looked so genuine.

"Well, gentlemen. We'll have to see what we can do for you all."

Fronto nodded.

"However, that may have to wait. That's the other thing. On the way back here, we skirted round the edge of the Belgae. All of them. Judging by the relaxed atmosphere in the camp, I presume you're not aware of them?"

Caesar frowned.

"I have scouts out far and wide. They were last reported about twenty miles distant… They can't be anywhere near yet? We'd have had reports."

Fronto shook his head and pointed at the tent's doorway.

"They're out there. What looks like half a million of them to me. And they're so close that if you pissed off a high ladder you could probably hit them!"

The general's frown deepened and he leaned forward, placing the flats of his palms on the table.

"How close?"

"Two miles. Maybe a little further. And I can tell you this: there are a bloody lot of them." He turned to the prefects behind him.

"How many d'you reckon, Decius?"

The prefect frowned.

"I reckon their camps cover about eight miles or more."

Fronto nodded.

"Something like that. And they've burned everything they've come across between Bibrax and here. I think you've got a big fight waiting for you just out of sight."

Caesar growled.

"Then either my native scouts are defecting to the Belgae or the enemy have caught and killed every last one of them."

He smashed his fist on the table.

"How can I have been so blind?"

Fronto smiled.

"Simple. I wasn't here."

The general gave him a weak and humourless smile.

"What's the terrain like between here and there, do you know? I'm planning blind, here."

Fronto shrugged.

"A couple of low grassy humps and the odd belt of trees, and then a wide plain."

Galeo shook his head and stepped forward.

"If I may, sirs?"

The general and his legate nodded at him.

"Well it looks like a plain at first glance from a distance, where we marched past, but I saw tell-tale signs. That plain's a marsh at the moment. I think it probably gets flooded by the Aisne over winter and spring and stays swampy until high summer. There's reeds in clumps, and there are herons perching and flying around. It's never quite dry, I'd say. In fact, I think that's why the Belgae made their camp where they did: the marsh lies between us."

Decius made a sour face.

"Got to be plagued by insects there."

A nod.

Fronto frowned.

"How come you noticed all this? Looked like a green pasture to me."

Galeo smiled.

"I come from the wetlands at the coast near Aquileia, sir. And I know my birds, sir."

Caesar nodded.

"Then there's no clear field of battle near the enemy. They'll have to come round the edge of the marsh. That should even up the odds a little."

He stood silently for a moment, tapping his thumb on his lower lip absently and then looked up suddenly, as though he had forgotten the officers were there.

"Mmm? Oh yes, sorry Fronto. I think you four had best go bathe, change and get some rest. I'll be calling a general meeting of the staff some time this afternoon, but I'll send for you then."

He frowned again.

"On your way out, have someone go and find Varus and send him to me. I have a job for the cavalry."

Fronto nodded and, saluting, the four officers filed out of the tent.

Bees buzzed and added their gentle hum to the background noises of a military camp at rest. Fronto smiled. It was a nice time of year. Better savour the next hour or two, since the next few days promised to be busy.

"Well I don't know about you three, but I'm looking forward to rinsing out my mouth with some good, old-fashioned Roman wine for a change. Care to join me, relaxing in the laconicum with a nice wine?"

"Laconicum?" Decius raised an eyebrow.

"Alright," Fronto grinned, "the river, if you must know!"

* * * * *

Quintus Atius Varus inhaled deeply, sucking down the warm fragrant air of early summer. Barbarians the Gauls and the Belgae might be, but they had some lovely land up here in the north. The air seemed to be fresher than it was back home in Italy; lighter and cleaner. He glanced around him at the cavalry, two alae of regulars.

His orders were clear. Examine the terrain between the two armies and report back, preferably without engaging enemy scouts or outriders. Oh, a job like this could be done by scouts for the Romans, but from what Caesar had said, his scouts kept mysteriously disappearing, so the task needed a little more force this time.

Varus smiled.

And, of course, he and his men would be able to report the terrain with a soldier's eye, rather than the basic geography relayed by a native scout.

The crest of a hill loomed ahead, crowned by a thin row of poplar trees as if nature's own crest surmounted the helmet of the land. Steering the steed with his knees, he made for the avenue of trees. They were spaced evenly, planted by the design of some unknown hand, rather than naturally seeded.

As they approached the rise, Varus gave commands using hand and arm motions. The two alae peeled off to either side and came to a halt in formation. Off to the left, a large thicket cut off the view of the plain stretching away, and a similar knot of tangled trees lay to the right. Motioning to the officers, he walked his horse gently toward the crest. The two cavalry prefects trotted up to join him as they reached the top.

Varus whistled through his teeth quietly.

"Shit, that's a lot of Belgae!"

The three riders, largely sheltered from view by the thin avenue of trees, looked down the slope with a growing sense of awe. A sizeable marsh began at the foot of the slope and stretched away to within a few paces of the Belgae. The swampy ground was enclosed off to the left by a ridge, along which Fronto and his men must have come this morning. The other end, however, meandered off to the edge of the Aisne River with which it was almost level. Varus' trained military eye spotted the possibilities. That area looked marshy, for certain, but it was the area that had now dried out and sealed off the water inland. It would be easily crossable by cavalry and would probably present no great problem for infantry, but you would not want to actually fight there, just in case.

The impressive thing, though, that seized Varus's gaze and held it, was the camp of the Belgae. He had been sceptical of the reports from Fronto that the force covered a width of eight miles. It sounded such a long way.

And yet, looking down from here, the line of camps stretched from the river bank to the crest and was perhaps two miles thick as well.

"What would you say, Casco? Does that look like three hundred thousand Belgae?"

The prefect beside him shrugged.

"Respectfully, sir, it's damn near impossible to tell when they have no formation."

The prefect on the other side of him shook his head.

"Not that many, sir. They're spread out."

Varus turned and raised an eyebrow.

"Oh, there's a lot, sir, don't get me wrong, but not a third of a million. Remember seeing Ariovistus' army at Vesontio last year? Well I reckon there's about twice as many here. Ariovistus had about seventy thousand men."

Varus frowned.

"D'you know? I do believe you're right. It's a huge camp, but they're well spaced. I wonder whether they're trying to look bigger than they are? Must be… what? A hundred and fifty thousand at the most. Maybe half the Belgae we're expecting!"

Casco shook his head.

"Careful there, sir. Might be that they've left room for the other half, and there's more on the way."

"Hmm." Varus' frown deepened. Casco was right. This army could double in size any time, and the only way they'd know is if they kept a permanent eye on it.

"Maybe that's why they're killing off Caesar's scouts. They don't want the general to know where they are until they've met up with the other half of the army."

He shook his head.

"Shit. That means we need to do something about this, and fast. Let's get back to camp."

He turned his horse to walk her slowly back down the slope to the ala below and stared in horror. Warriors were pouring out of the thicket to the right and the corpse to the left in their hundreds. An ambush.

"Form up!" he bellowed as he started to gallop down the hill to his men, the two prefects at his back. The Belgae had known exactly what they were doing. They did not need this many men to pick off the occasional scout, and the warriors emerging from the undergrowth were, to a man, armed with long spears. The bastards must have been watching them for a while and preparing.

"Can we outrun them?"

Varus glanced at Casco.

"If we can't," he replied, "then we're all dead!"

As they reached the bottom of the slope, Casco shouted "Orderly retreat to the camp."

Varus stared at him for a moment, and then shouted in the loudest voice he could manage: "run!"

The first few of the barbarians were already reaching a position ahead of them. Behind lay the line of poplars and, beyond that, the marsh. No escape that way. The ground to either side of them was swarming with barbarians who had broken cover from the trees. Their only hope was to outrun the closing door of men ahead of them.

"Charge!"

Around him, his cavalry, now working on their own individual instincts rather than commands, rode as hard as they could for the closing gap, formation forgotten. Already a dozen barbarians had joined up ahead of them and were preparing themselves to unhorse the riders.

Without any need of issued commands, as soon as the first riders were within range of the barbarians, they raised and released their pila before drawing their blades. Many of the long, tapered missiles found their targets and the waiting barbarians clutched at their wounds, dropping their own spears.

The first rider found himself clear of the attackers, the nearest barbarian alive but pinned to the turf with a pilum through his thigh, just below the hip. For a moment, the soldier looked around in surprise and relief, but then the reality of his situation kicked in and he ignored the chaos around him and rode for Caesar's camp as though death itself fluttered at his shoulder.

Varus watched with dismay as the arms closed in front of them. Moreover, ahead in the distance, he could see a few Belgic horsemen. As far as he had been told the Belgae favoured infantry. He was not even aware they had cavalry! This was turning out to be a truly shitty day…

Ahead of him, two riders went down as the barbarians lunged with spears, one catching a rider in the gut and the other spearing a horse through the chest. Varus did not have time to wheel his horse or stop; besides, if he stopped, he was dead. This was one of those very few situations where 'every man for himself' was the only viable formation.

Taking a deep breath, he hauled on the reins and jumped his horse, arcing gracefully over the collapsing heap of men and horses. He counted all three heartbeats while he was in the air for what felt like hours, expecting at any moment to feel a spear jammed up through him or his horse.

And suddenly his hooves hit the ground once more. Without a single glance back, he thundered on. There were only a dozen or so barbarian riders; a mere reserve force to pick off the odd Roman who broke through the line, but they were off to the side and making a beeline to cut off the fleeing cavalry. Risking time to glance around him, Varus realised that perhaps twenty or thirty of his men had escaped the trap and were riding on. Far too many men were being butchered behind him, but there was nothing he could do about that.

"To me!" he bellowed.

Surprised troopers hauled on their reins and either steered or slowed to fall in with their commander. Varus cleared his throat.

"Riders off to the left. They'll intercept us before the hill. They've got to stop us escaping if they want to keep their numbers unknown. Take them down!"

The resolute grimaces on the faces of his men were born partially from the desperation of their situation, but the commander knew well how much they were now also being driven by the need for revenge after the butchering of over a hundred of their colleagues.

Indeed, as the Belgic horsemen closed on them, Varus began to feel a little more confident. The barbarians were clearly unused to mounted combat and unsure of their skills, for all their vicious demeanour. Varus' men, on the other hand, had set jaws and gripped their blades with white knuckles. There would be no quarter given by the survivors of this ala.

The attack was swift and efficient. The Belgae were hacked, stabbed, pushed from their saddles and left a bleeding mess, their surviving horses fleeing the scene and, among the Romans only one man down and two wounded.

Varus glanced behind him at the howling barbarians, cursing themselves at failing to spring their trap correctly.

The cavalry commander smiled to himself. Wait 'til he had seen Caesar and gathered his entire mounted division. Then the bastards would have something to howl about!

* * * * *

It had been two hours. It felt like half a lifetime, but in actual fact it had been just two hours since Varus had last been here. He glanced ahead at the line of poplar trees on the hill and could just make out the heaps on the grass in the distance that were all that was left of some of Caesar's best horsemen.

The general had surprised and irritated Varus. Instead of being incensed and planning retribution and extreme violence as the cavalry commander himself, Caesar had merely stroked his chin and muttered "unfortunate…"

Bloody unfortunate? But in a curious way, now that he looked back on it, the general was right. Insensitive, but right. They had lost a number of cavalry, but they had found out a great deal about not only the landscape, but about the enemy into the bargain. While the Romans were facing odds of perhaps five to one, they were considerably better than the ten to one they were expecting. Once word of that had begun to spread in the camp, the atmosphere had improved no end. It had taken only a few moments for Caesar to decide on his course of action, and only a few more for Varus to set it in motion.

Leaving only a small group of mixed regular and auxiliary cavalry in camp, Varus had divided the main mounted force into three sections. The first had set off first, riding hard along the river bank to the west, and skirting round behind the ridge. They should be able to completely bypass the Belgae, and then they would be free to head north and search for the rest of the enemy. The second had been given the most dangerous task: to head east along the river bank and across the edge of the marsh and actually harry the front lines of the enemy. They would not only be able to test what they were up against, but also to confirm whether the ground was viable for an assault.

And the third section, commanded by Varus, was the punitive group. Heading directly for the centre and the line of poplars, Varus would revenge himself on the barbarian ambushers. With a smile of grim determination, he used gestures to relay his commands to the prefects following him. As he pointed silently, two large groups peeled off from the main force and rode off east and west at a tangent.

The remaining force, around eight hundred strong, marshalled in the centre at the base of the slope. At further commands they split into two units, wheeled their horses until they were back-to-back, and then began to walk their steeds at a slow, steady pace toward the woods to either side.

"Bastards had better still be in there, eh sir?"

Varus looked over at Casco and nodded.

"They are. I can feel it. Nemesis is with us today."

Another command rang out, and the ranks of cavalry raised their pila into a throwing position. Moments later they heard the sound of the conflagration starting. The two groups that had separated had set fire to the furthermost edge of those concealing thickets. Smoke rose ominously from among the foliage and Varus watched with growing satisfaction.

A long moment passed and then the shouting began. At first, shouts of alarm, and then some of panic. The blaze tore through the dry woods, leaping from tree to tree like a wave.

As the Romans sat tensely, the first desperate warrior burst from the undergrowth. The look of relief on his face quickly slid away to be replaced once more by panic. Having escaped the dreadful fire sweeping through the thicket, he now found himself facing hundreds of angry Roman cavalrymen. He opened his mouth to shout a warning back into the woods and the first pilum caught him full in the face before he could issue a sound. The second pilum took him through the chest and hurled him back to the grass.

"Don't waste your throws! One at a time, and mark your man."

Another figure appeared from the woods, and then another. Quickly now, warriors began to emerge, some choking from the effects of the smoke that roiled under the green canopy. And yet it was less like a military action or even a punitive attack than like a hunt, or even a game. Not a single figure managed to break the tree line and walk four steps before he was hit by a pilum; sometimes two.

The steady flow of men escaping the flames grew over a long moment and then began to decline. Certainly there must be a lot of corpses there by now. The front rows of cavalrymen had cast their javelins and more that had been passed from the rear ranks. Probably four hundred pila had gone. Allowing for wasteful throws and misses, there would likely be two hundred and fifty to three hundred barbarians littering the grass before the woods. Likely more had been consumed by the flames that were now visible. Almost the entire wood was ablaze at this point, and the firing units with their extinguished torches were now riding to rejoin their commander.

Varus smiled coldly. On the assumption much the same had happened at the other side, behind them, that would be six or seven hundred dead barbarians. A fitting revenge for the hundred and fifty or so Roman dead below the hill. Caesar would be pleased, anyway.

He waited until his men were ready and then gave the order to form up.

Before he turned his horse away from the field, he gave a last regretful look at the littered heaps of men and horses. If only they could sort out a burial detail, but that was a job for the infantry, and after the danger was over. With a sigh he gave the command to return to camp.

Prefect Lucilius gritted his teeth and briefly regretted accepting command of the right flank. His thousand horsemen, almost entirely composed of Gaulish auxiliaries, stamped and snorted and chattered behind him. The other prefects and decurions watched him expectantly.

Lucilius had commanded more than one ala of cavalry before. Indeed, at Vesontio last year, he had been one of Varus' most favoured officers, but that was in battle. This seemed wrong. Cavalry were used as part of a grand battle plan or to harry and mop up. No Roman general in his right mind pitted cavalry alone against a solid enemy force with no infantry support.

He shook his head. It was well known that Caesar thought in curves and not straight lines. The general assigned officers to largely permanent positions, which seemed to suit the infantry. He maintained a regular cavalry attached to his legions, which was unheard of, even among the great innovators like Marius and Scipio. But sometimes the general's decisions seemed just a little too dangerous; even bordering on the insane.

"How am I going to do this?" he asked himself quietly, glad that the rest of his officers were far enough back to allow him thinking room.

The terrain allowed for a safe riding width of perhaps seven or eight hundred paces; not much room to manoeuvre a large cavalry force, certainly. And even from here he could see the glistening and glinting of the streams and pools that dotted and crossed the grass. He offered a quick prayer to Fortuna that Varus knew what he was doing and that what faced him was just standing water and not swamp.

So... how to arrange a trial assault on the Belgae on a narrow strip of land between a reedy river bank and a swamp; a narrow strip of land that might, itself, be marshy and treacherous. And all of this in front of a waiting force of Belgae who had a clear view of them coming. Caesar and Varus must be mad! And Lucilius must be an idiot for accepting this command.

He frowned. On the bright side, given the narrowness of the assailable area, they would only be facing a thousand Belgae at a time. An idea was beginning to form. Turning, he waved to the nearest of his prefects, a thoroughly Romanised Aedui nobleman. The man rode out forward and joined him on the rise. In full Roman uniform, with short hair and a clean-shaven face, the slight accent to his Latin was the only thing that marked the prefect as a noncitizen. He had even taken a Roman name.

"Septimius… you know the tribes of Gauls and Belgae, yes?"

The prefect nodded soberly.

"Most of them."

"And these Belgae are supposed to be the most dangerous, violent and warlike of the lot, yes?"

"Them and the Germanic tribes, yes. When they're not fighting someone else, they fight themselves. It's all they do: fight."

"So…" Lucilius frowned. "It shouldn't be too hard to goad them into a fight then?"

Septimius laughed.

"I suspect it would be harder to force them to stand still."

"Alright, then." The commander smiled. "Let's go give them a fight. Sound the advance."

The prefect saluted and returned to his men. Moments later the musician on his horse at the rear blew out the call to advance and the alae walked their steeds forward. Lucilius remained stationary until the line reached him and then kicked his horse into action, falling in with the front line. Slowly, like the inexorable tide, the cavalry poured down the gentle slope toward the flat open ground before the Belgic lines.

Manoeuvring carefully in order to maintain formation, the cavalry stepped onto the flat, rotating into blocks that fitted the terrain.

"Here we go" muttered Lucilius quietly to himself as they moved into the damp, glinting grass. The first fifty paces or so were tentative, each rider warily watching the shallow pools and trickles as they walked their horses.

Lucilius glanced ahead, squinting to make out the lines of the Belgae. The barbarians were rushing around, gathering several men deep in a front line. As the prefect watched, spears were raised defensively. Any direct attack could be very short and very unpleasant.

His confidence grew as the cavalry trotted through the shallow puddles and pools and splashed across small streams. Varus had been right: the ground between the marsh and the river had dried out fairly well in the last few weeks.

The decision made, he smiled a determined smile and turned to the officers beside him.

"Sound the charge but rein in at a hundred paces for a volley. Pass the word; and no calls on the horn in case anyone there knows our signals."

The officers nodded and shouted the commands down the line to their decurions, who relayed beyond. Within a few moments the entire cavalry broke into a run, the front lines pulling away first, but the rest gradually falling in and catching up like a landslide. Lucilius laughed as he rode. This was the kind of mad stunt that old Longinus used to pull.

Rapidly, the intervening space between the two armies narrowed and the commander found himself so into the rhythm of the charge that he almost shot out ahead as his troopers reined in to a sudden halt. Clicking his tongue in irritation, Lucilius turned his mistake into a show, wheeling his horse sideways and flicking an insulting hand gesture at the Belgae. To either side of him along the lines of horsemen, the front two ranks let fly with their javelins.

The Belgae, confused as to why the Romans had halted their charge so suddenly, stared wide-eyed at several hundred javelins that suddenly arced out from the front lines. All along the wall of men, warriors shrieked as they were pierced and flung back into the crowd with the force of the blows. They were so tightly packed the Romans could not have missed.

The front line of the Belgae bulged ominously. Lucilius smiled. One volley and they were already wanting to break their lines and attacks. With a widening grin, he turned to his officers.

"Let's repeat the process a few times and see how fast we can get it. I want to piss these barbarians off enough that they'll do anything."

Nodding, the prefects and decurions passed down the orders, and the entire cavalry turned their back on the enemy and rode peacefully back across the wet, grassy ground.

Once they reached the slope at the far end, Lucilius waved his arm.

"Same drill. No orders or calls. Everyone knows what they're doing. Those men who've now cast their javelins to the back and make way for the next rows. This time I want that volley the moment you stop. Then straight back. Don't give them a target!"

The men around him grinned in anticipation.

"Alright. Charge!"

This time he allowed the troopers to charge past him and took a position at the rear, where he could observe the results.

True to their training and efficiency, the cavalry thundered across the open space and came to a sudden halt, a volley of hundreds of deadly shafts arcing out from the lines and dropping with horrifying accuracy into the mass of Belgic warriors. Without waiting to see the results, the cavalry wheeled and rode back to the far end of the grassy stretch.

Once again, the line of the Belgae bulged, this time in three places. Lucilius rubbed his chin reflectively. They'd get one more charge or maybe two before the barbarians decided they couldn't take it any more and broke formation.

"Again, but quicker!"

This time, he stayed on the lower reach of the slope and observed from a distance. The Belgae had best attack soon anyway. They only had enough javelins for probably three more volleys.

He watched with satisfaction as the same manoeuvre produced the same result: hundreds of dead warriors and bloodthirsty pushing and shoving as the Belgae nobles fought to prevent their tribesmen running after the Roman horsemen. With a grin he surveyed the ground near the enemy line while his troopers returned. The repeated charges had churned up the wet grass leaving slick and dangerous mud. That should be helpful. A cavalry trooper would be much more stable in that mess than a foot soldier.

He smiled at the officers as they steered the mounts with their knees and readied for another charge.

"They're ready to break. A dozen or so followed you last time. But I don't want them following right across the field. Same drill again, but this time, when you've released the volley, retreat fifty paces, form up for action and draw swords."

The officers saluted and relayed the orders to their men.

With the fourth charge, Lucilius accompanied the cavalry once more. The charge reached the churned mud, the horses whinnied to a halt, the javelins arced out, and the Belgae, with a deafening roar, broke their line and ran forward waving spears, swords and axes. As ordered, the cavalry pulled out of reach and formed up to await the onslaught.

Clearly, the barbarian warriors had broken the orders of their chieftains. The boar-head standards and horns and the shining golden helmets of the few visible noblemen remained tightly in position. But hundreds had been unable to contain their rage any longer and had run forwards.

As they ran, screaming, Lucilius watched with keen interest, bordering on mirth. The warriors reached the churned mire left by the hooves of the Roman cavalry, and many slid, tripped or fell. As they climbed to their feet, they were forced to move slowly and painfully through the thick, sucking mud, hauling their feet out and then sinking them back with a squelch. The entire bloodthirsty attack had slowed to an embarrassing plod.

"Take them."

The men to either side walked their horses forward and began to swing with their longer cavalry blades, arcing like bloody scythes left and right, maiming and killed the desperate Belgae wherever they found them. It was a massacre, plain and simple; a harvest of living bodies.

Lucilius watched as the barbarian attack dissolved into pure butchery. Within a hundred heartbeats the only Belgae who were left standing were the lucky few at the rear of the attack who were now fleeing the field back to their own line as quickly as the mud allowed. A few of the more eager troopers were advancing to take the stragglers.

"Call for regroup!" Lucilius shouted.

The cornu rang out a moment later, and the troopers wheeled their horses and returned to their alae. With a satisfied smile, Lucilius calculated the numbers. He could assume at least a hundred dead from each of the four javelin volleys, and at least a couple of hundred more here in the mud. Six hundred Belgae dead at a highly conservative estimate.

He laughed out loud as he surveyed the muddy mess.

For eight Romans. Now *that* was going to please the general. Mars be praised, it certainly pleased Lucilius.

"Sound the withdrawal. There won't be any more barbarian pushes for a while now. Time to head back to camp and report."

A decurion nearby laughed.

"And maybe we can resupply with javelins and have another go!"

As the cavalry reached the top of the slope, Lucilius smiled in surprise and saluted. Varus returned the gesture and eyed the returning cavalry with a raised eyebrow.

"Had fun, Lucilius? Looks like you hardly got dirty?"

"We've given them a fairly bloody lip, sir. I'll tell you all about it on the way back."

Varus nodded as the two cavalry forces fell into formation together and began the trek back to Caesar's camp.

It was hours later when the third cavalry group finally came into sight of the main gate. Varus leaned over the parapet where he had been waiting anxiously for word of his men and waved at the lieutenant.

"What did you find?" he asked, eyeing with interest the tired but apparently undamaged cavalry force as they slowed to a walk.

"Nothing, sir" the prefect reported, sighing. "We've been miles and miles and miles. No sign of anything. Just in case, I sent one ala off with orders to do a sweep over a ten mile radius beyond where we were, but if there's more Belgae coming, they're at least a day away."

"Did you have a more exciting time, sir?"

Varus laughed.

"It's been a good day. We've dented the Belgae and confirmed we're safe from reinforcements as yet. Get yourselves into camp and rest. I need to inform the general."

Chapter 8

(Caesar's camp by the Aisne River.)

"Lilia (Lit. 'Lilies'): defensive pits three feet deep with a sharpened stake at the bottom, disguised with undergrowth, to hamper attackers."

Fronto grumbled under his breath and leaned forward over the table, fixing Caesar with a steady gaze. As so often happened, the other officers in the room had melted into the background, trying to blend in with the tent leather in an attempt not to become involved in the argument.

"But it's a waste to play a defensive action now. We need to press the advantage we have!"

The general glowered at his senior legate. His brow had furrowed, and he had become quite pale; a sign that he was deeply angry and reaching the end of his tether.

"We don't have an advantage, Fronto. They outnumber us about five to one. Only an idiot charges into those odds!"

The legate's rumble rose to a steady growl, and he barked back at his commander.

"It's five to one now! Wait until you've faffed for a while building walls and shuffling the legions around and you could find it's ten to one. The advantage I'm talking about is that is not more than five to one! We should strike while the iron's lukewarm!"

Caesar's eyelid flickered alarmingly. Tetricus, standing behind Fronto, could see the warning signs in the general's demeanour, though Fronto apparently either could not tell or did not care. Either way, this had to stop. Tetricus stepped forward to intervene, but the two arguing commanders ignored him.

"Fronto, I put up with your astounding insolence because you really are one of the best legionary commanders Rome has to offer, but I'm rapidly reaching breaking point with you. There will come a time when you are more trouble than you're worth." He snarled. "Pray it's not today!"

"You…" Fronto drew a deep breath, ready to launch into a tirade. Tetricus reached out and grasped his shoulder, hauling him to the side and defusing the building stress in the man by slapping him so hard on the back he was momentarily winded.

"Caesar," the young tribune said calmly. "I believe we can put together adequate defences in a few hours. I propose a compromise. Fronto may well be correct in his estimate that the Belgae will only get stronger, but I also see the wisdom in being as prepared as possible."

He glanced sideways at Fronto, who was staring angrily at him.

"All we need is something we can fall back into if we run into serious trouble. Instead of fully enclosing stockades and gates, towers and so on, which would take more than a day, I propose this:"

He leaned on the table where Fronto had previously been and drew an imaginary map of the terrain with his finger.

"We're sort of on a loop in the river here. In front of us is a nice flat area where we can marshal the troops. All we need is one good defence across it… say a nice deep and wide trench with just two or three causeways crossing it. Might even put some lilia in place."

Caesar shook his head.

"That's not enough. If the Belgae come in force, they'll just swarm over it. I will not allow my army to be destroyed in detail after all I've achieved."

Tetricus shrugged.

"Once the ditch is there, and I think we can have a deep ditch that crosses the flat ground from riverbank to riverbank in about five hours, we can look at raising a palisade perhaps. More than that, if we install a small fort at each end of the ditch, we can have a marvellous cross-storm of missiles in the middle."

Balbus stepped forward from the shadows around the edge of the tent.

"He's right, general. If we put our artillery in emplacements at either end, there won't be a finger width of flat land that's out of range of a shot. Once that's done, we can look at the possibility of marching on the Belgae, but we know we'll have a good safe line to fall back to."

Caesar rubbed his eyes and pinched the bridge of his impressive nose.

"Alright. I will concede to a reduction in the planned defences, but I have no intention in engaging in combat until we are clear that the advantage is ours, and there is no viable alternative."

He turned to Tetricus.

"You seem to be full of ideas, tribune. Gather your engineers and get to work."

As Tetricus saluted and made for the exit, the general regarded his legates.

"I want every spare man working on this to get the defences as tight as possible and as fast as possible. While that's happening, have your artillery from each legion taken to the left and right of the proposed site, so that they're ready to move into place as soon as the platforms are ready."

He gestured at the door, and the officers saluted, nodded and filed out.

"And the cavalry, Caesar?"

The general looked up to see Varus hovering in the doorway.

"Form your men on the plain in front of the works. The entire infantry is going to be occupied with the construction, so the cavalry are the main defence against any sudden assault."

Varus nodded professionally, though Fronto noted the brief flash of disapproval on the man's face.

The general turned to the only figure remaining in his headquarters tent.

"And you? Just get out of my sight!"

Fronto saluted half-heartedly and muttered under his breath "gladly!"

As he allowed the tent flap to drop back into position, he breathed deeply of the air outside the headquarters and then strode across the grass to where Labienus and three other members of the senior staff stood in deep conversation.

Fronto wandered up and stood next to Labienus.

"Maybe we should just go attack them anyway."

Labienus raised his eyes to the sky.

"Fronto, your mouth is going to open too wide and swallow the rest of your head one day. I swear it must already have swallowed your brain. Crassus can get away with talking to Caesar like that, because he's richer and his daddy is so important."

He gestured up and down at Fronto.

"But you? Your command is all you really have. Don't mess it up."

There was a chorus of nods from the others and Labienus laughed weakly.

"I, for one, don't relish the thought of fighting the rest of this campaign without your help."

Fronto kicked at the turf.

"We need to persuade Caesar to attack; we can't wait until every barbarian north of the Alps is gathered together against us. He's too worried about how this all looks at home and not worried enough about what might happen right here."

Labienus shrugged.

"Problem is, even if we could persuade him to attack, the ground around here is just not suitable for a battle. I couldn't even begin to decide how to go about it."

Fronto nodded.

"I know. Can't just take an assault to them because of the marsh. Not enough room either side of the marsh to take seven legions without stringing them all out and making it easy for the Belgae. Can't lure them onto the plain in front of the fort, cos they'll not come. They're just waiting and growing in numbers. The only option would be to actually decamp and move to see if we can find somewhere that's less defensive."

He frowned.

"Why did Caesar choose somewhere like this? There was never any hope of conducting a proper battle here. It's a place just made for defence."

Labienus shrugged.

"Maybe Caesar never intended to fight here?"

Fronto slapped his head in irritation.

"That's it. Should have realised the old bastard had something up his sleeve."

He realised the others were looking at him in expectation.

"He's waiting for something. He's not bothered about the growing strength of the Belgae. Only an idiot would wait while they got stronger… unless he's waiting for something more important, and whatever it is must be important enough that he thinks it'll make this battle either easy or unnecessary."

With a smiled, he patted Labienus on the shoulder.

"I'm going to find out what it is."

The senior staff officer grasped Fronto by the shoulder.

"Be careful and deferential. If you go blundering in there with accusations and demands, you're going to find yourself shipped off back to Rome by the end of the day."

Fronto smiled.

"I wouldn't go. You all need me too much."

Labienus raised his eyes skywards again as the legate turned and strode back towards Caesar's tent. Without knocking or calling out, he lifted the flap and entered. The general was still sitting behind his desk, pinching the bridge of his nose as though suffering from a powerful headache. Caesar looked up at the sudden intrusion.

"What is the name of Venus do you think you're doing, Fronto?"

The legate smiled what he hoped was a disarming smile, actually the one his sister always said made him look constipated.

"Alright, Caesar. I've worked it out. I know you're waiting for something, but we really need to know what. Your officers are quite capable of planning actions both offensive and defensive, but if we don't know what's going on, we can't plan for anything."

Caesar narrowed his eyes, and Fronto continued.

"Look, I don't know what the secrecy is about, but I can tell you that just wandering along as though you haven't a care in the world, settling in behind fortifications while the population of the northern world gathers nearby is just going to make you look either indecisive or cowardly."

Caesar's eyes flashed dangerously.

"I'm not saying that's what you are, general, but that's what people are going to think. If, as I assume, you have a good reason for waiting here, you need to tell people what it is."

The general shook his head.

"I cannot afford to have certain things become common knowledge ahead of time, Fronto. My army is riddled with treacherous Romans trying to undermine me and Gallic sympathisers who leak information to the Belgae. I trust most of my officers, but this incident with Paetus has just made me question how far that trust can really be extended."

Caesar sighed and leaned back in his chair, rubbing his temples.

"You, Fronto, are the most insolent, arrogant and obstinate man in my army. And don't think I haven't contemplated sending you back, many times…"

He leaned forward.

"After all, no commander, no matter how clever he is, is worth the trouble we have to put up with from you. But that's only half of it. There is hardly an officer in my army I can trust fully. All of them have some political game going on at some level… except you. And that's why I can't have you arguing with me and gainsaying me in front of the others. I need them to know you're with me and to understand why I don't send you home."

Fronto shrugged.

"If that's the case then at least confide in me. You know damn well I'm not going to go shouting your plans to the Belgae or sending letters to the senate."

He laughed.

"Hell, I never even get round to sending a letter to my sister!"

Caesar sat back again, thoughtfully.

"The reason, Fronto, that I was getting so damned angry with you just now, is that you already know the answer to this! And you are the only person in the whole army that does already know. Focus, man. What could I be waiting for?"

Fronto blinked.

"What?"

"The Aedui" Caesar said with a sigh. "Divitiacus and his tribesmen are busy hacking and burning their way through the lands of the Bellovaci. They're closing on our position as we speak."

Fronto grinned.

"Caught between two armies. Now I see what's happening. You want to hold off until the Aedui are close and you can pin them and crush them in one fell swoop!"

Caesar sighed.

"When will you realise that I'm not completely helpless, Fronto?"

* * * * *

Fronto stood on the causeway with Tetricus and Priscus, peering up and down the defensive trench that cut a line across the flat ground before the fort, just under a mile away. The shadow in the trench was dark and deep as the sun sank quickly now toward the western horizon.

"Are we really going to hole up here and wait for the Belgae to get stronger?" Priscus grumbled. "You may have had your fun at Bibrax, but my lads are itching to kick a few Belgae."

Fronto smiled.

"I'm sure you'll get the chance shortly. Caesar's got something up his sleeve. Just be patient."

Once more he shaded his eyes and examined Tetricus' handiwork. The ditch was wide enough to roll a cart back and forth across the bottom and deep enough that a man could break his leg if he fell. It really was impressive for only a few hours work. Now, men were working on the inner side shaping a rampart from the excavated earth and planting a palisade atop it. On the berm between the mound and the ditch, men in small groups worked to dig and disguise lilia. At each end of the fortification, a small but heavily defensible fortlet protected artillery platforms onto which the ballistae and onagers were now being manoeuvred. All in all it was impressive. Probably unnecessary, given the approaching Aedui force, but then only he and Caesar knew that.

Priscus snorted.

"I hate defences and sieges. Give me a good open field and a sword any day."

Fronto opened his mouth to reply, but closed it again when he saw, over Priscus' shoulder, legate Balbus of the Eighth striding down to the causeway.

"Evening all. That's looking very strong."

The older legate nodded appreciatively as he looked up and down the defences. Fronto smiled.

"Afternoon stroll, Quintus?"

Balbus chuckled.

"Not quite. Now most of the work's done, Caesar wants the legions moved forward to the new line and camped behind it. I think he's worried that the Belgae think we've lost interest."

Fronto nodded.

"He doesn't want to commit to battle yet, but the last thing we want them to do is to leave. Are we dismantling the main camp?"

Balbus shook his head.

"The reserves are to stay in the camp."

"Reserves? We have reserves?"

Balbus nodded wearily.

"You've been busy, so you've not seen what's been happening. The two new legions have all but cut themselves off. None of the veterans will talk to them, because they're Gaulish foederati who don't speak Latin well. There have been fights and arguments; thefts and vandalism. It's turning into an administrative nightmare. My officers are spending most of their time policing the men."

He sighed.

"I spoke to Caesar about integration. I was seriously considering transferring some of the Eighth out to them and taking some of them back in return, but Caesar won't have it. He doesn't think it'll improve morale in general, so much as destroy the morale of the Eighth. It is entirely possible that he's right as well."

Fronto nodded, and Balbus squared his shoulders.

"So essentially Caesar's separating the forces. The Thirteenth and Fourteenth, as reserves, are going to stay in the camp while the other five legions move up to the new line."

"I suppose it's a solution for now. Things will have to change eventually though."

With a nod to Tetricus and Priscus, Fronto joined Balbus, and the two began to stroll back up the grass towards the camp.

They had walked less than fifty paces before they became aware of the sound of thundering hooves behind them. Stopping and turning, they saw half a dozen cavalry riding for the camp gate. Among them, Fronto noted the plume of a senior officer. Waving his arm, he stepped out towards them.

"Ho, Varus! What's happening?"

The commander of the cavalry steered his horse toward the two legates with a deft twist of his knees.

"We've got trouble. Another big force of Belgae has turned up a few miles further out."

Fronto narrowed his eyes.

"You sure they were Belgae?"

"What? Yes of course I'm sure."

"They couldn't be any other sort of Gauls?" Fronto probed gently.

Varus stared at him.

"What the hell have you been drinking, Fronto."

Gritting his teeth, he dropped from the horse lightly to the grass.

"No, these are definitely Belgae. At least ten thousand of them; maybe fifteen. And they'll be in camp with their friends in an hour or so."

"Damn it!"

Fronto ground his teeth.

"Caesar's plans are just going to have to change. At the very least we need to whittle their numbers down while we wait."

He looked up at Varus.

"Balbus and I are coming with you to see Caesar."

"We are?" the older legate said with mild surprise and then hurried to catch up with the other two, Fronto walking with his hands clasped behind his back and his head down, Varus leading his horse by the bridle as his troopers went to water and rest their steeds.

"We're going to have to goad them into sending some kind of force out somewhere we can meet them," Fronto murmured. "I don't suppose you could get your cavalry round behind them and destroy this relief force?"

Varus shook his head.

"Not really. Not in time. We'd likely end up trapped between two armies of Belgae."

"Then we're going to have to either provoke them into coming to us or find another way to pick off a number of them. Your man Lucilius did a good job earlier. Maybe he could think of something?"

Varus shrugged.

"Whatever we try, the terrain will be dangerous, and the Belgae will be well prepared."

He looked up into the purple sky.

"And it's too late to do anything tonight anyway. It'll have to be in the morning."

Fronto nodded.

"Fair enough. Gives us a night to work something out anyway."

He smiled at Balbus.

"Actually, I think I've changed my mind. I've seen quite enough of Caesar for one day. Priscus will deal with moving the Tenth, and I presume you've set Balventius to moving your lot. Shall we retire to my tent for a beverage or two? It seems like an awful long time since I've seen you socially."

Balbus chuckled, rubbing his fist.

"That it does. In fact, if I'm not mistaken, the last time I had to break your nose!"

Fronto smiled weakly.

"Yes, well..."

He turned to Varus.

"After you've reported to Caesar, come join us. We should talk."

Varus nodded.

"I'll find you."

It was a little less than an hour later, with the last glow of the sun finally vanishing in the west, when Varus, divested of his armour and weapons and looking tired though relaxed in just tunic and breeches, finally knocked on Fronto's tent.

"Come on in."

He blinked as his eyes adjusted to the low lamp light. Fronto's tent looked exactly how Varus would have imagined: the furniture was pushed back against the walls, heaped with dirty clothes and junk, his armour in a pile near the door where he had dropped it, and the centre of the tent covered with rugs and cushions, all set around a low table on which sat a pair of dice, several piles of sesterces and goblets and jugs of wine.

In addition to Fronto and Balbus, the training officer of the Tenth, centurion Velius, and Aulus Crispus, legate of the Eleventh, sat around drinking and laughing. With a smile, Varus sank gratefully into a pile of cushions.

"Gentlemen."

As he sat, Fronto leaned back, and his face became serious for a moment.

"Is there anyone around outside?"

Varus shook his head.

"Not nearby. Why?"

Fronto sighed.

"There's something I'm not supposed to tell anyone, but I'm going to anyway."

Balbus raised an eyebrow.

"Very mysterious. You shouldn't pass on secrets, Marcus."

Fronto laughed quietly.

"I don't think it should be a secret. Caesar wants it kept under wraps because he's starting to get paranoid about people in his army being untrustworthy or leaking information to the Belgae."

He cast a glance round the room and smiled.

"But I'd be willing to bet my career on you lot."

It was true. Balbus had no political leanings and Velius was a career centurion with no position in Rome. There was no guarantee that Crispus and Varus had no other agenda but, apart from the fact that they owed their commissions to Caesar, something about the pair of them just sat well with Fronto. He would be prepared to trust any one of these men with his life.

"Thing is… I know why we're sitting tight and not engaging the Belgae."

He leaned back, noting with interest the intrigued look on the faces of all of his companions except Balbus, who merely nodded thoughtfully.

"The Aedui" he stated and leaned back.

Balbus nodded again. "I had a suspicion" he confirmed. "Didn't want to voice it, since Caesar clearly intended to keep this quiet, but there was a glaring hole in Caesar's attack plan, and there was only one logical solution."

Fronto smiled.

"You're ahead of the game, Quintus. Yes, Divitiacus and a sizeable Aedui army have been traipsing through the western edge of the Belgae lands, burning as they go. The Bellovaci tribe, I think it is."

Crispus smiled and poured himself another drink.

"So Caesar's waiting for the forces to join up? Or just to have them at the other side of the Belgae as a threat. Might be able to end this entire campaign peacefully if we can trap the Belgae in a vice and threaten them."

Varus shook his head. "We'll still have a battle on our hands. I've seen these Belgae in action now. They'll not lie down and give in. The only way we're ever going to beat them in a straight fight without more legions is by being inventive and outthinking them."

"Agreed," Fronto added. "I saw them at Bibrax, and they're not the sort of people to give up without a fight. We only succeeded because of a few clever moves."

Balbus scratched his head, deep in thought.

"So I assume Caesar set all this in motion long before we even left Vesontio. The Aedui must have started moving the same time as us."

Fronto nodded. "Caesar sent riders out to Divitiacus the same time he sent those couriers to Rome; to his sister."

He stopped for a moment, frowning. Varus took a swig from his goblet.

"Caesar sent riders to Rome?"

Fronto waved a hand. "Hang on. Yes. It's a long story and one you might be better off not knowing."

Balbus shook his head.

"Too late now. You've already told him enough."

The older legate turned to the cavalry commander.

"Paetus; the camp prefect?"

Varus nodded. "He's involved with one of Caesar's opposition in Rome."

Velius spluttered over his wine as Varus stared.

"True," admitted Fronto. "Caesar was all for getting rid of him one way or another, but it's not really Paetus' fault. He's been used; he's not really a traitor, so we found a way to use him ourselves. We turned him back on his patron in Rome. Caesar's going to have him…"

Suddenly, Fronto stared and then slapped his head.

"Balbus, I think I've been stupid."

A questioning frown.

"I should have realised. When I talked to Caesar a while back about Paetus and the couriers, for a moment he acted as though he hadn't a clue what I was talking about."

He ground his teeth. "And that's because he hadn't. He'd forgotten what he told me. He never sent anyone to Rome. The couriers he sent out were to the Aedui!"

Balbus' frown deepened. "That means that Paetus' family are still in danger. No one's watching over them after all. Would Caesar really do that? Are you sure about this, Marcus?"

Fronto started to climb to his feet.

"Quintus, I'm beyond sure. We've got to warn Paetus not to go along with Caesar. He'll be endangering his wife and children."

Balbus grasped his wrist and pulled him back down to the cushions, a dark look on his face.

"Too late, Marcus. Caesar had Paetus send his messages to Rome while you were off fighting at Bibrax…"

Fronto let out a low animal growl.

"That heartless, cold bastard."

The vicious edge to his voice made Varus and Crispus start with surprise. Fronto slammed his fist on the floor.

"The old bastard deliberately had Paetus put himself and his family in danger. He could easily have stopped it, or protected them as he said he would. But no! The miserable old bastard just had Paetus sign a death warrant on his own family. If that Clodius is as nasty a piece of work as I hear, he'll not flinch from gutting a woman and children."

Balbus' jaw line hardened.

"Not only that, but Caesar actually waited until you were safely out of the way before he set it in motion. I expect he thinks that you'd try and stop it."

He sighed. "Which, of course, you would."

Fronto continued to growl quietly. "So do we tell Paetus?"

"What good will that do?" replied Balbus. "There's nothing he can do about it now. I suppose it's possible you could persuade Caesar to send the riders that he never did, but I don't think so."

Fronto shook his head, a determined look on his face.

"I can do one better than that. I just hope there's still time."

He turned to Varus.

"I need half a dozen men with fast horses; Romans, too. Not Gauls. Think you can spare them?"

Varus nodded, uncertainly.

"The cavalry strength reports are always a mess anyway. What are you planning?"

"I've got family in Rome as well, and a bored sister with money. If Caesar won't do anything to protect Paetus' family, then it's up to me."

Varus sat back. "Pour me another glass of wine. I suspect I'm going to need it."

* * * * *

As the sun made its first appearance over the treelined hills to the east and the dew settled into the damp grass, Varus vaulted into his saddle. The cavalry section was quartered in a stockaded area near one end of the defensive line, close to a wide causeway crossing, and the pre-dawn morning had seen the camp alive with troopers, both regular and auxiliary, preparing for action. Caesar had called Varus to him in the middle of the night, and the cavalry commander had blearily attended to be informed that the cavalry would be going into action first thing in the morning.

Since then, Varus had had no time for sleep. Giving the call early, he had managed to marshal the entire mounted division in front of their stockade while it was still dark. Now, as he prepared to ride out and attempt a repeat of the cavalry's previous successes, he slung his shield on its strap over his back and narrowed his eyes at the five men sitting astride their horses awaiting orders.

"Sorry to take you out of the action. I'm sure you were looking forward to giving the Belgae a battering, but I need people I can trust with this."

Reaching into his tunic, he withdrew a scroll in a protective leather wrap, sealed with wax. Hesitating for a moment, he reached out and proffered it to the nearest rider. As the man took the scroll and tucked it away safely inside his cloak, Varus withdrew a second item; a small purse of coins. Handing it to the men, he fixed them with a serious gaze.

"This should be enough to see you to Rome and back comfortably, using mansios wherever you can. Remember: you're couriers for a legate, so steer clear of any trouble spots and stay as safe and inconspicuous as possible. Repeat your orders for me?"

The man with the tightly-wrapped scroll nodded.

"We're to deliver this to the House of the Falerii opposite the temple of Bona Dea on the Aventine. It's to go only into the hands of one of the two ladies of the house; no servants. Get there as fast as we can and then return to Durocorteron to find out where the army has moved to. Talk to no one about where we're going, what we're doing or who we're doing it for."

Varus nodded. "And if neither of the Falerii ladies are there?"

"Then we're to ride on to their villa in Puteoli and deliver the message there."

Again Varus nodded, satisfied. "This is very important. Lives rest on your success. Now get going, and good luck."

The men saluted and then rode from the stockade towards the bridge across the Aisne at the rear of the huge camp. Varus watched them go and sighed. How the hell did he get caught up in intrigue like this? It was Fronto, he thought, almost laughing. The man was like a hub around which trouble gathered. Gods would be frightened to get too deeply involved with Fronto.

Another smile, and he turned and rode back to join the cavalry prefects behind him. “Alright, gentlemen. Let’s go and show the Belgae how we make war.”

Squaring his shoulders, he kicked his horse into motion and led the large cavalry contingent of Caesar’s army, fully equipped for battle, through the gate in the stockade and toward the crossing point of the ditch.

The mile or so to the marsh passed peacefully, the dawn chorus twittering its song to the thousands of riders as they trotted, grim-faced, past nature’s morning spectacle. As the sun gradually rose higher, it washed the landscape of gentle rolling hills with a pale, watery light.

Varus prepared himself. Though he had seen the lay of the land several times and knew the Belgic position well, until he reached the scene, he really could not decide how to proceed. Would it be best to attempt a repeat of Lucilius’ action to the east? Perhaps it would be best to take the army round to the west and try to skirt them until they could reach appropriate ground beyond the ridge? He was even tempted to send a few scouts into the marsh to see if it was shallower than it looked. If the cavalry could cross the marsh it would certainly make things easier, though that was extremely doubtful.

His face hardened as they reached the plain where two of the recent actions had taken place. In the hours since the last attack, the Belgae had retrieved their dead, presumably to bury them and raise a mound somewhere back near their encampment. The Roman dead, of course, remained where they fell, starting to putrefy. The sooner they could get the Belgae to fight, the sooner this would be over, and they could retrieve their own dead and give them a proper funeral.

He mused again. His orders were to try and get the Belgae to march on the Roman lines but, if they continued to refuse, to harry them and reduce their numbers. Easier said than done, given this terrain.

As they reached the foot of the low hill, he looked up at the familiar line of poplars and then turned back to his men. Signalling a halt, he gestured to the senior prefects and together the officers rode to the top of the hill to confer and make plans.

The line of poplars offered some protection and a clear view across the marsh at the lines of the Belgae. As Varus reached the crest, he drew up sharply.

"What the?"

The prefect by his side stared. "Where the hell are they?"

Ahead, the marsh stretched out as a barrier of dangerous ground. Beyond lay the camp of the Belgae, stretching across the plain, almost empty and seemingly abandoned. Peering at the mess and squinting, Varus could make out a number of warriors gathered in small groups.

"There can't be more than a few thousand men there in the whole bloody camp!"

The man by his side said, in much the same shocked voice "but where have the rest gone?"

'Good question', the commander thought to himself.

"They can't have got far" he murmured as he squinted at the camp. "There are far too many fires burning there for them to have been travelling for long. They can't have been gone more than two or three hours, I'd say."

This was the highest point within reasonable reach, but the view was fairly restricted by the charred and blackened areas of woodland and thick undergrowth to either side. Frowning, he glanced round at his officers.

"Any of you men good at climbing trees?"

There was a lot of metaphorical shuffling of feet and finally Septimius, the prefect of the Eighth's cavalry sighed.

"Alright, sir. I'll see what I can do."

Walking his horse a few steps, he hoisted himself up until he was standing on the saddle and reached for the nearest solid branch of the tree. With a grunt, he hauled himself up into it. Varus watched him climb, deftly, higher, quickly reaching the narrower, more flexible branches. Above the commander, the tree swayed, twigs and leaves dropping and fluttering down among the officers. After a moment, Varus stepped his horse back, so that he could see the armoured figure hauling himself ever higher. With a crack, Septimius stopped, having reached the highest safe point.

"What can you see?" shouted the commander.

"Shit!"

"What?"

"They're on the other side of the river!"

There was a great deal of rustling and cracking as the prefect clambered and slid back down among the branches, heedless of the cuts and scratches he was acquiring.

"They're what?" demanded Varus incredulously.

The prefect dropped lightly from the lowest branches and landed on the grass with bent knees before standing straight.

"They must have found somewhere safe upstream and crossed during the night. They're maybe an hour away from the bridge at the most on the other side!"

"Oh shit." Varus spat on the floor. "They'll be able to sever our supply lines and cause havoc."

In the privacy of his head he offered a quick prayer to Fortuna and added '...and hopefully they haven't intercepted Fronto's couriers!'

He turned back to Lucilius. "You did a nice job here yesterday. Think you can repeat your success and clear up?"

The prefect nodded. "Give me a few alae and I'll leave that camp charred and covered with Belgic bodies!"

Varus slapped him on the shoulder. "Take yours and three of the auxiliary alae. That enough?"

"More than enough" agreed Lucilius through gritted teeth.

Varus nodded.

"Then I've got to take the rest back to camp and warn Caesar. He'll not have time to mobilise the legions. Sabinus is going to have to defend the bloody bridge on his own!"

Without bothering to give orders, Varus wheeled his horse and began to charge, hooves thundering, back the way they'd come. As he passed the cavalry, his troopers stared in surprise at their commander storming past with an expression of great concern. Moments later, their prefects returned.

Lucilius gestured to several decurions and then pointed off to his left.

"You lot! Form up your units over there. We've got a few thousand Belgae to maim."

As the selected units hurried to move their units into position, Casco, prefect of the Ninth, waved his arm expansively at the rest of the cavalry and then pointed to the retreating figure of Varus.

"Back to camp at a charge. We've an army to save!"

Chapter 9

(Caesar's camp by the Aisne River.)

"Gaesatus: a spearman, usually a mercenary of Gallic origin."

Fronto rushed from his tent at the alarm call blared out by the command cornicen. Struggling with his cloak for a moment, he gave up in annoyance and let the crimson article drop to the grass outside the tent flap, leaving it waving in the breeze. As he ran to the general's headquarters tent, he saw the other legates and officers rushing to the rallying point. As he reached the patch of grass outside the tent at the same time as Crispus, he bent double and clutched his knees, breathing heavily.

"What the... hell's happened?"

As he glanced around, taking everything in, he noticed two horses tethered by the tent flap.

"Varus is back? What happened to the cavalry?"

Crispus shrugged, also taking in ragged breaths.

"I've no idea, Fronto."

As Balbus came to a halt beside them and Labienus appeared, pink-cheeked with the effort of running, the general suddenly threw back the leather tent flap and stepped out into the sunlight with Varus at his shoulder.

"Gentlemen, form up your legions. Galba? I want the Twelfth to take command here and man the defences. Several alae of cavalry should be returning to join you shortly."

He took a deep breath.

"The rest of you, get your troops moving back to the bridge at the quickest march you can manage. The Belgae have apparently found a fordable crossing point and come round behind us during the night. Sabinus is about to be attacked at any moment by a force of probably a hundred and fifty thousand Belgae on the other side of the river."

Fronto blinked.

"The sly bastards! How long have we got?"

Varus stepped forward.

"It's been maybe a half hour since we saw them, and they were less than an hour away then."

"We'll never get the legions there in time, Caesar" the legate spat. "Even if we drop everything but weapons and run, we'd be lucky to get to the river in time, but it'll take hours to get the men across that bridge too. The legions simply can't get there in time."

Varus nodded.

"He's right, Caesar. We should send a dispatch to Sabinus and tell him to get out of there as fast as he can. We'll have to follow the Belgae and bring them to battle somewhere else."

"No!"

The force of Caesar's tone surprised them. The general had gone pale, and his teeth ground together.

"No. It's critical that we stop them here. My plans are being changed for me, and I won't have that. I can't leave this place right now, and if we let them loose they have free rein with the Remi; they can burn their crops and attack and loot their settlements. What use Fronto's hard work getting the Remi on our side if we let them go now?"

A thought seemed to strike the general, and he smiled at his legate.

"Fronto."

"Sir?"

"Think you can repeat your Bibrax triumph back at the main camp today?"

Fronto frowned.

"You mean take the missile troops and actually engage a vast army of Belgae with them? There were maybe thirty thousand Belgae there. There's five times as many here! Respectfully, only a mad arsehole would try it!"

Caesar smiled a lopsided smile.

"Well?" he prompted.

A grin slowly slid across Fronto's face.

"I'll need more men this time. There's a lot more Belgae."

Caesar nodded.

"Get every light auxiliary unit from every legion. All the archers, slingers and spear throwers. They're all unarmoured light troops." He addressed the assembled legates in front of him.

"Go now and get all your light auxiliaries to form up on the plain as fast as you can."

Another thought seemed to strike him as the legates turned to head back to their legions.

"Labienus? You take temporary command of the Eighth. Balbus? I want you to go with Fronto and take command of the Thirteenth and Fourteenth in the camp. They could be useful."

Balbus nodded, though worry darkened his eyes. Fronto could understand that. They were about to take two untried legions and the lightest of the auxilia into battle against a foe that would seriously outnumber them."

The general turned back to Fronto.

"Get there as fast as possible and engage them, Fronto. You don't have to defeat them; just hold them there until the rest of the legions can engage."

Varus cleared his throat.

"Caesar? The cavalry can get there in time to help as well. Permission to accompany Fronto and his men?"

The general nodded.

"Very well, Varus."

He regarded the three commanders in front of him.

"The bridge would slow the rest of the legions too much, but if the Belgae can find another way, so can we. I shall take the Eighth, Ninth, Tenth and Eleventh as fast as we can along the river to the east. If a hundred thousand barbarians can ford it in a few hours, the legions should be quicker. You three keep them busy at the bridge, and we will come round behind them and seal off their escape route. Once we have them trapped between us, I think things will quickly go our way."

Fronto nodded. A quick glance and he could see how quickly and efficiently the Roman commanders had organised their legions. The main forces were already forming up. The light auxiliary units were being rushed out to the side, where they were gathering in a much looser formation, waiting for their commander.

Caesar smiled.

"Good luck gentlemen. I shall see you on the south bank."

The three officers saluted and, as the general strode off toward the regulars, Fronto turned to Varus and Balbus.

"Varus: collect your cavalry and break speed records in getting to Sabinus. Tell him we're on the way and not to do anything stupid! Balbus? You'd best take a horse and get to the fort. You'll need to tell Plancus what's happening a few times until it sinks in and then start the legions moving across the bridge as soon as you can. We'll need all of you on the other side of the water where it's flat; it's the only terrain legionaries and cavalry can operate safely in."

Varus grinned. As Caesar's cavalry commander, he was aware that he theoretically outranked all the legionary legates but, for some reason, if felt natural to be ordered around by Fronto. The man had a talent for leadership. When he shouted, even the senate would stand to and obey.

"My pleasure. See you at the fort."

Fronto turned to Balbus.

"Be careful with them. We don't know how well prepared they are for real battle."

Balbus smiled.

"It's about time they got the chance to find out. Hurry along now, Fronto. You'll have to catch us up quickly."

As Varus and Balbus rushed off to find a horse for the legate and rejoin the cavalry, Fronto sighed. He was legate of the Tenth Legion, and here he was, deep in the campaigning season, and he had hardly spent any time with the Tenth at all. Priscus was itching to get involved in a fight, but all he got to do was the day to day tasks of legionary command. Fronto, on the other hand, was about to undertake his second hard fight of the season, commanding auxiliary troops only. He regarded the force gathering nearby and smiled. Fortunately, promotions and transfers had been delayed in the current circumstances, so at least he knew he was fighting alongside good men.

As the units were formed up, he quickly ran back to his tent and grabbed his sword, shield and helmet. He stopped for a moment and looked down at the red cloak lying outside the door. He had ignored it and run across the fine material with muddy, hob-nailed boots twice. He smiled sadly at the messy item. What was it with him and cloaks? Jamming the helm on his head, he started to jog down to the gathering units.

There were perhaps three or four thousand men there altogether. Mostly Numidians, either armed with short bows or spears, along with the familiar Cretan archers and the deadly Balearic slingers. Much like the force he had at Bibrax, but more than three times the size.

"Decius!"

The prefect turned and grinned as Fronto bounded up the gentle incline towards him.

"D'you know, when I was told all the auxiliary foot troops were being called to service, I had a feeling I'd see you shortly, sir!"

Fronto laughed.

"You remember those Belgae we fought off? Well now we get to kick them and all their mates around a bit."

He squared his shoulders and straightened his sword by his side before addressing the force gathered around him.

"Senior officers to me!"

A dozen or so prefects rushed out of the press of men and came to attention at the front, saluting. Fronto noted the knowing looks on the faces of Galeo and Pansa. What was this reputation he seemed to have acquired?

"Men? We're about to go into action alongside the Thirteenth and Fourteenth legions and the cavalry against more Belgae than you can wave a shitty stick at. I need to see the same kind of strength and bravery I saw at Bibrax. But we need to run to get there in time to save Sabinus and his men."

He took a deep breath.

"So no dawdling! Prefects? Get your units back to the main camp at a run and form up above the river."

The officers in front of him saluted and started bellowing commands at their men. Fronto watched as the lightly-armed and completely unarmoured men began to move off at a steady jog toward the south. As the nearest unit of Cretans started to run, Fronto sprinted alongside and fell in next to their prefect.

"Enjoying life in the limelight, Decius?"

Momentarily, he concentrated on the turf in front of him as he felt that familiar twinge in his ankle. Damn it. Almost two decades of fighting with the legions and he had sustained no lasting injuries. Then one bloody fight last year and he gets bitten in the ankle by a mad German woman and almost hamstrung. That ankle had never been quite right since. He became aware that Decius had replied while he concentrated on the ground. Ah well. At least his nose felt good these days.

"I'll need brilliant ideas from you lot before we engage. The way I reckon it, there's going to be a hundred and fifty thousand mad, bloodthirsty Belgae on the other side of the river, and all we've got will be a couple of thousand veteran legionaries under Sabinus, ten thousand green, untried legionaries under Balbus and Plancus, maybe five thousand cavalry under Varus, and three thousand missile troops. That's... what? Twenty thousand against a hundred and fifty? Slightly unnerving odds, eh?"

Decius grinned as he stared off into the distance.

"Maybe, but we've got fortified defences, a narrow bridge to defend and the height of the northern bank for advantage."

He turned his grin on Fronto.

"And, of course, we've got us!"

Laughing, the two men ran on alongside the Cretans with their bows.

* * * * *

By the time Fronto reached the camp, standing on the high ground and overlooking the bridge and Sabinus' fort, the action had clearly already begun. In this lofty position, Fronto swallowed hard as he viewed a disaster of epic proportions in the making.

Sabinus had his cohorts secure yet trapped behind the walls of the small but defensive fort. There was no hope of him being able to sally forth and do any damage at this time, as the near side of the fort was bounded by the river, quick flowing and the darkness of the water suggesting dangerous depths. The other three sides were being assailed at close range by a veritable sea of shouting Belgae. There were, indeed, so many barbarian warriors that the observers had to look carefully to make out the fort walls under the press of bodies. The rearguard force that Sabinus had been left with fought desperately over their defences, stabbing and slashing madly at anyone they could reach. In Fronto's professional opinion, Sabinus' force would be gone in half an hour, and the fort left as kindling. From the look of things, the Belgae had moved faster than Varus had expected. They must have been here before the other Romans arrived.

Balbus' reserve force would be precious little help. The Thirteenth and Fourteenth legions were still mostly on the north bank, a small group desperately trying to create a bridgehead at the far side in the face of many thousands of barbarians. They were failing dismally. If Crassus or Caesar had been here, they would likely have placed the blame firmly with the new, green, Gallic legions. Fronto, on the other hand, could see this for what it was. Two legions crammed into a narrow space, desperately attempting to break out in the face of impossible odds, most of them still trapped on the bridge or the near side. The Eighth or the Tenth would be doing no better in these conditions. Had Fronto been in charge of the Belgae, he would now be trying to collapse the bridge, but at least that thought seemed to have escaped the barbarian chieftains. The bridge was big and strong, but not big enough to host a battle.

Varus had clearly arrived just in time to get himself cut off and trapped. His cavalry had made it across the bridge in the face of the charging barbarians and were now milling about in the middle distance on the edge of the Belgic army, too isolated to try anything truly useful. As Fronto watched, he could see them doing what they could to harry the enemy, skirmishing and casting javelins into the middle of the mass, but little they could achieve would make any real difference without infantry support. At best they would annoy the Belgae and whittle down their numbers a little.

The way things were currently going, the fort would fall to the Belgae in around half an hour, the dead would pile up at the far end of the bridge, and the legions would remain blocked up until it finally occurred to the barbarians to destroy the entire structure, drowning a few hundred legionaries and rendering the rest ineffective. The cavalry would engage in quick bursts, but once the Belgae completely held the far bank and had rendered the river uncrossable they would turn and massacre Varus and his men before waiting for Caesar to arrive.

A disaster.

Fronto paced along the crest as his missile units began to fall into formation, the rear ranks still arriving. Something had to be done, and fast. Damn it!

A familiar voice called out from nearby.

"Looks like shit, sir, eh?"

Fronto turned to see prefect Pansa shading his eyes and taking in the scene.

"This makes shit look good, Pansa. Got any ideas?"

The prefect shook his head.

"We can start picking them off from here with arrows, slingshot and spears, but it's going to be like being bothered by insects for that lot. No way can we make a difference in time to save anyone."

Decius came to a halt nearby.

"Going to have to widen the crossing, so our legions can get over."

Fronto turned in surprise.

"How the hell do you propose that?"

Decius shrugged. "I really don't know, but that's what we've got to do. If we can get more men over there, we can create a proper bridgehead. If that happened, they could then force the Belgae back between the bridge and the fort and start setting up a proper line while everyone else crossed. After that, it's battle as usual."

Fronto shook his head.

"Makes sense, I suppose, but it doesn't solve how we get more men across." He frowned as he looked down at the chaos. "Rafts? Boats?"

Decius shook his head.

"Too slow. We'd have to build the rafts, and then only a few could cross at a time. Sabinus would be dead long before we could get there."

Somebody noisily cleared their throat so close behind Fronto that he jumped slightly. He turned to see prefect Galeo staring off toward the huge camp above them, a thoughtful frown on his face.

"Would you kindly not sneak up on me like that!" he snapped at the prefect.

"Hmm? Oh, sorry sir. Think I've an idea."

The other three officers turned to him.

"You want to get the men across? Well you either have to go over, which means a bridge or boats… or you just move the river."

"What?"

"A dam" the prefect replied, still staring up at the camp.

Decius smiled.

"Go on, Galeo."

"Well… I reckon that bridge we built down there is good and strong. It was built to support the weight of several loaded supply carts. The piers of the bridge are quite close together." He pointed up at the stockade atop the camp's rampart. "And we've got a massive ready supply of great big logs."

Fronto frowned.

"That's bloody dangerous. What happens if we break the bridge? Then we've done their job for them."

Decius nodded. "That's not the only danger. What if you succeed and the water level rises enough to reach the bridge and flows over the bank?"

Galeo smiled.

"Then a hundred thousand Belgae drown. Doesn't sound like a problem to me."

Fronto's face slowly split into a smile.

"Galeo, you clever bugger, you! You're in charge of the dismantling. Get the Gaesati up there and start work tearing down the stakes... they can't hit the Belgae from here anyway." He turned to the others.

"Get all the archers and slingers concentrating on that mass of Belgae near the bridge. Send any spearmen up to Galeo. I'm going to find some men from the Thirteenth or Fourteenth to help."

As the prefect started shouting out commands, Fronto descended the slope toward the bridge. The journey was short but perilous, with rabbit holes pock-marking the steep turf incline to trip the unwary, and his ankle occasionally giving a little 'twang' of pain. As he slid and ran he took note of the disposition of the legions.

Balbus had led the Thirteenth into the front. In fact, as he carefully scanned the other end of the bridge, he could occasionally spot the legate's plume bobbing around amid the violence. He shook his head. Balbus used to be careful and command from a position of safety. The longer he spent with Fronto and Crispus and the others, the more reckless he was becoming. Still marshalled on this side of the bank, hanging back from the action, were the Fourteenth. As he watched occasional pila arced out from the reserve legion toward the Belgae on the far bank, falling harmlessly into the swift current.

"Men of the Fourteenth!" he called forcefully as he finally reached the shore level.

The legionaries turned, and the nearest men saluted.

"The next soldier who throws a pilum into that river will have one jammed up his arse. Don't waste weaponry. And I know some of you don't understand me, so if you do, make sure you pass that on!"

A plume wobbled around at the far side and then a gap opened in the lines as Plancus, red-faced and angry, strode back towards him.

"What do you think you're doing, Fronto? These are my men, and I ordered them to harass the enemy with pila."

Fronto growled.

"Most of them can't even get half way across, Plancus. No one stands a chance of hitting a barbarian. Save your weapons. We're going to pull off a little trick in a moment and give you men a chance to get across and into the action. When we do, get over there and help solidify that bridgehead and drive a connecting line to the fort."

The legate stared at him.

"Look, Plancus. This is your first command and your first action. I know they're your men, but I've been commanding legions for twenty years. Take my advice and use it."

The young officer glared for a moment and then nodded.

"Where do want me and what signal will you give?"

Fronto pointed.

"Form up on the downriver side of the bridge, about twenty men abreast. You'll know when to go, if this works."

Plancus saluted stiffly, and Fronto gave him a half-hearted response.

As the young officer began to manoeuvre his legion, Fronto pushed further through to the rear of the Thirteenth Legion, massed around the bridge and waiting to cross.

"Any of you lot engineers?"

The men of the Thirteenth looked around in surprise and saluted the senior officer.

"Come on, come on…" he shouted.

A stocky legionary at the rear with an extremely unfashionable but plainly Gallic beard shrugged, the braids at the side of his head scraping along the edge of his helmet. In a fairly thick Gallic accent, he spoke up.

"Had some training sir. A few of us have, but we've not really had the chance to put it to use."

Fronto grinned at him. "That's about to change, soldier. Get a dozen or so good men together and come with me."

As soon as the Gaulish legionary and a few of his compatriots reached him and saluted, Fronto pointed up to the camp, where several sections of palisade had already visibly gone.

"Up there, come on."

A few moments later, he reached the top of the slope with his party. The new recruits of the Thirteenth looked on with interest as an officer and a number of ebony-skinned auxiliaries worked on dismantling the legions' camp. The engineer frowned as he saw two of the palisade stakes dropped to the ground and let roll down the hill where they disappeared into the river with a splash.

"What are they doing, sir?"

Fronto pointed at the stockade.

"We're going to roll the timber down into the river to dam it at the bridge."

"That won't work, sir."

Fronto turned on him. "Why not?"

"Well, the timbers are big enough, sir, but they'll just bounce around on the surface and some will just float under the bridge end-on. It just won't work, sir… take it from me."

The legate fumed, rubbing his temples. "Well we've got to do it somehow."

The legionary shrugged.

"It's vaguely possible we could drop a section of the palisade as it is down from the bridge? That would dam the river pretty well." He frowned. "But can I ask what you're wanting to dam the river for, sir?"

Fronto pointed at the Fourteenth Legion, lining up on the bank downstream of the bridge.

"Need to lower the water level so the legions can cross in bulk, rather than being jammed tightly onto that bridge."

Again, the legionary shook his head.

"But if you dam the river at the bridge, sir, with that current, you'll only have maybe the count of a hundred, and then the river will flood the flat land above the bank before flowing back round the dam. Basically you'll be putting the entire battlefield ankle deep in water and mud, and there'll still only be time to run a few men across. And think of how dangerous the river bed might be, sir? Could be deep mud."

Fronto rounded angrily on him with a growl.

"Then what do you suggest? I'm running out of time very quickly, and you're just tearing down any idea we have."

The legionary frowned. "We'll just have to go over the river, sir. Safer, dryer, and probably quicker."

"What? How?"

The man gestured at the palisade.

"If we stop tearing them apart, you can see the stockade is already solidly bound. The whole thing is tightly-roped together. Standing upright, it's a stockade. Lay it flat, sir, and it becomes a bridge."

Fronto blinked. "That's genius! Can you do it?"

The legionary tapped his chin.

"I'd say we want ninety feet of stockade to be sure we reach across. We want to check the rope binding and maybe strengthen or repair it where needed. Then several men are going to have to cross, dragging one end by ropes. Then they have to secure it to the bank. They can do that using some of these stakes that have already been dismantled. Then men at this end haul it tight and secure the near end. It wouldn't take the weight of a cart, and you'll have to limit the number of men that cross at a time. I'd say not more than thirty or forty. But a lot safer than a dam."

Fronto grinned. "And can you do it quickly?"

The man nodded.

"With enough men. Give me a century and it'll take about a quarter of an hour to take a section down and check the bindings; then get it down the hill and into the water. A moment more to get it across and then quarter of an hour to secure it at both ends. I'd say half an hour at the quickest. Is that fast enough, sir?"

Fronto shook his head. "Maybe... maybe not. It'll certainly be tight."

The legionary shrugged again. "Can't think of a better way, sir. The dam won't work, though. I do know that."

Fronto's brow furrowed. "If we're cutting it that fine, I need to get as many men across as possible. Can you string more than one of these across?"

"Given enough men, I don't see why not, sir, but the men swimming across and securing the bridge will need to be protected from the enemy while they work."

Fronto smiled.

"Alright. Go up and explain it quickly to Galeo. Him and his men will get started. Get three sections of palisade down. We'll string them across between here and Sabinus' fort. The walls of the fort will protect you from the enemy when you get across, and you can secure the ropes to it. Might make it quicker. We'll give you cover as you work. Once you get across, shout to the defenders and they can take down sections of the rear wall, so we can get the legions across and straight into the fort. I'll go back down and send you up a cohort."

The legionary saluted and ran off up toward the auxiliary prefect where he worked at the stockade. Fronto watched him go, impressed. Caesar had underestimated these noncitizen legionaries. Glancing down at the scene below, he realised that Sabinus had pulled much of his force away from the rear wall by the river to bolster the beleaguered men at the other three walls. As he scanned the shoreline, frowning, he turned to the auxiliary archers and their commander nearby.

"Decius!"

The prefect looked back up from where he was pointing out targets to his men.

"Sir?"

"Sabinus' rear wall is unprotected, and there are a few Belgae trying to get round on the river bank. Discourage them, will you? And shortly we'll be trying something there, so have your men concentrate on keeping that rear wall completely clear of barbarians."

Decius nodded and smiled, turning back to his men. There were small groups of Belgae making their way along the bank toward the badly-defended riverside ramparts. Moments later, as Fronto watched, arrows began to find their targets and barbarians toppled into the water with a splash. The current down by the bridge began to take on a pinkish hue.

Without waiting any longer, he ran once more down to the men of the legions below.

"Plancus!" he bellowed. The young legate turned from his position by the bank.

"Change of plan. Get your men to the river opposite the fort."

Without waiting for acknowledgement or reply, he ran across to the soldiers at the near end of the bridge.

"Whichever cohort's near me, get up that hill and join in. They'll tell you what to do. Now go!"

The signifers and centurions pushed their way through the mass and started to run up the hill, the legionaries following their standards. Fronto took a deep breath and ran across to the ground opposite the fort. Briefly, and nervously, he looked back up the hill at the archers loosing their arrows overhead, but the missiles were coming down with deadly accuracy on the opposite bank and picking off the last barbarians brave enough to try the difficult approach.

He watched with unease for long moments, tapping his fingers nervously on his scabbard and then, turning, squinted past the ranks of archers to check the activity at the top of the slope. Once again, he was impressed with the quality of these men. Already the three sections of palisade were unearthed and being gently moved down the slope. Even as he watched, the archers parted to allow the engineers and legionaries through with their makeshift bridges. Gods, they were fast.

"Hold on, Sabinus. We're coming..."

* * * * *

Quarter of an hour later, Fronto was still standing on the north bank, twitching at the urgency of their mission. He watched with growing tension as the legionary engineer, whose name he had discovered was Biorix, tied off the last rope securing the far end. Now all three bridges were attached to the opposite bank. Tapping his foot impatiently, he watched the engineers carefully hauling the bridge ropes as tight as possible and then tying them to the stakes that had been hammered into the ground here. Opposite, three large holes had been broken in the fort's riverside rampart.

He clucked his tongue irritably and was about to shout something when he saw Biorix waving at him. With a sigh of relief, he turned to the legion assembled behind him.

"Get across. Twenty men to each crossing at a time for now!"

The legionaries stormed onto the makeshift bridges and Fronto watched with sudden alarm as the wooden walkway dipped and disappeared below the water. However, it took but a moment for him to realise they had only sunk a little under the weight of the men. The soldiers, nervous though they were, crossed in water only ankle deep. As the first men reached the far side and ran into the fort, a familiar figure in burnished armour and with a red plume appeared in one of the gateways. Sabinus was directing the new arrivals to plug the worst gaps in his defences.

With a sigh of relief, Fronto turned to Plancus.

"Looks good. I'm going across. I think we can just settle now into getting one century across at a time."

The young legate nodded, staring with clear nerves at the submerged and shuddering bridge. Ignoring him, Fronto joined the next group of men to cross. Splashing along the thirty paces, he grinned as he climbed up the embankment and Sabinus slapped him on the shoulder.

"Thought you'd never get here, Marcus!"

Fronto breathed deeply.

"We nearly didn't. Clever engineers, eh?" He gestured back across the river.

"Indeed. What's your plan?"

Fronto blinked. He had not got as far as a plan. Just getting here had been his plan.

"Well Caesar's on his way with the other legions. We need to drive a wedge between the Belgae and the river, so that the Thirteenth can form a bridgehead and secure the bank. Once that's done, we can marshal the men and begin to actually do the job. You need to get runners out around the Belgae somehow to pass instructions to Varus, and others back across to the missile troops. If Varus can start trying to help thin them out towards the bridge and the prefects above can concentrate their missiles on the area where the Belgae are thickest, we can divide the men between maintaining the defences here and joining up along the bank with the Thirteenth at the bridge."

Sabinus laughed.

"Oh… nothing simple, then?"

Fronto shook his head.

"We're still up against enormous odds, but now we can actually start to bring tactics into play.

Sabinus nodded. "I'll get the messengers out and get back to the walls. You concentrate on things by the river, yes?"

Fronto nodded. As the next group of men crossed the bridge, he called them over. Their centurion stepped to the front.

"I need you to head along there between the wall and the river, and when you get to the end start to push out into the Belgae. Don't try and engage properly. I just want a shield wall that moves slowly outwards. Reserves will be coming up to support you. We're going to keep pushing them back until we control the whole bank and meet up with the Thirteenth at the bridge, alright?"

The centurion saluted and nodded. Without a word, he and his men picked their way along the difficult terrain towards the open ground on the river bank. Fronto watched them go and then turned his attention back to the bridge. The next century had just arrived. The legate pointed into the fort.

"To the walls!"

The men saluted and ran off into the fort. Fronto turned back to the bridge and smiled. Plancus was coming across with the next group, stepping lightly as a dancer, as though there were sea monsters beneath the surface. As the young man, visibly relieved, arrived on the bank, Fronto clasped hands with him.

"Plancus… can you take over here if I join in the action? I'm sending alternate units into the fort or along to the bridgehead."

The young man nodded, letting out a deep breath. With a quick glance at him, Fronto gestured to the centurion who had just crossed.

"You men are with me!"

Without waiting for a reply, he started to make his way speedily along the river bank. Ahead, he could see the legionaries fighting desperately at the edge of the river. As he ran he saw with dismay one of the men slip in the midst of combat and drop into the river like a stone. Weighed down with chainmail and helmet, there was no hope for the man. Fronto gritted his teeth as he saw how hard the men were fighting for such little ground. He and his reserves finally reached the rear of the century of men, now already whittled down to a third of their number.

"Push!" he yelled, and threw himself in among the soldiers, clearly greatly to the surprise of the Gaulish legionaries. The reserves joined the line, and the extra weight began to press back the Belgic warriors. With grim satisfaction, as they slowly heaved the line forward, Fronto noted how the victorious faces of the barbarians slipped to uncertainty as they found themselves being pushed backwards into the press of their own men. Fronto grinned. An idea was forming, but he'd have to be fast. These bastards were vicious. The Roman numbers in the push had almost halved again already. He leaned across to his right and barked hurried instructions at the centurion nearby. Behind them, another century of men joined the fight.

"Push them back!" he bellowed to the Roman force in general. He was almost at the front now. Almost close enough to reach one of the hairy bastards with his gladius.

Spotting the centurion that had accompanied him into the fray, he quickly leaned across and repeated his instructions. The man nodded and began to move off to the left. Fronto waited a moment for his instructions to have been disseminated among the men present, during which another century joined the rear. Their ranks were now growing faster than they were being whittled down, and they were forcing the Belgae back, but the push was getting ever harder, since the barbarians were being heaved into the press of their fellows.

"Now!" he cried.

Simultaneously, two thirds of his force changed direction and pushed off to the left, in line with the fort's western wall, while the other third pulled back from where they had been pushing along the riverbank. The whole Roman front line swung like a gate, back along the shore to the fort wall. The sudden push deep in their lines and the opening space next to the river caused a natural momentum unfortunate for the Belgae. Unable to hold their ground, pushed back by the inland advance and their own great press, a large number of the Belgae found themselves pushed out of the force, into the open space and then beyond, where the shoving carried them straight on, over the bank and into the fast current of the river.

A cheer went up on the bridge several hundred paces downstream as over a hundred Belgae washed past beneath them, screaming as they were carried away from the field. The few wealthier barbarians who wore the heavy armour and helmets of the Celtic noblemen splashed briefly before disappearing without trace.

"Reform!" Fronto called.

As suddenly as they had changed direction before, the Roman left pulled back, and the right pushed out once again to their original solid line. Now, the diminished force of Belgae by the river gave Fronto's force sufficient room to begin pushing in earnest. Laughing like a maniac, Fronto launched into the front line, hacking and stabbing with his sword, lost in the simplicity of combat where complicated thought could be replaced by instinct.

Bolstered by a continual supply of legionaries from the rear, Fronto's force continued to expand the line in an arc, pushing the Belgae back. Stepping back from the action for a moment, Fronto smiled with satisfaction. They had now fought their way almost half way along the fort's wall, allowing Sabinus to redeploy a number of his men from that side. As he watched the nearest gate opened, just behind his advancing line, and more reserves poured from the fort. The press of Belgae in the narrowing area of riverbank they controlled were now shouting desperately. As their concentration had been drawn toward Fronto's vicious assault, Balbus had taken the advantage of their lack of attention and finally broken away from the bridge, the Thirteenth pouring into the field and forming an arc like Fronto's, pushing the barbarians further back from the river.

As the moments passed, Fronto grinned. The advancing forces from the bridge and the makeshift crossing were close now, the Belgae pushed back to the flat land on the other side of the fort. With a deep breath, he once more threw himself into the front line, shouting encouragement at the legionaries to either side. A roar went up, and the advance redoubled in effort, Belgae now trying to turn and flee among their own ranks.

'Lucky', Fronto thought to himself. For all the Romans had finally gained the riverbank and forced the Belgae back, they were still outnumbered by at least five to one. The Belgae had descended into chaos. Had they the discipline of the Roman army, they would right now be driving Fronto back into the water, instead of trying to get out of the way. The number of casualties Fronto's advance had suffered spoke volumes about how dangerous a foe these barbarians could be when they had the bit between their teeth.

He clenched his teeth and offered a small prayer to Nemesis that the bastards kept on running.

Another cheer went up and the forces of the Thirteenth and Fourteenth legions finally met on the bank, joining forces and turning the two expanding arcs into one great, solid line advancing over the grass on the disordered Belgae. Professionalism took over among the centurions and the desperately pushing line quickly reformed into a traditional legionary shield wall, supported by second, third and fourth lines, with more reserves falling into place and rapidly forming a fifth.

This was starting to look like a proper battle now, rather than a mad advance, though only because the enemy were already trying to leave the field. A voice nearby called out his name and he turned to see Balbus, grinning, his forehead spattered with blood and, judging by the long cut close to his temple, much of it was his own. Fronto shook his head.

"Quintus, you crazy bastard. Why are you at the front?"

"Why are you?" the older man shouted back, laughing. Leaving command of the push to the centurions, Fronto and his fellow legate fell out of the line to the rear and stretched.

"I saw Sabinus at the fort. He's alright. I left Plancus with him, so the prat can't do much harm."

Again, Balbus laughed.

"I loved your swinging gate manoeuvre. My lads laughed like Bacchus when they saw all those flailing barbarians washing away underneath. I even saw one of the men pissing over the side of the bridge on them as they went past. Should have disciplined him, really, but to be honest, it was just too amusing!"

Fronto grinned.

"Let's just hope this panic keeps up. If they realise they're still more than five to our one, things could go very badly for us."

Balbus nodded, sobering up.

"Best keep them running then."

Fronto smiled.

"Where's your helmet?"

"Bottom of the river, I think. Ah well. Cita owes me a few favours. I'll get another one without going through the rigmarole."

"Sir?"

Fronto and Balbus both instinctively turned. Behind them, Decius stood with three of his auxiliary officers.

"I beg to report, sirs, that we are now out of range of the cowardly, spineless, piss-poor barbarians. I've ordered the auxiliaries across to the fort where we can keep up the good work from the walls and free up legate Sabinus to bring his legionaries into the fight."

Fronto's grin widened.

"Very good, Decius." He turned to his fellow legate. "Balbus? You know Decius? He's one of yours."

Balbus nodded uncertainly.

"I've seen you around, prefect, yes. That's some fine work today."

"Thank you, sir."

He smiled and stretched wearily.

"There's more, though. From the hill we saw the standards of the legions behind the woodland to the left over there. Caesar should be here in about an hour and a half with the rest of the legions, but it looks like the rear of the Belgic army is already on the run. I doubt there'll be many left here by the time the general arrives."

Balbus frowned.

"Caesar wanted us to hold them here. Could be trouble in store."

Fronto ground his teeth.

"I'm here to fight and to win. The only way they'll stick with this now is if we start to pull back and hand them the advantage. I'm not going to do that, Balbus."

Smiling grimly, he took a firmer grip of his sword.

"Coming?"

The older legate flexed his hand several times. That finger he broke on Fronto's nose still locked up painfully occasionally. He sighed, which turned into a smile, and then gripped his own blade.

"Why not?"

Chapter 10

(Battlefield on the south bank of the Aisne River.)

"Aurora: Roman Goddess of the dawn, sister of Sol and Luna."

"Cloaca Maxima: The great sewer of republican Rome that drained the forum into the Tiber."

Caesar, pale faced once again, pulled his horse ahead of the vanguard of officers.

"Fronto? Where, pray, are the Belgae?"

The blood-spattered legate, still gripping his sword, his helmet crest in disarray, smiled grimly and gestured all around him with a sweep of his arm. The general's colour drained a little further.

"Fronto! I wanted the Belgae trapped here. I wanted to wipe them out, for good."

Fronto shrugged.

"With respect general, the only way we could have kept that many here is to let them carve us into new shapes. We were teetering on the edge of complete disaster and, frankly, I think it's quite impressive, given the odds, that we pulled this off."

The general shook his head and pinched the bridge of his nose. "And now they're south of the river, they've got free rein to attack our supply lines and destroy Remi lands!"

Balbus shook his head.

"I don't believe so, Caesar. As they fled, they went west. They were trying to get far away from us and yourself. I think they're following the river and trying to find a way to get back across and head north again."

Caesar grumbled.

"And then the Belgae will fall back and regroup to face us again."

Fronto grinned.

"A lot less of them, though. We won you a solid victory here, Caesar."

The general ground his teeth.

"Trying to give you orders, Fronto, is like trying to nail a shadow to a wall!"

The legate's grin widened.

"That was not meant to be funny!"

Behind the general, Labienus cleared his throat and leaned forward over his horse's neck.

"Apologies for interrupting, Caesar, but I think we need to decide on a course of action quickly and worry about recriminations later. The Belgae are getting further away all the time, but they could stop and reform damned quickly."

The general let his stare of disapproval linger on Fronto a moment longer, and then straightened.

"Quite right, Labienus. Send for my Belgic scouts. We need to infiltrate the fleeing mass and try to determine what their next move will be. But as soon as our scouts are with them, we'll need to follow on and harry them. We certainly don't want to give them time to reorganise themselves."

He climbed down from his steed and handed the reins to the nearest legionary.

"For now, I shall return to my headquarters. Fronto? This is your mess. Kindly sort it out."

Fronto rolled his eyes and sighed as the general, with Labienus at his shoulder, made his way among the bodies to the bridge and back toward the huge camp on the hill.

"Alright then." Fronto gestured to a centurion he spotted nearby, who looked up in surprise.

"I want those three temporary sling-bridges to be supported, strengthened and secured. We can't guarantee that the Belgae won't change their mind and come back for more, so I want movement of troops easy. Find some engineers and get it done."

Scanning the nearby ranks, he singled out another centurion.

"We need to get these dead piled up and cremated. Two piles. One for Romans; one for the Belgae. No disrespect though; they may be barbarians, but they're warriors who fought well and died in battle. Give everyone the same send-off. You'll need to co-opt another century for the detail. There's a lot of bodies."

The centurion saluted and cleared his throat. "And survivors and wounded among the enemy, sir?"

Fronto nodded thoughtfully.

"Medical care for those who can be saved. Round up the prisoners and put a guard on them… and do the same for any that are caught in the vicinity afterwards. At the very least, they'll fetch a few coins for us in Rome."

Scratching his head, he looked up toward the legions that Caesar had led by his circuitous route and who, abandoned by their general and no longer required for battle, were standing awaiting further orders from the staff officers at their head. The familiar face of Gnaeus Priscus, primus pilus of the Tenth, grinned back at him from the ranks. Fronto raised his voice and pointed at his second in command.

"Priscus! Get Pomponius out here."

There was a brief ruckus in the ranks of the Tenth, and the young centurion and chief engineer of Fronto's legion strode out to meet him.

"Sir?"

"Just on the off chance that the Belgae come back for more, I want the fort defences on this side of the river extended to form a long boundary. I'll leave the details to you. Take as many men as you need."

Frowning at the assembled legions, standing quietly, he cleared his throat.

"I want the Tenth to remain on this side of the river with the Thirteenth and Fourteenth and make camp once the bodies have been moved and the new defences built. While that's happening, those of you who aren't needed can go and break camp near Tetricus' ditch and haul the gear back here. Priscus? When I'm not around, you come under Sabinus' command."

The primus pilus nodded, eying the battle-worn Gaulish legions warily.

Fronto turned and waved his arm at the assembled work parties.

"Oh, and if you find a posh and probably dented officer's helmet in the river, have it sent to legate Balbus!"

There was a ripple of laughter and Fronto turned to his counterpart from the Eighth Legion.

"Let's go see if we can console the general. Our victory seems to have pissed him off a little."

Balbus nodded, but before turning to leave, he glanced across to see the Tenth Legion going about their business, while Rufus and Crispus started moving the Ninth and Eleventh back toward the river crossings.

"Balventius?"

The primus pilus of the Eighth stepped out of the mass of officers.

"Sir?"

"Get the men back to camp. I have a feeling we'll need to be rested shortly."

The scarred veteran barked out a harsh laugh.

"I bloody hope so, sir. All this action and the veterans haven't seen a bit of it yet!"

Balbus grinned at his friend and second in command, before turning to leave the field with Fronto. As they approached the sturdy bridge, so recently a scene of such carnage, they spotted Sabinus leaning over the parapet and staring down into the water.

"Mortal thoughts or some such?"

The senior officer looked up in surprise.

"Oh, hello, Fronto… Balbus. Just taking a moment to relax and breathe the air. Above the water's the only place around here that doesn't smell like dead meat. I don't suppose either of you has a stock of wine with you?"

Fronto grinned.

"I can always find wine."

"It's true," Balbus laughed. "He can feel when it's nearby!"

Fronto turned for a moment.

"Hmm. I told Priscus he was under your command while I'm not there." He shrugged. "Ah well. He knows what to do without us interfering."

He smiled at Sabinus.

"When you roll down the hill later tonight back to your quarters, you'll find I've left the Tenth, Thirteenth and Fourteenth all assigned to you. Don't want a repeat performance, eh?"

As the three men continued on along the bridge, Fronto spotted the Gaulish engineer, directing a small party of men strengthening the slung bridge supports.

"Biorix?"

The legionary saluted as he saw the three senior officers. Fronto fished in his pocket and placed half a dozen silver coins on the flat top of the end bridge pile.

"When you're done, use this to get wine for you and your lads. Well done."

Sabinus raised an eyebrow.

"A Gaul? What did he do?"

Fronto laughed.

"He's the one that managed to get us across the river in time to save your arse!"

Sabinus smiled and, fishing in his own pocket, added another pile of coins to the top.

"And when you've got drunk on Fronto," he called out, "get drunk on me, my friend!"

Biorix grinned and saluted once more before getting back to work. The officers strode on up the hill toward the camp.

"At least you've given us an easy rear entrance now!" Sabinus laughed, pointing at the demolished camp rampart.

The three men reached the top of the hill, climbed across the rampart amid the torn chunks of palisade and walked through the camp towards the officer's section. Fronto patted Sabinus on the shoulder.

"Go find my tent. There's a jar in there and some of that bloody awful beer that Crispus likes. I've got to go and see Caesar, and then I'll find more wine and join you."

Balbus frowned.

"Want some moral support?"

Fronto shook his head.

"I'll be fine. See you shortly."

The other two officers waved at him and disappeared off through the ranks of tents, but Fronto made for the large headquarters in the centre. For a moment he dithered, unsure whether to knock or just stride inside confidently, but his plans disintegrated at the call from within.

"Come in Fronto, and close the flap."

He stepped inside to see Caesar lying on his bed in the shade, no lamp lit to banish the dark.

"Caesar?"

"Headache" the general said, by way of explanation. Fronto stared into the dark as he let the leather flap drop into place, plunging them into stygian gloom. He blinked a couple of times and then slowly felt his way round the tent until he found the seat he knew to be there and sat down.

"You do know that this is actually a lot less of a problem than you made out, Caesar, yes?"

There was a moment of silence and then a tired voice said "go on…"

"Well, I've been thinking about the geography of this. Divitiacus and his Aedui are wading through Bellovaci territory, so they're actually more to the west than the north. In actual fact, the Belgae are now more directly between the forces than they would have been near the marsh. In fact, if the Bellovaci learn about the Aedui, they'll likely abandon the army to go home and defend their lands."

There was a sigh.

"I suppose so. I was just looking forward to a single definitive victory."

Fronto smiled in the dark.

"That was never going to happen among the Belgae, Caesar, and you know that. Everyone says that when they've no common enemy they fight each other. That sort of people aren't going to give up in one big force. We'll probably be fighting them tribe by tribe long after the big boys are under our heels. The way to do it is not in one big battle, but to put them down one tribe at a time and, if possible, to turn them into allies as we do it."

"Yes, you're right, of course."

"Caesar?"

Fronto's voice took on a worried tone. A headache was one thing, even one strong enough to make the general delegate all duties and retreat to his tent, but for him to meekly accept Fronto's advice without an argument, a quip, or a little pomposity was truly unheard of.

"Are you alright?"

"Yes, Fronto!" Slightly irritable now. "Of course. Now, what else?"

Good. That was more like Caesar.

"I've seen to everything here, but I'm assuming that we'll probably be moving on shortly, and I doubt we'll be back here, no?"

Another sigh.

"Would you like me to handle your scouts and spies while you recover?"

"That would be good, yes. Thank you, Fronto. Now I think I should sleep."

Fronto stood in the darkness and turned, using the tiny sliver of grey to navigate his way to the door once again.

"Be well, Caesar."

Trying not to open the flap wide and admit too much light, Fronto left the room and spied the dozen Gallic-dressed horsemen standing respectfully a distance away, beyond Ingenuus' men who guarded the tent.

"You speak Latin, yes?"

"Yes," confirmed the nearest man.

"I don't know what Caesar usually asks you to do, but the general is sleeping, and I'm to brief you. We need you to get back among the fleeing Belgae. Spend a few hours among them and find out their plans. Then get back here as soon as you can and report to Caesar or myself. Be subtle and careful. Clear?"

The men nodded.

"Good. Then go."

Without watching them leave, Fronto turned and strode back towards his own tent.

"Wine!" he said, slapping his forehead. Veering off to the side, he strode in the direction of the quartermaster.

* * * * *

The morning was pale and watery, as was Fronto, blearily emerging from his tent like a cave dwelling creature coming out of hibernation.

"What is it?" he grumbled, rubbing his bristly chin and blinking. This was going to be a powerful hangover.

"The scouts are back and Caesar's called for his officers, sir."

Fronto stared at the young guard in front of him; one of Ingenuus' men, neat and smart, who had obviously been on guard.

"Urgh." Wincing, Fronto excavated a lump of crusted sleep from the corner of his eye.

"Of course… the general's had a long sleep, so he's up at Aurora's arse!" He became aware of the smirk the soldier was trying to hide. "Lead on!"

As he shuffled along behind the guard in the direction of Caesar's tent, he saw Balbus approaching with Varus. The latter was clean-shaven and bright, but the older legate was clearly enjoying this morning as much as Fronto was. He smiled. On the bright side, they'd both be feeling better than Sabinus who, this morning, probably wished he was dead. The two legates shared a look and entered the tent.

Many of the staff and senior officers were already present and seated. Fronto and Balbus walked around the edge and sank gratefully into their chairs. The general tapped impatiently on the table and then cleared his throat.

"My scouts have returned and confirmed the situation, gentlemen."

He tapped on the map behind him, indicating the territory to the west.

"The surviving force, numbering probably around a hundred and twenty thousand has made for the lands of the Suessiones. There they plan to disperse to protect their own lands and wait to see what our next move is. It would appear that the Bellovaci have become aware of the Aedui in their lands and have already gone off ahead on their own."

The general paused and registered the surprise on many officers' faces at news of their Gaulish allies.

"I am sure of Divitiacus' ability to deal with them on his own, so I intend to concentrate on the rest. We will not give the Belgae enough time to pull a huge army together again, but will move on them swiftly, one tribe at a time. But in the first instance, while they're still largely together and disorganised, I want to damage them further. We are only a day behind them and can easily catch up."

He smiled grimly.

"I want to follow them closely and keep harrying them. I want to encourage them to panic and disperse and, as soon as they have, we will make for the Suessiones' capital at Noviodunum, where we will bring that tribe and any allies that remain to battle and either absorb or annihilate them. Once that is done, all of the southern Belgae will be under our control: the Bellovaci, Suessiones and the Remi. Divide and conquer, gentlemen… divide and conquer."

There was a shuffling noise at the rear. Fronto turned to look, and he and Balbus almost let out an explosive burst of laughter. Sabinus was sheepishly stumbling around the periphery and looking for a seat. He resembled one of the homeless drunken old soaks that lived in the outfall pipe of the cloaca maxima in Rome. There was a general good humoured murmur, though Fronto turned and watched the disapproving frown on the general's face.

Caesar cleared his throat.

"So this is what you will do: Varus? You will take the cavalry and harass the enemy as they flee. You will need to split into three forces to herd them in the correct direction along the river, so... Pedius and Cotta? I am assigning you to Varus on cavalry duty."

He gestured at Varus.

"I want you out there and engaging them in the next few hours. As soon as we're done in here, get the cavalry moving. Keep pushing them west into the Suessiones' land. And don't bother having them decamp first. Just get going."

Varus nodded professionally. Fronto smiled. The young cavalry prefect he had seen at Vesontio last year had evaporated, to be replaced by this professional veteran who had just had two of Caesar's most senior staff officers placed under his command.

The general wheeled.

"Right behind them will be half the army. The Eighth, Ninth, Tenth and Eleventh are all fresh and at full strength. Those four legions under their commanders will move out immediately after the cavalry at the fastest possible pace. Again, they need to take only their weapons and armour. Leave the decamping and transport. Just get caught up. Varus will be keeping them busy until you arrive."

He turned to the officer on his left.

"Labienus? I'm putting you in overall command of that force. The legates all know what they're doing..."

He cast a pointed look at Fronto and Balbus.

"... despite current appearances... but I want a cohesive strategy and that means an overall command system. Kill as many of them as you have to with as few losses as possible. Don't let them change course, and don't allow them to form up into a proper army again. You will need to play this carefully to keep them moving. Be a shepherd and only cull where necessary."

Labienus nodded and the general straightened.

"The Twelfth has been mopping up the survivors by the marsh and burying the dead. Galba will return shortly. Once he is here, the Twelfth, Thirteenth and Fourteenth will break camp and accompany the slow-moving artillery and baggage. I will stay with them, and we will transport all the gear of the cavalry and the other four legions until we meet up and find the place for our next campaign camp."

He folded his arms and scanned the crowd in the tent.

"Is that all clear? Any questions or comments?"

Fronto cleared his throat.

"With respect, Caesar, there are still quite a few Belgae unaccounted for. According to the numbers you got from the spies and the Remi before we moved into Belgae lands, we've only come across half or two thirds of them. We can be fairly sure the rest aren't out to the west. If the Bellovaci are rushing that way to protect their lands, then there's no allies out there. We know they're not south, 'cause that's where we came from. They can't be west as that's all Gallic and Germanic lands and we'd have heard. That means they're north, and when the legions follow the survivors, they'll have free rein behind us."

Caesar frowned and rubbed his neck.

"So what are you suggesting, Fronto?"

You need a rearguard, Caesar. A strong rearguard. All your cavalry will be out west, and you'll be weighed down by the wagons. I'd suggest you send three legions west, not four. Then have two legions accompanying the baggage and artillery and two playing rearguard. In fact, I'd be tempted to keep a small cavalry unit to act as scouts and outriders for the column."

Caesar nodded.

"I suppose that's sensible. And we need to be sure of our supply lines anyway. Very well. I'll keep the Eleventh and Twelfth for rearguard and the Thirteenth and Fourteenth with the baggage. The Eighth, Ninth and Tenth will go west under Labienus."

A quarter of an hour later, Fronto was standing, still grey, bleary and unshaven, by the standards of the Tenth in their shrine. Priscus sat on the altar to victory, an act that was highly sacrilegious, and folded his arms.

"So we're actually going to have a chance to fight?"

Fronto nodded.

"It's not going to be much of a fight. We're just pursuing a fleeing army and nipping at their heels. Varus and his cavalry left a few moments ago. Caesar wants the three legions ready to move, unburdened by crap, within the hour. I want the Tenth out front and ready in half that time. We've a reputation to maintain, Gnaeus."

The primus pilus laughed.

"You're certainly living up to yours. If you want us to look good, go bathe and shave while we decamp. You smell like a latrine, and you look awful."

"Thanks again."

The legate sighed.

"But a bath does sound good. Right, I'll go bathe sharpish, and I'll see you on the 'parade ground' out front in three quarters of an hour."

The primus pilus nodded and tapped the nearest standard.

"I'm looking forward to it. So is Balventius. We talked last night. To be honest, we're all a bit sick of watching auxiliaries and Gauls hogging all the glory. Are you sure you remember how to command a legion? You've been an auxiliary prefect for the past few weeks, really."

"Shut up!"

Fronto glowered at his subordinate's grinning face and, turning, left the legion's command tent. Watching the upheaval around the camp, he strode down the slope to the river. Finding the shelf by the water's edge that the legions had flattened and decked out with planks for this purpose, he wandered over to the large wooden chest that lay on one side.

The container was unlocked and opened to reveal jars of olive oil, strigils, and clean sponges. Fronto stretched and began to remove his tunic, breeches and various accoutrements. The early morning chill brought out gooseflesh as he stood, naked, on the wooden platform. Reaching down, he grasped the olive oil container and proceeded to tip it out into his hand and rub it into his cold flesh. In a nice civil bath house within the empire, the process was relaxing and refreshing; often with the help of a slave and, in the better establishments, accompanied by wine, bread and cheese, and music. The experience in the field was a little less relaxed.

He shivered as he hurriedly rubbed the oil into his calf. At least it led to remarkably quick and efficient bathing. Once he was fully oiled, he replaced the oil container in the chest and, picking up the strigil, stepped off the wooden surface and onto the discoloured turf nearby. Slowly, he worked at removing the oil and grime with the curved blade, the gloop falling away in gobbets to the grass. Finally, he finished his routine and stepped forward and down into the water.

As part of the work the engineers had done on this temporary bathing complex, a set of steps had been carved and decked down into the water, and a floor of wooden beams sunk into this side of the river, replacing the reeds and sucking mud that would have greeted him.

Biting his lip, he stepped into the cold water, his toes curling at the sensation. A little further and his shins and calves complained. Then the knees; the thighs; his abdomen and then with one quick splash, he submerged completely, dropping to sit underwater on the wooden floor. He sat for a moment, adjusting to the refreshing cold, and then pushed himself back up.

He crested the water with a splash and stood, chest deep, raking his fingers back through his hair. Rubbing his chin and neck, for a moment he considered whether he should leave it. Beards may not be popular in Rome, but they were fairly common among soldiers on campaign; especially with all these Gallic recruits.

"No. Roman it is!"

He shook his head and wiped the excess water from his eyes, stepping forward to the pile of gear on the wooden shelf. His dagger probably needed work, but it'd be sharp enough for a cursory shave. A closer one could come later, as he was short on time right now.

He reached across and pulled at the coiled belt. The knife was gone.

Instinct made him use bent knees to launch himself back out into the water, just as the figure leapt from the reeds and undergrowth to the side.

Six feet out into the water, almost at the edge of the wooden platform, Fronto stared. It was a girl. Well, more of a woman than a girl, probably in her mid twenties and clearly Celtic. Her long strawberry blonde hair was plaited and braided and she wore a long tunic or dress of pale blue wool, belted in the middle with expensive-looking bronze, though stained with mud and blood.

Her eyes were sharp and clear, and she brandished Fronto's knife and waved it in his direction threateningly.

"What in the name of Venus?"

He eyed her warily. She was pretty, certainly, and clearly strong in both mind and muscle, but that was not always a good combination. His mind flashed briefly back to a pretty looking young German woman who tried to tear his tendon out with her teeth. Frowning and setting his jaw, Fronto wondered how to proceed.

The woman gabbled something off in her tongue. Fronto looked her up and down once again. She was clearly one of the Belgae, but how the hell did she get down here? They did not usually bring their women onto the battlefield, as far as he remembered. And she was clearly a noble or a woman of wealth from the bronze and gold belt and jewellery that adorned her. Perhaps she was a chieftainess? One of these warrior women rumour spoke of among the Celts? The barbarian version of an amazon? Taking a step forward, she kept the knife defensively between them and scooped up his clothes, leaving only his boots.

"Dress!"

He was so surprised at the sudden use of Latin that he merely stood and blinked. She had a strong Belgic accent, but there was no doubt about it. She could speak his tongue.

"I said dress! I know how to use this!"

Fronto shrugged and moved toward the river bank, his body still submerged to the chest.

"I honestly don't know what you're hoping to achieve here, but your very best option is to run like Pluto himself is jabbing you in the arse. I expect you've heard horror stories about what Roman officers do to captives; I know I have; but, to be honest, I'm not the rape and murder type. I'd rather you took my knife and buggered off, so I can get dressed and go have a bite to eat."

The woman tipped her head to one side slightly.

"Many of your words are not familiar to me, Roman. Now, dress!"

Fronto emerged from the water, naked and pale. As he had hoped, the sudden appearance of naked masculinity caught her attention for a moment. It was involuntary and only momentary, but it was enough. As the legate rose from the surface, she failed to notice the stick in his hand; a sturdy pole that had been jammed into the riverbank by some helpful soldier, possibly to hang a cloth from.

The stick came out of the water at a fast swing, whacking the woman on the wrist, and causing her to lose her grip on the knife. In a momentary panic, she dived for the blade, but Fronto was there first. She backed away, edgily, watching his every move.

"Damn it" he grumbled.

He frowned at her. Why did stupid things like this always happen to him?

"Pick up my gear!"

She did so, nervously.

"Now throw me the breeches."

Carefully, she separated them out. He was expecting her to hurl them at his face, but instead the clothing was tossed gently over to him.

"I'm going to trust you not to do anything stupid while I put these on."

Keeping a close watch on her and gripping the knife, he let the stick fall to the platform and used his free hand to pull on his breeches. He looked up in surprise to see the girl laughing.

"Something funny?"

"I think the water… it must be very cold, yes?"

She laughed again, and Fronto cursed the colour that rose involuntarily in his cheeks.

"Hilarious, I'm sure."

He fixed her with a steady glance.

"I have no intention of hurting you, young lady, and I can see that you're intelligent, wealthy, and strong. So I'll try not to be condescending."

A deep breath.

"You have a choice. You can run. In fact, that's probably your best choice. You'll not catch up with your army, but you can probably make it to one of your allies' oppida. The Remi, I've noted, are particularly friendly and generous."

He looked up the hill at the fort.

"Actually, that's not your best option. It's your only option. You stay here, and either one of the men will find you, which I can't guarantee would be pleasant, or you'll end up with the officers and Caesar will likely either take you as a hostage or make you a prize to go back to Rome."

He pointed east along the river.

"Run away, girl. Run home."

The woman shook her head.

"Many wolves around the hills. And bandits. I will not make it to a town. I come with you. You will protect me from your men."

Fronto laughed.

"I think not. I've got enough to do. Enjoy your countryside."

With one long look at her, he sheathed his knife and shrugged into his tunic.

Slipping his feet loosely into his boots, he tied the belt round his waist, closed the chest, and, ignoring the woman standing, bewildered, by the water, he turned and climbed the hill toward the fort.

He was half way there before he became aware of the sounds of ragged breathing close by. He stopped and turned angrily.

"Look, lady… will you just piss off back to your own people. I'm on a tight schedule."

The woman stopped in her tracks and stared at him. He let his gaze stay on her for a moment and then turned his back and walked on, to the crest and over the rampart where the palisade had been torn down. The camp was in chaos, tents being torn down and men on the move everywhere.

Wherever Fronto passed, the legionaries halted in their work to stare. He was not in his armour, though his fine tunic with the embroidered edge marked him as an officer, but he was well aware of the reason for their stares, since they were not directed at him, so much as just behind him.

Across the camp he strode, causing ripples of interest, until he reached the gate. The guards came to attention and foundered for a while, unsure of how to deal with the Belgae woman leaving their camp hot on the heels of a senior officer.

Sure enough, Priscus had the Tenth formed up and ready to move, while the Eighth was falling in nearby under the shouted commands of Balventius. As Fronto strode towards them, Priscus stepped out from the front of the legion.

"Sir?"

He waited until he was out of earshot of the men.

"What's this?"

Fronto shrugged.

"She won't stop following me. How ready is everyone?"

Priscus gestured to the camp behind him.

"Here come the Ninth now. We'll be ready to move in less than quarter of an hour."

Fronto nodded.

"I'll be back by then."

Striding back into the camp, he made for his tent to finish getting ready. As he passed the rows of tents being struck, he spotted a familiar face: Felix, the primus pilus of the Eleventh Legion. With a sigh of relief, he stopped.

"Felix?"

"Sir?"

"I've a favour to ask of your commander. Could you take this young lady to Crispus and ask him to look after her while the army moves out?"

The woman started to shake her head, but Fronto grabbed her arm.

"Look. If you won't leave, then do as I say. We're marching hard and fast into battle again. You need to stay with the baggage where it's safe. The commander of the Eleventh is a friend and an exceptionally good man. He will look after you."

She looked unsure for a moment, but finally nodded, wearily. Fronto heaved a sigh of relief and strode off toward his tent. Women!

* * * * *

Fronto watched as a rider raced back towards him. The valley was peaceful, and the afternoon sun had burned off the mist of the morning and left an exceedingly pleasant day to march through. During the journey, Fronto had been disturbed to discover several times that he had drifted off into his own private little dream world that often involved the young lady from the river bank. He growled to himself.

"Must be going soft."

He looked up at the horseman as he thundered to a halt.

"What is it, trooper?"

The man bowed awkwardly on horseback as the legate stepped out to the side of the column, which continued to march past at double speed.

"Commander Varus begs to report that the Belgae are splitting up. The front of the army seems to be making for an oppidum we can see in the distance. Basically fleeing, sir. The back end is being harried by us, sir, but the commander is going to break off and try and intercept the vanguard before they can hole up in the town. He asks if the legions can pick up pace and close on the rear of the force to trap them?"

Fronto nodded.

"I think we can manage that. How far behind are we now?"

The man pointed at a low hill around half a mile distant.

"Just beyond there sir. Shall I convey your acknowledgement to Varus?"

Fronto nodded. "Get going. We'll be along in a few moments."

He turned to one of the soldiers marching along closest to him.

"Fall out of rank. Go find commander Labienus and tell him we're only half a mile away and Varus needs us to close in on the rear now."

The legionary saluted and ran off. Fronto jogged back to the front of the Tenth, the vanguard of the army, and found the primus pilus staring rigidly ahead.

"Priscus? We've half a mile to cover in just a few moments. Get the men into a run, but keep it together. I'm going to warn Balbus and Rufus and get them to catch up."

The primus pilus nodded and turned to his men.

"Time to engage lads. Triple time, now. No dawdling! We've got Belgae to flatten!"

The Tenth broke into an accelerated pace, racing now toward the hill that obscured the force of Belgae. Fronto jogged back along the lines of his men to the head of the Eighth Legion. Balbus waved as he approached. The Eighth was already moving apace.

"We saw your lads pick up, so thought we'd best join in. Just ahead then, yes?"

Fronto nodded. "Past that hill. Can you drop a message back to Rufus?"

"Already done it," the older legate grinned. "Let's get a battle line formed."

Turning from Fronto, he addressed his men.

"Pull out to the left, alongside the Tenth! Quadruple time!"

Fronto grinned as he watched the Eighth peel out to double the line. Balbus smiled.

"I'll drop word to Rufus and get him to pull right. Let's be ready, eh?"

Quarter of an hour later, the legions finally caught their prey. By the time ranks had closed and formations made, the Belgae had fled as fast as they could. Varus and his cavalry were out of sight in the distance, harrying the Belgic vanguard, but the bulk of their army, almost a hundred thousand strong ran for their lives toward the high walls of the distant oppidum.

Fronto turned to Priscus as they jogged.

"Shield wall time. Let's run over them like a cart over a rabbit."

Priscus grinned.

"Form up as you run… Ad aciem!"

With the practiced ease of a veteran legion, the Tenth, having marched fast for half a day with no rest, and still at a run, rearranged into solid battle lines. The command was echoed to left and right, and the Ninth and Eighth joined the line.

Taking advantage of the tiny gap left for them, Fronto and Priscus fell into the line and formed up with the rest. The Belgae were fleeing, but in a disordered rabble, which slowed and confused their ranks.

With a roar, the lines of legionaries, Shields locked and swords ready, barged into the retreating lines of Belgae. Those few who resisted the panic and realised the sudden added threat turned to face their pursuers, wielding their heavy Celtic blades, but to no real avail.

The charge was immense. Swords jabbed and slashed as the shield wall suddenly met resistance but continued to move, regardless. The legionaries did not delay to check whether their opponents were finished as they fell to an initial blow, but rather marched over the fallen bodies and on to the next warrior they found, leaving the wounded Belgae to be trampled to death by the stomping feet of fifteen thousand men.

Fronto looked to his left, where he stood in the second line, stabbing out between his men's shoulders, and saw Priscus, laughing like a demon, as he waded into the enemy. He sighed and settled into the routine of a legionary advance. It was so familiar and simple after weeks of commanding unusual units in strange circumstances. He had almost forgotten what it was like and what to do when placed on a real battlefield with regular veterans.

Priscus shouted at him.

"We'll never manage to stop them getting to the town!"

Fronto shook his head in the press.

"No, but we can whittle down their numbers by quite a few thousand before they get there."

The advance of the line had now slowed. The press of men ahead was too great and tightly packed, and the legions dropped back to the traditional slow advance of the shield wall, systematically butchering anyone before them.

Nodding to himself with satisfaction, Fronto allowed his legion to pass around him and retreated through the ranks until he reached the rear of the Tenth, where he stepped out into the open air with the relief of a long-confined man. Just ahead he could see Labienus on horseback, accompanied by several tribunes, watching the advance.

"Titus… Sorry I didn't give you the opportunity to give the orders. There just wasn't time."

Labienus nodded, frowning.

"Not a problem, Fronto. I'm a little chilled by this butchery though. The Roman way is to face them head-on and fight like men. It doesn't sit well with me attacking fleeing warriors."

Fronto sighed.

"I do know what you mean, but they still outnumber us at least five to one. We need to even the numbers a little. It's not like they sued for peace, after all. They're just falling back, and the moment they group together again, they could hit us like a hammer!"

The two men watched the carnage below, and it took a moment for them to notice the small group of riders thundering back toward them.

"Is that Varus?"

Labienus frowned and shaded his eyes.

"I believe it is."

They sat and watched as the half dozen cavalrymen made their way to the command unit and finally came to a halt, breathing heavily, their horses snorting and stamping.

"Gentlemen?"

"What's happening, Varus?"

"The Belgae are falling apart now. A large bunch; the Suessiones, I assume, made it to the oppidum, though we must have killed hundreds on the way. The Bellovaci are out of reach, way ahead and making for their own lands, but we can leave them to the Aedui if what Caesar says is true. What you have below is about sixty thousand warriors from mixed tribes but, if you look ahead, they're already splitting up and going their own way. We can't follow them all."

Fronto nodded. Already, the force Priscus was busy pushing into was fragmenting, the Belgic warriors running in a dozen different directions. The shield wall was stretching to reach the enemy. At the top of his voice, he bellowed “Melee!”

Below, the legions bust forth into individual combat, fighting any target that presented itself, but even that would shortly be useless. He shrugged. They had reduced the Belgae by thousands in one afternoon with hardly any casualties to show for it. Why did it worry him that he felt less satisfaction with it than when he had led a few non-Roman archers to victory at Bibrax?

“Well, I suppose we make camp in the valley until Caesar arrives. Let’s hope he’s in a better mood this time.”

Chapter 11

(On the plain outside Noviodunum.)

"Vineae: moveable wattle and leather wheeled shelters that covered siege works and attacking soldiers from enemy missiles."

"Immunes: legionary soldiers who possessed specialist skills and were consequently excused the more onerous duties."

Caesar tapped his fingers irritably on his belt as he strode up and down before the staff officers. Fronto sighed once again as he looked past the general to the seven legions marshalled in readiness between the officers and the walls of the Suessiones' oppidum.

"Time is of the essence, gentlemen. I want Noviodunum in our hands by nightfall. The other tribes are fleeing back to their lands, and we need to move against them before they have enough time to prepare for another full engagement. We do not have time for a great siege or protracted campaign of starvation. I need the men to get in there as soon as possible."

Fronto cleared his throat.

"I've spoken to both Tetricus and Pomponius, and they are adamant that any assault against that place without proper preparations is a complete waste of time."

Caesar stopped pacing and glared at him.

"It's not my fault, general," Fronto spread his hands defensively, "but the engineers know what they're talking about. I know you're in a hurry to move on, but the job will just have to be done a certain way."

There was a low rumbling from Caesar's throat.

"No, Fronto. Today! It has to be today. Now, in fact… so give me ideas, not arguments."

Fronto settled into a growl once again. This was sheer idiocy.

"The only ideas we have involve siege engines, general. There's just no way to cross that ditch safely. It's too deep and too wide. And the walls beyond are too thick and too high. You can throw a million men against the place, and you'll just waste a million men."

Plancus raised a hand and stepped forward, causing Fronto to shake his head in dismay.

"Then we must concentrate on the causeways across to the gates in the wall. Battering rams. We can break down the gates."

Caesar nodded appreciatively, but Fronto's growl resumed.

"Bollocks."

"I beg your pardon?" Plancus demanded in a high-pitched shriek.

"Those causeways are wide enough for forty men abreast at most. Factor in a battering ram and you've barely got room for the men on either side to operate it. And no one to protect them."

Caesar was looking back and forth between the two of them quietly.

"So use vineae!" screeched Plancus.

"If you could fit bloody vineae over those causeways, do you not think I'd have mentioned it? The causeway is too narrow!"

He turned to the silent officers behind him.

"Am I repeating myself, or am I actually not saying anything? Can you hear me? Are any words coming out?"

The legate of the Fourteenth had gone purple.

"So we'll have the men on either side of the rams form a roof with their shields then!"

Fronto grinned. He was starting to enjoy this.

"While the battering ram trundles on propelled by what? Moles? The breeze? Listen to me, Plancus…"

He illustrated his words by speaking with exaggerated slowness and waving his arms.

"The… cause… way… is… too… na… rrow!"

Plancus was actually vibrating slightly.

"Then what do you suggest, Fronto?"

He smiled.

"You know the answer to that. A siege."

Caesar shook his head.

"No, Fronto. That's not good enough. I want Noviodunum today. We will conduct a grand assault with all seven legions against the main gate. The auxiliary units will provide shots to pick off the defenders atop the walls. The legions will cross the causeway and the ditch wherever they can, and we will have that gate down with a ram as soon as it can be brought across, and the walls down with grapples. It can be done. To your units, gentlemen."

Fronto and Crispus stalked away from the general under the aggravated gaze of Plancus, as the legate of the Tenth kicked at the ground irritably.

"It can't be done. I've known the engineers long enough to know that when they say it's a waste of time, it's not wise to ignore them."

Crispus nodded unhappily as the command cornicens behind them blew out a series of commands. Fronto watched the legions ahead begin to move slowly forward, the auxiliary archers rushing around the edge to find positions from which they could loose. A huge treetrunk ram was being manhandled by a century of men and taken down to the rear of the regulars as they moved. Fronto slowed his walk and Crispus raised an eyebrow.

"You're not joining your men, Marcus?"

Fronto growled again.

"Waste of time. I can't do anything to help, and Priscus knows how to keep the men as safe as possible. Frankly, I want nothing to do with this."

For a moment, he pondered, then lightly punched Crispus in the upper arm.

"Unless you feel the urgent need to die in a ditch with your men, come with me."

Crispus frowned and turned to follow Fronto as he veered off to the side. On a slight rise to the east stood the supply train and wagons of the army. Sitting, looking rather bored amid carts full of dissembled machinery, were the members of the legions' engineering details assigned to the wagons and, as Fronto expected, Tetricus stood atop the nearest, staring in dismay at the legions marching on the high walls of Noviodunum. He saw the two legates approaching and sighed.

"I hope you've brought some wine, Fronto. This disaster is going to be hard to watch sober."

Fronto shook his head.

"Sadly, no. I'm here to pick your brains."

"You can have them!"

Fronto gave a weak laugh.

"The only legate down there stupid enough to believe they can do it is Plancus. Everyone else is going to do what they can to preserve the men they have. I know damn well that Priscus is going to see that I haven't joined him and take it very carefully. It'll be over in a lot less than an hour, for certain. So you need to start thinking."

"What about?"

Ways to get in there without wasting any more troops. This assault's doomed and, as soon as Caesar realises that, we need to present him with the quickest possible way of taking the place before he decides on another frontal assault.

"Oh shit. Will you look at that?"

Fronto and Crispus turned as Tetricus pointed across the intervening ground to where the assault was taking place. The legions had reached the oppidum's defences, and the men were carefully skidding and dropping down into the wide ditch. It was like watching a waterfall of people disappearing over a horizon. But that was not the thing that Tetricus was drawing their attention to. Somehow, during legions' journey across the intervening space, Plancus had managed to manoeuvre the Fourteenth to the centre of the force, where Balbus' Eighth should be.

The green legion was marching across the causeway. Fronto watched with mounting dismay as the front lines reached the gate and began to mill about hopelessly waiting for the battering ram that was being slowly transferred through the force to the front. Men were dying so thick and fast there it looked like the Fourteenth might disappear altogether.

To each side, men had crossed the deep ditch in reasonable formation and were now forming testudos to protect them from the many falling missiles dropped by the defenders. As they watched, soldiers hurled grapples toward the wall tops. Remarkably few reached the height of the walls and those that did were instantly dislodged and fell back into the ditch. The units of auxiliary archers had let off a few initial volleys, few of which had even crossed the parapet, but had now wisely packed away their bows and were also watching unhappily. Once the legions were in the ditch, they had fallen prey as much to the Roman arrows bouncing off the wall tops as to the defenders' own missiles.

As they watched, a massive rock was tipped over the parapet and fell out of sight into the ditch, where it likely killed several men and injured many more. Another glance at the causeway confirmed Fronto's fears that the Fourteenth may well be gone before they could bring the ram to bear on the gate.

"Screw this."

"What?" Crispus and Tetricus turned to look at him.

"We're going to get Caesar to stop this madness." He turned to Tetricus. "And you are going to come up with some ideas on the way to impress him."

Without waiting for them, Fronto stormed at speed back down the slope toward Caesar.

Arriving red-faced with his two companions, Fronto pulled himself up to his full height before the general.

"What?" the man asked absently, looking past the legate at the distant fracas.

"Right..." stated Fronto. "You hate being gainsaid, but you know me well enough to know that I always have good reasons for what I do."

Caesar nodded vaguely. Fronto carefully positioned himself so that he was in the way, aggravating the general a little more.

"You have to stop this. It's a disaster. If you don't sound the recall now, in half an hour you'll have six legions instead of seven and the ones you have left will be seriously understrength. They're getting massacred over there! A few days of siege and you could take the place without all of this."

Caesar was shaking his head.

"Look, general. This is a waste of good men. If you lose half your army here, what's going to happen when you meet another large army of Belgae? They're dropping rocks the size of haystacks on your men!"

"Plancus promised he'd take that gate!"

Fronto grasped the general's shoulders.

"Plancus has the brain of a boiled herring! He's lost about a thousand men in a thousand bloody heartbeats down there. Stop them now!"

Caesar stared in surprise at the officer who had dared to manhandle him. Suddenly, he seemed to wake from a daze.

"You're right, Fronto. You always are..."

He turned to the cornicen standing behind him.

"Sound the recall!"

* * * * *

Fronto carried the wax tablet across the ground by the hastily-erected command tent to where Caesar stood, looking unhappy. He tried to ignore the glare he was receiving from Plancus, despite the fact that it gave him such a warm glow.

"Apologies, Caesar. It's not good news."

The general ignored the sounds of the legionary camp being assembled around him. The seven legions and associated extras had split off and were each constructing their own camp in a circuit around the large hill that was the oppidum of Noviodunum. All the legates and staff officers were, however, here in the camp of the Tenth.

"We lost over two thousand men in quarter of an hour?" Caesar said despairingly as he examined the figures. "That's the heaviest loss I think I've ever heard of in such a short time."

Fronto nodded soberly.

"Tetricus has drawn extra men from the legions and started work on all fronts. There are more vineae being constructed as we speak. By noon tomorrow, we could probably shelter a legion under them. He's got three towers being constructed too... one for each gate. We should be able to get them close enough, so long as we keep throwing water on them, so the Belgae can't set fire to them. But he's most concerned with his ramp."

"Ramp?"

Caesar frowned. "He never mentioned a ramp before."

"That's what he took the existing vineae for, Caesar. He used them to build basically an 'aboveground tunnel' that goes from out of the enemy's range right to the edge of the ditch."

"What for?" Caesar looked nonplussed.

"For the ramp, sir..."

He smiled.

"Tetricus is having tons of rubble transported under the vineae to the ditch, where it's being tipped in. He's filling the ditch in, but more than that, he's starting to angle it up so that by the time it's crossed the ditch it'll be at the top of the wall nearly."

The general stared at him.

"But that would take weeks, wouldn't it?"

Fronto grinned.

"Tetricus says three days. And it's nice and safe, as the men are all working under cover of the vineae. He reckons that by noon three days from now, we can hit them at each gateway with a tower, and should be able to get men in their hundreds up his ramp and over the wall under cover all the way. It's worth the slight delay."

The general nodded, still bewildered.

"A ramp?"

"Yes, Caesar… a ramp. He says the Belgae keep gathering on the walls and pointing."

"I'll bet they do. I've heard of siege ramps before. Seen one used once, even. But never seen a ramp built across a ditch before…"

"He's a clever bugger, that Tetricus" Fronto agreed.

As Caesar stood quietly, staring down at the casualty figures in his hands, Plancus cleared his throat.

"If I may, Caesar…"

"Mmm?"

"I think it would do the morale of the Fourteenth good if you were to thank them for their efforts earlier. We may not have succeeded, but they fought hard."

Caesar frowned.

"I don't think so, Plancus. That would demean the other legions, and to be honest, I'm really not in the mood to give a rousing speech."

Fronto nodded.

"And when you've known soldiers a little longer, you'll know what they appreciate, Plancus." He turned to the general. "Caesar? Permission to break out wine rations for all off-duty legionaries as soon as the camps are complete?"

Caesar nodded.

"Good idea. Let's regroup and try to turn today to some good. And when Tetricus is done for the day, can you ask him to visit me? I'd like him to go over his plans with me in detail."

Fronto nodded and strode away, once more basking in the vicious looks Plancus was casting at him. It occurred to him that it did a man good to have someone to hate; defined him in some important way. Normally, it would be Crassus of course, but with the man being out west or possibly dead, it was nice that Plancus had stepped up to take his place.

He was still pondering on the differences between the two equally dislikeable officers as he headed for the quartermaster, when he heard his name being called from behind. Turning, he spotted Balbus and Sabinus walking fast to catch up with him. He waited for them and smiled as they fell into step.

"Do you really have to wind Plancus up like that?" Balbus asked lightly. "It means he spends the next three hours bumbling around miserably, looking for someone else to take it out on."

Sabinus laughed.

"It's funny the way he keeps putting himself forward for things. He seems to be completely unaware that everyone knows he's an idiot. What's on your agenda, Fronto? It seems to me that we lucky ones have actual free time. Perhaps we could relax with a drink somewhere?"

Fronto smiled and nodded, his gaze straying back up the slope to the officers gathered in a knot around Caesar and coming to rest on Crispus, who had left the group and was strolling in their direction.

"There's nothing I'd like more, but I have something to do first. My tent should be up and furnished within the hour. I'll meet you there then."

The others nodded and went off their own ways, leaving Fronto standing quietly as Crispus caught up with him.

"What's up?"

The young legate smiled.

"I think, perhaps, that we need to discuss your 'captive'?"

Fronto went blank for a moment, frowning, and then light dawned on him.

"Hardly a captive. More like a limpet. Where is she at the moment?"

He turned and walked on toward the supply wagons where Cita would be surveying the store situation as Crispus fell in beside him.

"I have two of the tribunes of the Eleventh keeping her safe and sound and a couple of the immunes tending to her needs." He smiled a sly smile. "Or perhaps you would rather tend to her needs, Marcus?"

Fronto glared at his companion and rolled his eyes.

"I'm not looking for someone to jump on and ravish, Crispus. I'm in the middle of a campaign. Besides, I suspect my mother and sister would have a heart attack if I brought home a Celtic girl."

Crispus laughed.

"I was not aware that you cared that much about improprieties, Marcus."

"Shut up."

Crispus' face became serious for a moment.

"You do need to decide what to do with her, though, Marcus. We cannot campaign with one of the enemy under our protection, no matter how pretty she might be."

Fronto nodded.

"I've been thinking about that, but it all depends on the next stage or two of the campaign. I can't just release her into the wilderness. That would be cruel, with wolves and bears out there. But we can't take her with us. If, when we've taken Noviodunum, we can subdue the Suessiones without having to raze the place and enslave them all, I can deliver her to them to look after. They're all Belgae, so they'll probably look after her until she can go home one day. Unless they decided that death is better than being allies with Rome."

Crispus nodded thoughtfully.

"That's a pretty big if, Marcus. We have to take the place first and, since they have already cost us several thousand men, I cannot see Caesar edging toward the merciful."

Fronto frowned as he thought of the general and his mind flipped back through past victories, coming to settle as it often did, particularly in the night, on the image of that day last year by the Saone where the Tigurine had been slowly and methodically executed under Caesar's orders.

"Then we will either have to persuade him, or she'll have to stay with us until the next tribe or town we deal with that can and will take her."

The two fell silent for a moment, and Fronto looked up as they approached the supply wagons.

"Cita? The general has agreed to a requisition of wine stores for the legions. Can you arrange it?"

The quartermaster's jaw firmed.

"For Bacchus' sake, Fronto, don't you ever think of anything other than wine? You do know we're on campaign here? I have a very limited stock of luxuries like wine, and it's a massive pain in the backside trying to replenish my stocks."

"So?"

"Every time you requisition wine, I have to send a resupply list back with an empty cart all the way to Vesontio, where I had the foresight to set up a storage camp. They send us the wine and then do the same thing, sending their list to the decurions of Geneva, who actually sell us the wine, at a reduced military rate if they're feeling generous. Then they buy in more wine from Cisalpine Gaul, across the Alps."

Fronto shrugged.

"Your point being?"

"My point being that every time you withdraw more than a few amphorae of wine, we have to utilise a massive resupply system that relies on more than a hundred people, stretches fully half a thousand miles and, by the time that wine is in your hand, it's cost a month's pay for many people. Think about the cost and difficulties before you start blithely handing out luxury goods to the men!"

Fronto smiled.

"Nah. That's your job, Cita. Mine's to keep the men happy."

He ignored the glare he was receiving from the quartermaster and his grin widened.

"But, on the other hand, since it's costing so much each time, we'd best make it worth it. Have another five or six amphorae sent to my tent, will you?"

As Cita started to shake, slowly, Fronto tossed him a loose sestertius and turned with Crispus to wander back toward his headquarters area.

Several hours later, Fronto exploded with laughter and had to wipe the wine from his chin as Sabinus ended a tale of misspent youth with a sidesplitting punch line. The officers seated around the legate's tent rocked with mirth.

Sabinus grinned at his companions. By the time Fronto's tent had been put up and his gear set out inside, almost a dozen officers had gathered to relax in the notorious officer's company. Crispus wheezed and took a deep breath but, as he opened his mouth to speak, there was a heavy knock at the door.

Fronto cleared his throat.

"Yes?"

A legionary, ruddy-faced and out of breath, leaned in through the doorway.

"Sir? We have movement at the gate of Noviodunum. The duty centurion asked me to find you..."

Fronto stood, wobbling gently, his legs unsteady after an hour cross-legged on the floor.

"Thank you. We'll be along presently."

As the soldier retreated and let the tent flap fall shut, Fronto struggled into his boots and the men around him hurriedly replaced their drinks on the table and hauled themselves upright.

"What do you suppose this is?" Crispus queried. "They can't be trying sorties against us, surely?"

Fronto shook his head.

"No. Let's go have a look."

The officers finished suiting up, adjusted their accoutrements, and strode in a businesslike fashion out of the tent and through the newly completed camp. A moment later they arrived at the gate and gazed across the grass to the impressive oppidum. A small party of men, three of them on horseback, were slowly approaching the Roman force.

Squinting, Fronto spied the traditional animal standards and bronze equipment of Belgic noblemen and their guards. Likely these were top men among the Suessiones. Briefly his memory flashed back to Bibrax.

"Gods, I hope someone there speaks Latin."

The officers gathered around the open gate parted as the familiar voice of Labienus called out "make way for Caesar!"

The general strode out to the front to stand between Sabinus and Fronto.

"Ambassadors. They perhaps hope to make terms?"

Fronto shrugged. He fervently hoped so. A siege was a messy way to make war, and they could do with the tribes in the south all being at peace with Rome. He looked up again as the Belgae closed and reined in. One of the three riders, an old man with white-grey braided hair raised his spear in a non-threatening fashion, holding it sideways and casting it to the floor in front of the group.

"Roman. The Suessiones seek an end to this. Call off your war dogs and we will discuss peace."

Caesar smiled his empty smile.

"Why should we discuss peace with an enemy when we have the advantage? You seek peace only because you see our ramp, our towers and our determination. You know Noviodunum will fall soon and fear drives you to bargain."

The old man's brow furrowed.

"You would keep fighting? So that the Suessiones are no more? Be sure that if you do, many Romans will not leave here. We are Belgae and brave. We offer peace, but if you insist on war we will make the price of our oppidum the highest Rome will ever pay."

Caesar frowned.

"My terms are simple, then: total and unconditional surrender of the entire tribe to the will of Rome. Then we call off our attack."

The old nobleman sighed.

"And our most beautiful women, our strongest men…" he sneered unpleasantly "… and our prettiest boys will be sent to Rome as slaves. This is less acceptable than death. We will agree peaceful terms, but we will not sell ourselves, Roman."

Caesar took a deep breath and gave a feral smile.

"Equally, when we are in such a strong position, you would not expect us to clasp arms with you and forget our thousands of dead? I will retire to consider what I am willing to accept and return within the hour. You," he said arrogantly, "will wait here until I return. If you do not, then I will consider that to be a decision to fight on and we will recommence our siege."

Without waiting for a reply, Caesar turned and strode off back to his headquarters, the senior officers hot on his heels as the duty centurion and his men fell in and closed the gate behind them, leaving the disgruntled Suessiones staring at a closed door.

* * * * *

Caesar shook his head.

"After the damage they have done to us, and with our current position of strength, I refuse to smile and welcome these barbarians into the fold. By rights, they should be begging for their lives on their knees now and, instead, they have the audacity to make demands of us?"

Fronto glanced across at Galronus, the most senior of the Remi serving with the auxiliaries. The man, strong and tall and every bit as impressive as the son of a chieftain should be, was glowering at Caesar.

"My father want Suessiones treat well. Friend with Rome!"

The general rumbled deep in his throat.

"Your father, Galronus, does not dictate the policy of the Roman military. If the Suessiones wanted alliance with Rome, they should not have chosen to go to war against us. For Venus' sake, it's their leader who was elected to prosecute the war!"

Crispus cleared his throat.

"Perhaps, Caesar, this is an opportunity to build bridges rather than walls?"

The general's head snapped round to glare at the young legate.

"Very pretty rhetoric, Crispus, but I am faced with two options. Firstly, I make peace with them and let them side with Rome, and to balance the thousands of dead they have caused, we draw a small number of auxiliary soldiers from them, and maybe a hostage or two. Secondly, we take Noviodunum, put the Remi in charge, and sell the Suessiones and all of their goods for an enormous war profit that may well pay for another year's campaigning?"

The room went silent.

"Yes, I think that's a fairly clinching argument, gentlemen."

Galronus stood angrily.

"Rome want friends with Remi? Remi want Rome friends with Suessiones." He folded his arms and then spread them in a breaking motion. "Rome not friend with Suessiones? Rome not friend with Remi. Remi go home!"

Caesar's face took on a dangerous hue and Fronto stood and strode across between them, turning to the Belgic nobleman.

"Galronus? Your point is made. Please, go outside and calm down. Have a drink. Kick a horse or something. Just cool down."

He jostled the resisting man to the tent's entrance and heaved him bodily outside, pinning the flap closed. He turned to see mixed emotions on Caesar's face.

"Sorry, Caesar, but any moment you or he would have said something we'd all later regret!"

The general continued to glower. Fronto walked forward and took a central position. He had never been a great speaker, and his rhetoric teacher had given up in disgust, but when you had a great point to make, he knew the centre of the floor was where to make it.

"Caesar, you can make money from them as slaves and from booty, but it's a short term win. I can give you three reasons why you should choose to come to terms."

He held up his hand and touched one index finger with the other.

"One: terms are negotiable. You can gain auxiliaries who know the other tribes and the lands to the north; men who have been in the intimate council of the enemy; even taking the man who led their army on as an ally. The intelligence you can gain is phenomenal. If they feel you are treating them with fairness, they may be amenable to giving you booty willingly, and resupplying you. You may find the benefits that you can argue for outweigh what you can just take."

Caesar's glower had faded to a vaguely thoughtful frown. He gestured to Fronto to continue.

"Two," the legate said, touching his middle finger this time, "word of this will spread. If you show mercy and care, other tribes may be swayed to our side without a fight. Whereas, if you tear the Suessiones down and destroy them, you will remove for all time any hope of the other tribes seeking peace. I've fought these Belgae four times now this year already, and I don't believe that they'll react to violent treatment by becoming scared and meekly surrendering. If they see you take out vengeance on a defeated tribe, I think you'll find they'll react with ever greater violence."

He waited and watched Caesar's frown deepen.

"Three."

Here was the biggest gamble, as he touched a third finger. "The future. I don't know whether we'll be here next year fighting more Celts or whether, once the Belgae are with us, the whole land will settle, and we'll be able to call the whole of Gaul Roman, but either way…" he swallowed. "Either way, one day Gaul will be Roman and what we do now will either help hasten that or delay it. If we want Gaul a peaceful, contented province, we have to start dealing with them correctly even now."

He finished his little speech with a dramatic sweep of his arm and looked around at the assembled faces, pleased to note the nods here and there among the officers, the thoughtful looks on almost every upturned face, and the sheer pride in Crispus' young eyes. He dropped his arms to his sides and gazed levelly at Caesar.

For a long moment, the general sat silently, staring at him, and then suddenly burst into genuine and noisy laughter.

There were nervous laughs scattered around the tent from those who did not see the joke but feared for their careers if they were not seen to follow Caesar. Fronto almost smiled as he watched

Plancus wrestling with himself, laughing madly while he frowned, unsure why he was doing so.

Finally, Caesar slapped his hand down on the arm of his chair and wiped his eyes.

"Fronto, you are absolutely priceless. I can see why you never went into politics. A magnificent collection of points you made, but you deliver great ideas in common language, while gesturing like a hawker of meats in the forum. And you're sweating so much your tunic's actually changed colour!"

More laughter. Fronto sighed and merely waited for it to finish.

"Fine!" Caesar smiled. "You win me over. I can be as merciful as I can harsh. Let's go see the Suessiones and see what they can offer."

Fronto's shoulders dropped with relief and, as the general left the tent, the other officers filing out behind him, a number of them slapped him on the back or grasped his arm as they left. Lastly, Crispus and Balbus joined him, and the three left the tent.

"Magnificent, Marcus" Crispus grinned. "You had the general convinced by the end of your first point. That last one though… worthy of Scaevola himself."

"Who the hell is Scaevola? You're in danger of slipping back into rhetoric yourself!"

Balbus laughed.

"He's right, though. That was very good. I didn't realise you thought that far ahead. I never assumed you thought beyond the next drink or the next fight!"

Fronto frowned.

"I just hope he doesn't demand too much and push the Suessiones into a fight anyway. Do we really want to go and watch negotiations?"

Balbus shook his head.

"I don't, but I think Caesar might expect you to be there, given the role you just played."

"Oh, he doesn't need me. And I have a jug in my tent that's still half full. Cita would moan at me if he thought I was wasting his precious wine."

Almost an hour had passed with Fronto, Balbus and Crispus lounging in the tent, working through Fronto's now copious stock of wine. The mood had been light and frivolous since the meeting at Caesar's tent.

Crispus grinned at Fronto.

"So… about your woman, Marcus?"

Fronto grimaced.

"What about her?"

"Well I can't devote the senior officers of the Eleventh for the rest of the campaign to babysitting a girl for you. You need to decide what to do. Are you going to leave her here?"

Fronto shrugged.

"Can you have your tribunes deliver her to the elders in Noviodunum? She'll be safe there, once the treaty's been ratified."

Crispus frowned.

"We can do that, certainly, but she trusts you, Marcus. It should be you who takes her if she's to go."

Fronto shook his head.

"I think not. The bloody woman attaches herself to me like a limpet. If your tribunes take her, she might stay there. Not with me though."

Crispus smiled.

"Very well. I shall arrange it for the morning. But you may regret it on the cold nights in the hills…"

Balbus laughed.

"What is it with you, Marcus? Woman just want you."

The three were still laughing when there was a knock at the door. Before Fronto could call out, however, the familiar voice of Sabinus from outside addressed another man.

"It's Fronto's tent. Don't stand on ceremony."

Fronto grinned as the staff officer flung the leather aside and stepped in.

"Are you still sober, man of the hour?"

Behind Sabinus came Tetricus, with the tall figure of Galronus of the Remi stooping to enter and bringing up the rear.

"Others will be along shortly" Sabinus stated. "Your man Priscus is busy arguing with Cita over wine and beer…"

"Oh, good…" smiled Crispus vaguely.

"But I thought you'd like to know that we are now officially allied with the Suessiones. They're supplying us with troops, gold and provisions and lots of information. Their leader's gone to consult with Caesar."

Fronto smiled.

"Good sense does sometimes win out, then."

Sabinus nodded.

"So, I think we'll be here for a few days now and, since you and I might be called on at any time to go deal with official matters, let's make the most of this evening."

He sat down and grabbed three mugs from the table, passing one to Tetricus and one to Galronus. The engineer watched happily as the staff officer filled the mug.

"Hadn't even got a third of the way out into the ditch with my ramp, let alone got the towers built. Caesar reckons that as soon as they saw what we were doing, they gave in. Says he's going to give me a phalera for my efforts. It's rare that an engineer gets decorated!"

Sabinus nodded.

"Certainly is. Well deserved though. That ramp idea of yours gave us the Suessiones without a fight."

"Thank you" a voice said.

Fronto turned to look in surprise at the Remi nobleman, who raised his mug in salute.

"Remi and Suessiones thank legatus Fronto."

Taking a deep swig from the mug, the man reached up and unfastened the finely-crafted golden torc that hung around his neck. With a smile, he held it out to Fronto. The legate stared at it for a moment, so Galronus nodded and gestured with it.

"Fronto says thank you" interjected Sabinus, passing the torc on. "Now that's enough giving of presents. Tomorrow we'll probably be ironing out treaties and training Belgae, so for now, let's get good and drunk before your primus pilus gets here with his dice and takes me for everything I own.

PART TWO: PRIDE OF THE BELGAE

Chapter 12

(Roman camp outside the fortified oppidum of Noviodunum)

"Duplicarius: A soldier on double the basic pay."

The early afternoon sun glinted off the standards and equipment piles of the Tenth Legion. The camp had settled into that limbo during a campaign when there was currently no direction or action, but the constant threat of it.

Despite Caesar's earlier desire to press on with the campaign, he seemed to have changed his mind, and over two weeks had passed since the deal had been struck between them and the Suessiones, during which time the senior officers had been closeted away, leaving the legions and the auxiliary units to their own devices.

Fronto had been called regularly to staff meetings, though his input had been minimal, he being entirely uninterested in facts, figures and agreements regarding supply, levying of new auxiliaries and the terms and conditions of the alliance. Fronto had taken every possible opportunity to slip away and relax, though most of the people he would generally relax with were also required to attend those meetings.

He had tried to get into the oppidum to make use of the local taverns as the lower ranks were doing when off-duty, but had spotted that Bellovaci woman again in the square with a face like thunder and had hurriedly left without a drink.

And so he had been forced to turn elsewhere for a drinking companion, and had been pleasantly surprised at the good company he had found entirely by accident.

Galronus of the Remi smiled at Fronto as he shook the dice.

"My Latin getting better, yes?"

Fronto nodded.

"It was never bad, but you'll be fluent in no time. Long before I learn any of your tongue, anyway."

Galronus laughed.

"Your language easy. My language hard."

"No argument from me." He sighed. "When the hell is Caesar going to move on, I wonder. A few weeks ago he was hopping from foot to foot, willing to throw away good men just to get moving and wade into the Belgae… no offence meant, Galronus… but now he's spending all his time in talks with the king of the Suessiones and the legions are getting bored."

The Remi nobleman grinned.

"I think your speech make him want to be friends with Belgae?"

Fronto shook his head.

"You don't know the general. He's about as sentimental as a sword-point. He only went along with what I said because it was advantageous to him and I made it clear. Besides," he sighed, "I've noticed that the Belgae don't generally seem interested in peace with Rome."

He leaned forward, drawing close to Galronus.

"The strange thing is: we've had some hard fights so far, don't get me wrong, but not what I was expecting from what people say of the Belgae. Half the northern world is frightened of you, yet we actually had a harder time fighting Ariovistus, or the Helvetii even."

He noted the faintly offended look in the nobleman's eyes.

"I mean no offence. It's just that the massive army we fought by the Aisne could have pounded us into the ground but, the moment they lost the overwhelming advantage, they just ran and kept on running while we carved slices off their arse."

Galronus nodded thoughtfully, so Fronto drew a breath and went on.

"And the Suessiones gave up without a fight, despite the fact that they were theoretically in charge of the whole affair."

Another nod, and the Belgic warrior leaned back, taking a swig of frothy beer from his mug.

"The Suessiones unsure. Remember, Suessiones are our brothers. Many not wanted to fight Rome in first place. Amazing works of Tetricus tipped balance in council against ones who want war. This why we want mercy for Suessiones from Caesar."

He shook his head.

"Big army running is different. You think they flee, but they not flee. They return to own lands. Belgae not used to fighting together in big army. All fight better as own tribes. You see?"

Fronto nodded.

"I see, but they're wrong. The only way they could beat Caesar is if they all gather together. As smaller individual tribes, we will beat them. It's a foregone conclusion. But one thing still worries me..."

"Yes?"

"Well even that huge army we fought by the Aisne that's now dispersed was maybe half the army that had been reported building to Caesar. So where's the other half? We've seen nothing of them yet."

Galronus' expression darkened.

"North. Many enemy wait to north. There the worst. Small tribes Rome meets here fight and lose, or ask Caesar for peace. Not in north though. Atrebates... Aduatuci..." his voice lowered menacingly. "Nervii..."

Fronto frowned.

"The Nervii are bad then?"

The nobleman nodded emphatically.

"Most dangerous tribe in world. Nervii are rabid dogs. They already threaten to skin leaders of Remi alive for friends with Rome, and they do it too if they get chance. Nervii skinned King of Menapii when he made deal with Germans, in front of wife and children. Nervii vicious... but Atrebates cunning. Nervii and Atrebates together is trouble for Rome. And with Aduatuci, who very German..."

Fronto sighed. He really had almost convinced himself that the Belgae were going to smile and turn to join Rome in light of recent events, but it now looked like this was the veritable calm before the storm.

The tent fell silent as the two men considered the future, until a moment later there came a knock at the door.

"Yes?"

The flap was pulled aside, and Priscus and Balventius, the lead centurions of the Eighth and Tenth Legions strode in. Priscus looked unhappy, but Balventius' face would have frightened Vulcan himself. Fronto looked up, worried.

"What's happened?"

"We've had two riders arrive" Priscus announced, reaching for the jug of wine that habitually occupied the surface nearest the door of Fronto's tent. "An Aedui scout went to see Caesar. He wasn't absolutely knackered, so I assume the Aedui are close. And if the Aedui are close that means they're dealing with the Bellovaci, which means that Caesar's probably going to move us."

"And?" prompted Fronto, still looking at Balventius' glowering face dubiously.

"And another rider came in just now from the south" grumbled Balventius darkly, reaching for the wine and pouring himself a large mug.

Fronto frowned.

"If we're likely to be moving shortly, I suggest that you two might want to water that down. Won't look good if you have to call the muster and you're swaying."

Balventius growled and drank deep, pouring himself a second mug.

"The other rider was one of Varus' men; one of the ones you sent to Rome, to your sister?"

Fronto stared.

"No. It's been… what… just over three weeks? He'd have had to do sixty miles a day. He'd have killed his horse!"

Balventius nodded.

"They rode hard to get there, but sent one man on ahead on the way back. He's been riding like the wind and changing horses at every mansio or Gaulish village. When he arrived, Varus told him to find me, because you'd be in with Caesar. I, of course, knew better."

The primus pilus sat heavily in an empty chair and drank down a second mug of wine in one long gulp.

Fronto growled.

"For Dis' sake, Titus, tell me what happened!"

"The riders delivered your message, and your sister gave them a reply and sent them off as fast as they could to get to you."

He held out a scroll, its wax seal neatly snapped in half.

"You opened a private sealed message from my sister to me?" Fronto stared, astounded.

"In the circumstances, it was likely to be important to me."

Balventius shrugged.

"For Gods' sake, Fronto, stop moaning and read it!"

The legate unrolled the scroll and ran his gaze down the message. As he did so, Galronus unfolded his legs and started to climb to his feet.

"This private…"

Fronto grasped the man's wrist and pulled him back down.

"Oh, Nemesis!"

Balventius nodded and passed the mug of wine over to him.

"What the matter?" Galronus asked.

"Oh, shit."

As he reached out and took a deep pull of the wine Balventius had handed him, the tent flap was thrown open and light streamed in. Fronto squinted into the bright sunshine.

"This is private…"

His voice tailed off as he recognised the bald, moon face of Balbus silhouetted in the doorway.

"Caesar's calling the legions to order in a few hours, Marcus, but he wants you at the meeting now."

Fronto growled.

"The cowardly, lying, shit-heeled bastard can damn well do without me."

Balbus stared and let the flap drop into place behind him.

"What's up?"

Fronto threw the scroll at him with some force.

"We were too late. Paetus' family paid the price for being friends with the great Caesar."

Balbus' face fell. He started to unroll the scroll, but instead placed it on the cupboard top.

"What happened?"

"In detail? 'Cause she's given me plenty of detail? The kids were drowned in the Tiber, as was the old man. But as for his wife, Calida…"

Balbus held his hand up.

"I think I know all I want to, and I can guess the rest. This'll destroy Paetus altogether. Do we tell him now?"

Balventius reached out for the wine again from Fronto and shook his head sadly.

"We'll have to. Fronto's rider almost killed himself trying to get here fast to give us the news before the official courier arrives to find Paetus. I think we'll have a day or two at most. It's not a nice job. Anyone want to take it on?"

The room went silent, the three other Roman officers averting their gaze as Balventius looked back and forth between them. Galronus frowned.

"I not understand. Maybe too private for me, eh?"

Balbus noticed the Remi nobleman for the first time with surprise.

"It's a little complicated, my friend, but there are people in Rome and even here in the army that would like to see Caesar fail. And a particularly nasty individual in Rome has just killed one of our men's wife and children."

Galronus nodded.

"Like Nervii. I was tell Fronto about them. Nasty."

Fronto sighed.

"I'll tell him, Balventius."

The primus pilus shook his head.

"I wasn't serious, Fronto. This is my job…"

The legate cut him off with a low growl.

"I'm not going to face Caesar right now. If I do, there's a distinct possibility I might re-enact the death of a king in the hands of the Nervii. I wonder what the general would look like without his skin?"

Balbus grabbed his wrist.

"Don't do anything stupid, Fronto. If you're going to see Paetus, just do that. Tell him everything, but try to keep both of you calm and be sympathetic. And stay the hell away from Caesar for a few days. I'll tell Caesar about it."

Fronto nodded unhappily and turned to Priscus.

"You're in command of the Tenth for the moment. I have other duties. If Caesar wants to see the legate of the Tenth, that's you. Understand?"

Priscus nodded as he reiterated Balbus' words.

"Stay calm and don't do anything stupid, Marcus."

"I am calm," Fronto growled as he stood and retrieved his belt and scabbard from the cot. "I am calm like death."

Without a glance back at them, he strode purposefully out of the tent.

* * * * *

The legions had been on the march again for eight hours, and Priscus was starting to worry that Fronto had snapped. While the officers had attended Caesar's campaign meeting and the legions themselves had prepared to break camp, Fronto had gone off to find the camp prefect. Paetus had been extremely busy, and it had taken a great deal of dragging to get him away from his tasks. After that, Fronto and the prefect had disappeared into the man's tent, where they had remained for the night, the only sign they were still alive being the request for alcohol sent to the quartermaster.

The next morning, Priscus had formed up the Tenth and started them moving with the rest of the legions and still Fronto had been nowhere to be seen. With thousands of men to command and get moving, Priscus had had no time to enquire of his superior. Fronto had put him in temporary command of the Tenth, and the primus pilus knew that meant that Fronto would be absent for a while.

But now? Eight hours travel and no sign of him?

He really was beginning to worry. Priscus knew his commander better than any other man, and Fronto, for all his practical, worldly attitude, was actually a lot more soft and emotional than most people realised. Priscus had always suspected that was what lay behind the fact that Fronto was still single and uninvolved in anything political. He was so damn prey to his emotions that he deliberately steered clear of things that he knew would mess him around.

"Sod this" he announced to nobody in particular. Turning to the signifer of the First Cohort, he made a sour face.

"Keep going. I'm dropping back for a few moments."

Without waiting for a nod or salute, Priscus fell out of line and strode back past the marching column at a brisk pace. The men moving past like a sea of tramping feet gave the impression that he was running, though in truth he maintained only a fast march.

Behind the First and Second Cohorts, he passed the various mounted tribunes attached to the Tenth, including Tetricus, who raised an eyebrow at him. He ignored them and marched on. No time to chat and the tribunes had been as busy as him this morning, so they'd be no help. Besides, he had seen them several times and, if they'd known anything about Fronto, they'd have commented.

Back past the rest of the cohorts, and Priscus continued to ignore the engineering detail with their artillery on the carts.

"Aha!"

Up ahead, the command section of the Eighth Legion marched, with a break of just fifty paces or so from the rear of the Tenth to allow the dust to drop below shoulder height. Legate Balbus sat astride a horse, keeping pace with his men. The tribunes of the

Eighth rode just behind and accompanying their commander, with Balventius behind them, his face indicating how much he enjoyed staring at the rear end of a tribune's horse for eight solid hours.

Priscus came to a halt and opened his mouth to speak to Balbus, before quickly remembering the proprieties of addressing a senior officer in front of his tribunes. Time and circumstance had drawn some of them closely together across traditional rank divides, but it was not wise to advertise that.

"Legatus?"

Balbus looked down in surprise to see Priscus turning to keep pace with him.

"Can I help, centurion?"

"I'm trying to locate legate Fronto, sir. Haven't seen him since he… ah… left the meeting last night."

Balbus frowned.

"Really? I just assumed he returned to the Tenth."

Balbus turned to a tribune beside him.

"Adrattus? Take my horse and walk on. I have something to attend to."

As he dropped from his horse with a litheness that belied both his age and his frame, the tribune took the reins in surprise.

"So," Balbus frowned as the two men turned and began to stride back along the line once again. "Someone will have seen either Paetus or Fronto this morning."

He laughed, though Priscus noted the lack of genuine humour in it. "Knowing how Fronto can put it away, I expect he and Paetus are grey and unconscious and draped over a supply cart. Let's go find out."

Unconvinced, Priscus nodded, and the two men marched on, past the Ninth, Eleventh and Twelfth legions. Despite their nature as new and largely untested legions, the Thirteenth and Fourteenth had been placed as rear guard, partially for protection, but largely, once again, to keep them separate from the non-Gallic legions.

Priscus shook his head as he thought about it. It still pissed him off that noncitizens with braided hair and yellow beards who spoke a language that sounded like a sink emptying could march with pride in the name of Rome and collect the same pay, shares of booty and benefits as men born in Latium of longstanding Roman families.

And yet, these men had saved Sabinus and his men by the Aisne. Though he had not been there to see it, he had observed the aftermath, and tales had passed round about both the ingenuity and bravery of those men. He growled again. How could he expect the legions to treat them appropriately when he could not even think about it himself without his prejudices getting in the way.

And there were still incidents. Only yesterday, a legionary from the Thirteenth had been caught in the temporary latrines by an unknown group and had been beaten within an inch of his life. Priscus had seen the man making his report. He had been a mess, his bronze-coloured beard and hair stained further red by the blood that poured from his mouth and two or three cuts on his head. His arm had clearly been broken, and his uniform, up to the waist, was a colour that clearly indicated he had been thrown in the latrine ditch afterwards. And yet the man in good Latin, though with a noticeable accent, had claimed to have not seen any of their faces.

Pride. It was, more than anything, the backbone of the legions. Pride. And these Gaulish recruits had enough of it that they were willing to accept a near-fatal beating to preserve it.

He turned to Balbus as they passed the rear ranks of the Twelfth and approached the staff and the wagon train.

"We've got to do something about these legions. Got to get the Thirteenth and Fourteenth in with our own lads."

Balbus nodded.

"I know. The problem is that they've not had a chance to fight alongside each other yet. I think the other legions resent the fact that the only action that's worthy of note among the legions so far was carried out by the new boys. I'm hoping that, once they all have a chance to take the field together and watch each other's backs, they'll settle down."

Priscus grunted.

"So long as they do actually watch each other's back. I wouldn't be too sure right now."

The two of them slowed as they reached the command section, and while Priscus saluted the senior officers Balbus looked up at them. Caesar raised an eyebrow.

"Lost your horse, legate?"

There was chuckling among the officers.

"Looking for Fronto, Caesar. I presume you haven't seen him?"

"No" the general confirmed, a shadow passing across his eyes. "Not even when I asked to…"

Without pressing the subject, Balbus nodded and, stopping, turned to Priscus.

"This is pointless. We need to speak to the lower ranks. They're more likely to know where Fronto is than the officers."

Priscus nodded.

"I have an idea."

With Balbus at his heels, he strode on to the baggage column and frowned at it. Pursing his lips, he turned to the legate by his side.

"Something's wrong here."

Balbus shrugged.

"Looks normal to me."

"No." Priscus shook his head. "I've seen the supply train of an army a hundred times. This is different. Look:"

He gestured at the front wagon.

"This wagon's full of tent gear. For the camp when we stop."

"Yes?"

"Front wagon's always stockade posts and defensive equipment; in case camp needs to be set up quickly. Need the defensive works closest to the legions… tents go up after that."

Balbus shrugged.

"So someone changed the order or made a mistake."

"No. This is Paetus' job. He always oversees the wagons. He's a bit of a martinet over it. We've had words about it before now. This was organised by someone else."

Ignoring the look of impressed surprise on the legate's face, Priscus strode over to the first wagon and located a duplicarius legionary in charge of the cart.

"Who oversaw the wagons this morning?"

The legionary saluted hurriedly.

"Prefect Cita, sir."

"And where is Cita now?"

The soldier looked a little panicky, as though convinced he had done something wrong. Balbus had seen that face many times on a subordinate as they addressed the primus pilus of the Tenth. Priscus had something of a reputation.

"Five or six carts back, sir, with the luxuries wagons."

Priscus nodded and, turning, beckoned to Balbus. The two strode on past the loaded wagons until they saw the familiar hulking figure of Caesar's chief quartermaster. Cita was a large man; not fat, but with a bulk distributed well across his frame. His lantern jaw was always dark, as though the man needed to shave several times a day. He scratched his short, curly hair with a stylus in one hand while trying to concentrate on the figures displayed on the wax tablet in the other, despite the bouncing of the cart. Priscus waved at him.

"Prefect?"

Cita looked up from his figures and frowned.

"Priscus... legate? What can I do for you?"

Priscus pointed toward the head of the column.

"I'm looking for Fronto and Paetus. Have you seen them?"

Cita nodded unhappily.

"You want the medical carts at the rear of the column." He noted the sudden alarm in their faces. "Don't panic, gentlemen. Fronto's alright. Very, very, very drunk, and a little light headed, but alright."

Balbus turned to ask a question of Priscus, but the primus pilus was already striding toward the other end of the long column of carts, travelling three abreast. It always astounded him when he saw them just how many wagons were needed to keep an army this size supplied on the move. The wagon train took almost an hour to pass fully. Truly, without men like Cita and Paetus, a marching column may well fall apart.

He caught up with Priscus and eventually they arrived at the medical wagons: eight empty carts at the rear that served to carry the non-walking and non-terminal wounded. He tried not to think about just how crammed those eight large carts were, and scanned them, trying to locate Fronto or Paetus.

"Here!"

Priscus waved him over to one of the rear carts. A space had been cleared, the legionaries almost sitting on top of one another to make room for the senior officer among their number. In many cases, that would be through fear and obedience. Balbus suspected, given Fronto's reputation, that in this case, it was through love and respect.

Fronto lay in the cleared space with Florus, the young capsarius from the Tenth, tending to him. Balbus opened his mouth to enquire, but Priscus beat him to it.

"Florus? Talk to me?"

The young man looked up and frowned.

"I'm a little concerned about the legate, sir. He's clearly still suffering the effects, let alone the after-effects of whatever he drank last night, but I'm not sure how much of his barely-conscious condition is the alcohol and how much is the wound."

Priscus growled.

"What wound?"

"Well sir," the young man answered earnestly. "When he was found this morning, he was completely unconscious and reeked of wine, but when the legionaries turned him over, they found a wound on the back of his head. There was blood on the frame of the chair by the door, and they believe he must have fallen, drunk, and struck his head on the way down."

The young, rosy-faced man leaned closer conspiratorially.

"But I'm not convinced of that, sir."

Balbus bent closer to join the low conversation.

"What do you mean?"

"Well," Florus shrugged, still carefully cradling the legate's head against the jarring motion of the wagon, "I can't show you the wound right now, but I had a good look at it before I bound it this morning; before he went in the cart…"

"And?"

"And the wound is not consistent with having fallen on a campaign chair, sirs."

He lowered his voice again, so that Balbus had to strain to hear.

"The wound was inflicted by something rounded and heavy and at a reasonable force, and I think from the looks of it, it was inflicted from behind and above."

"Paetus!" Priscus growled. "Fronto was found alone?"

"Yes sir."

"But in Paetus' tent?"

"Yessir."

"And, were I to suggest, would you say the wound could have been inflicted by this?"

As Balbus and Florus watched, Priscus lifted his sheathed sword and displayed the heavy, rounded pommel at the top of the hilt. Balbus stared, but Florus nodded. "That was my thought already, sir, though I didn't want to voice it until after the legate had woken."

Balbus shook his head.

"He will wake then?"

"Oh yes, sir. He'll be delicate for a while and have a bad headache, but some of that's from his own self-abuse, begging your pardon, sirs. The wound was enough to render him unconscious, but no more. I wouldn't be comfortable releasing him for duty for a few days, though."

"Paetus!" growled Priscus once again.

He turned to Balbus.

"I think we'd best inform Caesar that Paetus has attacked Fronto and fled." He frowned. "Question is: where's he fled to?"

* * * * *

Divitiacus of the Aedui and several of his nobles rode out ahead of the vast Gallic force that was milling around on the plain ahead. As he approached the head of the Roman column, the staff officers arrived from their position further back along the line while the men sighed and rested their feet from the four day march along the river valley into the lands of the Bellovaci.

"My lord Divitiacus" Caesar greeted the Aedui chief with as deep and respectful a bow as he could manage on horseback. Divitiacus gave him a traditional Roman military salute. "General."

"What news of the Bellovaci?"

The Aedui chieftain pulled his horse alongside the general and shrugged.

"We have fought and burned our way from Lutetia all the way here, Caesar. The main force was absent, fighting you, though even their women and children fought us as best they could. It was tragic really. I dislike having to take war against women."

Caesar nodded.

"It is tragic, and all soldiers try not to, but sometimes civilians will just not listen to reason and must resist. I hope you have not incurred too many casualties?"

Divitiacus shrugged again.

"Hardly any until the Bellovaci returned to their lands. About a week ago we started to meet actual warriors in small tribes. We have fought and defeated each small army we came across, but were always surprised at their low numbers until yesterday. Then we discovered where they have all gone."

Caesar raised an eyebrow.

"They are in the greatest oppidum they control; a town called Bratuspantium, about a mile down the valley from here. There they've held against us for four days and have caused us a lot of deaths. We outnumber them, but they're in a strong position and won't sally forth to deal with us."

Caesar nodded.

"But now the Aedui will join Rome on the field and the Bellovaci will tremble before our might."

Divitiacus shook his head.

"I'm afraid not, Caesar. The Bellovaci will not sue for peace as others have. They are too proud. Their warriors would rather die than submit to Rome. Even their women and children, as we've seen."

Caesar frowned, thoughtfully.

"But it will take days to remove them from an oppidum, even with my best engineers. If they will not come out to meet us and they will not accept treaty, then we must make them bow before us!"

Priscus caught a glimpse of the general's face as he addressed the Aedui chieftain and he knew that look. He hardened himself for whatever he was about to overhear.

After a moment, Caesar turned to Labienus and Sabinus, both of whom sat ahorse behind him.

"I assume Fronto took prisoners after that fracas by the Aisne? Are any of them Bellovaci?"

Sabinus nodded.

"Almost a hundred, some pretty badly wounded though. They're chained up at the rear of the supply column, in the charge of the Thirteenth."

Caesar nodded.

"In a moment we're going to move out to Bratuspantium. While we do, have the prisoners brought forward under guard."

Bratuspantium was, as had been intimated, an impressive fortress, with thick, high walls and a wide ditch, as defensive as Noviodunum and more besides. The Bellovaci lined the walls, with archers, slingers, stone and spear throwers ready to repel any threat. They were clearly no more concerned about the arrival of seven legions of Romans than they were about the large numbers of Aedui that had been whittling down the defenders through extensive attrition for days now.

Priscus stood in his accustomed position at the head of the Tenth and the front of the Roman column, with only Caesar's staff between him and the defences of the Bellovaci. From here he could see the prisoners being marched along the side of the column; mostly the walking wounded, with occasional old men and the braver women who had accompanied their tribe into battle.

A good job Fronto was not here. The legate was conscious now, but would remain with the medical staff until tomorrow morning for observation. It was, Priscus thought, a damn good thing. There was a man accompanying the prisoner column who the primus pilus recognised; a man whose job it was to extract information from a reticent source. Every legion had such a man, though they were rarely called upon. This one, Manlius of the Ninth, had a reputation that surpassed the others, and which made him Caesar's first choice for that least pleasant of activities.

The Gauls of the Thirteenth Legion marched the prisoners out ahead of the column, to where Caesar and Sabinus stood, alongside Divitiacus. Priscus was close enough to hear the low conversation between the army's leaders, intended to be unheard by the legions.

"What do you intend to do?" Divitiacus sounded nervous.

"I shall persuade the Bellovaci to peace."

"You will execute their fellows?"

"In a manner of speaking…" Caesar turned that frightening feral smile on him and then, as the prisoners were lined up, he cleared his throat and called out in a voice loud enough to reach the walls of Bratuspantium and be heard within.

"Leaders and warriors of the Bellovaci…"

He gestured with both arms widely.

"You have shut yourself in a trap. My army will slowly close that trap and squeeze you to death, if that is your will. I have been warned that you will not surrender to the will of Rome and that you will not fight us in open and honourable warfare. Therefore you leave me no choice but to use every weapon at my disposal to make you accept our will."

He turned and gestured to Manlius, who began, with the aid of two legionaries from the Thirteenth, to hammer a huge stake into the ground and bind ropes to it.

Caesar nodded, stony faced.

"I give you this first great chance to prevent further bloodshed and to make peace with Rome. What is your answer?"

There was a resounding silence in answer to his call.

"Very well. Continue, centurion Manlius…"

Priscus watched with growing unease as an old man with a leg wound was drawn, limping, from the column of prisoners and tied tightly to the stake. His worst fears were confirmed when Manlius collected from his kit a small flask of oil and drizzled it over the old man's head. The torturer stopped in front of the prisoner and gave him an unpleasant grin. Priscus felt like applauding as the prisoner spat a mixture of oil and saliva in the centurion's face. Centurions like Manlius gave the rank a bad name. The job might be a necessary one at times, but there was no call for anyone to enjoy it so much.

Priscus looked away as Manlius worked the firesteel with a flicking noise. Keeping his head erect and straight, the primus pilus focused instead on Divitiacus of the Aedui, whose own face had become a mask of horror. Yes…a damn good job Fronto was not here right now. There was a sudden explosive noise just out of his field of vision to the right, accompanied by an agonised shrieking.

Caesar, he noticed, barely blinked.

For two hundred and twenty six heartbeats, they stood in silence like a still painting on the wall of a villa, locked in the seemingly eternal torture of a relative innocent. Two hundred and twenty six heartbeats, though! Priscus knew, for he counted each heartbeat past while Caesar stared at the oppidum as Divitiacus stared at him. And throughout each tick in his mind, the sound of burning slowed and quietened to become the crackle and hiss of crisping flesh and burning fat.

Priscus' teeth ground as Caesar once more addressed the Bellovaci.

"That is one of your people. Possibly the father of one of you on the walls? He is dead. Painfully, horribly, and unnecessarily dead. Because you will not listen to reason. I offer peace and an end to this horror. What is your answer?"

There was a silence once more. Caesar placed his hands on his hips and drew a breath, but Divitiacus stepped in front of him.

"General, this is not war. This is torture and murder. Let us tear down their walls instead. It is slow, but it is war!"

Caesar's eyes flicked briefly to him and then back to Bratuspantium.

"I have almost a hundred other fathers, wives and children here" he called, "and be sure that before we reach the end, my legions will have rounded up others; farmers and woodsmen of your kin that live nearby. I will do what I must to end this war today."

He waited as Divitiacus shook gently, and turned to Manlius.

"A woman this time. Quartered."

Priscus took a very deep breath and kept his head rigidly straight, his eyes on the officers. Off to his right, he heard the sound of a woman being restrained and then, slowly and horrifically, even over her screams, he could hear the sound of the saw. Behind him among the men, someone vomited.

Divitiacus growled at the general.

"I will have none of this, Caesar. If you persist in this madness, the Aedui will leave."

Caesar turned the coldest, most snakelike expression Priscus had ever seen on the leader of the Aedui.

"You are treaty-bound with Rome. If you leave this field you will break that treaty, and I will be forced to deal with the Aedui instead. Do you value your ethics enough to make an enemy of Rome and myself?"

For a long moment, Divitiacus wavered, and then finally nodded and, turning, went to join his army who were looking on this display of Roman might with a mix of astonishment and horror. The screaming had stopped, and Priscus could hear the sounds of several things being dragged across the grass. He winced as Caesar once more addressed the Bellovaci.

"I tire of asking, so this will be the last time I speak to you. You have only to accept Roman law and this will end. Until you do so, I will continue to deal with your kin." He turned and addressed the men beside him, but loud enough to be heard as far as the walls.

"Manlius? Continue your work. Be creative and very visual. Allow a count of fifty only between victims. Sabinus? Have a party of three alae of cavalry sent out to round up any of the Bellovaci they can find outside the city. Labienus? Have camp set here. We may be here for the night."

Once again, Divitiacus left the folds of the Aedui and marched across to the general.

"Caesar? What can we do to stop this?"

The general glared at his ally.

"The Aedui have no more part in this. You will remain here until Bratuspantium falls and, once the Bellovaci are with us, you will retire to your own lands and stay out of trouble. Unless I call for you again, the Aedui are forbidden from forming an army."

Divitiacus stared at him.

"And be grateful that I am sending you back. Rome needs strong allies, not weak ones!"

The two leaders stood, locked in an embrace of mutual dislike and distrust as the screaming started once more behind them.

The purple twilight dwindled as Priscus sighed and walked over to the medical cart where Fronto lay recovering. The sun had set only a quarter of an hour ago, and there was still a deep cerulean glow about the valley. Fronto groaned.

"Where the hell have you been? I hope you've brought wine."

Priscus shook his head.

"No wine for you for a few days. Got some for me though. Need to celebrate… or something."

"What's happened?"

Priscus sighed again.

"The gates of Bratuspantium opened an hour ago, and the Bellovaci submitted unconditionally to Caesar's whim."

Fronto smiled and then winced at the pain on his scalp.

"The old bastard. He may have dropped Paetus in the shit, but he can still win over the enemy, can't he, the silver-tongued old snake?"

"I suppose so" agreed Priscus soberly, picturing the scores of charred and dismembered bodies he had watched being shovelled into a pit on the way here.

"Yes, I suppose so."

Chapter 13

(River valley outside Samarobriva)

"Samarobriva: oppidum on the Somme River, now called Amiens."

"Mare Nostrum: Latin name for the Mediterranean Sea (literally 'Our Sea')"

Fronto frowned as the column came to a halt once more and Priscus grumbled irritably next to him. They both shaded their eyes again to see the small party of riders making their way toward the Roman force from the open gate of Samarobriva, capital of the Ambiani.

"Just the leaders, I'm sure of it" the legate noted, his frown deepening. "Not even an honour guard. What the hell is going on? Is this really the Belgae?"

Priscus shrugged noncommittally.

"Are you complaining about not having to besiege that place?"

Fronto shook his head.

"Well no… just what did Caesar do to the Bellovaci, 'cause whatever it was apparently frightened the shit out of their neighbours?"

Priscus grasped Fronto's shoulder and leaned close enough to whisper in his ear.

"How much do you trust me?"

"With my life, you know that."

"Then take my word for it... you don't want to know, and it'll do no good getting all riled up about it. Suffice it to say that it was one of those 'Julian moments' that you despise."

Fronto rumbled deep in his throat.

"I can well imagine. Ah well. Nemesis always marks those that need taking down. Either Caesar really does have the blood of Venus, or one day Nemesis will have her way with him."

Priscus smiled.

"Very pious, I'm sure. I don't know about Nemesis, but I'm pretty sure there are a few senators that would like to wedge their foot up his arse."

Fronto grinned at his second in command.

"Alright. That's an end to it. We're his army, after all."

They turned to look ahead once more, and Fronto's suspicion was confirmed. Four of the party of five riders wore the accoutrements of senior noblemen, their gold and bronze torcs and jewellery marking them as extremely wealthy. The fifth, Fronto noted with surprise, and a little suspicion, wore a dark grey robe belted at the waist with a great flax belt, intricately woven. He wore no jewellery, but his long hair and braided beard were as black as his eyes, colouring that Fronto had not yet seen among these northern tribes. The man carried a staff whose tip was carved into the shape of a dragon.

"Druid!" whispered Priscus with indrawn breath. "This could be trouble."

The sound of hoof beats drew their attention and Caesar, Sabinus and Labienus arrived from their position further back.

"What can you see, Fronto?"

"Looks like four chieftains and a druid, general. No guards."

"Curious." Caesar turned and frowned down at Fronto. "I like my legates to look important. You should be on horseback."

Fronto shrugged; he hated riding on marches. It was not that he felt guilty particularly, though that was a part of it. More it was that he was not that good a horseman, and found it quite difficult to make the beast walk at the same pace as the legions.

"The jarring hurts my head, Caesar. Wounded, remember?"

The general's face darkened momentarily as he was reminded of Paetus' treachery and subsequent violence and disappearance.

"Very well, but at least stand straight. This could be important."

The officers tidied themselves subtly as they waited for the five riders to close with them. Finally they did so, and Fronto noted with interest how the four chiefs came abreast and bowed slightly to Caesar, while the druid stayed apart and sat glowering haughtily.

"Gentlemen" Caesar said clearly, "I presume you are the chieftains of the Ambiani?"

The druid nodded, his mouth turned down at the corners with a sour expression.

"They are. They do not speak Latin, so I am here to translate before I leave this place."

Caesar opened his mouth to speak and then glared sharply at Fronto as the legate interrupted.

"You're not staying around, your druid-iness?"

"The Ambiani have abandoned their pride, and so I abandon the Ambiani. And I have no wish to spend any more time than necessary with the men who shamed my brother Divitiacus..."

Caesar started.

"Your brother?"

"My brother druid."

Fronto turned to stare at Priscus, whose face was an equal mask of surprise.

"Divitiacus is chief of the Aedui?" Fronto said, unsurely.

"Chieftain and druid. A man usually of vision, though by putting his trust in you, I fear his vision has abandoned him. Yet now you have forsaken him, and he will return to the old ways, I hope. This is immaterial. I am not here to pass the time of day with you, Romans. Let my companions speak, and then I can leave."

Caesar frowned for a long moment and then nodded.

There was a brief, slightly heated exchange in their own language between the chiefs and the druid, and then the dark eyed man sat high in his saddle.

"My lords the leaders and kings of the Ambiani wish to submit their land, their kin and all of their goods to the will of Caesar to do with as he sees fit, in the hope that the general will show them mercy and kindness and look upon them, not as enemy or victim, but as friend and ally."

The man almost spat the last words, the bitterness clear in his mannerisms.

"For myself, I expect nothing of the sort. I hear of what you did to the Bellovaci. Our pride is greater than yours, as, I believe, are our morals."

Caesar sighed.

"I understand your distrust and even your hatred. Druids are an insular and distrustful group. But I mean no harm to any who will join me in making these lands a safer place."

He ignored the sneer on the druid's face and Priscus was extremely grateful the general was facing away and could not see the look on Fronto's.

"However," the general went on, "I do not believe that you are an appropriate spokesperson or translator for these chiefs as you do not have their interests at heart. We have men of the Belgae with us who can translate."

He turned and addressed Labienus.

"Ask Galronus of the Remi to join us, will you?"

Labienus rode off down the column, and Caesar turned once more to the druid.

"You can consider yourself relieved of your task, or honour, or obligation, or whatever it is that keeps you here with the chieftains. Go wherever it is you wish to go, and I hope that we never meet again."

"I echo your hope."

The druid explained the situation quickly to the chiefs, gave the Roman column one long, hard, look and wheeled his horse to ride off. There was a pause for a few moments, during which the four Ambiani looked unsure and regularly turned to see the lone figure riding away down the valley. Fronto turned to Priscus.

"Druids and chieftains arguing and splitting up? I can't decide whether that's a good thing or a bad one…"

Priscus grumbled.

"Bad. That means he's going somewhere where they still hate us to stir them up."

The two men fell into a thoughtful silence until, a moment later, the familiar figure of Galronus cantered to a halt beside the commanders. He exchanged brief words with the four chiefs and they nodded.

"Good, Caesar. Chiefs know who I am. I translate for you."

The general nodded.

"Thank you. Firstly, please inform the Ambiani that I am grateful for their offer. I accept peace with them and accordingly would like to extend them the same terms as we came to with the Remi. That they defy their own druids to join us is an honour and deserves to be treated as such."

Galronus smiled and nodded, turning to repeat Caesar's words in the guttural language of the Belgae. As the four men listened, Fronto noticed a sag of relief among them. They had been unsure of Caesar's reaction and genuinely frightened for their people. Once again, Fronto wondered what Caesar had done to press so much fear into the Belgae.

The chieftains gabbled something in reply, and Galronus turned to Caesar.

"Ambiani very grateful for Rome's friend. They want agree all terms. They meet in council chamber this evening with officers to arrange details."

Caesar nodded.

"However, before we settle the legions for the night, I need to know the lay of the land, so that I can best decide how to proceed when we leave Samarobriva. What can they tell us of the surrounding tribes?"

Again, Galronus translated, and the four men entered into a deep, involved conversation for a short while as the Roman officers stood patiently, watching the exchange.

"Chiefs say" the Remi leader replied finally, "land east of here Viromandui land, but not just Viromandui there. They say big force east of here. In Viromandui land is army of them and Nervii. You get to east of Ambiani land and lesser chiefs there have more knowledge of Nervii."

Caesar frowned.

"The Nervii? So soon? I thought we would be able to forge more alliances and consolidate our hold before we had to face them."

Galronus shook his head.

"Nervii come south for Romans into land of Viromandui."

"What can you tell me of the Nervii?"

Galronus shrugged.

"Nervii hate Romans. Nervii hate Germans and Gauls." He laughed. "Nervii hate Belgae... Nervii hate everybody."

"So we'll not find anyone willing to treat with us to the north?"

Again the Remi noble shook his head.

"Nervii not trade with Gauls or Romans. No wagons go there. Nervii not accept foods or drinks. No wine or even beer among Nervii. They say luxury make men weak..."

"Sacred Bacchus" Fronto exclaimed to Priscus, but loudly enough to be heard by the staff. "We've come a thousand miles north only to find the bloody Spartans!"

There was a chorus of stifled laughs among the front ranks of the Tenth Legion and Fronto instantly regretted his outburst as the general gave them all a sharp look. Ah well. Let the men laugh now. Sounds like they would not be laughing when they met the Nervii.

"Nervii already condemn all Belgae for joining Rome. They threaten to kill any Belgae warrior who not fight Rome. You never speak to Nervii, Caesar. When you meet them, you fight."

Fronto nodded, more soberly this time. On the bright side, that sounded better: a straight fight. No political wheedling, no pretence, and no sieges; just two armies in a sea of grass, battering each other repeatedly until one was dead. A test of military might.

Caesar turned to the staff.

"Make temporary camp, gentlemen. Tonight we thrash out alliance details with the Ambiani, but tomorrow we march to meet the Nervii."

He became aware suddenly that the front ranks of the Tenth were listening intently. The general had almost forgotten the ordinary soldiers were there, and that would never do. One must always play to the crowd if one wanted to leave the arena a hero. He jacked his voice up a notch.

"We will take Roman law and power to the Nervii and, when we have defeated them, Rome will acknowledge us heroes and all the lands from the Mare Nostrum to the coast of Britannia will call us either ally or master!"

A cheer went up from the Tenth. You had to hand it to the sly old bastard… he knew how to work an audience. Only a couple of hundred men of the First Cohort in the Tenth would have heard that, but the word would pass and by nightfall his speech would be replaying in the mind of every soldier on the plain. And the bugger had been devious enough to include the phrase 'ally or master', both mollifying the Aedui and Remi in the column, and reminding them of the importance of their alliance.

The coming days would be interesting ones.

* * * * *

The legions had been on the move again for three more days, continuing eastward, through Ambiani territory and ever deeper into Viromandui lands. The scouts had been circling ahead of the column throughout the journey and what had begun as a positive, adventurous undertaking had now settled into the lull and quiet of an army that, having lost the initial impetus and lust for battle, was now settling into thousands of private worries about the coming conflict and the danger it brought.

Fronto shaded his eyes to stare once again out to the front. Somewhere out there, a hundred thousand Belgae were waiting to make minced meat of any Roman that came within reach.

A shape swam into focus. No... several shapes. On horseback.

Fronto frowned for a moment and then held up his hand to halt the column. He turned to the six tribunes marching along behind him. They looked generally unhappy about being relegated to traipsing along without their horses but, as Tetricus had pointed out to the rest of them, if Fronto was on foot, it would make them look lazy and feeble if they were to ride. Tetricus raised an eyebrow.

"Something up, sir?"

"Get word back to Caesar and the staff. Riders approaching."

The tribune nodded and turned to Priscus. Oh, he could run alongside the column and find the staff, but there was nothing in the world that moved faster than word of mouth. He told Priscus, who told his lead man, who passed the word back, and so on, through hundreds of lines of men until it reached the optio at the rear of the legion, who approached Caesar and, saluting, informed the general of the approach. By the time Tetricus could have reached the staff, Caesar and his closest consorts were already slowing as they reached the vanguard.

There was a tense moment as they waited for the riders to come fully into view. And when they did, relief swept over many a man. Three of Caesar's outriders with a native on a fourth horse. As they reined in, the general addressed them in a clear voice.

"What news?"

One of the scouts, a member of the Remi serving under Varus' auxiliary units, saluted and spoke in clear, though accented, Latin.

"This man is one of the Ambiani. He is wounded and was fleeing, sir. He is from a village on the banks of the Selle River."

Caesar shrugged.

"Yes?"

"The Selle is about ten miles north, Caesar. Not a wide or deep river, but it's the border of Ambiani lands. But, Caesar..."

"What?" demanded the general irritably.

"He says the Nervii are on the north bank awaiting us."

Caesar frowned.

"Did he say how many?

The man shrugged.

"I tried to ask him sir, but all he said was 'all of them'. And not just the Nervii. He says he saw the standards of the Atrebates and the Viromandui and several small local tribes." He said there are too many to count. Like a field of wheat."

The general nodded thoughtfully, though Fronto frowned.

"No sign of the Aduatuci?"

The scout blinked in surprise and Caesar turned to glare at the legate.

"The Aduatuci, Fronto? Explain?"

Fronto shrugged.

"They're a Belgic tribe from the east where…"

"I know who they are, Fronto! My tent is littered with maps in case you hadn't noticed. Why would you expect them?"

Fronto looked momentarily taken aback. Galronus had told him about the Aduatuci, but had not told Caesar? Was there a reason? Probably Galronus never got invited to briefings and never got asked. 'Can't drop him in it', he thought to himself.

"I heard the Remi levies talking. Apparently the Aduatuci are solid supporters of the Nervii. Closest thing they have to allies. They're very Germanic and they hate us. From what I've heard, I'm just surprised they're not here. Perhaps we should be worrying about where they are?"

Caesar fixed him with a long glance and then frowned.

"I'd love to know where you hear these things, Fronto. I have men posted specifically to listen for gossip among both the legions and the levies, and I never heard any such thing..."

'Interesting' thought Fronto. The fact that the general might be trying to infiltrate his own army had never occurred before, though it really should have done. He expected nothing less from the man.

"How sure are you of your facts, Fronto?"

"Positive, general. If the Aduatuci aren't with the Nervii, then they're either still on the way, or they're waiting somewhere to close the door behind us when we meet the enemy."

Caesar nodded.

"Thank you for your assistance, Fronto. Timely as ever."

The scout cleared his throat.

"There is something else, Caesar."

"What?"

"The man says he saw the enemy rounding up all the local farmers. All the women, children, old men and so on have all been sent north. They were herded in hundreds on carts. The only people for many miles in any direction are either us, enemy warriors, or occasional Ambiani farmers who have been dispossessed by the Nervii."

Caesar grumbled under his breath. Fronto turned to Priscus, an unasked question in his eyes, but the primus pilus merely shrugged.

The general leaned forward.

"All their noncombatants are beyond our reach, then?"

The man nodded.

"They've been taken past a swamp, Caesar, to the north. It could take many days and many lives to find a way through to them."

The general leaned back again and then turned to address the staff and senior officers together.

"Very well. We are ten miles from an enemy that outnumbers us and is prepared for us. They are so prepared, in fact, that they have withdrawn all noncombatants beyond our reach to remove any leverage and to clear out the locals that could cause trouble. This means we must be prepared for anything. If the Nervii have prepared this much, they have likely prepared more. We might encounter traps laid in the ground, siege engines, defensive works or anything. I have noted that the recent farms we passed have been harvested early; something I might note that none of my scouts seem to have spotted. An early harvest suggests to me that the Nervii have already removed any possible supplies we might draw from the natives, so we will be required to rely on the rations we carry, alongside anything that can be hunted and foraged as we travel. In other words, be alert and be prepared."

He turned back to the scouts and gestured Labienus to join them.

"Take the chief engineer from each legion, along with two alae of cavalry and tribune Tetricus of the Tenth. Move ahead to the river opposite the Nervii and check the ground very, very carefully. Find the absolute best position for a camp and I want to know every blade of grass around that site. Once you've done so, return to the column immediately. As soon as we get there, I want camp set up immediately. I need to engage them on good ground, but they outnumber us two or three to one, so I want a good defensive position ready to begin with.

Fronto stepped out from the front ranks of the Tenth.

"Caesar? If I might suggest, it would be worth having some of the Remi forward there too. They know the enemy and their customs, and they know the land better than us."

The general nodded.

"Have Galronus join the advance party."

Fronto nodded.

"I'd like to accompany them too, Caesar. I have an odd feeling about all of this."

Caesar shook his head quietly.

"No, Fronto. We're about to go to war against a very prepared enemy. Did you not hear what I've been saying? I want all of my legates to stay with their legions. I keep the same man with the same legion season after season for a reason, Fronto. You are tied to the Tenth like Balbus is tied to the Eighth. It makes you better officers and it makes them better legions."

"I'd still be more comfortable if I'd seen for myself what lay ahead, Caesar. As I said: I have a bad feeling."

The general laughed.

"Keep your old woman superstitions under control, Fronto. Sacrifice a goat if you can find one, but I want you to stay with the Tenth until we are sure of what's happening."

Fronto grumbled but stepped back into line.

* * * * *

Paetus frowned and rubbed his chin. Once, as a young officer out in Hispania during the revolt of Sertorius, he had grown a beard. It was just easier on campaign, and the Hispanics all seemed to be bearded anyway. But since he had achieved higher position and returned from that campaign, he had never considered it again, until now. He had made the decision to leave very suddenly in the middle of the nightlong session with Fronto.

He felt bad about that. Fronto was one of the few truly decent men in Caesar's army. He found himself thinking on that traitor Salonius from last year and wondering whether perhaps it was

Salonius who had been the decent one, and not Caesar. Clearly not Caesar, in fact. But anyway, he had decided he had to leave so suddenly and so urgently, fuelled by grief and drink, that he had pommel-bashed poor Fronto, dropped the sword and ran. Unfortunately, that had left him in just his tunic, breeches and boots with no weapons or armour.

Getting out of the camp had been ridiculously easy. He had fallen in at the back of a group of off-duty legionaries who were leaving the fortification with a pass to go visit the oppidum, where the locals had thrown their taverns open to their new Roman allies, and had peeled off from the group once beyond and in the dark.

Of course, that idiotic decision made under the influence of Fronto's wine had resulted in him standing in a clearing in some woodland perhaps three miles from the camp, rapidly sobering and wondering where the hell he was and where he was planning to go. He did not even know which direction he had been heading, until a short stroll through the woods had left him on the south bank of the river.

He had sat there, his mind gradually clearing, watching the dark waters rush by like his life seemed to be doing, and tried to think; tried to reason and decide what to do. Unlike many men of noble families in Rome, Paetus had actually fallen truly in love with his wife. Oh, he knew that her family were a liability; especially her idiot father, but she was truly a beautiful rose that had grown from that bed of dung. And while he could not care less what had happened to the old soak, Calida cared; he was her father after all, and for Calida's sake, he had looked after the fool. And now all of this had spun around and turned on him. He had lost his beloved Calida and the children, the future of the line. And three men were to blame.

Calidus, the old arse, with his drinking, debauchery and gambling, that had brought his family to the brink of total poverty and had landed him in debt to one of the most notorious gangsters of Rome. He was the man who had actually started this whole mess. But there was no way for Paetus to take out his frustrations on his father-in-law, who would now be feeding the crows in Rome.

Then of course, there was Publius Clodius Pulcher, the man who had given the orders to butcher Paetus' family. Clodius had to be punished, but that was a task for the future. The man was rich and powerful and guarded by many henchmen. Moreover, he was hundreds of miles away in Rome and currently far out of reach. Not forever though. By the waters of the Aisne, Paetus had vowed that one day he would find and kill the man. Personally. Enough to stare into Clodius' eyes and tell the vicious shit why it was that he was dying.

But there was a closer, more immediate problem. The third man. A man in whom he had placed his trust and the lives of his family, and who had turned around and betrayed him, leaving Calida and the children to die at the hands of thugs without lifting a finger when he'd had the opportunity and the resources to save them easily. Yes, Caesar must suffer too. But that, again, was a thorny problem. Seven legions now stood between him and Caesar. Had he been thinking straight that night with Fronto, he would have bashed the legate and then taken the sword to the headquarters and cut the general's throat there and then.

But then he would be executed and unable to revenge himself on Clodius. A complex problem. He would have to finish Caesar in Gaul first; get him back to Rome so that he could devote all of his time and the remaining funds of the family to bringing the two men down. But first he must stop Caesar, and that meant stopping Rome.

It went against the grain to betray his people but then, as he continually reminded himself, these were no longer his people. These were Caesar's people.

And so, his decision made, Paetus had crossed the Aisne, dangerously and alone at first light and, cold and wringing wet, had started to traipse north.

For the first few days, he travelled slowly and carefully, moving from copse, to wood, to gulley, to brush, being certain to avoid any signs of life. He knew the geography here as well as any Roman. During interminable briefings in Caesar's tent he had stared again and again at the maps of the Belgae lands. Straight north would take him through the lands of the Suessiones and then along the dangerous edge between the Bellovaci and the Remi. That in itself was perilous, but at least once he was ten miles north he would be free of Roman scouts, as Caesar travelled west to meet the Aedui.

Paetus' journey would cross two more rivers and then into the lands of the Nervii and their allies. He would make for Nemetocenna, the only oppidum important enough to be marked on Caesar's map, though to which tribe it belonged he had no idea.

And gradually, over the days of aching legs and stumbling through scratchy thorns, Paetus' resolve had hardened like a diamond, more and more; his confidence had grown, and he had begun to travel in open ground. As the sun rose and set time and again on his slow and uncertain journey, Paetus had changed, though he could not see it himself. His ample frame, fattened from years of living well and little or no exercise, had become already visibly leaner and thinner. Days of privation and non-stop movement had his muscles calling out for release, but he did not stop; daren't stop.

So now, the Paetus who stepped in the early evening into the circle of fire light, was bulky, but muscular, his clothes torn, stained and dirty and barely recognisable as Roman, let alone as military garments, his face part-hidden behind a thick beard and his hair tatty and unkempt. Calida would have shrieked had she seen him.

The barbarian warriors, four of them in all, sat around a central camp fire, their weapons driven point-first into the ground by their sides for easy retrieval, spears gathered in bundles and horses tethered to a sapling. The smell of roasting pork was almost tortuous to Paetus in his current condition, having lived for days now on only a few berries and a raw rabbit he had been lucky enough to take by surprise.

A twig cracked beneath his foot, and the Belgae lurched to their feet, twisting, their muscular arms hauling great blades from the dirt as they did so.

Paetus held both his arms wide, the flats of his palms facing the barbarians in a gesture, he hoped, of peace and surrender. By the Gods, they'd been fast. He was sure the one who grasped a spear could have turned, thrown and impaled him before he had even put his arms out. But not only were these Belgae sober and sombre, they were alert and shrewd. Their first moves had been merely preparation as they apprised themselves of the situation and decided whether the man should die immediately or not.

"I presume it would be a long shot to suggest that any of you speak Latin?"

The men crumpled up their faces in incomprehension.

"You speak Roman?" he translated himself, shrugging.

One of the men, presumably the leader of the scouts, frowned and asked him something in the guttural tongue of the Belgae.

"I don't understand" he replied, trying to make appropriate motions with his hand and his ear. "I need to speak to a leader? A man who speaks Latin?"

Incomprehension.

"Chief?" he asked desperately. "Druid?"

He sighed at the blank mask that was his companion.

"I was trying to get to the Nervii? To the oppidum of Nemetocenna?"

A spark of understanding glittered for a moment in the man's eye.

'Thank Jupiter' thought Paetus to himself and smiled in relief as the fifth and unseen Nervii scout hit him hard across the back of the head with a branch.

* * * * *

Paetus awoke slowly, his vision returning as the scene around him swam into focus. There was a throbbing in his head like he had never felt. He went to reach for the back of his head, where he suspected there was a wound, but discovered his arms were bound behind his back at both wrist and elbow. He focused.

He was lying on a stone-flagged floor covered with straw. It was dirty and itchy, but dry, which meant he was inside somewhere. Yes… he could make out the rectangles of light that were windows. And the breeze… of course the barbarians did not seal their windows with blinds and drapes like the 'civilised' Romans. There was heat from somewhere though. He stretched, trying to look all around and examine his situation. He was in a low building of some sort of wood and mud mixture, with a thatched roof. No sign of stonework here; the structure was apparently one room, roughly twenty feet by fifteen, and decorated only with rough timber table and chairs and a fire pit blazing away in the centre.

Though he was alone in the room, he could see the door, which rested over an finger width from ground level, leaving a thin line of light that displayed the shadow of the legs of a man, presumably on guard. Paetus wriggled, trying to find a reasonable position to stand, but the scouts had bound his ankles and knees as tightly as his arms. At least they had not gagged him.

"Hey?"

There was no answer. Paetus realised he had actually hardly made a noise at all. He drew a deep breath and forced his parched and unused throat to rasp out loudly.

"Hey you? Anyone there?"

There was a shuffle outside and conversation in the low, guttural tone of the Belgae. Paetus wished he had spent some time on this campaign learning their damned language, but then who knew he would need it? The shadow legs moved, leaving a straight line of light.

He lay there in the silence for a long moment wondering what was happening and was just considering calling out again when he heard the crunch of footsteps on gravel approaching the building. He tried to look as confident and defiant as he could, though truly he was beginning to wonder about the wisdom of his chosen course of action.

The door swung open, Paetus' pupils shrinking to pinpoints in the bright morning light that flooded in through the door momentarily before three figures blocked the aperture. Two men entered while the third remained outside, closing the door.

"I am not here as your enemy" Paetus announced. "You can loosen my bonds. I sought you out and have no intention of running."

There was another exchange in their tongue, and then the two figures settled, cross-legged on the floor before him.

One was a man decorated with bronze and gold and wearing the highest quality furs and wools, clearly a chieftain. The other... well even cross-legged it was clear the man was extremely tall and well built. But there was more... he was familiar. His long, grey hair and beard, the white robe, the flax circlet and the broadsword and staff. In a flash of déjà vu, Paetus recognised the druid that had addressed the meeting of chiefs at Bibracte last year. A Roman hater, for sure. That could go well for him... or it could go hard.

"What are you doing here, Roman?"

Paetus sighed and relaxed slightly.

"It is," replied Paetus sadly, "a very long story. But fortunately, the story and my motives are irrelevant. I am here to help you."

The chieftain asked the druid something in their language once again, and the druid replied. A translation, presumably.

"You are one of the Roman commanders. We are not stupid. The beard does not hide your stink. You are still alive because I am intrigued. Boduognatus here wants to skin you and fly your flesh from a standard when we find your legions. He is a simple man. So, unless you are done with your skin, talk to me, but talk fast and keep everything to the point. I must translate your words and speaking your tongue makes me retch."

Paetus nodded, uncomfortably in his current position, but he was fairly sure that nothing he could say right now would make them treat him like a man. That could change, though…

"I am no longer Caesar's man. I am Roman, yes, and I will not aid the Belgae in bringing war against Rome, but Caesar is not Rome. I believe it is not unknown for Celtic tribes to develop a 'blood feud' that causes constant war. Suffice it to say that Caesar and I now have a blood feud."

"You chatter like a mindless bird. I said keep it to the point. You say you hate Caesar. I believe the phrase you seek is 'the enemy of my enemy is my friend'? I have heard this said by Romans, and it shows, I might add, a very narrow view of motive."

Paetus shrugged.

"Whether you agree with it or not is not the issue. I am willing to help you destroy Caesar's army and drive him from your lands. It is in my interest that Caesar is unsuccessful in his conquest and is forced to return to Rome a failure."

The druid frowned.

"While I may say that I seriously doubt your honesty, and I have absolutely no reason to believe what you tell me, I will warn you that if you can interest us enough to make me prevent your death, Boduognatus here will certainly make sure of the truth of this. It will be extremely painful and possibly disfiguring, so I advise you if you are lying to tell me so now."

Paetus gritted his teeth. He had not considered the possibility that they would torture him. Possibly death if they did not believe him, but torture? He hardened himself. He was set on a course of action and to bring down Caesar he would give an eye and an arm if he needed. Nemesis would be with him.

"I am telling the truth. I have a plan of attack that will give you enough of an edge to take Caesar's army and crush them into the dirt. Are you willing to listen?"

The druid held another brief conversation with the Nervian chieftain, and then turned back and nodded.

"Speak."

"Caesar has seven legions, as well as auxiliaries and cavalry."

"We know this. We know all about the legions and their commanders and the traitorous Belgae and Gauls who serve with them to the detriment of their own peoples."

Paetus nodded.

"Do you know the marching order?"

The druid frowned.

"You are so strictly controlled that you even march in a set order?"

"Yes." Paetus smiled. At last he was getting somewhere. "That is how you can beat Caesar. It will all depend on the land. You will have to find a barrier that they must cross; probably a river. When they reach it, Caesar will have five legions to the front. Each legion will be marching eight abreast, with the Tenth Legion being the vanguard. Behind them will come the Eighth, then the Ninth, the Eleventh and the Twelfth. After these legions will be the commanders, with the bulk of the cavalry contingent. After them is the baggage train, which is long, slow and cumbersome. And behind that, the Thirteenth and Fourteenth legions, the rest of the cavalry, and the few auxiliary units attached to them."

"I fail to see how this helps us."

"Wait," Paetus said with a predatory smile. "It is simple. When the column reaches an obstacle that requires the army to stop for a while, the front legions will begin to construct a camp. Gradually, as the other legions catch up, they will join in and then enter the camp. If you place warriors in cover somewhere to the sides and wait as you count off the first five legions and the baggage train comes into sight, you have three advantages."

He looked intently at the druid, who was now listening, rapt. Good.

"Firstly, the front legions, who are the five veteran ones and are your most dangerous opponents will be trapped against the river and surrounded by the Belgae. Secondly, the only reserves are a way back beyond the baggage train and will take time to catch up and engage and, even when they do, they are newly-raised legions who are not experienced in true warfare. Moreover, they are Gauls by birth and perhaps could be persuaded to revolt if the circumstances are right."

The druid had an unpleasant glint in his eye now. The chief was asking him something, but the druid ignored the man, waving a hand at him dismissively. Paetus was impressed. He knew these priests held a powerful place in the northern societies, but to have the authority to silence a powerful chieftain with just a gesture? If only the druids could be persuaded to the Roman view. Still, he had almost won them over.

"And thirdly, and most importantly for both you and I, the command staff will be there, jammed between the Twelfth Legion and the supply train. And if you time things exactly right and are very, very disciplined, like a Roman army would be, you could get Caesar. Cut the head from the snake and watch the body wither, my friend."

He saw the druid flinch at those last words and worried for a moment whether he had just ruined his whole argument by insulting the man. But no. He sighed and relaxed as the druid turned to the chief and they had a very heated conversation. Finally, the huge man turned back to Paetus.

"If what you say is true, we could end the Roman invasion of our lands in one quick move. A decisive battle. Probably at the Selle River. The Romans are busy putting down the cowardly Bellovaci dogs right now and will then turn north. They will have to cross the Selle at some point and, when they do, we can be waiting for them."

Paetus smiled and nodded.

"A river they must cross? Yes. That would be it."

The druid frowned.

"What do you ask in return for this important knowledge, Roman?"

Paetus smiled.

"Three things. Three very small things."

He watched the man's face carefully.

"When the battle is concluded, and the Belgae are free, I will be freed and given food and horse to return to Rome."

The druid shrugged noncommittally.

"Also, when you attack, I be allowed to watch. If Caesar is to die, I want to watch his blood spill to the earth."

The druid nodded.

"I can do better than that, Roman. If this comes to pass, I will put you in the front of the attack with them."

Paetus opened his mouth to object, but realised that arguing would be of no use with this man.

"And thirdly, when it is over, and I am to leave, you give me Caesar's head to take with me."

The druid held a brief consultation once more with his chieftain and the two nodded.

"On the condition that all of this plays out as it should, we will agree to your terms. However, before that may happen, the chieftains must all agree on the same course of action which, given this information, is likely, but far from certain."

He smiled unpleasantly and gestured to his companion.

"And, of course, before the matter is taken before the chiefs, Boduognatus here must be sure of the authenticity of the information."

Paetus started and turned to look at the chieftain, who had slowly, and with a horrible rasping noise, pulled a long and surprisingly jagged knife from its sheath.

He swallowed nervously.

'For Calida. Nemesis protect me.'

Chapter 14

(Approaching the river Selle)

"Dolabra: entrenching tool, carried by a legionary, which served as a shovel, pick and axe combined."

"Bacchanalia: the wild and often drunken festival of Bacchus."

The column waited, shuffling its feet in anticipation as the officers, having gathered at the head of the column, went into a last tactical discussion before the army passed the last half mile to the chosen site.

"Caesar, I'm still concerned about the absence of the Aduatuci," Sabinus said quietly.

Fronto nodded. The same thought had gone through the mind of every senior officer in the army. He stared at Caesar.

Fronto had wrestled with his conscience over the matter of Paetus several times since the night the man had vanished. While he was still angry with Caesar over the betrayal, now was not the time for a confrontation. The entire army was in dangerous enemy territory. Besides, Paetus had not stuck around to make his point, but had disappeared, presumably back to Rome.

He cleared his throat.

"I've spoken to both the Remi and Bellovaci auxiliaries serving with us. They all say the Aduatuci are the ones to watch. The Nervii are vicious and tough, but the Aduatuci are much the same and cunning besides. What if the Aduatuci are sweeping round behind us?"

The general nodded.

"I'm hoping that the Aduatuci are either late, or are not coming at all to the aid of the Nervii, but you're both right. We do need to be prepared. I want a few changes made. As soon as the column begins to arrive at the Selle, have the cavalry sent across the river to harry the Nervii and their allies."

The general cleared his throat and vaulted from his horse. As the other mounted officers joined him, he began to draw in the flat dirt with a handy stick.

"This is the lay of the land according to our scouts."

He drew a wavy line across the patch and tapped it.

"The river. Only about twenty feet wide here and not more than about three feet deep. Crossing it should not be a problem, but that means it's not a problem for them either."

He marked out several areas with hatching on the near side of the river.

"There are a lot of areas of copses and scrub, but the scouts have checked them out and they're empty and too overgrown to hide any real number of men."

He drew a set of arrows to denote slopes.

"There's a gentle decline down to the water at this side, and then a low hill opposite with areas of woodland around the crest. My scouts estimate around a hundred thousand of them on the other side of that rise in a camp, which suggests they've been there a while."

He drew a large mass there.

"Presumably they either believe they can keep their numbers hidden from us, or perhaps they're worried about our artillery range and are keeping out of direct line. Either way, so long as they remain safely behind that hill, we have time for the entire column to arrive and to set up camp here."

He drew a square on the slope descending to the water.

Fronto nodded.

"It's a plan, general, but there's a few suggestions I could make too."

"Go on?"

Fronto sniffed. "Well, if you're sending the cavalry out front to deal with the enemy scouts across the water, that means the staff will have no escort and protection. You'll be a lovely little target riding along slowly between the legions and the wagons. One good archer could effectively remove the high command."

Caesar blinked.

"You think they actually could try such a thing?"

Fronto shrugged.

"Who knows, but I think that, given the odds here, we ought to play it as safe as we can. My suggestion would be to get the staff distributed among the legions, yourself included. That way, not only are you much harder to target, but you're well defended too. And it might give the lads a bit of a boost to see the staff alongside them. Especially on foot."

Caesar frowned for a moment and then nodded.

"It's a good idea, Fronto. See to it."

"And the other thing," Fronto said, glancing back over the lines of men, "is that when the legions begin to make camp, usually we have a screen of cavalry and our men have time to rearm if threatened. With the cavalry away, we can't afford to have all of our men busy moving earth sods and not easily armable. I would suggest that each man keeps his armour and helmet on while they work and their shield and weapons within arm's reach. I would like to know that every man can defend himself at short notice."

Caesar frowned.

"You're being uncharacteristically careful, Fronto?"

The legate shrugged.

"This engagement's making me nervous. Something about it makes my skin itch. Nemesis is trying to tell me something."

Caesar smiled.

"Then tell her to speak up."

There was a chorus of nervous laughter; Fronto's nerves were beginning to spread to the other officers.

"Very well," Caesar nodded. "All that we can do, we will do. It's in the hands of the Gods now, and let Venus who, as you all know, is my grandmother," more genuine laughter this time, "let her protect us all."

Fervent nods around the circle of men.

"Let's get the final phase of this march underway, then. Right, Fronto. Where do you want us?"

Fronto shrugged.

"I don't suppose it really matters. There are, what?" he performed a quick head count. "There are twelve officers who need to distribute among the legions, ignoring the legates. That's two a piece and perhaps one a piece with the Thirteenth and Fourteenth at rearguard."

Caesar nodded.

"I will join the Twelfth at the rear of the legions, just before the baggage."

The rest of the officers went quiet and looked at each other expectantly.

"Oh for the love of Venus. What is it with you men and these new legions? Sabinus? You go with the Thirteenth. They saved your life. Cicero? Go with the Fourteenth."

He smiled a grumpy smile.

"Can the rest of you decide what legion to travel with or does uncle Marcus have to smack some bottoms?"

Sabinus laughed.

"Just as you say, Marcus. Sorry… uncle Marcus."

With a laugh, the officer mounted his horse once more and rode off toward the rear of the column. After brief discussions, the various officers split up and moved to their new positions, those stationed further back riding, while Labienus and Brutus walked their horses forward to the Tenth alongside Fronto.

As they reached the legion, Labienus accosted one of the legionaries in the front line.

"Take our horses back to the baggage train and then return to position."

The legionary saluted, took the reins, and strode off down the line of men with the three officers' horses.

Labienus settled into position with the tribunes at Fronto's shoulder. Brutus stood next to him, smiling calmly. Fronto grimaced.

"All ready? We're the vanguard."

Brutus, in his late twenties and fresh faced, squared his shoulders.

"I look forward to it, Marcus. No offence, Labienus, but being stuck in staff meetings was not what I was looking for when I joined Gaius."

Fronto raised his eyebrows. Nobody referred to the general by his praenomen.

Labienus frowned.

"What do you mean?"

"Well, I was looking forward to leading a legion. Thought I'd get a chance to play legatus and actually take part, but Caesar's a very distant cousin and his wife coddles me. Between my own family and Calpurnia, Caesar daren't put me in a dangerous position. They keep me trapped and tied up in red tape. I'm actually quite looking forward to this."

Fronto grumbled

"It's still a bad idea. This is not going to go well, I tell you."

Labienus laughed.

"Give it a rest, Fronto. I can see his point. I haven't actually been in close command of a legion myself for many years, since the Cilician campaign in fact. It'll do us good."

Fronto had to laugh.

"How can we possibly lose, with this much enthusiasm?" He turned to the Tenth's lead cornicen.

"Give the call to march. Let's get there and see what Nemesis has in store for us today."

The musician saluted and blew a complex series of notes that was picked up by the cornicens of the individual centuries throughout the legion and then the other legions to the rear. With an unstoppable gait, the men began to march.

Fronto relaxed a little as the familiar pace and noise settled around him like a comfortable blanket. At least here and now things were normal, expected, and he knew exactly what to do.

Smiling, he took a deep breath, inhaling the heady scent of the summer wildflowers. Soon all he would be able to smell was blood and steel, so he carefully registered every facet of that smell and filed it away in his mind for reference. Funny really, he had not realised how bad his nose was until Balbus had broken it again and Florus reset it. He smiled. Good things came to you in curious packages some times.

He would have to give Florus a gift when this was all over.

* * * * *

Varus reined in alongside Fronto. The cavalry had been riding in force alongside the Tenth for the last leg of the march, their number stretching out across the land to either side as far as Fronto could see. It really was quite impressive.

"Time to go, Fronto" the commander said, his voice even and professional. "Our scouts say the river's just over that rise. We need to get on ahead and cross the water to give you time to build the camp. Do it quickly though. There's several thousand of us, yes, but there are a hell of a lot more of them."

Fronto nodded.

"We'll be ready as fast as we possibly can, Varus. Don't do anything too brave and stupid, though. If you land in serious shit, regroup with the legions."

Varus returned the nod.

"Good luck, gentlemen."

"And to you."

In a manner that ought to have been noted by those members of the legions distrustful of their newly-raised Gaulish brethren, the cavalry were arrayed as a loose mass of men, with the few regulars in Roman red mixed in among their Gallic auxiliary counterparts, as though they were considered equals.

Now, however, the cavalry commander gave a quick hand signal and his mounted cornicen blew out a series of calls and, like an organised sea of men and horses, the vast array of cavalry around the head of the Tenth moved with intricate precision into their new formations. The auxilia became separate alae once more, with the sparse regular cavalry settling into smaller units between them. It was a spectacle to see, like the ridiculously expensive mechanical toys that Greek merchants sold in Rome.

Moments later, rather than a mass of horsemen gathered around the Tenth, three rows of tightly organised cavalry alae trotted ahead of the column. At a further signal, they broke into a run, leaving the bulk of the Roman force behind in a cloud of dust.

Just as Fronto and the officers of the Tenth crested the rise in view of the enemy and began the descent to the site chosen for the camp, Varus and his cavalry reached the water and splashed across it.

As reported by the scouts, the north bank of the river rose in a slope almost the mirror image of the one to the south, though a little higher and crowned with areas of woodland. At the top of the hill a few Nervii on horseback waited in one of the more open spaces and, as soon as Varus' men hove into view, vanished over the crest.

The cavalry ploughed into the river, the water spraying high to the side of each man, churned and thrown by their hooves and soaking the whole force, and Belgae warriors appeared over the top of the hill. On the Roman cavalry splashed, reaching the far bank and climbing from the water quickly, reforming into units as soon as the ground allowed.

With yells of command from the officers, the cavalry charged once again in formation up the slope, more and more of the Nervii and their allies pouring forth over the crest and issuing from the areas of woodland across the summit.

With cries to a variety of Gods, the Romans and their auxiliary counterparts closed the distance to the enemy, Varus in his accustomed position at the front edge of the charge. He smiled. They may be brave, but the same mistakes were inevitable in every damn battle with every damn Celtic army. No discipline; no preparation. It all came down to the personal bravery and skill of each individual warrior. How could they ever hope to…

Varus' thoughts came unstuck with terrifying suddenness as the Roman charge, sure of their prowess and their superiority, met with the hidden pit traps carved in the side of the hill by the waiting Nervii in the preceding days and disguised with wicker screens covered in leaves and dry grass.

Varus' horse, his pride and joy for five years of campaign, snapped its neck instantly as the front legs disappeared into the hole and the head hit the turf opposite. Varus, his mind reeling hopelessly, was thrown from the four-horned saddle and hurled twenty feet or so up the gentle slope. His world exploded in a white-hot burst of pain and shock. As he cartwheeled over and over before coming to a painful halt, he saw flashes of his men disappearing into the disguised pits alongside the screams of men and horses both.

With a crash, he came to rest. Experience and professionalism took over, and he found his feet, despite the pain of his various cuts and grazes, what felt like a dislocated right shoulder, and almost certain concussion. He had fared better than some of the men he could see as he stumbled, spinning in pain and confusion, to his feet. His eyes scouted the turf nearby, searching for the sword that momentum had snatched from his grasp. No sign of it, but his gaze latched onto the discarded blade of one of his companions. He stumbled towards it and bent to retrieve it with his left arm. The first wave of cavalry had now passed, some number falling foul of the hidden pits, but many more passing them and engaging the enemy. The second wave thundered up behind and slowed enough to avoid falling foul of the same obstacles as the first.

Varus turned and tried to take in the entire situation. This was one almighty screw-up… Fronto had been right with his bad feeling. These Nervii knew exactly what they were doing and were more than prepared. What should have been a cavalry charge that shattered the resolve of the front line of the enemy had, instead, turned into a bloodbath, the surviving members of the first wave of attack now being systematically unhorsed with long spears and, where that was not possible, the Nervii and their allies were simply butchering the horses beneath the riders.

Varus spun around at a loud 'crack' and fresh horror overcame him. To the left and right the enemy had pushed aside wicker screens at the edge of the woodland to reveal massive tree trunks lying along the crest of the hill. A rolling tree trunk could do enough damage, but Varus realised with cold dread that the architects of this nightmare had left the sharpened stumps of all the branches attached, creating a rolling mass of spikes that even now had begun its inexorable descent toward the river. The second wave of attack foundered instantly, the officers shouting directions that were being entirely ignored by the men. Those who could were making for the far left and right flanks to try and evade the rolling nightmares. Others crowded into the killing zone at the centre, where they were butchered by the enemy infantry as they neared the crest.

Varus turned to start crying out orders and found himself face to face with a warrior at least a foot taller than himself and as much again broader across the shoulder. The barbarian raised a huge Celtic blade to strike down at the cavalry officer.

The commander lifted his unfamiliar, stolen blade in an arm unused to wielding a weapon in an attempt to block, and the sheer force of the blow ran down his arm to the shoulder, numbing the joints. He flexed his right hand and tried to roll the shoulder, wondering whether he could change sword-arm, but that one was most definitely out of action. Staggering back, he almost dropped the blade again. Lights and colours were still flashing behind his eyes. He really was in no fit state to fight.

The man raised the great sword once again, this time for a massive overhead strike that would likely shatter Varus' own before continuing its descent and separating him in two. In a flash of instinct, the cavalry commander lashed out with his foot, delivering the man a hard blow in the groin.

Shock suddenly filled the man's eyes, yet, while Varus waited for him to drop the blade and double over, the barbarian gritted his teeth and fought the pain, once more raising the great blade.

'What the hell were these people made of?' he thought to himself as he stepped back. The man advanced on him again, the sword still raised high. Another step back. Varus was beginning to panic. He had no idea what was going on behind him and what he was backing towards, unwilling as he was to take his eyes from his assailant.

There was the distinct possibility he might walk straight back into the pit down which his poor horse had gone…

He smiled grimly.

"Alright, you bastard. Come with me."

As the barbarian growled and once more stepped close enough to bring the blade down, Varus slipped out of his reach yet again. The man was beginning to become vexed and yet, the commander had to give him credit, he had not only overcome Varus' unpleasant attack, but had held enough discipline to keep his blade raised, rather than madly swinging down at a man who was keeping just out of reach.

Back another step; back another step; back another step…

And suddenly Varus' heel came down with nothing under it. Had he been unprepared, he would have toppled back into the pit, but that was not the case; he was well prepared. He regained his balance as the great barbarian smiled a horrible smile at him and begun to swing his blade downwards.

Ignoring the agony in his arm, Varus threw himself forward and into a roll, directly between the man's legs. Lucky he was such a big fellow, really. The warrior staggered, trying to counterbalance the momentum of the swing that was now suddenly carrying him forward into the pit by arching his body backwards.

With a vicious smile, Varus came out of his roll, standing poised. Years of falling from horses had trained the commander exactly how to control a fall and a roll. In a matter of a heartbeat he had gone smoothly from standing in front of the warrior to standing behind him.

The Nervian swordsman glanced in surprise over his shoulder.

"In you go."

With hardly any force, Varus gently pushed at the point between the man's shoulder blades. With a squawk, the great warrior disappeared into the deep hole. Varus turned and looked at the chaos around him. It was odd. The Belgae had not pressed the attack, but were now picking off those cavalry who were still fighting at the top, and thrusting their long spears into the wounded Romans on the ground. They were making no attempt to advance down the slope toward the river.

Perhaps they were fighting a defensive strategy? Waiting to see what the Roman infantry across the river would do.

Realising that the space around him was opening up, he scoured the grass until he found a fallen cavalry spear, which he collected before turning and heading back to the pit.

The warrior, bruised and irritated, was using the carcass of Varus' horse to start his climb out of the hole.

With immense satisfaction, Varus reached the edge, raised the familiar thrusting spear, and brought it down as hard as he could. The leaf-shaped blade entered the barbarian in the 'V' between shoulder and collar bone and pushed deep through the interior of the man's torso, reappearing just above the other hip in a spray of blood.

The man actually looked astonished. Again, Varus found himself wondering what these Nervii were made of.

Leaving the spear protruding from the dying man as he uttered his rustling death rattle, Varus grasped his sword and took in the situation with a professional eye. Fronto had obviously been prepared to support the cavalry for, though the legions were already heaving sods of earth around across the river, the auxiliary units of archers that seemed to be the legate's pet units these days had taken position on the far bank and were loosing off missiles that were, despite the incline and the distance, remarkably accurate, ringing off Belgic helmets and thudding into Nervian shields.

Gritting his teeth he tried to locate all the cavalry standards. Much of the first wave had been destroyed by the pits and rolling logs. The latter, only two trees, had left a swathe of horrific destruction down either side of the hill before splashing into the water and floating off downstream. A sizeable group of the second wave have fallen foul of the rolling menace, but most of them and the third wave had escaped unharmed and were either milling round in confusion on the near bank or rallying to their standards to one flank or the other.

Varus glanced quickly at the line of Belgae. He wanted to call them Nervii, but they might not be. He could not tell the difference between one Belgic tribe or another. Who could? The enemy were shouting taunts at the cavalry but were holding their solid line. There was something expectant about the way they worked, almost as if they were about to leap into action some way. He had to do something about this. There was nothing he could do to save the wounded being calmly executed at the summit, but he had to do something.

Jogging down the hill, his mind still hazy and pained, he fixed on the dragon standard of Galronus of the Remi. Thank Mars... a familiar sight. He ran on and, as he approached, the auxiliary officer hauled on his reins to control his prancing mare.

"Sir?"

Varus coughed with the effort of his run.

"We need to do something; need to give Fronto time to get the fort built, and I want to see what the Nervii are up to behind that crest."

Galronus nodded uncertainly.

"More traps yet? We attack, we die?"

Varus shook his head.

"They've used up their traps. If they had anything else, they'd have used it by now. They're planning something, and we can't give them time to carry it out. Fronto's got to get that camp built. Sound the rally. Get all surviving units back here and formed up. You!"

He gestured at the nearest regular cavalryman.

"Sir?"

"Go help Fronto with the camp. I need a horse."

The man looked uncertain for a moment and then nodded, dismounting. As Varus vaulted into the saddle, the trooper ran back down the hill and waded into the water, relief now flooding over him that he would not have to try that ascent again.

As the cavalry units formed up on the call, Varus sat tall in his saddle.

"I know no one's particularly keen to try that again, but we need to give the legions time to set up the defences. So… we're going to charge, but we're going to do it like this: Two columns, five riders across. The only place we know there aren't pits are where the logs rolled down, so we'll use those paths as a guide. We charge up those narrow corridors and then, once we're thirty feet from the enemy, separate out one horse width and allow the second row to filter in so that we become a ten-man front. Watch out for those spears though. They're deadly with them. So hang your sword on the saddle horn and go in with your own spears. Anyone who's no longer got their spear, take rear positions in the formation. Use the spears and try and pick them off without getting too close. Once we've taken down the front spearmen, you can draw your swords and go crazy. Alright?"

There was an affirmative shout around him. The atmosphere was aggressive. While nobody relished the thought of that charge once again, the general anger over the Roman losses was fuelling the need for revenge.

"But don't get carried away. Listen out for the call from your cornicen. The fall back will be given either when Fronto gives the signal that he's sorted, or we are so deep in the shit we have to. Be heroes, but not suicidal ones."

* * * * *

Fronto gave the cornicen a nod as the Tenth descended the slope to the river Selle. The engineers that had been sent out with the advance party of scouts had already placed poles with flags to mark the positions of the wall corners, along with the gates and, as the musician blew out the orders, the Tenth at the front of the column dispersed as they arrived on site and moved left to take position on the western perimeter where the professionalism of the Roman army took over. The engineers dropped their shield and pilum somewhere easily retrievable and began to mark out the edge of the rampart and ditch with string, while their assistants ran along the lines with groma setting new flags to mark drainage culverts and so on.

Even before the lines were measured, the ordinary soldiers collected their dolabra from their pack and began to dig the ditch in positions where they knew it to be without markings, and to pile the excavated earth behind on the line of the future rampart.

By the time the Eighth Legion began to arrive on the scene, the Tenth was already at work on the western ditch. At a second series of calls from Balbus' command, the Eighth marched straight ahead and began to work on the northern line. More calls could be heard over the next few moments as the other legions gradually arrived on the scene. The Ninth flanked Fronto on the western wall, curving round to the south. The Eleventh joined Balbus to deal with the north, the most important line, facing the enemy. Finally, the Twelfth appeared to deal with the eastern rampart.

The section toward the enemy would be completed first. By the time the baggage train and then the Thirteenth and Fourteenth arrived, most of the work would be complete.

Fronto watched for a while with a professional and marginally-interested eye. It was always fascinating in a way to watch engineers at work, no matter how many times you'd seen them do this before. But right here and right now, Fronto felt about as useful as a eunuch at a Bacchanalia. A legate's duty was to set the overall orders for his legion. Once it came down to carrying out those orders, the centurionate took over, and all he had to do was stand around and look pretty. Well he knew he did not look particularly pretty, so it was time to find something useful to do.

He turned to Labienus, who was examining the ground across the site.

"Can you take charge here?"

"Take charge of what?" laughed the staff officer. "I'm about as important as you right now."

Smiling, Fronto turned and strode out toward the water, ahead of the works. Assuming things were proceeding according to plan, he had concentrated on the Tenth and had barely glanced across the river. Now though…

"Oh shit!"

He turned and pushed his way back past the surprised legionaries, hacking away at the ground and already making their mark, a foot-deep, three foot wide trench opening up along the northern and western lines. He spotted Labienus and Brutus deep in conversation.

"Varus has hit trouble!"

The two men turned and squinted past the works. The slope was too gentle for them to easily see over the heads of hundreds of working legionaries.

"Can't see. What's happened?"

"He's in the deepest of shit."

Brutus frowned.

"Do we mobilise the legions?"

"No." Fronto frowned. "We need to get the camp built as soon as possible. I'll deal with it."

Running along the line of the ditch past surprised legionaries, he finally spotted what he was looking for: a whole group of white-garbed men standing around, looking bored. The auxiliaries had no place in the construction of a camp and were in position on the periphery, not on guard so much as keeping out of the way.

"You!"

Fronto ran up to the nearest man, a Numidian archer.

"Sir?" the man replied in heavy-accented Latin.

"Go and tell every auxiliary archer officer you can find that legate Fronto needs them down by the water."

The man looked nonplussed for a moment and then saluted, turned, and ran off. Scanning the group, the legate spotted prefect Galeo tapping his fingers on his sword hilt irritably.

"Bored, Galeo?"

The prefect turned and smiled when he saw Fronto. He opened his mouth to reply, but Fronto beckoned.

"Got a job for your lads. Come with me."

As Galeo gave the order, he ran to join Fronto who was already jogging back down the slope. Moments later the archers were catching them up. One of the benefits of light, unarmoured auxiliaries was the speed with which they moved. Fronto stopped just outside the line of working men and pointed.

On the opposite hill, carnage was taking place. As Galeo followed his gaze, he saw a great tree trunk descend, flattening everything it rolled across, wiping out a group of panicking cavalry and then disappearing into the river with a splash.

"Where do you need to be to reach them?"

Galeo shrugged.

"We can hit them from near bank."

"Then do it!"

As the prefect ran forward with his men, who began to stretch strings and release deadly missiles high across the opposite slope, Fronto turned and looked back and forth between the camp and the cavalry mess. Several of their shots were striking home at the Belgae, and the threat alone seemed to be making the enemy pull back to their initial line.

"Sir?"

He turned to see Decius approaching with his archers. Other units were pouring through the lines of legionary workers.

"Get your men to the bank and concentrate your missiles on anywhere the Nervii are looking like they're about to break."

The prefect nodded.

As he turned back to the works, other prefects rushed past with their units. There was no need for further commands. The officers could see where they were needed.

Fronto grumbled under his breath. Pit traps, rolling logs, disciplined lines. These were not simple barbarians. These bastards had tactics. Possibly they'd even learned from what the Romans had done to the Belgae at Bibrax? He'd had a feeling of foreboding about today, and now it was being borne out. Just from an initial glance across the river, he guessed that Caesar had lost a quarter of his cavalry in one horrible move. Bloody ridiculous. And they'd hardly seen any of the enemy yet. There were maybe five hundred men on that ridge. And no standards or chieftains.

Turning to the men working behind him, he spotted Pomponius, measuring something incomprehensible.

"How long 'til the basic defences can be up?"

Pomponius looked up in surprise.

"I'd say about half an hour, sir. It's an enormous camp, but there's five legions working on it."

"I have a feeling it's going to be a close thing at best."

* * * * *

Paetus smiled as he adjusted the strange, yet surprisingly comfortable bronze helmet on his head and re-slung the extremely heavy Gallic blade at his side. He had asked for armour and been laughed at. Only the nobles got armour, apparently. Not the ordinary warriors. In fact, as he had learned in the days leading up to this, their warriors often went into battle naked as the day they were born, save the whorls and swirls and other marks they daubed on their skin.

He drew breath sharply as one of his many now-healing knife wounds caught uncomfortably with his baldric. He had assumed they were trying to frighten him by telling him they would put him in the front line of the attack, but here he was, hiding beneath the eaves of the wood, surrounded by thousands of smelly, sweaty, often disturbingly naked, Nervii. He had learned since receiving the 'trust', such as it was, of the chieftains that the Aduatuci were due to join them but were late and may not make it here before the Romans. He looked up at the sun. Too damn late now, for certain.

The cavalry had already met with the Viromandui and the Atrebates on the hill and Paetus' carefully-worked surprises had devastated the initial Roman charge. Well, they'd met the visible Viromandui and Atrebates, anyway.

But the Nervii lay waiting to spring his main trap.

For a long moment, Paetus paused. He was a Roman, though dressed and armed like this few would realise it. It was his duty and pride to march, and fight, with the legions and yet here he was, about to bring about their downfall; cause the vicious deaths of thousands of soldiers and all in the name of… no. Not in the name of revenge, he reminded himself… in the name of justice, and that was what Rome should stand for!

I could call off the attack. One shout and I could save the legions and ruin the Nervii.

Just one shout.

But that would save Gaius Julius Caesar too.

* * * * *

Varus nodded in satisfaction. The second charge had been what he had hoped for the first time. The two columns of cavalry bellowed up the safe zone where the logs had rolled down and met the forces of the Belgae just below the crest, engaging in careful, spear thrusting combat. Once in combat, the two forces expanded out sideways to meet up, creating one heavy front against the barbarians. And then the most unexpected and peculiar thing happened.

The Belgae on the ridge dropped their spears, turned and fled. Around him, riders cried out in triumph and raced over the summit, the officers yelling encouragement. But Varus paused. Something was not right here. These men would not flee. Not after what they'd managed to do. They knew damn well they could crush the cavalry if they worked it well.

Varus's eyes bulged.

"Retreat!"

He tried to locate the cornicen but the man had joined a group heading over the crest. Once more he yelled for a retreat at the top of his voice, but the triumphant cries of the men and officers drowned him out and only a few surprised troopers nearby heard him.

"For the love of Mars, retreat!"

His heart thumping, he carefully edged his mount up so he could see over the crest in the bare area between the woodlands. His men were chasing down the fleeing thousand or so infantry from the ridge, but there was no one else there. Where was the army of a hundred thousand or more?

"Oh no…"

Guttural cries all around and behind him filled him with dread, and he stared. Large groups of Belgae came running out of the woods to either side, carrying something. Each group bore between them, sweating and cursing, a fence or screen made of sharpened stakes, tightly bound together, almost like a caltrop that was six feet high and twelve long. As he desperately wheeled his horse in panic, the Belgae began to drop their horrible screens into lines, creating one long defence that would clearly prevent the cavalry from returning to the battle.

"Rally! To the camp!"

As the few hundred men he could see turned and rode back downhill, Varus scrunched up his eyes and let out a string of violent expletives. This was the problem with using Gallic auxiliary cavalry. No matter how much you tried to drill legionary discipline into them, they still had that mad Celtic need to go racing into battle and run after glory and victory. That was why most of the few regulars were still here with him and had not crossed the summit alongside the auxilia.

Well, the cavalry were lost to him for now. Thousands of men were cut off and it would be some time before any of them managed to get back. If the Belgae had planned this much, damn certain that they'd made sure all easy routes of return were sealed.

As his mind raced, he heard a roar and his bones filled with cold dread. The copses and areas of woodland around the hilltop had not just been home to a few careful surprises… they'd harboured to the whole bloody Belgic army. What the scouts had deemed impenetrable woodland had apparently been cleared of undergrowth and had hidden thousands of warriors. From either side of him, a sea of Belgae swarmed out from the eaves and thundered down the hill towards the river.

Fronto would never have time to finish. The legions were lucky, in fact, that he had suggested they worked in their armour, for they'd only have time to grab their weapons and shields and then this mass of men would be on them. 'Hell, I hope Fronto's seen them.'

He squinted across the shallow river valley to the camp workings.

"Oh hell, no!"

The legions were clearly aware of the danger and were already grasping weapons and dropping their entrenching equipment, but that would not save them. Already the Eighth, Ninth and Tenth were getting into position where they had been working, but the

Eleventh and Twelfth were a different matter, and had only just begun their work.

Beyond them, the lines of wagons were slowly appearing over the crest of the hill and somewhere far behind them were the other two legions.

But what filled him with dread was the sight of other huge groups of Belgae rushing out of the trees to either side of the camp; trees that had been swept only a few hours ago by scouts and deemed impossible to hide men in due to the deep undergrowth.

Either the scouts had been horribly mistaken, or the Belgae had worked damn quick.

Varus smashed his fist on his pommel in anguish. He was being ignored by the attackers pouring down the hill between him and the river. He and his few remaining companions presented no great threat, but that huge charging force of Belgae now stood between him and the rest of the army.

Chapter 15

(Construction site by the river Selle)

"Corona: Lit: 'Crowns'. Awards given to military officers. The Corona Muralis and Castrensis were awards for storming enemy walls, while the Aurea was for an outstanding single combat."

Publius Sextius Baculus, veteran of four great campaigns, recipient of the corona castrensis, the corona aurea and the corona muralis and Primus Pilus of the Twelfth Legion, spat on the floor and lifted his vine staff, bringing it down on the back of the legionary's legs, hard enough to leave a stinging pain but no damage. The centurion smiled grimly. The lad should be grateful he did not use the other arm; there was a dolabra in that one!

"Every rock you drop slows the camp down, so every rock you drop gets you another belt!"

The legionary bit his tongue to prevent himself yelping, saluted hurriedly and collected the large fallen rock. Baculus, never entirely trusting any other man to do the job correctly, had taken charge of the procurement party from the Twelfth himself.

A century of men, his century no less, had split off as soon as they arrived on site and left the rest of the legion digging and heaving sods of earth, while they moved hurriedly to the eaves of the nearby woodland to collect supplies.

Fifty or sixty of his men, under the control of his optio, had begun cutting poles and stakes to supplement those that would be arriving in the wagons shortly; were probably being unloaded as he pondered, in fact. He could see pairs of men now, carrying heavy lengths of timber between them and heading back towards the camp.

The rest were gathering rocks the size of a man's head and piling them up on shields to carry back. The rocks would be utilised to line drainage culverts in the rampart and various other sundry uses.

He smiled again. Last time they'd made camp, he had left the job to one of his junior centurions and they'd brought back what looked like saplings and gravel. Never delegate something important, as he always said.

He scanned the woodland and nodded with satisfaction as he saw men carrying boulders back toward the heaps nearby.

A flicker of movement caught his eye as he turned. He squinted into the woodland. There it was again. Just a little flash of movement back in the woods. No one would make anything of it. It could easily be an owl disturbed by the work, but Baculus had survived on the front line of more battles than he cared to remember and this was something wrong. Without waiting to confirm his suspicion, he swept his vine stick, cleared his throat and bellowed: "To arms! Rally to me!"

Around the eaves of the woods, the men of the Twelfth, drilled almost obsessively under Galba's command the preceding winter, reacted with perfect military precision. There was no panic; no shout of alarm. The men merely dropped the timber and rocks they were carrying and pushed their way through the woodland to get back to their centurion. Baculus nodded with satisfaction and, as his men began to congregate around him, squinted into the woods once more. This time he could see several signs of movement. And they were getting nearer. Blue. Blue meant Celts. Blue trousers... blue skin.

"Form up on me!"

He spotted the men coming out of the woods and did a rough head count. He could see around fifty or more men. Given that the century had been under strength for most of the year, he was not missing many of his men.

"Can't wait around for dawdlers, lads. As soon as everyone you can see is here and armed, we fall back to the legion; slowly and calmly, like... there's rabbit holes and all sorts around here and one man falling could end it for all of us."

"What is it, sir?" a legionary asked. "I can't see anything."

"Belgae, lad. And lots of 'em. Back in the woods, but getting closer."

He glanced around at his men. The last stragglers, being hurried along by his optio, arrived and collected their swords and shields, tipping the piles of rocks off and to the ground.

"Fall back at a slow march!"

The First Century of the Twelfth Legion formed up in solid military fashion, and began to step slowly back toward the defences, a couple of hundred paces behind. As they passed from under the last foliage and out into the open, the first of the Nervii burst forth from the deep woodland. Behind him, Baculus could hear the cries to arms going up around the camp. It could be that the Twelfth had seen the century in full kit backing away from the trees, but it was much more likely, given that a large group of Belgae were rushing forward from these woods, that there were many more around the battlefield. This could be trouble.

As they moved carefully back across the open ground, a veritable sea of Celtic warriors poured forth from the woods.

"Double pace now, lads."

As the unit backed rapidly across the open ground, Baculus risked a moment to glance around and take in the entire situation. They would make it to the lines before the Nervii reached them, but only just. There must be thousands upon thousands of the bastards in these woods, so the camp construction would have to be abandoned. They could not hope for relief from the two Gaulish legions either… they would not get here for a while yet. There'd be no help from the other four legions or the cavalry either. From his good position on the slope, Baculus could see the enemy pouring out of the woods opposite where they'd keep Priscus and Grattius' legions busy. And the cavalry had gone. There were thousands more barbarians pouring down that slope to cross the river and keep the other two legions busy. The Twelfth was screwed; on their own.

A momentary glance and he realised that one of the larger groups of Nervii were making for the near end of the baggage train as they were being settled at the top end of the incomplete camp. Nothing he could do about that. Have to leave that to the Thirteenth and Fourteenth when they arrived and hope there was some baggage left.

The Twelfth had rearmed, but the units had become shuffled and mixed as the men had worked hurriedly, taking any position where a task needed to be done. Now they were rushing around trying to locate the standards of their unit in the mass of men. Baculus growled and took a deep breath, bellowing loud enough to be heard all along the rampart.

"Forget finding your own units. Fall in to the nearest standard and form up!"

On the embankment, he heard legate Galba echoing the command to the men. Not a bad leader, the legate. A bit fanciful, as they all were, but sensible and with enough brains to defer to his centurions when need be. He was grateful, as the First Century finally neared the Roman line, with thousands of screaming Nervii hot on their track, that the legate had had enough foresight to open up a space in the lines for Baculus and his men to fall into.

He could almost smell the breath of the fetid bastards as he reached the embankment and rejoined the Roman line. He cursed for a moment. He had been so damn busy making sure his men were prepared, rearmed and observed military etiquette, that he had not had time to find his own sword and shield. Idiot. They were lying in the eaves of the wood back there.

With a growl, he looked down at his hands and frowned. He gave the vine staff an experimental swish, shook his head sadly, and threw it on the ground, hefting the heavy dolabra in both hands, trying to decide whether the Nervii would enjoy the pointed side or the wedged blade side most.

And suddenly the Nervii were on them. They travelled with more speed than the Roman legions, most of them unencumbered by armour and, a surprising number, even by clothes. Jabbing with long spears or swinging large blades, they rushed the shield wall of the Twelfth.

"Hold the line!" Baculus yelled.

Suddenly the world around him exploded into action and noise, Nervian warriors stabbing and hacking, trying to land killing blows between and around the shields of the defenders, while the legionaries, fighting alongside men they hardly knew from other units under unfamiliar standards, held the line like the consummate professionals they were.

Suddenly, in a series of events that lasted mere moments, the attacking mass of the Nervii opened up just to Baculus' left and, in the narrow space this afforded, a naked man, armed with two wicked looking knives ran forward and leapt onto the legionary to his left. The barbarian was dead moments after he landed and before even the gap in the Nervii had closed, but his plan had already worked. Though the legionary who was the target of his insane attack dispatched the blue-painted warrior as he scrabbled at the shield, the man had driven his two blades deep into the leather and wood and, as he died, still gripping the knives, the sheer weight of the body tore the shield from the soldier's grasp.

This gap in the wall became the sudden focus of dozens of Nervian warriors, who leapt into the fray, trying to kill the man and, more particularly, the centurion next to him. Spears jabbed and blades flashed as the legionary desperately tried to turn the attacking weapons aside with his sword. A spear thrust caught him in the shoulder and pushed him back. Baculus growled once again.

"Reform the line!"

As his order was carried out, the wounded man being hauled back through the line and the second row of men edging forward to try and reform the wall, Baculus stepped out in front of his men. The sheer audacity of the move, walking out from the defensive line without even a shield or sword, took the Nervii by surprise enough that a small circle opened up round him.

"Right, you fatherless sons of whores… who's first?"

A laugh went up behind him as the line solidified and the wounded man was removed from combat during the brief pause in fighting afforded by Baculus' surprising act. The Nervii jostled for position, all tensing ready to attack this madman, but none of them quite willing to be the first to try.

Baculus grinned and hefted his dolabra.

"My turn, then."

Lifting the heavy multi-purpose tool above his left shoulder, he gave it an almighty swing, blade-edge first. The close press of the Belgae meant that none of them had time to duck back out of the way and the powerful swing smashed through arms, faces and weapons in a complete arc, Baculus being almost unable to stop the weapon, such was the momentum.

A noise went up through the warriors that was half groan of dismay and half howl of fury. Six barbarians collapsed in the front row, clutching broken wrists or hands or dead on their feet with shattered skulls.

Baculus had expected them now to close in and take him but, to his astonishment, the circle around him widened. That would not last long though, and he was an easy target out here at the front. Sure enough, the mood among the enemy changed rapidly, and a spear thrust from the crowd caused him to lurch to one side or risk a head wound.

"That the best you've got?"

He raised the dolabra over his right shoulder to swing, and the warriors pressed back again away from this insane Roman. He let loose and took another swipe with the edge of the weapon, this time extending his arm as far as he could. The tool curved round in a wide, unstoppable arc, smashing more heads and limbs. A roar went up from the enemy and finally they pressed forward to kill him, trampling the latest half dozen victims who were still collapsing.

A sword thrust pierced his side below the armpit, and he winced for a moment as the iron pushed through his muscle and grated along his ribs. With a growl, he let the dolabra drop and grasped the hilt of the blade, wrenching it back out of his flesh. The warrior whose sword it was blinked in surprise as the apparently immortal Roman officer pulled the hilt from his hand and, with an almost negligent flick cast the heavy blade vertically into the air, catching it by the handle as it swung around and then hefting it professionally, backing away from the thrusting spears towards the line of his men.

With a grin of malice, he swung the great blade, taking out two more of the Nervii, as the shield wall behind him opened up and he was pulled back into the safety of the legion. Every time he took a deep, ragged breath, the pain in his ribs ripped through him like fire and he struggled for a moment to deliver commands before giving up and allowing the men to ferry him through the lines to the rear.

Legate Galba shook his head in wonder as the optio in the rear line helped the wounded centurion from the mass of men and then turned back to his work. There was a huge rent in the chainmail and leather armour at the man's side, and gouts of blood were issuing from it.

"Centurion Baculus, I don't know whether to congratulate you or have your mind looked at. That was unbelievable."

Baculus grunted.

"It's like fighting a bunch of girls, sir."

He turned and looked up and down the line. The Twelfth was holding well, but the pressure was increasing and the numbers of the enemy were a little discouraging from this vantage point on the slope.

"I see there's some trouble up by the standard of the Firth Cohort. Regards, sir, and I'll be off."

Galba stared at him.

"You're bleeding to death, Baculus. You're done for now… get to the surgeon."

"Bugger the surgeon, sir."

With a salute and without waiting for Galba's flapping mouth to make a sound, the primus pilus turned and strode off toward the wavering standard, pausing further down to collect a sword and shield that lay unclaimed on the grass. Galba shook his head and beckoned to one of the Capsarii who waited at the rear to deal with minor wounds.

"Follow the centurion and when he stands still long enough, stitch that wound of his up. He might not stop, but I'd like to stop him bleeding to death in the meantime."

The capsarius saluted and ran off after Baculus.

Galba frowned and shook his head yet again. This was starting to look a little dangerous. He could only hope the other legions were bearing up as well as his own, or better. He scanned the lines for his commander and spotted Caesar alongside Cicero and Pedius, remaining back from the line of combat and in deep conversation. For a moment he considered joining them, but truly, he had his own problems.

* * * * *

Fronto watched the screaming tribesmen running from the eaves of the wood to the west. He had been quite lucky really. He had been in a position to view the disaster that had befallen Varus and the cavalry on the north bank and, the very moment he saw the Belgae pouring out of those woods and down toward the river and the working legions opposite, he had known damn well there would be more on this side waiting to close the trap.

He had run back to the wall, yelling 'to arms', much to the surprise of the other officers of both the Tenth and the Ninth. Soldiers were retrieving weapons and shields before their centurions could issue further commands and, by the time the first warrior had left the shelter of the trees, the Ninth and Tenth were formed up on the partially-constructed rampart, fully equipped and ready in a shield wall.

Good job, really, given how many of the bastards there were. Fronto glanced around at the situation and shook his head, then turned to Labienus.

"We've got it best, really. There's more of them heading for the centre than here and the Twelfth's on their own on the other wing. I just hope the wagons get settled in quickly so that the Thirteenth and Fourteenth can support us..."

His voice tailed off.

"The wagons."

Labienus shrugged.

"They won't be trying for the wagons. There's no point at this stage."

Fronto shook his head.

"I know, but there's more. Look!"

He pointed to the higher end of the slope, where the wagons were arriving, now hurrying as fast as they could to get into position in the camp, safe behind the legions. Labienus followed his gaze and noticed with dismay further groups of Belgae beyond the camp's defences, heading down toward the staging area where the wagons were gathering at the planned south gate of the camp. The number of warriors in that attack was smaller, but they were coming from both sides and converging on the wagons, which were undefended and behind the main fight.

"What the hell are they doing? The wagons are immaterial right now."

Fronto shook his head more irritably.

Clever little sods aren't after the wagons. They know that's where the command party was. Bloody good job you all split up among the legions. You'd all be dead before we could get to you."

Labienus nodded, staring.

"How do they come up with such things? None of the other Belgae seem to have been half as prepared."

Fronto growled.

"Galronus said the Atrebates, the Aduatuci and the Nervii were the ones to watch. He was bloody right."

He frowned and rubbed his temple.

"Someone's got to deal with them. Can you take command here? Lead the Tenth?"

Labienus nodded. "Of course, but what will you do?"

Fronto smiled.

"I'm going to take the Sixth Cohort only and go save the wagons and guard our rear."

Labienus shrugged.

"Sounds dangerous, but good luck."

Fronto grinned.

"Titus, we're in the middle of a battle. Danger's kind of the norm, don't you think?"

He scoured the rear ranks of the Tenth and spotted their chief centurion.

"Lucretius? Call your cohort to order and follow me!"

The centurion, a veteran with snowy-white hair that made him look considerably older than he truly was, saluted, and began shouting orders to his subordinates. Moments later, he strode back from the assembling cohort.

"What's up, sir?"

Fronto pointed up the hill to where the enemy were already now converged on the carts, which had come to a stop, the column being held up by the attack.

"Trouble with the wagons. We're going to save the day, as usual, Lucretius."

The centurion nodded and turned to his men.

"At the double-time, to the wagons! Prepare to charge on arrival!"

Fronto smiled and drew his sword. As the legionaries began to half-march, half-run towards the wagons, he fell in beside them. He and Lucretius picked up their pace to reach the front of the relief column as they ran. The centurion grinned at his commander.

"Did you know that the soldiers think you actually look for trouble to get involved in, sir?"

Fronto laughed.

"It's not a long way from the truth, Lucretius."

As they closed on the enemy, they could see in much more detail what was happening. Two columns, each of perhaps seven or eight hundred warriors, had broken cover after the main attack and made straight for where they assumed the staff officers to be. Having arrived, they had either discovered their error and decided to attack the wagons instead or, more likely, had not yet discovered, in the large staging area of wagons and riders, that the command unit were not present.

Next to Fronto, Lucretius bellowed "Attack!"

The cohort roared as they swept past the officers. Fronto was momentarily taken aback, expecting the traditional slowly advancing shield wall. But then, Lucretius was right. Adapting to the situation, a shield wall would be no good here as the warriors swarmed around and over the wagons, killing their drivers and the oxen drawing the vehicles.

Taking a deep breath and raising his shield protectively, Fronto shouted a quick prayer to Nemesis and, aiming for the nearest wagon's assailants, ran forward.

There was no strategy to the attack. As men to both left and right struggled, the result was, for Fronto, a foregone conclusion. There were maybe fifteen hundred Belgae here, but there were five hundred Romans, and they were more disciplined and better equipped.

Fronto reached the wagon and saw a Nervian warrior with a spear thrusting up at the rider, who was squirming in his seat, trying to avoid the vicious point. The legate ran up behind the attacker and drove his gladius to the hilt in the man's back just below the right shoulder blade. The body went limp and fell to one side. As it did, Fronto juggled his sword into his shield hand and grabbed the falling spear. With a grin, he passed it up to the wagon driver.

"Pick a few off!"

The man grasped the spear gratefully and began to thrust down with it into the warriors at the far side as Fronto returned his sword to the correct hand. There was a noise behind him, just a faint grunt, and pure instinct led the legate to duck to the left and spin. As he did so, the warrior that had been closing behind him thrust out his sword into the empty air where, a moment earlier, Fronto's kidney had been.

The man lurched forward in surprise as his blow foundered, and Fronto stepped neatly in from the side and drove his blade into the man's neck just at the base, above the man's tunic. It took some effort to haul the sword back out of the man as he collapsed, dead instantly, his spinal cord severed.

Fronto glanced around. There were a number of men nearby who presented ready targets and were not currently occupied by the legionaries, who were working their way efficiently toward the wagons.

He lunged for the nearest man, obviously one of the wealthier warriors, for he could afford a helmet and was fully dressed in good quality clothes. The bearded barbarian took a stance that surprised Fronto, reminding him more of the crouch of a gladiator circling his opponent than a Celtic warrior in the midst of a pitch battle.

"Oh, come on!"

He stabbed at the warrior with his gladius and the man desperately turned the blow aside with his large, unwieldy Celtic blade. Fronto readied himself for a counter-attack and stared in astonishment as the warrior turned and fled among his own men.

"What the hell is going on?" he asked of nobody in particular.

The situation here was rapidly coming under control. The Nervii who had attacked the column of carts seemed to have lost heart and, as Fronto casually dispatched another warrior, they broke and ran; not from the field, but to join their comrades who were pressing the legions. Fronto looked up at the man on the cart who was wielding his spear with great relief.

"I presume you can handle things now?"

"Yes sir."

Fronto nodded.

"Get all the wagons marshalled here and as soon as each one's in position, get the drivers and staff armed and in position to protect them from any other attack."

The soldier saluted.

"Oh," Fronto added as an afterthought, "and send someone back past the train to the Thirteenth and Fourteenth legions and tell them to pick up the pace. Tell them we've engaged the Belgae and we're in the shit. They need to join the Twelfth on the right flank as soon as they're here, alright?"

The man nodded and turned to his companions to begin calling out the orders.

Fronto nodded, satisfied with the situation at the rear, and located Lucretius and his standard bearer and cornicen.

"I think we're probably done here. The rearguard will be here shortly, and I doubt there's any more enemy units lurking around the rear. We should get back to the Tenth."

The centurion nodded and gestured at the cornicen, who sounded the recall. Pausing only to dispatch the few surviving fallen Belgae, the Sixth Cohort rallied to the standard and formed into centuries. Lucretius gave further orders and the cohort turned and moved off at a fast march to rejoin the fighting on the left flank, with Fronto running alongside.

As they reached the rear ranks of the Tenth, Fronto was surprised to see Labienus and Brutus in conversation with Caesar. He growled under his breath.

"Lucretius, get to work."

The centurion saluted and then filtered the Sixth Cohort back into the lines of defenders, bolstering the numbers, while Fronto marched irritably across to the group of officers.

"Problems?"

Caesar turned to him and blinked.

"Not problems, Fronto. All my senior officers are with the legions and I need to be apprised of the situation."

Fronto growled.

"The situation is that we're in the shit. Labienus is supposed to be commanding the Tenth while I was away, not reporting to his commander. The situation's a bit perilous for wandering around the battlefield and passing the time of day."

Caesar glared at him and ground his teeth, but before he could speak, Fronto pointed back in the direction from whence the general had come.

"The Twelfth are seriously outnumbered, hard-pressed, and have no support. In that position, morale plays as much a part as strength, numbers, or discipline. How much of a morale boost do you think it gave them to see their commander desert them and wander off across the battlefield to go chat to another legion?"

Caesar's opening mouth closed again. For a moment he looked astonished, and slowly his anger was replaced by grudging acceptance.

"What do you suggest, Fronto?"

"If you hold any hope of pulling our arses out of the fire today, we need the Twelfth to hold until the relief arrives. It might do them some good if all their officers pitched in and helped. In fact, we've got enough officers here, really. I could use Labienus, but Brutus might be of use over there."

Caesar nodded slowly.

"I agree, yes. A show of bravery and 'mucking in' from the officer corps. Come, Brutus."

With the briefest of nods at Fronto, the general and his young companion strode back across the battlefield towards the beleaguered Twelfth Legion. The legate watched them go and then turned back to Labienus and rolled his eyes.

"Shall we get back to the real work?"

Labienus smiled at him.

"Only you could get away with scolding your commanding officer like a naughty child, Fronto. You do make me laugh sometimes."

* * * * *

Paetus stared at the man in front of him. He had known Fronto for years and the legate had not even recognised him. Oh, certainly he was wearing Belgic gear and he had grown a beard, but surely that could not disguise him that easily?

The plan had failed. That was clear from the moment the two ambushing units of Nervii had left the woods. The wagons had rolled into view and the warriors had charged, but there was no mounted command unit, just the rear end of the Twelfth Legion and then the carts. The bastard had changed the marching order. How did he know?

It had not stopped the Nervii and their allies anyway. They'd missed the opportunity of removing the commanders but, given the amount of preparation that had gone into this attack and the level to which they and their allies had now committed themselves

there was no point in changing plans or calling off the attack. They outnumbered Caesar's army and had the advantages of surprise and preparation. They could win this anyway, without taking down the staff.

The disappointment to Paetus was crushing. Now he would have to stay through the entire battle to make sure that Caesar did not escape alive. Tricky, though, as it was possible that, even when the Nervii won, they would take issue with Paetus for the failure of his plan. Still, he could worry about that when it happened. Right now, he had other issues…

Fronto.

The legate of the Tenth faced him with gladius and shield like a true soldier of Rome, unstoppable and efficient. Paetus felt the panic rise in his throat. Oh, he had trained as a soldier, of course, but for many years now his days and nights were a constant flow of comfortable chairs, scrawling figures on wax tablets, and planning from behind a desk. It had been years since he had even drawn his sword and the recent exercise he had undergone could not replace the fighting skills and instinct he had long since lost.

He dropped into what he hoped was a combative stance. Since Fronto had not recognised him, he might get away with this. Hell, he really did not want to kill Fronto, even if he thought for a moment that he could. Fronto was one of very few people in Caesar's army who actually seemed to care.

The legate grinned at him, and the smile was horrible. Paetus could suddenly understand how Fronto achieved his reputation and respect. It was a wonder the enemy did not flee just at his scowl.

In a blur of movement, the legate lunged at him. It was like watching a snake uncoil he was so damned fast. In a desperate move, Paetus swung his sword at Fronto's attack and managed by some miracle of luck to knock the blade away. He stared for a moment at the legate and, turning, ran like a cowardly child from a bully, back to the west.

Around him, several other Nervian warriors were now fleeing the scene, though they were doing so with determined looks and there was evidently no fear or cowardice involved as they ran to regroup with their countrymen attacking the legions. Paetus, unnoticed among their number, ran on and, as the warriors turned and joined the Atrebates who were busy swarming over the defences of the Ninth and Tenth, the frightened prefect continued on past them and into the woods from where the attack had been launched.

* * * * *

Crispus pushed his way through the lines of his men, the noise around him deafening as the Eleventh fought for their lives among a press of screaming, bloodthirsty warriors. The legate, educated and bright, thin and well-groomed, was currently a sight that would have sent his mother into fits.

Fronto's influence was clear to those around him these days. His tone had matured as he deliberately fought to keep his mannerisms military and forthright, where his family had always taught him to hold himself as an orator. He now moved with the deliberate and powerful certainty of a soldier. But mostly, the change was clear in his appearance.

The bronze cuirass, embossed with the head of Medusa, now carried more than a dozen dents, one of which had actually punctured the metal. Some of the leather pteruges hanging from his shoulders and belt were missing or cleaved off halfway. His tunic was smeared and dirty, and one sleeve hung raggedly down, his sword and shield bore the rents, dents and viscera of a warrior in the fiercest of battles.

And the men around him cheered as he passed; a commander so close to, and beloved of, his men that Crispus could do no wrong. He grinned at a centurion as he pushed past.

"Just like harvest, eh, Publius?"

The centurion laughed.

"Reapin' time, sir…"

Crispus continued on, his eyes fixed on the crimson plume among the helmets ahead.

"Balbus?" he called, and the heavy-set legate of the Eighth turned toward him as he raised his shield to ward off a blow. The older officer, himself involved in the front line of combat, noted the approach of his peer from the Eleventh and pulled back from the worst of the fighting, allowing the line around him to close up.

A moment later, the two officers had retreated from the men desperately defending the low, partially-constructed rampart against the tremendous force that had swept down the hill and across the river. Even though that central army was the largest concentration of the enemy on the field, Crispus could see the reserves of the Belgae waiting on the north bank to see where they were needed.

"It would appear that these barbarians will not break, unlike the Belgae we've faced before."

Balbus nodded.

"They're a hardy lot, and I think we'll have to kill the lot of them. There'll be no surrender." He sighed. "My main worry is that this could go either way. There's a lot more of them than us, but we've got experience, equipment and formation. It's worryingly possible that we'll all just keep hacking at each other til there's nobody left on either side."

Crispus nodded.

"We've got to do something. We have to turn the tide and start pushing them back rather that just holding them off."

Balbus shrugged.

"There's precious little hope of that. The Twelfth are pinned down and unlikely to hold unless the reserves arrive, and we're facing a large force, with another behind it. Even Rufus and Fronto are too beleaguered to do anything."

The younger legate shook his head thoughtfully.

"Not necessarily. That's why I pulled out of the line and came to find you. I've been scanning their ranks, and I noticed the standards."

"What about them?" Balbus asked, intrigued.

"Those facing us are not Nervian ones, but the wolf standards of the Viromandui."

"How in the name of Minerva do you know that?"

Crispus shrugged.

"I spent some time with the Remi auxiliary officers early in the campaign, talking to them about their countrymen. It seemed wise."

"Alright, so we're facing the Viromandui then."

"Mostly, though there are, I believe, Nervii supporting them; and the reserve across the river are Nervii. I don't know what tribes Fronto and the others are facing, but that's not my point."

"Then what is?" Even Balbus, a tremendously patient man, was beginning to become tetchy with the loquacious young legate.

"Well, my friend, as our centurions wear crests for identification and are accompanied by the signifers, the Belgae leaders wear gold and armour and tend to be found around their own standards."

Balbus frowned.

"So we know where their leaders are, then."

Crispus smiled.

"And if we know where their leaders are, and we can manage to get to them, there's a possibility that we can break the spirit of the tribe."

Balbus' face split slowly into a wide grin.

"The Twelfth can't do much with that information, but we have to tell that to Fronto and Rufus. Come on."

The two legates almost ran across the empty interior of the camp toward the Ninth and Tenth, who were deeply embroiled in combat.

* * * * *

Varus stared down the slope at the horrible events unfolding across the water. The legions were clearly in trouble. As he watched, he saw a unit pull away from the flank and run to aid the baggage train that had suddenly come under attack. He growled and looked around himself. He and the thirty six surviving cavalrymen on this side of the Belgae's barrier had rushed to the wooded edge of the slope during the initial confusion and hidden themselves from the view of the enemy.

Thousands of Belgae lay between them and the river, let alone the legions beyond. There were still thousands of cavalry beyond the hill where they had charged blindly, but the part of the Belgic reserves that had formed the fence from the spiked barriers were now manning it with long spears to prevent Varus' men from rejoining the battle.

He could not see what was going on, but he knew his officers. By now the alae would have reformed out of sight over that hill and would be moving either east or west along the river to find a way to bypass the reserves, cross the river, and rejoin the battle.

But in the meantime, that left thirty seven horsemen in a perilous position, hidden from the view of the enemy reserves and cut off from their compatriots. He ground his teeth and nudged the trooper next to him.

"Did you see that?"

"Sir?"

Varus pointed at the far side of the battlefield.

"Those men who attacked the wagons and got driven back? Most of them rejoined their nearest group, but a few fled into the woods."

"I didn't see sir. But they'll eventually get caught. Even hiding in the woods." The man sighed. "Unless we lose, of course..."

Varus grunted.

"This is the narrowest and shallowest stretch of the river for miles, yes?"

The man nodded. "That's what I heard, sir."

"Think we can find another way across?"

The trooper looked unsure. "Who knows, sir? But we could have a look? Better than sitting here and waiting for them to see us."

Varus nodded. That was certainly true. They were hidden here, but for how long?

"Pick a direction. Upstream or down?"

The trooper shrugged.

"Down, I guess, sir. That way, if we can get across, we might be able to find those runaways you saw."

“Then downstream it is.” Varus turned and addressed the assembled riders in tones just loud enough to hear but quiet enough to not provoke the interest of the Belgic reserves.

“Alright lads. We’re going to pick our way through these woods. I know it’ll be tough, but if the Belgae can hide great log contraptions in there, there’s likely room for us to work our way through. And once we reach the far side, we’re going to descend the slope to the water’s edge and head downstream until we can find a way to cross.

There was a silent chorus of nods. None of the men wanted to wait in the eaves of the wood to be spotted by wandering barbarians. As quietly as possible, the three dozen cavalrymen began to step their mounts through the woodland.

The trees were well spaced and the undergrowth almost entirely removed or trampled down by the Belgae. The going was surprisingly easy, as long as they kept their heads down and watched where they walked.

The journey seemed to last forever, each man holding his silence and most holding their breath. Gradually the sounds of desperate battle faded with distance and the dampening effects of the trees, until Varus decided they’d travelled far enough west and turned to move down the slope. All was eerily quiet, save the whispering of the leaves and the rustling of the occasional creature.

The trooper behind Varus risked speaking in a low voice.

“What do we do if we break cover and they’re there waiting for us, sir?”

Varus shrugged.

“We fight like madmen, and we die like Romans.”

The gradient gradually increased as they descended and slowly the trees began to thin out until finally Varus stepped his horse out onto open turf and looked up to the blue sky. Behind him the other troopers quickly and quietly left the woodland, dropping down towards the water.

The commander frowned as they approached the barrier, and he examined the river with an eye to its crossing. It was deeper and faster here; that was clear from one look at its dark, glassy surface. But it was also too wide to jump. They would have to find another place further downstream to try.

He scanned the riverbank, but further ahead the woods came down to the water’s edge and barred the path to cavalry. He growled.

No way forward and no point in sneaking back up through the woods to where they had been trapped in the first place. They'd have to make their way slowly back along the water's edge toward the battle and hope they could find a crossing point before they ran into the Belgic reserves.

Today was turning out to be a very bad day. Maybe Fronto was right, placing his faith in Nemesis, rather than Fortuna.

Chapter 16

(Battle of the Selle)

"Pilus Prior: The most senior centurion of a cohort and one of the more senior in a legion."

Fronto grinned at Balbus and Crispus.

"It's stupid. It's dangerous; even suicidal and totally stupid."

Balbus smiled at his friend.

"You like it."

"You're damn right I like it. We've got to do something to break this, or we're going to end up just overwhelmed by sheer numbers."

He frowned.

"Are you going to try the same thing?"

Crispus shook his head.

"I don't think so. We've got the reserve force facing us as well. If we break the Viromandui, they're going to turn and run straight into the Nervian reserves and then we'll end up fighting both lots at once. We have to wait until you succeed, then you can get behind the reserves and we can push the Viromandui. If it all works we can end up surrounding them and pushing them into the river."

Fronto nodded.

"Then I'll see you when it's over."

As his two fellow legates turned and headed back toward their struggling legions, Fronto strode across to the small force of reserves from the Tenth who were standing tensely waiting to plug any desperate gaps.

"Find the primus pilus and centurion Velius and tell them I need to speak to them immediately."

As men saluted and pushed off through the crowd to find the officers, Fronto spotted Labienus and waved to him. The commander strode over.

"I was thinking perhaps I ought to be getting my hands dirty, Fronto, rather than standing here like a fifth wheel."

"I've a more important request for you. I'm about to do something suicidally reckless, and you need to take command of the Tenth again for a while."

Labienus frowned.

"What are you up to?"

Fronto laughed. "I hate repeating myself, so I'll wait until Priscus and Velius are here. I can see them coming now."

The two centurions pushed their way out of the press of men and marched up the gentle incline to the waiting officers. Fronto looked them up and down. Hardly an inch of them was not dented, dirty and covered in blood. Velius strode with his hands behind his back. Fronto frowned and, as the centurion came to a halt in front of him, he drew his hands out in front.

"Can I give you a hand, sir?"

Fronto and Labienus stared at the severed appendage in the grizzled veteran's hand as Priscus exploded into laughter. Velius grinned and cast the article to the ground nearby before straightening to attention.

Fronto sighed.

"Your sense of humour leaves something to be desired, Velius. I've got a plan."

Priscus raised an eyebrow.

"And naturally, whatever idiocy you have in mind includes us?"

The legate nodded.

"I've been speaking to Crispus, and he's come up with an idea. We can see the standard of the enemy. He says they're the Atrebates on this flank. Don't know how he knows that, but he does. There are three groups of standards out there, and that means their leaders are likely beneath those animal heads. We think that maybe, if we can wipe out their commanders, we can break their spirit and make them run. The standards are relatively close to our lines, so we'll have to go straight head-on, rather than try to flank them and come from behind."

Priscus shook his head.

"It's bloody dangerous. It relies on men actually getting through the enemy, surviving long enough to kill what will likely be tough royal bodyguards, and then the Belgae actually being sensitive enough about it to run. Even if we succeed, it might just make them angrier."

Fronto nodded.

"That is a possibility, as is death. But the thing is: we're screwed anyway if we don't do something. Three groups, each led by one of us, while Labienus takes over the Tenth."

The commander stared.

"The whole reason we have a chain of command, Fronto, is so that vital officers can delegate this kind of thing to the people who are trained and paid to do it."

Fronto grinned.

"There are precisely three people in the Tenth that I trust to pull off this kind of manoeuvre, and I am one of them." He turned to the chief training officer of the legion. "I'd have liked to choose the most dangerous men we have, Velius, but there isn't time. What do you think?"

Velius shrugged.

"Pick any century. They're all full of madmen. You're infectious, you know."

Fronto nodded.

"Then pick a century each. Velius, you take the standard on the far left; Priscus, the centre. I'll take the right, as I want to signal Balbus and Crispus when we're done."

Labienus shook his head.

"You know this is mad, Fronto."

The legate nodded.

"Mad and necessary. Have fun."

He turned and strode off to the right flank of the Tenth. Scanning up and down the ranks for a centurion, he spotted the familiar white hair of Lucretius wiping his brow, his helmet off. Lucretius' century were in the rear line and currently unoccupied.

"Lucretius!"

The centurion turned and saluted, coming to attention.

"You and your century want to join me on a suicide mission?"

"Is that really a choice, sir?"

Fronto laughed.

"Not really. We're going to break out of the line, make for the nearest enemy standard, and kill their leaders."

The centurion grinned.

"That'll shake 'em, sir."

Without waiting for orders, he turned.

"Sixth Cohort, First Century: Report to the rear!"

The seventy or so remaining members of Lucretius' century fell out of the line and assembled in formation and at attention in the open space of the camp's interior. As they did so, Fronto strode to the rear line directly opposite the standard he could see wavering, bronze and shining, above the enemy, and accosted the closest legionary.

"In a moment, the whole line will have to part to let a century through. We're going to push out of the line. Pass the word down to be ready."

The soldier saluted and spoke hurriedly to the men around him, as Fronto turned back to the century behind him. Lucretius was standing to attention with his men.

"Alright, here's what we're going to do" he announced. "The line's going to open as we march through towards the front. As soon as we're three men back from the enemy, I want the century to drop into testudo formation, four men wide. Lucretius and myself will take central positions at the front. The moment we're in formation and the front line opens, I want a charge, maintaining that formation. We can't afford to open any gaps, as we'll be surrounded by the enemy. That means the rear will have to take position and walk backwards..."

He gestured at the optio. "That's your position. Bear in mind you're going to have to charge backwards. Can you do it?"

The optio shrugged.

"Can't guarantee the line will stay closed while we charge, sir. We'll do our best, but I can guarantee that as soon as we slow to a march, any gap will close."

Fronto nodded.

"Do whatever you have to. They're a dense mass, so they probably won't have room to drop to the ground and attack under the shields. We just need to get there. Once we're there we kill anyone well-dressed, armoured, or holding a standard. If we can do that, we form up and hold tight until the legion marches to meet us. If this works, Labienus will push the legion forward as soon as he sees the standards go down. If we're lucky, we'll still be alive when they get to us."

The soldiers of Lucretius' century continued to stand, stony faced, not a single man showing a hint of fear. It always made Fronto proud to see the quality of his men.

"Alright. Form up, four abreast."

He collected one of the spare shields from the armament piles behind the ranks of men, stepped next to the centurion and smiled.

"See you in Elysium then, eh?"

Lucretius nodded.

"Hopefully a few years away, yet, sir."

Fronto gritted his teeth and raised the shield, drawing his sword.

"Open ranks!" he called to the Tenth, and the lines of men pulled aside like a tide retreating over wet sand, leaving a space for the column to march through. As the two officers led the column into the lines of legionaries, the discipline of the Roman military once more impressed itself on him. Row after row of densely-packed legionaries stepped aside and opened a path as they advanced forward through the ranks of the Tenth.

After what seemed like an eternity of marching, Fronto saw the fighting ahead, the front ranks of his men lunging, stabbing and shield-barging; even head-butting where the opportunity presented itself. As he watched, lucky barbarian blows landed between the shields and figures fell, only to be replaced by a legionary from the rank behind, causing a line of men of that cohort to step one rank forward.

And then there were so few men in front of him that he could see the contorted, hungry faces of the enemy as wool-clad or naked warriors swung with swords or stabbed with spears.

"Testudo!"

With a crash of shield upon shield, the century fell into formation, four shields forming a front wall, with each man along the side creating a solid shield wall down the side. Unusually for a testudo, there were not enough shields to create a complete roof, but this particular manoeuvre was unlikely to come under arrow shot. Fronto held his sword up and ready to shove through the narrow gaps afforded by the curvature of the rouded-rectangular, bull-emblem shields.

Suddenly the front ranks of the Tenth opened and Fronto found himself face to face with a screaming, naked, blue-painted Celt.

"Charge!"

The century, still in formation, picked up to a fast pace and slammed into the enemy who were trying desperately to make use of the sudden opening to break the shield wall.

The sheer momentum of seventy heavily-armoured men running with shields to the front carried them into and through the first few ranks of the enemy, Belgic warriors staring in surprise and panic as they were quite literally battered to one side and ploughed out of the way.

After a moment's initial push, however, the pace of the testudo began to slow, as the momentum waned and the mass of enemy bodies around them increased. Now began the work that was the forte of the legion. As the testudo moved forward at a slow, heavy plod, Fronto began to lash out with his blade through the available narrow openings. He could barely see what he was attacking, his view was so restricted by the protective shields, but he felt the blade bite into flesh time and again.

Slowly, pace by pace, the century moved on, deeper into the mass. Legionaries would be dying, he knew. They'd be lucky if they lived long enough to reach the standard, let alone kill the men around it. Of course, the discipline and training of the Roman military meant that each time a soldier fell, he would be replaced by his nearest compatriot. The testudo would gradually shrink as their numbers fell, but the wall of shields would close after each death.

Fronto felt something clatter off his helmet. Damn, that was close.

Behind him to the left there was a shriek, and for just a moment he felt the ominous expanse of air where a man had been, and then a moment later another man was in that place, and there was the reassuring 'clunk' of a replacement shield slotting into the gap.

How long would this take? He could not spare the time to look around and see how far they'd come and, even if he could, he would not have been able to see past the rows of legionaries with shields and the press of barbarian warriors beyond.

He would…

Suddenly the world next to him opened up to chaos. A well aimed blow had landed between the curved shields and had carved a great gouge in Lucretius' face. The centurion was dead before his knees buckled and he hit the ground. Fronto and the other front man to his right swung their weapons like madmen to prevent the assailant from managing to pull apart their formation and then thankfully, suddenly, the soldier from the second row managed to step forward over the fallen officer's body and slot his shield into place.

Fronto grimaced. The loss of any man was always unfortunate, but the loss of a good veteran centurion was particularly lamentable, though common, given the impressive mortality rate among the centurionate.

Suddenly, through the narrow gap between shields and over the heads of wild, screaming barbarians, Fronto saw a golden boar on a pole waving back and forth. They were almost there.

"I see it lads! Push!"

With renewed vigour, the depleted century barged and heaved their way forward through the enemies and suddenly Fronto found himself face to face with a man in a bronze breastplate and a strangely-horned helmet, screaming wilding and gesturing with his sword. The area around the leaders of the Atrebates was relatively open, giving them enough space to deal with the job of commanding their army, such as it was.

"Now, lads!" he cried. "We've got 'em. Open up and form a protective circle."

As Fronto moved his own shield to the side and prepared for straight combat, the remaining men of the century opened up behind him in a crescent, pushing their way in among the Atrebates' command party while maintaining a curved line of shields against the rest of the enemy.

Fronto kept his eyes on the nobleman or bodyguard or whatever he was, but cast a quick, satisfied glance past him to see that other men were already engaging another well-dressed man and the standard bearer.

The warrior, a bulging-eyed man with red cheeks and an impressive moustache, screamed violently and lunged with his sword, too restricted by the sudden press of Romans to make a good swing with it. Fronto threw the shield in the way, and such was the power of the man's blow that the blade tore through the shield and wedged in among the fractured wood and leather. Almost contemptuously, Fronto twisted the shield and ripped the sword from the surprised barbarian's hand.

As the man stared and then reached in a panic for the smaller blade at his belt, Fronto took the opportunity of an undefended opponent and lashed out twice, quickly, with his gladius. The first blow caught the man in the belly, the second in the arm as he spun. The chief or guard was as good as dead now. He would certainly be dead within the hour at the latest, but this whole push was all about the look of things. The Belgae had to see their leaders die, ignominiously and in pain.

Fronto stepped forward and towered over the slowly-collapsing man, raising his sword for a killing blow when a sudden explosion of white-hot pain in his left arm spun him around. A well-thrown spear had ripped through the protective layers at the top of his shield and had gone straight through his arm, breaking the bone in the process, and into his shoulder next to the armpit.

It was a lucky blow for the victorious Celt but, really, luckier for Fronto. Half a hand higher and it would have gone straight through his neck. Fronto winced and gritted his teeth, trying not to shout in pain. The command group of the Atrebates was gone, and the legionaries had formed into a protective circle around him and the three other soldiers that had dispatched the leaders and their companions.

As he spun around in pain, he noted, even in his predicament, that the circle was tightening as the men created a solid shield wall against the enemy. Somewhere back at the Roman lines, the cornicens called the advance and a roar went up.

Fronto dropped his gladius to the floor and reached round to grasp the spear just below the head. His mind was beginning to feel a little fuzzy. He made an unsuccessful attempt to pull out the spear and grunted in pain, collapsing to his knees. Suddenly, hands were helping him up.

"Gettoff! Just get this bloody thing out of me."

"Are you sure, sir?" a legionary enquired quietly.

"Get it out!"

There was a commotion going on among the Atrebates and Fronto caught out of the corner of his eye the sight of pila arcing through the air and coming down among the barbarians. He gritted his teeth and let out a whimper as two men pulled on the spear shaft and the blade came out of his shoulder with a 'slurping' sound, followed by a gobbet of blood.

"Lie down, sir."

"What?"

"I'm the capsarius for this century, and I know what I'm doing, sir. Lie down!"

Fronto, starting to feel distinctly faint, collapsed to the floor, the jarring of the shield on his broken and impaled arm making him shriek.

As soon as he was down, the capsarius picked up a heavy Belgic blade and took a swing downward, severing the spear shaft close to his arm. The shock that ran through Fronto drove him into immediate and blissful unconsciousness, and he was still in the dark bosom of Morpheus while the capsarius grasped the spear head and pulled the shaft through the arm, removed the shield and splinted and bound his legate.

Around him, the defensive circle tightened again as the surviving eighteen men of the century tried to defend their position against an angry, but increasingly panicky enemy.

* * * * *

Labienus was close to the front of the charge. Whoever Fronto's second most senior centurion was, the man had been adamant that Labienus should not be endangered and had argued him into staying in the third line. What was it with the Tenth? It was as though Fronto's insolence and disobedience had spread like a disease through his men.

After only a few heartbeats of argument it had become clear to Labienus that he was not going to win this one, even if he ordered the man to stand aside.

As soon as the call had gone up, every soldier who still had access to a pilum had cast it in a shower of deadly iron. The dismay at the death of their leaders and the capture of their standards was already shaking the morale of the Atrebates. The sudden horrifying rain of missiles caused an uproar and, by the time Labienus shouted the order and the Tenth began to push forward, the Ninth following suit on their left, panic was beginning to grip this Belgic tribe.

Like a slow tide, the Roman line moved through and over the enemy who tried to retreat for a long moment in an orderly fashion with a view to regrouping, before news reached the rear of the Celtic force that their leaders were dead, their standards gone, and they were now being pushed back.

Firstly the rear groups of Atrebates began to peel off and flee toward the water's edge, and then more and more broke away like ice in the first warmth of spring. Gradually, the trickle of fleeing warriors turned into a river, and then a flood, and suddenly the Tenth were no longer pushing the Atrebates, but pursuing them.

A roar went up among the men, and they began to pick up pace behind the fleeing enemy. Their enthusiasm and pace were so powerful that they almost engaged with the last dozen defenders around their legate before hurriedly peeling off and flowing around them after the enemy.

Labienus bellowed after the centurions "Steady! Form a line again!"

He watched for a moment as the officers reined in the more enthusiastic men and reformed into centuries as they drove on down to the river. Now, the Ninth was alongside and creating an impressive front. Labienus continued to observe the action for a moment and then approached the weary and battle-scarred survivors. He spotted the prone figure of Fronto, and for a moment his heart skipped a beat. Then, as he watched, he saw the legate's chest rise and fall. A soldier crouching next to him came to attention.

"Legate Fronto has been wounded sir. I should get him to the medicus."

Labienus nodded.

"Will he be all right?"

The capsarius gave a non-committal shrug.

"He should live, sir, but he might lose the arm."

The staff officer shook his head sadly and thought back with fresh perspective on that centurion refusing to let him take a place in the front line.

"Get him back there straight away and tell the medicus to do whatever he has to."

Leaving the tired and wounded men of the heroic century to escort Fronto back to the hastily-organised hospital, basic trestle tables in the open air, Labienus jogged after the Tenth to catch up. As he ran, he spotted the primus pilus running at an angle to intercept him.

"Priscus. Glad to see you made it."

"Only just, sir. You and the lads got there just in time. There were about ten of us left."

The centurion was bleeding in a dozen places, though none seemed to be bothering him. Labienus was, as always, impressed with the quality of the centurionate.

"And Velius?"

Priscus shook his head sadly.

"Seen no sign of him, sir, but it looks like no one survived there."

As they caught up with the rear ranks of the Tenth and marched along behind them, Labienus took the opportunity to glance to his right and see what was happening in the centre of the field. It appeared that the panicked retreat of the Atrebates had had a knock-on effect on the Viromandui, and the Eighth and Eleventh legions were even now beginning to move, pushing their Belgae opponents back slowly towards the river. He could not see as far as the Twelfth, but could only hope that the reserves would arrive in time to help them.

Ahead, the Tenth and the Ninth had reached the water and were busily butchering those Atrebates they caught trying to cross. The centurions gave a call and the line stopped. Labienus turned to Priscus and raised an eyebrow.

"Why?"

Priscus shrugged.

"They know that any further, and they leave the main field of battle. They're awaiting orders."

Labienus nodded and looked to the left to see legate Rufus and the primus pilus of the Ninth marching toward him.

"Rufus."

"Sir. The Atrebates are beginning to reform on the far bank. What are your orders?"

Labienus nodded.

"Then we need to break them before they get too courageous again. Pass the word down to the officers. Let the men have a wild, bloodthirsty charge but, if that breaks the enemy, make sure they know to rein in and form up near the crest of the hill."

Rufus nodded and walked back along the line of men. As Priscus passed the word down, Labienus looked up across the river and could see some sort of obstacle at the top. The enemy were going to be trapped. That meant they'd have to either surrender or die at the top. He took a deep breath and waited. Calls went up from one of the Ninth's cornicens and were picked up by the other musicians, throughout both legions. A chorus of centurions and optios bellowed simultaneously.

"Charge!"

Labienus watched tensely as the men waded into the water and sloshed across the river as fast as they could manage The first man to reach the far bank was felled by a massive swing with a Celtic blade, the second and third with spears, but then the bulk of the men reached the bank and began to stab and hack at the enemy.

Fresh dismay swept across the Atrebates, and they fled up the hill, their army breaking up once again like ice. At the rear of the legion, Labienus took a deep breath and then waded across the river behind his men, drawing his sword as he went.

The Ninth and Tenth swept up the gentle slope opposite. Labienus' fears that the enemy would be trapped by that strange blockade and fight to the death like cornered rats seemed unfounded. As the rear ranks of the Atrebates reached the obstacles, they hauled the great defences aside and, joining the warriors who had manned them, fled over the hill.

Labienus struggled out of the water onto the bank in time to see the last of the Belgae they were chasing disappear over the crest as the legions formed up just below them.

A voice off to the left attracted his attention, and he spun, wielding his sword, before he realised who it was. Varus, accompanied by a number of cavalrymen, came trotting out from behind a cover of trees.

"Labienus! You have absolutely no idea how grateful I am to see you."

"Varus?" Labienus blinked. "We thought you were gone or dead."

"Thankfully not. Most of the cavalry got cut off, but I'm hoping they're on their way back down. Where are you going now?"

The staff officer shrugged.

"There's still best part of ten thousand warriors up there. Got to either get them to surrender, kill them or disperse them. And Caesar'll want captives."

Varus nodded.

"I'm heading back across. Thanks for the rescue."

Labienus smiled.

"See you soon."

Drawing a deep breath, he set off once more up the hill after his men. They would have to gain control of the Belgae's camp over the ridge and take prisoners. Then they could turn round and take on the Belgic reserve from behind and trap them at the river.

He had almost reached the rear lines of the legions, when Rufus came running back down to him.

"What's up?"

Rufus grasped his shoulder and, spinning him around, pointed back across the river. The wagon train had still not finished arriving, and the reserve legions were not yet in sight. The Eighth and Eleventh were fighting a vast number of the enemy right on the bank of the river, but the Nervii reserve had taken advantage of the sudden gaps in the Roman line and had crossed the river. Even now, as he watched, the Twelfth Legion on the flank, already outnumbered around five to one, were suddenly hit by fresh waves of the enemy, this time from behind.

The Twelfth had a nominal strength of five thousand men, but it looked worryingly to Labienus as thought there were not more that fifteen hundred left. And that was where Caesar was. As he watched, the Twelfth reacted with astonishing efficiency to this new threat, closing up so that the rear ranks turned and became a second battle line. They were now entirely surrounded, cut off and hopelessly outnumbered.

"Sacred Mars!"

Rufus nodded.

"What do we do? Head back?"

Labienus shook his head.

"Can't leave ten thousand Atrebates in control of their camp and with room and time to reform into a unit. You stay and deal with them. Capture as many as you can. Get them to surrender if you can."

He ground his teeth.

"I'm taking the Tenth back to try and relieve the Twelfth and save Caesar."

* * * * *

Centurion Baculus stood gritting his teeth in the press of men. Around him his legionaries fought like lions against unbelievable odds as wave after fresh wave of Nervii fell upon them, hacking, maiming and screaming guttural curses. In the small circle afforded him temporarily while he sorted his latest wound, the veteran officer crouched, settling the shield in most comfortable position possible on his shattered left arm and used his good arm to remove his belt. Wincing, he used the belt to strap the shield tightly to his useless arm, holding the buckle between his teeth as he pulled it tight. Standing once more, he tried to lift the great defensive item, but the arm was too weak. A constant stream of crimson drips fell from his useless fingers. Still, at least he had a shield.

Once more he collected his sword and hefted it. To his left there was a crunch and a gurgling scream as a thrown spear arced over the front lines and came down in the middle of the Roman press, straight through the chest of a legionary.

"This is getting ridiculous!"

Baculus pushed his way back through the press of men.

"Come on, lads. They're only barbarians. Fight harder."

Ignoring the shocking pain in his arm, he pushed through the struggling men and spotted waving plumes a little to his right. About bloody time the legate got involved! Galba had been directing things as well as anyone could, given the circumstances, but really the Twelfth was as organised as it could ever hope to be now, and what they needed most was men with swords.

With a grunt of satisfaction, he pushed his way over to the commander and was surprised to realise that the man standing next to the legate in the line and jabbing madly with a sword, smashing his shield into the faces of howling barbarians, was the general himself. Caesar was already dirty and spattered with blood, his white tunic and crimson cloak making him stand out among the darker garb of the legionaries. This whole campaign could go to shit if Caesar fell to a well aimed blow. Who would pay to keep the legion active then? Pompey? Doubtful… and certainly not the senate.

With another grunt, this time of irritation, he made his way quickly over to the two officers and pushed his way in next to the general. If anyone was going to make sure the general survived, it had to be someone Baculus trusted, and the only person he truly trusted to fight well and not die was himself.

He moved a legionary aside and took the position, stabbing down at a warrior who was trying to swipe at their unprotected legs.

The general beside him cast him a sidelong glance.

"Thank you, centurion."

"Sir."

"You've just been back from the attack?"

Baculus nodded.

"Sorting a wound, sir."

Caesar smiled as he smashed his shield into the contorted face of a Nervian warrior.

"What's your estimate of our chances?"

Baculus gave a grim smile.

"We're in shit, sir. I was on the mound back there, and I couldn't see more than three or four centurion or optio's crests. I think the officers are nearly all gone. We're down to just over a thousand men now. There's a tribune back there that's busy bleeding out. We're surrounded on all sides, and the rest of the army's all engaged elsewhere. Unless the reserves get here, we'll be gone in less than a quarter of an hour."

Caesar's expression became grim.

"That's a bleak estimate, centurion."

"Just realism, sir."

Baculus had to break off from the conversation again as three warriors leapt at the line. One hit Caesar's shield and knocked the general back heavily enough that the man wobbled and almost lost his footing before heaving the attacker forward again using his shield. The others hit Baculus' shield so hard he felt his arm almost detach and narrowly avoided blacking out. The third forced his way between the two.

As the men in the row behind them dealt with the warrior who had broken through, Caesar looked Baculus up and down.

"You've been wounded twice, centurion."

"Six times" the man replied with a straight face.

"And you don't appear to be able to move your shield arm."

"Broken, sir."

The general laughed.

"If I had a hundred men like you, centurion, I'd live in no fear of the Nervii."

"Look there!" a voice shouted.

Both men turned to Galba in surprise. The legate was pointing over the enemy from their position on the slight rise of the incomplete rampart. They followed his gesturing and squinted. A fresh wave of Celtic warriors had appeared around the edge of the woodland nearby; mounted warriors, shouting fresh cries in their unintelligible language.

"They'll likely cut off the reserves" Galba said, his voice leaden and flat. Baculus shook his head in wonder at how this debacle had come about and leapt forward just in time to dispatch a warrior who had lunged at the momentarily distracted general.

"I don't think so…"

Caesar sounded unsure, but slowly a smile spread across his face.

"Look. There are legionary regulars among them. It's Varus' cavalry!"

As the three officers fought desperately to keep the line from the howling warriors before them, they caught glimpses briefly over the enemy. Varus' trapped cavalry had found a way round and back across the river and now came hurtling down behind the Nervii, where they began to harry them, attacking in a charge that swept past the Belgae and picking them off before pulling back out of reach and forming up for the next attack; standard Roman skirmishing tactics.

Baculus drew a deep breath as yet another blow trimmed a chunk from the edge of his shield and gouged a long but shallow line in his upper arm.

Caesar turned at the sound and, as he did so, one of the Nervii facing them swept his long Celtic blade down and across beneath Caesar's shield. Fortunately for the general, the man's aim was imperfect and the bone-breaking, limb-severing sword edge clipped the very base of the general's shield and jumped, scoring a deep rent across his calf in a blow that would, otherwise, have removed his leg. The general disappeared with a squawk and a crash, falling backwards into the press on his buckling leg. Two legionaries immediately went to his aid, while a third stepped in to take his place between Baculus and Galba.

The legate growled.

"Where the hell is Plancus with the reserves?"

"Sir?" a voice called.

Both Baculus and Galba shouted "Yes?" neither willing to take their eyes from the enemy, as they continued to block blows with their shields and stab and swipe at any flesh they could identify before them.

A legionary appeared behind them.

"Sir, the wagoners and engineers are marching across the camp, armed like us!"

Baculus laughed.

"Looks like the reserves are having their job done for them by a load of fat carters! We're going to be rescued by the support staff!"

Across the gently-sloping camp, three hundred legion-retained civilians, retired legionaries and engineers had dragged swords, shields, helmets and pila from the supply wagons and were marching in an impressive imitation of a legion toward the rear of the Nervii.

At the front, Sabinus and Cicero, freshly arrived at the field and determined to do what they could to salvage the Twelfth, shouted orders and tried to keep their strange, newly-commissioned unit in formation.

The 'century' pulled up with reasonable efficiency forty or fifty paces from the enemy, presented a shield wall as the rear Nervian ranks turned to deal with this new threat, and cast their missiles.

Though few of the ancillary staff had any training, the mass of pila arced up and came down among the mass of angry warriors, causing deaths and cries of dismay. With a roar, a group of warriors veered away from the mass and charged the small group of false legionaries.

The men presented a passable wall and planted their feet apart to withstand the crash as the Belgae barged into them, reeling back momentarily and then putting all their strength into holding the line while they stabbed madly at anything they could. There was no finesse or plan to the attack but, in the press of enemy bodies, it was near impossible, even for the untrained, to fail to land a blow.

More of the Nervii began to turn to this new unexpected attack, and within a couple of dozen heartbeats, the support column was being overwhelmed in a similar fashion to the Twelfth. Across the rampart and beyond the battling remnant of the legion, the cavalry began to pull back. The Nervii had finally decided to deal with the incessant gnat-bites that were the cavalry attacks, and had sent a large group of spear bearers to deal with them.

Baculus pulled himself back from the frontline, allowing a legionary to take his position. The general was upright, but being supported by one of the men. The primus pilus, a tall man already, pushed his way to the highest stretch of incomplete rampart, a mere two feet high, but enough to look over the heads of the legion and take in the situation. The hope they'd felt at the arrival first of the cavalry and then of the support staff slipped away as the centurion realised just how little difference it had really made. They were still outnumbered at least ten to one and the legion was losing a dozen men every fifty beats of the heart, despite their defensive stance. The cavalry had been forced to withdraw and were now forming up to charge, though the spear-bearing enemy would make minced meat of them if they tried it. The support staff, brave though the move had been, were now being systematically exterminated by the Nervii rear lines. Even as the primus pilus watched the rear lines of wagoners fled the scene for the relative safety of the wagons, leaving two unknown officers desperately holding together a rapidly disintegrating unit.

He turned to see what was happening elsewhere. The Eighth and Eleventh were embroiled in fierce fighting on the river bank, and their engagement could still realistically go either way. The standards of the Ninth were waving at the top of the hill opposite as Rufus and his men cornered the Atrebates and began to exact a heavy toll on them.

But the standards of the Tenth were descending the hill back towards the river at a run. He smiled and turned to the beleaguered men of his legion.

“Hold it just a little longer, lads… Fronto and the Tenth are on the way.”

Lucius Vorenus, pilus prior of the Second Cohort in the Thirteenth Legion, growled. A long-serving veteran who had been pulled in to the command structure of the newly-raised Gallic legion, Vorenus was sick to death of his men being sent to nursemaid the baggage, or left to guard the camp. It was clear that the rest of the army saw the two new legions as inferior, and that prejudice extended even to the centurions such as himself, who had more experience than many of the taunting bastards. Vorenus had been there under the elder Crassus fifteen years ago when they’d put Spartacus and his slaves down and now he was leading a unit that were not even expected to truly take part in anything.

And almost a quarter of an hour ago the Thirteenth and Fourteenth had received word that the battle was already happening; that the other legions were in the shit. The staff officers Sabinus and Cicero had immediately ridden off ahead at breakneck pace to see what they could do and to confirm that the reserves were on the way.

And what had ‘commander’ Plancus done about it? Kept them at a steady march so that they were fresh when they got there.

His growl deepened in intensity. The bloody battle would be over when they got there at this rate. The legate of the Fourteenth, currently the only commander in the rearguard and leading both legions, was so concerned over looking good when he arrived that the reserves would be too late. Taking a deep breath, he ran forward to where the primus pilus strode ahead.

"Pullo?"

As he fell in alongside, he noted an equally sour look on his peer's face.

"We're going to have to do something."

Pullo nodded.

"I know. But you're suggesting we disobey the direct orders of a legate."

Vorenus grimaced.

"I'm suggesting we disobey the direct orders of an arsehole. You're the primus pilus. I'm just the pilus prior. It's up to you to give the order."

Pullo sighed.

"I was enjoying being back in service. Seems a shame to end my career so quickly."

He took a deep breath.

"But you're right. We've got to pick up the pace. Get back to your men."

Vorenus nodded and, as he jogged back along the lines of the First Cohort to the Second, he heard Pullo shout "Time to get into action lads. Triple pace, now!"

The Thirteenth Legion surged forward with a rhythmic crashing of arms and armour and thudding of feet.

Somewhere back with the Fourteenth, legate Plancus would be having a fit.

Chapter 17

(Battle of the Selle)

"Contubernium (pl. Contubernia): the smallest division of unit in the Roman legion, numbering eight men who shared a tent."

Baculus staggered under another blow and swung wildly with the enemy blade he had ripped from the hands of one of the dying barbarians. Lifting the heavy sword with a bone-weary arm, he used the sleeve of his tunic to wipe away the stream of blood flowing from the wound on his now-unprotected head and blinding his right eye with a crimson veil. He staggered slightly, his leg cut in four places and now with barely enough strength to hold him up.

"We have to do something. There can't be more than eight or nine hundred of us left."

Caesar, having fallen back from the front line and landing occasional blows between the shoulders of his men while supported by another legionary, nodded and glanced at Galba. The legate was as hard-pressed as anyone else here, fighting for his life alongside the common soldiery. It occurred to the general that the greatest leveller among men was a life-threatening situation. In any other circumstance, even in the thick of battle, he would have been required by propriety to haul Baculus over the coals for addressing him in such a manner. In the situation in which the two men currently found themselves, even the idea was laughable.

And, of course, Baculus had fought like a titan.

"You're right, of course. Step back from the line..."

Baculus did as he was bade, dragging his leg and barely able to stand. As the man breathed in ragged rasps, and used the great Belgic broadsword as best he could to support himself, the general collared Galba and hauled him back from the front line.

Legionaries fell forward to replace the two men immediately, desperately defending the diminishing line.

"I need suggestions" the general said. "We've lost three quarters of the legion, most of the officers and standard bearers. With enemies on all sides, the Twelfth is just shrinking and will shortly disappear, with us in the middle."

Galba shrugged.

"We need support. But the problem is that even if the reserves show up and attack the Belgae, unless the enemy actually break and run for it, they won't be able to get to us. We'll still be gone by the time the relief reaches us."

Baculus pointed.

"Looks like the Tenth are coming back across. The Ninth must be in control over there. We've got the cavalry trying to help us, the support staff and the Tenth, and the reserves must be nearly here by now. They must have been told ages ago now."

"Yes," Galba said, "but none of them can actually reach us. They can attack the Nervii on another front, but that might not help us at all."

Caesar frowned.

"Then we must move the world around us."

"Sir?"

The general smiled.

"If the relief cannot reach our position, we have to move the entire legion mid fight; find a different position."

"But sir…" Galba said, "We're completely surrounded."

"Then we'll just have to push hard. This is my plan: It appears that the Eighth and Eleventh have the enemy pinned against the river. They cannot afford to stop that push, or their own opposition could regroup. But the Eleventh is at this end of the field. If we can link up with them, they can give us support, and we will be the flank rather than on our own."

"I can see that, general, but how can we get to them?"

Caesar smiled.

"The plebeian way… brute force and ignorance."

Baculus wiped the free-flowing blood from his eyes again.

"We send all the standards in that direction and reorganise. The northern edge takes the lead and actually pushes through the Nervii until we reach the Eleventh. At the same time, the other three directions go as defensive as possible, almost a testudo, and pull back so that the whole legion gradually moves north until we join up with the others."

Caesar gave a rare, very genuine grin.

"That's the sort of thing."

Baculus saluted, almost collapsing as he lost the support of his arm.

"I'll start moving the standards forward now, sir."

He turned, but his leg, so pale from blood loss it had taken on a blue tint, buckled and gave way beneath him, causing him to collapse to the floor. He grasped the belt of a nearby legionary and used it to haul himself up.

Caesar looked him up and down and shook his head, smiling.

"I don't think you will."

He rapped a nearby second-line legionary on the shoulder. The man turned irritably and, as he saw who it was, came to a cramped salute in the press of men.

"What's your name, soldier?"

"Naevius, sir!"

"Well, Naevius… I'm putting you in charge of your primus pilus. He fights like a lion, but he's so badly wounded he can hardly move. Your task is to make sure he stays calm, away from the action, and alive long enough for me to be able to decorate him when this is over. Got that?"

The legionary saluted again and then grasped the centurion to support his weight. Baculus glared at both he and the general and then sighed and gave up, just before his legs did. Caesar turned to Galba.

"This will need every ounce of courage and pride your men have, legate. I need you in the middle of things, shouting encouragement. I, on the other hand, will be at the front, with the standards."

"Sir…" Galba shook his head. "You can't do that. You're the only person on this field that we really cannot afford to lose."

"That, legate, is very charming and a little sycophantic. Given our circumstances, if we don't do something big, it will make no difference how important any of us are."

Galba nodded. If the slight put-down in the general offended him, he showed no sign.

"Very well, sir. I shall head to the rear of the column and try to hold the legion together as we move."

Caesar smiled.

"Signifers? To me… Rally on me!"

As the general turned and began to push his way through the rapidly-diminishing unit, the standards of various centuries bobbed through the crowd, converging on the northern area of the struggling unit. Once the general had reached a position in the third line of men, he waited for the signifers to arrive. There should have been fifty nine standards throughout the full legion. A quick count and he could see twenty four… no, twenty five. Taking a deep breath, he called out.

"Call out if you are a signifer for the First Cohort!"

Seven voices replied.

"And the Second?"

Four men.

"Third?"

Six voices.

"Fourth?"

Not a voice was raised above the background din of battle.

"The Fourth Cohort is gone?"

He sighed. What he had thought he could turn to a rousing speech was, instead, drawing attention to the losses they'd encountered and the danger that none of them would live to see the sun go down. Change of tactic…

"The Twelfth has valiantly held a flank against overwhelming odds on its own!"

Rousing… it had to be rousing.

"The Gods themselves would tremble before the spirit and might of this legion, who I have been proud to fight alongside."

There was a chorus of low cheers.

"But now, it is time to save ourselves; to preserve what remains of this glorious unit. We must push aside this sea of unwashed and bloodthirsty apes as a stable hand sweeps aside the excretions of a horse, and we must join with the Eleventh. I will lead this push, alongside the signifers of the Twelfth. We will show the Nervii that they may throw a million barbarians at us, but we are Rome, and we will not be snuffed out!"

A massive cheer went up as he finished. In a final, defiant gesture, he jabbed his gladius high in the air, turned and pushed his way into the frontline. The gens Iulia could disappear into obscurity with the death of its greatest son on this bloody field, but if the great Caesar was to die in battle, it would be in the thick of it where he would be remembered. The wound in his leg throbbed and, if he held his leg at certain angles, threatened to collapse him, but he gritted his teeth. Baculus had been fighting with far worse.

"Push! Make for the Eleventh!"

With no apparent regard to his personal safety, the general gritted his teeth, raised his shield, and threw himself into the fray. To either side, the men of the legion renewed their attacks, heaving with their shields, no longer holding them as steady as possible to fend off blows, but rather to bodily push the lines of the Nervii back away from them. Slowly, almost interminably, the wave of frothing barbarians gave slightly, and the men of the Twelfth managed a single step forward.

"Again!"

As the men heaved and pushed, slashing and stabbing as room allowed, there was another shift, like the collapse of sections of a cliff into the sea. The legion surged forward a few steps, taking advantage of the opportunity. Caesar stepped forth himself, carefully, aware of the wound in his leg that threatened to fell him with every pace, in line with the front wall of men, ducking and stabbing at a barbarian who lunged for his face. The man howled as the general's sword slid deep into his chest, grating slightly between the ribs. As Caesar tried to pull the blade back, the front mass of Nervii shifted again and the warrior fell backwards behind his fellows, taking the officer's very fine blade with him.

"Damn it!"

The general raised his shield slightly. He could reach round and take a sword from one of the men behind him, but the action might leave him open to attack. Instead, he braced his legs, grunting at the pain as the wound on his calf pumped out his precious lifeblood. Ignoring the pain and discomfort, he leaned in against his shield, keeping his head down enough that he could only just see over the bronze edging strip of the scutum below the guard of his helmet. Taking a deep breath, he bellowed "Push!"

Trusting to the men beside him to achieve a similar force, the general put every ounce of his weight against the shield, planting his legs behind him and heaving against the turf. Behind him, a quick-thinking signifer took advantage of the fact that the general was ducked and low, and raised the standard with its ornamental spear point, stabbing with it over his commander's head and impaling the face of one of the barbarians.

"Good man! Keep going!"

The general, down in the darkness behind his shield where no one could see him, suddenly realised that he was grinning like an ecstatic boy. There was something truly refreshing about the prosecution of a battle when you were one of many compatriots with a simple, straightforward task, no matter how hard that task might be. His mind found a clarity it rarely managed in the knowledge that, right now, all that was required of him was to push and survive until he found there were Romans in front of him instead of barbarians. No plans, no treachery, no bureaucracy or argument. Just men relying on each other and all pushing the same way.

Briefly, for one moment in the heat of battle, Caesar found that he understood men like Fronto and Labienus. There was a simplicity and a purity in battle that held a lure when compared with the thorny complexities of politics and was not always any more dangerous.

"Come on, men. Just a little further."

Of course, he had no idea how far they must go; possibly further than was realistically possible, but something had to be done.

Once again there was a roar and the Roman line heaved forward, stepping forward once… twice… three… even four paces. The general risked looking up for a moment, ducking back urgently as a great blade swung past, almost removing the top of his head.

He could see the standards of the Eleventh ahead. Straining, he listened over the roaring of his men and the general sounds of battle. Crispus and his officers were bellowing out commands, and the two legions were slowly converging as the Eleventh tried to push far enough to join with them.

He ducked once more and heaved, pushing at his shield, noting with concern that so much damage had now befallen the great wooden cover that he could actually see points of daylight through it. That could not be good.

Above him, the signum lanced out once more and stabbed into another barbarian.

Just a few more moments…

* * * * *

Labienus grimaced. It looked very much like they would not make it. The Twelfth was so seriously depleted, perhaps down to a quarter of their number, and still surrounded by a veritable sea of Belgae. Even if the Tenth ran like racehorses they would still have to fight their way through the Nervii to relieve Caesar's legion.

He fretted as he ran with the Tenth, still in good formation, down the slick and bloody slope of the north bank and began once again to wade across the river. Despite the trouble the Twelfth was experiencing on the flank, the day looked hopeful for Rome now. Rufus could deal with the Atrebates, even if it meant just chasing them off. Balbus and Crispus were still heavily embroiled in combat, but things were going enough their way that the Belgae had committed every man they had, with no reserves to be seen across the field. With the Roman reserves surely only moments away, the battle would be theirs.

But unless they did something quickly, the Twelfth would be gone by then, along with Caesar and any hope for a glorious end to the campaign. Without the general, a new governor would be selected for Cisalpine Gaul, the legions would be withdrawn, possible no longer funded, and everyone would go home, probably without much in the way of booty either. Sad, really, that so many men and their families' futures relied on the one patrician busy fighting for his own life.

Clambering up the opposite bank, he waved his cornicen over.

"Sound the muster. I need to think."

The musician put out the call and the Tenth and, as they returned to the south bank and began to form into their contubernia, centuries and cohorts, Labienus found a low natural mound and stepped onto it for the best view he could manage. What would Fronto do?

He could just make out a crest in the midst of the fighting that would be either Balbus or one of his tribunes, or perhaps one of the staff fighting alongside them. Up by the furthest end of the fighting he could make out a small unit who seemed very irregularly organised, being led by a couple of officers. No sign yet of Plancus and the reserves.

He fretted again. What to do? Labienus was a career soldier. Oh, he had dabbled in politics far more than Fronto, but only to secure military positions for himself. He had almost as much command experience in the field as Fronto and Balbus, so he damn well should be able to think of something.

He sighed as he realised the Tenth was almost formed behind him, and he would have to have an answer in a few moments.

It looked bad for soldiers to have to wait while an officer faffed and dallied.

He needed to see this from an objective view. He tried to imagine how an eagle would see the scene. The corner of the camp where the action was going on was like a disjoined 'L' where the long side was the strung-out line of the Twelfth, surrounded by the Nervii on all sides. The short side was the compact Eighth and Eleventh, fighting only on the one side.

He frowned and squinted at the legions in combat. He knew what he would be doing if he was in command of the Twelfth or the Eleventh. Surely they must have figured it out. Caesar and Crispus between them could outthink Minerva. They had to close up and form a solid 'L' with no gap. Then he had a plan.

Squinting, he watched carefully. Behind him, someone cleared his throat.

"Shh!" he said irritably.

Labienus frowned. He could not quite make it out in that complex press of human bodies. He suddenly became aware of the comforting figure of Priscus beside him.

"You got good eyes, Priscus?"

The primus pilus of the Tenth shrugged.

"Good enough, sir. Why?"

"Can you see any movement over there?"

Priscus frowned.

Moments passed tensely by.

"The Twelfth is moving down toward the Eleventh. Not sure how they're managing in that position, but I swear they're moving!"

Labienus nodded.

"I thought so. And I think the Eleventh is doing the same."

"I believe you're right, sir."

He cleared his throat again and spoke in a low whisper.

"Sir, the men are waiting for orders…"

Labienus nodded. As he turned, there was a satisfied smile on his face.

"Here's what we're going to do, gentlemen…" he said to his men.

* * * * *

Rufus stood at the very crest of the hill, where he could see every part of the battlefield. The Twelfth was still in trouble, but Labienus and the Tenth were closing to help and, best sight of all, a great number of men had appeared in the distance, moving alongside the wagon train on both sides, not at a march, but at a run. The Thirteenth and Fourteenth would take the field any moment. Good, because the rest of the fight would certainly have to go on without the Ninth.

He turned once again to look down on the scene.

The Atrebates had pushed aside the defences they'd created on the hill and returned to their camp, but Rufus' men were ahead of the game. His primus pilus, a veteran named Grattius and whom, he had been informed, had effectively controlled the legion before Rufus' appointment, had, the moment they reached the crest, split his men with a simple shout of "Bull horns!"

Immediately, the cohorts had split into three groups. As four cohorts formed into a traditional attacking line, two groups of three cohorts picked up to double pace and arced out to the sides in a long column, where they began to encircle the retreating enemy who were dithering in their own camp, unsure of what direction to flee, given that their world was now collapsing around them.

Rufus gave his primus pilus an appreciative nod of salute and stood back to watch the scene unfold like a carefully organised parade. Within a few moments, the enemy camp was surrounded by three lines of legionaries who, as soon as they were in position, formed a solid shield wall. Rufus smiled at the sheer speed that his legion had completely enclosed the fleeing Atrebates. Grattius was worth his pay several times over.

As the enemy warriors milled around uncertainly, the four cohorts in standard battle order marched forward to the edge of the slope where they towered over the enemy. The primus pilus turned to his commander.

"Sir? The command is yours to give."

Rufus stepped forward to the front of the battle-ready cohorts.

"Some of you will speak Latin" he bellowed. "At least enough to understand this…"

He took a deep breath and deepened his voice as much as he could, like an orator addressing an open air assembly or an actor in one of the greater theatres.

"This battle, your resistance and your war are over. Ended."

He waited for this to sink in; several heartbeats longer, in fact, hoping that those who understood him would pass the word.

"You have only two choices: surrender..."

He tried to make his voice as flatly menacing as possible.

"Or extermination."

There was a great deal of sudden discussion below.

"Surrender now and you will live. Many of you could go free."

He waited, tense, for some sort of spokesman to step forth among the Atrebates. Moments passed quietly, the only sounds the desperate yet quiet conversation of the enemy and the occasional clanking or grating of the arms and armour of the Ninth Legion.

And then suddenly, someone at the far side of the mass screamed something in the guttural language of the Belgae, and the entire mass charged, bellowing, at the enclosing circuit of shields.

Rufus shook his head sadly. Prisoners fetched good money in the slave markets of Rome. Corpses were only of use to the crows. He turned to Grattius.

"They've made their choice. Wipe them out!"

* * * * *

Labienus shouted orders as the Tenth marched against the enemy. They'd crossed the first part of the open ground at a steady pace but, as soon as he had judged the advancing edges of the Eleventh and Twelfth legions to be a hundred paces from each other, heaving and squeezing the Nervii out of the intervening space, he had picked up to double-time. If he wanted this to work properly, it had to be carefully timed.

They had now passed the rear ranks of the Eighth, to the cheers of Balbus' men, and were closing on the enemy. As they reached a distance of three hundred paces, he yelled his penultimate command.

At his cry the centurions and cornicens relayed the orders and the Tenth Legion suddenly expanded from a column into a line, which lengthened and continued to do so as they closed. Labienus' timing was impeccable. With an audible crash, the Eleventh and Twelfth legions met and turned their numbers outwards to the enemy in a joint front, while the Tenth, forming another junction with the

Eleventh, turned the ‘L’ of legions into a ‘U’. Suddenly, one side of the massed Nervii that had been slowly obliterating the beleaguered Twelfth were now themselves trapped between three groups of Romans.

Labienus grinned to himself; Fronto could not have done any better. The Tenth began to roll like a tide over the ranks of the Nervii who, he had to admit, bore the sudden change in their fortunes bravely. Many people would have run or downed their arms, but ten thousand Nervii trapped between three legions with no hope now of victory merely snarled and fought with renewed vigour.

He found himself for a moment actually impressed with these men. Fronto was right; if the future of Gaul was as a province of Rome, these men would one day make legions that could storm the very gates of Hades. The idea made him frightened and hopeful in almost equal measures.

* * * * *

The primus pilus of the Thirteenth Legion took in the view of the battlefield with a practiced eye. From his position at the head of the reserves and the top of the southern slope, he could just see activity on the far side of the river but, judging by the organised lines of men, their commanders had the situation well under control.

This side of the river, however, was chaos. Two legions, the Eighth and Eleventh by the looks of it, were engaged in heavy combat down by the river, and the Tenth was attacking the enemy on one side, the other remaining open. Must be the Ninth and Twelfth on the opposite hill then. Things were not going half as badly as the scouts had made out…

Then he noted the standards in the deep press of the enemy. Somewhere in the middle of that huge mass of barbarians, a standard of the Twelfth raised and dipped.

Alright then; perhaps there was a problem after all. He waved his cornicen over.

“Give the orders. We’re moving at a charge down the eastern side of the slope. The Tenth have the enemy hemmed in to the west, and the Eleventh from the north, so if we take the east and the Fourteenth come straight from the south at them then we can squeeze them to death between four legions. Best also have someone pass the plan back to the primus pilus of the Fourteenth.”

The cornicen saluted and gave the orders to one of the men who ran back along the line to update the other reserve legion on the situation. As the man disappeared, the musician began to blow the various command calls and Pullo took a deep breath.

"Charge!"

In the worst part of the field, Baculus stood in the thick press of men, a legionary holding him upright. The numbers of the Twelfth were still dropping. The tables had turned, and the Nervii were now in trouble, but even the threat of imminent defeat did not seem to be dampening their bloodlust. Trapped between legions, they just seemed to be fighting all the harder. At least now there were men from the Eleventh filtering in among them and bolstering the Roman numbers.

The soldier supporting his weight pointed out across the mass.

"Look, sir."

Baculus squinted for a moment and then nodded contentedly. The Thirteenth had arrived and, after a moment at the crest, presumably weighing up the situation, they were coming down toward the point where the enemy were thickest.

"The relief's here, lads. Don't want to give the new boys too much of a challenge. Let's kill as many more as we can before they get here!"

A roar went up around him, and the Twelfth fought on with renewed vigour.

He watched, grumbling beneath his breath for a moment and then gently pushed the soldier away from him.

"Buggered if I'm going to be sitting back and playing with myself when the relief arrive."

The soldier started to argue, but Baculus adjusted the shield on his useless arm, wincing at the pain in his leg when he crouched, and swapped the great Celtic blade he currently held for a familiar gladius. Hefting the latter, he stood with some difficulty, and half-limped, half hopped through the men toward the front line once more. Respectfully, though with his face displaying a mix of doubt and disapproval, an optio he vaguely recognised shuffled to the side as best he could in the press to make room.

Baculus immediately swung his torso so that the shield on his broken arm blocked a blow, and stabbed back at the man, almost toppling in among the barbarians as his leg buckled momentarily. Two men along the line legate Galba, previously obscured by the action, leaned across.

"What the hell are you doing back in the fight?"

The legate's attention was suddenly drawn away once more and he found himself fighting hard for his life as the primus pilus growled.

"My job, sir."

"You've been wounded a dozen times. Back off, centurion!"

"I'll back off when I reach two dozen, sir."

Glancing across the enemy, Baculus could see the standards of the Thirteenth now, bobbing around behind the Nervii and cutting their way in. His view was suddenly blocked by an enormous warrior, naked and painted with blue whorls, his great sword raised over his head for a downward blow. Baculus raised the shield as best he could, trying not to notice the way the arm strapped to it flopped from side to side, to ward off the inevitable blow, while stabbing at the man's exposed chest. As he felt the blade slide in to the enemy's torso, puncturing organs as it went, he noticed too late the spear point thrusting around the side of the man. In trouble from two directions, all he could do was try to duck to the side. The spear point ripped through the chain mail of his shirt and entered his body just below the bottom rib at his side.

He had no time to react to the sudden sharp pain, as the great heavy sword of the mortally-wounded warrior came crashing down on top of his shield with enough force to drive a man a foot into the turf. The shield cracked and broke under the strike, the bronze boss turning the blade aside and preventing what would otherwise have been clearly a killing blow. Unfortunately, the simultaneous timing of the attacks caused the centurion's leg to collapse once again under the weight and, as he fell to the ground, the spear ripped open the side of his abdomen in a spray of viscera and links of chain.

"Bast… bastard" he shouted, struggling to find his feet, but there was no longer enough strength in him to drag him upright. He felt arms beneath his shoulders and reluctantly allowed himself to be drawn back away from the action as another man stepped in to take his place.

He sat for a long moment on the turf, staring around him at the legs of the Twelfth Legion, constantly moving and straining in the press of battle. He was clearly out of the action now. In fact, he could not actually move his legs enough to change position, let alone stand.

Well, they would still either die as heroes or live as victors, but either way they'd have to do it without him for now.

He smiled as he started to count off on the fingers of his good hand the number of barbarians he had killed. He had passed twenty when he found he had noted one of them twice; the one with the axe. Well it was not a personal best, but he doubted many here would match the number. His grim smile widened. The primus pilus was a man who believed he should be better than any other man in the legion; else that man might deserve his job.

And, he thought more soberly, two leg wounds, two to the abdomen, one to the head and three to the arms. The legate was wrong; eight, not twelve, unless you counted minor scratches. He was definitely beginning to feel light headed; must be the blood loss. Grunting, he tore a long strip from his tunic and packed the wound in his side as best he could.

For a long moment, he wondered if there was a capsarius still alive among his men and then, blessedly, he blacked out.

* * * * *

Damiacus of the Aduatuci reined in his horse and held up a hand, lowering it, so the palm was flat to the ground and then sweeping it to the side. Behind him, a dozen of his best warriors drew their horses slowly and quietly to a stop and walked them alongside. The chieftain nodded, his face a mix of thoughtfulness and irritation. He had warned the damned Nervii time and again against rushing in too early; he had warned them against trying to protect too much land and had suggested a line of low cliffs that lay between the rivers Meuse and Schelde as the perfect land to lay traps and deal with the Romans. So what if they had to abandon some of their lands to the southern pigs. Once they'd skinned the Romans and sent the fleshless remains back to their mothers, the Belgae could retake their lands.

He snarled.

Instead, here he was, sitting atop a hill with a magnificent view over several miles, including a spectacular panorama of the debacle that Boduognatus and his Nervii had brought upon themselves. They had taken a chance and had failed. Had they listened to Damiacus, the Aduatuci would have been with them further east, but no. They were too impatient and had paid the price. The day belonged to Rome.

Now he would have to spit on the corpses of his 'countrymen' and call his cousins and their tribes across the Rhine to come and gut these catamites from the south.

He gestured to his men and the warriors turned and rode toward the advancing host of Aduatuci to order them back east. As they wheeled, they failed to notice the Roman scouts on a hill nearby, gesturing desperately at each other before they turned and rode back to their masters with the news.

* * * * *

Baculus came to suddenly in a commotion. He reeled and his head spun as he tried to remember where he was. Ah yes; the world came flooding back. He realised someone was helping him upright.

"What's going on?"

The legionary beside him grinned.

"It's over, sir. The Fourteenth have broken through and joined up with us. The Thirteenth and the Tenth are busy dealing with the remnant of the Nervii, but the commander of the Fourteenth has been asking for someone in charge, sir, and I can't find legate Galba."

Baculus nodded woozily and strained as he reached a standing position.

The soldier helped him limp slowly and painfully through the gradually dispersing ranks of the Twelfth who were now free from the press of the enemy and recovering their strength.

Ahead, he spotted a shiny breastplate and a crimson plume. He almost laughed at the parade-ready cleanliness of the commander, particularly given the fact that he himself was covered almost head to foot with dirt and blood and had lost his helmet some time ago.

"Report, centurion."

"Sir?" Baculus was genuinely taken aback. Who was this idiot? The commander, obviously a legate, removed the plumed helmet and placed it under his arm. He had big ears, Baculus noted, trying not to laugh.

"I want to see the commander of the Twelfth. Would that be you?"

There was no stopping it this time. Baculus laughed momentarily.

"Possibly, sir. Legate Galba was here somewhere, deep in the fighting, but he could be dead by now."

"Are you not going to salute?"

Baculus stared at the man.

"Can't sir. Wounded."

"Very well." The legate looked distinctly put out, which threatened to make him laugh again. "You appear to be diminished. How many officers do you have?"

Again, Baculus stared.

"I really don't know sir. Maybe half a dozen? I know we've lost two cohorts entirely, including the standards."

"You lost a standard?" The man's voice reached a high-pitched shriek.

"Not me personally, sir. That would be the standard bearer you're thinking of…"

He grinned. The officer glared at him, slowly tuning purple.

"When the general hears that you have lost a standard, he…"

Baculus watched with interest as the young officer's face dropped and very quickly turned from purple to white. It was a sharp colour change, the likes of which the centurion had never seen before.

"Legate Plancus," Caesar said, as he reached for Baculus' other arm and supported him, "I suggest you stop talking before you irritate me."

The young man's mouth flapped noiselessly, and Caesar smiled unpleasantly.

"As I expect you will observe from the fact that the Twelfth is missing four men in every five, that we are all covered in blood, both Roman and Belgic… and that centurion Baculus is so badly wounded that he cannot stand without aid…" he took a breath, leaving a leaden silence. "I expect you will realise that we have had rather a tough day, and I'm not as worried about the loss of a few gaudy baubles as I am about how long it took my damned reserves to reach the field and help us."

The last few words came out as a growl and Plancus flinched.

"Sir, we came as fast as I deemed sensible. Troops who are tired from running cannot fight as well on the field."

The general stared at him.

"You left us all to die because you wanted your men well rested? Get out of my sight, Plancus, and be grateful I'm not sending you home."

* * * * *

Baculus sighed and lay back on the sheet that was his temporary resting place. There had not been enough time to construct even a makeshift hospital and the wounded were being treated on carts where there was room and the ground elsewhere. Blankets and sheets from the medical supplies had been draped over the clear portions of grass at the top of the southern slope, and here lay those soldiers who had now been dealt with by the medical staff, but were too wounded to return to duty.

"What the hell?" a voice asked suddenly to his left.

He blinked and turned his head painfully. Legate Fronto of the Tenth was rubbing his head with his right arm.

"Where am I?"

Baculus smiled.

"With the wounded heroes, legate."

Fronto turned and tried to focus on him.

"Baculus, yes? From the Twelfth?"

"That's right, sir."

"Looks like they really did a job on you."

Baculus laughed and then winced.

"You too."

Fronto nodded as best he could.

"So does this mean it's over? We won?"

The centurion smiled.

"Pretty much. There were still a lot of them when I was taken away, but they were dying in droves by then."

"Good." The legate sighed and tried, unsuccessfully, to move his left arm. "I suppose this serves me right for asking why the Belgae were all pushovers!"

Baculus rubbed his eye.

"You might want to leave that arm alone, sir. I heard the doc talking. He's only fifty-fifty that you'll ever use it again and prodding and moving it probably won't help."

"Layabouts!" a voice cut across them.

They both craned painfully to look down past their feet at the source of the voice. Priscus stood in front of them shaking his head.

"Thought I'd best update you on the situation."

Fronto nodded as best he could manage.

"Go on."

"We lost about seven hundred men. Not done a full head count yet, but that's a good estimate. Among them were five centurions, three optios, a signifer and one of the tribunes."

Fronto sighed.

"Not good."

"It gets worse," Priscus said, his voice dark. "Velius has gone. Not found him yet, but we're searching the bodies, and we're not hopeful."

"Where are the lads now?"

"I've got some of them looting the enemy camp with the other legions. The rest are either collecting the bodies or herding the few prisoners we took. There aren't very many... maybe five thousand, all told. They fought to the death."

Fronto sighed again, and Baculus frowned.

"I don't suppose you know of the Twelfth's status."

Priscus nodded sombrely.

"Unfortunately, yes. They've already turned in a headcount. Your numbers are down to nine hundred and twelve, including officers. Only three centurions made it, and seven optios."

Baculus collapsed back to the floor.

"This was a total bloody shambles."

"Could be worse," Priscus sighed. "The outriders spotted scouts from the Aduatuci. They were only an hour away, and there were thousands more of them. They've turned round and run back to their own lands."

"Good," Fronto grumbled. "I'm rapidly getting sick of the Belgae."

* * * * *

Paetus cowered and shrank back amongst the Belgic warriors being herded like cattle between the trees and back toward the partially-constructed camp. Dozens of warriors, along with their druid, had left the field and disappeared into the woodland with a view to escaping the battle and finding somewhere they could recuperate before returning to their home. Paetus had gone with them. What else could he do?

All the way through those dark woods he had been deciding how best to deal with this. If he stayed with the Belgae, they would skin him alive when they reached safety; indeed, he was surprised they'd left him this long. But on his own, he'd not survive long either. The other option, to return to the army and deny any knowledge of what had happened, would be difficult to achieve convincingly. Plus it would leave that taste of bile in his throat.

But all his deliberation had been a waste of effort, for the moment they broke cover from the woods, Varus and a cavalry unit had them surrounded. Paetus had wondered what the druid intended to do about it, but somehow the man had vanished before the cavalry sprung their trap.

And now here he was. It was a testament to how much he had changed in recent days that the cavalry had herded him along without a second glance, assuming him to be one of the enemy. Things had fallen apart once more for him, and yet he was still alive; and as long as he was alive, that fiery thirst for revenge deep in his heart would continue to drive him.

Chapter 18

(Battlefield by the Selle River)

"Kalends: the first day of the Roman month, based on the new moon with the 'nones' being the half moon around the 5th-7th of the month and the 'ides' being the full moon around the 13th-15th."

"Haruspex (pl. Haruspices): A religious official who confirms the will of the Gods through signs and by inspecting the entrails of animals."

In the hastily-erected headquarters tent, Caesar leaned forward and cradled his fingers.

"Are we going to have to spend the next few months repeatedly pacifying every Belgic tribe that still has a complaint against us? I was under the impression that the Belgae's alliance would collapse if we broke the back of the Nervii?"

Galronus of the Remi shook his head gently.

"Nervii, Atrebates and Viromandui are greatest of Belgic tribes…" He paused, and looked a little saddened to Fronto. "Were greatest. And you destroy them. There is hardly man left who can fight; just women, children, old men. They not come to seek peace, for they broken and frightened, but you nothing to fear from them."

He pointed at the map on the wall.

"Now all of Belgae will take Rome as friend… except Aduatuci. You understand why?"

Sabinus, sitting to one side of the table, nodded.

"I think I understand. The Aduatuci are the last proud Belgae. They know that we are aware of their part in this, and they believe that we will not seek peace, yes?"

Fronto shook his head.

"It's more than that. The Aduatuci will shun the Belgae now and join the Germanic tribes. They descend from German blood and are as much German as they are Belgae. You've eliminated all the Belgic resistance now, and I think you can safely say that the Belgae are tamed. You can arrange terms and so on, but the Aduatuci will join with the Germans instead. Problem is: we need to deal with them before they get that chance."

Caesar shook his head.

"The Aduatuci have abandoned all the forts between here and their home. They've retreated to their oppidum. It makes no great matter whether they call themselves Belgae or German, or even Samnite or Greek. The fact remains that they are in no position to resist us now, and they know it. Given enough time to see the hopelessness of their position, they will fall before us and ask for peace."

Fronto glanced across at Galronus who was shaking his head.

"I don't think so, Caesar."

"What?"

Fronto tried to heave himself out of his chair, but he was still too weak from the battle and, with only one working arm, he just did not have the strength or the leverage. He sighed.

"If the Aduatuci consider themselves basically a Germanic tribe, and so do the Germans, there's a good chance that they will ally with the tribes across the Rhine against us. The Germans have had a problem with us since last year, and I can't see the Aduatuci having to do much prodding to push those tribes into open war again."

He looked around the room at the number of officers currently displaying wounds.

"And, given the fact that we just got the living snot kicked out of us and are operating very much below strength, we really can't afford to have another Ariovistus pop up and decide that Rome's getting too close to the Rhine again. If they rose against us, there's still time for them to come west before winter."

Caesar frowned.

"A worrying possibility, I will concede."

Fronto shook his head.

"It's very simple. We've got to get to the Aduatuci and take them out of the picture before they involve the Germans."

The general stood for a time, tapping his finger on his lower lip and finally nodded.

"Agreed. I was hoping this war was finally over, but we have to finish it before it becomes a German matter."

He looked around at the officers under his command.

"Labienus? I need you to take a force from the army. Not a full legion, as we may need them, but enough cohorts from wherever they can be spared to make half a legion, along with a few scouts and cavalry. Procillus and Mettius, I want you with him. The three of you, with a reasonable force, need to find and deal with the remnants of the Nervii and their allies. Send scouts out to every major oppidum of the Belgae and tell them Caesar calls their leaders to council at…" He paused and examined the map again.

"Nemetocenna is the main oppidum of the Atrebates and very much at the heart of the resisting area so far. Call all the tribes to a council at Nemetocenna by the kalends of Septembris. I am taking the rest of the army as soon as things are settled here to deal with the Aduatuci and we shall aim to return by then."

Labienus frowned.

"Caesar, is it not more important that you are here to deal with the politics of victory? Any number of us can take the battle to the Aduatuci."

The general shook his head.

"I have defeated, or allied with, all of the main tribes of the Belgae. When I return to Cisalpine Gaul and then Rome for the winter, I will have it known that Caesar has defeated the greatest of all the peoples of the north. My political enemies will be forced to acknowledge this. How will it look if I leave things incomplete and one of my subordinates fights the final battle for me?"

He looked around the room. Fronto tried very hard to become invisible, as he was sure his face would betray his own opinions on the matter.

"No. I will finish this myself. Labienus, you will send out your scouts and then take your force along with most of the baggage train and all of the wounded and journey to Nemetocenna. When you arrive you will impose Roman law on the oppidum. You will construct not just a temporary camp, but a fortress like those we built in Hispania, with defences, high walls and buildings within, rather than tents. Given the location of Nemetocenna at the heart of the Belgae, I want you to make a statement."

He smiled that hollow and humourless smile once again.

"And, when I return, I shall bring either the head of the Aduatuci, or the head of the head of the Aduatuci!"

He waved his hand dismissively.

"Go about your business, gentlemen. Every healthy man will be forming up under either Labienus or myself and leaving first thing in the morning. Labienus? I will leave you to deal with the post-battle matters. I need to plan."

The officers hurried out of the tent, Fronto moving as fast as he could to avoid being waylaid by the general. Outside, just out of audible range of the tent, Labienus was grumbling.

"What's up?"

"Too much to do with too few men. I think we need our own planning meeting."

He glanced over his shoulder at the various officers marching away down the hill.

"All officers to assemble in the remains of the Nervian camp opposite in quarter of an hour. Be there, or I'll find you!"

Fronto laughed.

"Don't know what you're giggling about" grumbled the staff officer. "You're coming too."

Labienus looked around at the expectant faces of the officers. The walk across the battlefield had not been a pleasant one. Many of the bodies still lay where they had fallen, including some Romans. Here, beyond the opposite ridge, the camp of the Nervii had been cleared of corpses when the men had looted it, but there was still an acrid and sickly-sweet smell that did not bear too much thinking about.

However, not only was this sufficiently far away from the headquarters for them to be undisturbed by the general, it was also away from where the men were busy clearing up the worst of the mess.

"Alright, tell me what the situation is. First of all, what's our total count of healthy regulars?"

Sabinus shrugged and opened the wax tablets he had brought with him.

"I can break it down for you, but the grand total is now sixteen thousand men fit for active duty out of a strength on parchment of almost thirty six thousand."

Labienus shook his head despairingly.

"Gods! I know we were already under strength to start with, but that means we lost roughly half the army this morning!"

Sabinus nodded silently. Every officer had been keeping himself occupied so as not to think too much on the numbers.

"There are so many dead, along with the auxilia," Rufus noted quietly, "that they're being separated into four groups for burning and burial to make it easier for digging the ditches and raising the mounds."

Sabinus straightened.

"Alright then. I'll take around three thousand of the men. I'll draw five centuries from each of the six stronger legions and take the entire Twelfth." He looked up at Galba. "I'm not meaning to take any glory away from you, my friend, but I rather believe that your men will appreciate the rest."

The stocky legate nodded.

"I agree entirely. But will you need three thousand? There should be no armies left to raise in the west."

Labienus nodded.

"Caesar probably hasn't thought it all out yet, but we'll have ninety per cent of the wagon train to guard, as he'll be wanting to travel fast and light. We'll have all of the wounded, which is a lot, to look after. He wants us to impose ourselves on Nemetocenna, which would be hard to do with a handful of men. He wants us to build a sizeable fortress…"

He suddenly stopped and tapped his temple.

"That means I'll need some good engineers."

Fronto smiled.

"I can provide them for you."

"Good. And, of course, there'll be prisoners to guard and booty to transport. To be honest, I think three thousand men's stretching things a little thin."

The group went silent again.

"How long til the legions have cleared away the bodies and buried everyone?"

Fronto shrugged and almost bit through his tongue at the horrifying pain in his arm.

"A few more hours. My lads are moving through the Roman dead like a swarm of locusts, looking for our training centurion."

Sabinus raised an eyebrow.

"Velius?"

Fronto nodded. Not been seen since we pushed into the Atrebates. I suspect he'll be found shortly.

"Sad."

The officers all lowered their gaze and eventually Labienus sighed and took a deep breath.

"Very well. Prisoners. How many have we taken today, and how many do we have in total?"

Crispus stepped forward from where he had been hovering on the periphery.

"I'm not at all sure how many we had originally. The moment we left Samarobriva, Caesar had the walking wounded, and some of the Gallic levies escort the prisoners back to Vesontio. I expect they are already on the way to the slave markets in Rome."

Labienus nodded.

"So now?"

"Now we have around six and a half thousand prisoners; a mixture of Viromandui, Atrebates and Nervii. Mostly Viromandui, though, since the others fought almost to extinction. Varus captured the command party, by the looks of it. He found the head man of the Nervii trying to sneak away through the woods along with some of his warriors."

Labienus laughed.

"Good. That should lend some weight to our demands when we get to Nemetocenna."

Fronto cleared his throat.

"Be prepared to carry out the peace on your own while Caesar carries out the war. I've seen the maps, and I know these Belgae and their sieges. I can't see a chance in hell of the general being back before at least the nones of Septembris, if not the ides."

Labienus smiled.

"Then I'll have to delegate some of it to you."

"Me?" Fronto shook his head.

"Yes, you. You're wounded and with only one working arm. You get to go with us."

Fronto grinned.

"If you think for one moment a broken arm is keeping me out of battle to sit and be talked to death by dozens of native chieftains, you've got another thing coming!"

* * * * *

Fronto stood impatiently watching his tent being erected. His furniture, such as it was, lay close by, waiting to be positioned inside. He had stopped them removing it all from the cart, though. Just the cot and a chair. It was hardly worth moving any more since the whole army would be departing at first light in one direction or the other and everything would have to be taken down and stowed in around ten hours.

Sabinus, given the task of overseeing the camp's creation in the absence of the trained and experienced camp prefect Paetus, strode across the open ground and watched with interest as the leather tent panels were fastened together and stretched across the wooden frame.

"Fascinating, isn't it?"

Fronto turned and raised an eyebrow. He realised he was absent-mindedly rubbing his bad arm again. How the hell could he not even waggle it slightly? It was obviously still alive, or it would not hurt so bloody much.

"What?"

"Watching the men setting camp. I've never really spent a lot of time watching it, but it's such a smooth, regimented system. Paetus has got the procedure drilled so heavily into the heads of the men that I'm not really doing anything useful. Just watching."

Fronto grumbled.

"You need to be careful saying things like that. In this army, that kind of comment could land you the job permanently."

"You're a ray of sunshine as usual, Marcus."

Another grumble.

"I have this horrible feeling…"

Sabinus frowned.

"Not sure I like the sound of that. You had a bad feeling about this, and we lost half the damned army."

The legate nodded.

"I'm torn. There's very little I can think of that I'd less rather do that go with Labienus and set up political allegiances and make deals and pacts. But on the other hand, Nemesis is making my head itch. There's something looming, and I think it's got something to do with the Aduatuci."

Sabinus laughed, though Fronto detected a definite edge to it.

"You're a practical man, Fronto. You always have been. Don't tell me you're turning into some sort of haruspex?"

Fronto laughed, but noted that subtly, at waist level, Sabinus had made the sign to ward off evil. He opened his mouth to say something suitably disparaging, but clamped it shut again as a voice from behind called his name. He turned to see Balbus hurrying up the slope alongside Priscus.

“What’s important enough to make you two run?”

Balbus heaved down air, his face rosy, and Priscus took a deep breath. Something about his expression set the legate very much on edge.

“You need to come see this, Fronto.”

Sabinus blinked. While it was generally understood and accepted that Fronto and his primus pilus had a somewhat informal relationship, to address his commander in such a fashion in front of two more senior officers was something of a breach of etiquette. What had Priscus so riled that he forgot entirely about propriety?

Fronto’s brow furrowed.

“Tell me.”

"They've found Velius. I wasn't kidding... you need to see it."

“It?” Suddenly Fronto was running in the direction from which the centurion had come, the other three hot on his heels. “Where?”

Priscus, quickly catching up, pointed off toward the woods to the west.

“How the hell did he get there? He must have fallen in the midst of the Atrebates, like I did.”

There was no answer from the primus pilus, but he picked up speed and jogged out ahead to lead the way. Sabinus and Balbus caught up with Fronto and the three men, in varying states of exhaustion, ran on after the centurion.

The way through the woods was easy. Fronto had not ventured to them since the battle’s end, but was aware that they had harboured a sizeable part of the Belgic army prior to the fight. There was hardly any undergrowth left, and what there was had been trampled flat.

Indeed, as the four men passed under the eaves, Fronto became aware of just how many men must have hidden here behind their wicker screens covered in leaves, preventing them from being seen by the Roman army on the slope. And not all of the footprints he could identify, some barefooted, some in Celtic boots and other in caligae, were heading to the battlefield. There were a number of tracks that told the story of the survivors of the Atrebates and the Nervii who had fled into these woods and picked their way quietly through them. Probably some escaped to run home to their families, but others fell foul of Varus' men at the wood's western edge and were now in chains.

Suddenly he became aware of conversation. Peering between the trees and plants, he spotted around a dozen legionaries with an optio in a small clearing. Priscus was making straight for them.

The legate found, as he stepped from the deeper wood into the clearing, that his pulse had quickened, and there was an uncomfortable lump in his throat. During the hours of waiting while the men searched through and retrieved all of the Roman bodies on the battlefield, Fronto had, sadly and slowly, begun to come to terms with the idea that Velius had gone. It seemed impossible when he thought about that grizzled face; the man had always seemed near indestructible but, realistically, it was actually astounding that only one of the three of them had died, given the suicidally reckless action they had undertaken.

But despite the enormity of it, he had just about come to terms. Velius was dead, and a new position had opened up in the centurionate of the Tenth. A new chief training officer would have to be selected. It seemed ironic that there was a good chance that whoever was selected would themselves have been trained by Velius.

Suddenly the legionaries parted, having spotted the officers approaching the scene, and Fronto felt the bile rise in his throat.

"Gods!"

The smell of meat, both raw and burned, assailed his nostrils. Sabinus, next to him, had gone white.

A frame had been hastily constructed by bending two saplings and nailing them to the boles of trees, resulting in a diagonal cross between two trunks. On the frame was tied the remains of a man, his headless body, missing both hands and feet and opened from neck to groin, hanging limp from the vines that held him. For a moment Fronto almost asked how they knew this was Velius, but then his roving gaze caught the sight of the head, impaled on a spear nearby.

The charring smell came from the ashes of a small fire, where the hands and feet and what was presumably a pile of internal organs had been burned, presumably in some sort of ritual. He averted his eyes. Looking at the head was making him an unpleasant mix of queasy and angry.

"Druids!" a voice barked.

His head snapped round to Sabinus, who was still pale, but now displaying a grim snarl.

"What?"

"Druids," the man repeated. "This is what they do: death rituals. This wasn't the work of ordinary men. I know the ordinary plebs back in Rome think all barbarians are nine feet tall and eat babies, but you and I know the truth. Look at Galronus. It's not Celts that do this; or even Belgae. It's druids that do this."

The legate could not find a reason to argue. Sabinus was probably right. And Fronto just could not think straight; was frightened to open his mouth in case the sight and the stench made him vomit.

Priscus took one look at the senior officers and addressed the optio and his men.

"Get this cleared up. All the body parts need to be put away in a bag for cremation and funeral, but the guts and all the wood... just burn it."

He took a deep breath.

"But leave the head. I'll bring the head."

The optio saluted, and he and his men began the grisly task as Priscus stepped in front of the three officers. Fronto blinked.

"Why the head?"

"Because that's what you need to see. That's why I brought you."

The primus pilus turned and strode in a businesslike fashion across to the head, sitting atop its spear and glaring at them, in a manner that looked disturbingly accusative to Fronto.

The officers walked across behind him, focusing on the head, while at the same time trying not to think too hard about it. Priscus, in a no-nonsense fashion, marched up to the grisly object and pointed.

"There."

"What?" Fronto frowned as he examined the remnant of his officer. It was extremely unpleasant, messy, and clearly a statement to the commanders of the Roman army, but it was equally clearly just Velius' head on a spike.

"The mouth." Priscus jabbed with his finger.

"What's that?" Fronto leaned closer, swallowing against the unpleasant smell and the bile that threatened to rise. There was something in the mouth of the severed head; something dark, smooth and oily.

Priscus shrugged.

"Don't know. Thought I'd better wait so that you'd seen it first. Want me to take it out?"

Fronto wavered for a moment. He was not entirely sure he wanted to know what the object was.

"Yes. Take it out."

The three men watched tensely as Priscus reached in and, slowly and carefully worked the object loose with his fingers before withdrawing it. As the small, oily object came loose with an unpleasant noise, a gobbet of thickened blood followed it. Once more bile rose into Fronto's mouth, and he had to turn and spit into the undergrowth. Velius' tongue had been removed to make room, probably burned in the fire along with the rest of the viscera.

"What the hell is it?"

Priscus turned the object over in his hands several times, frowning at the unpleasant liquids that ran across his knuckles.

"It's a bag. A pouch. Leather but waxed or oiled for waterproofing."

Fronto stared.

"So what's in it?"

Priscus stared down at the unpleasant article.

"I think finding that out's the commander's prerogative, sir."

Fronto stared at the small, shiny bag. Funny how the chain of command and all proprieties of officerhood came out when they were trying to decide who would do the worst tasks.

"I can't. I've only got one working hand."

Priscus glared at his commander for a moment and the clearing was blanketed in an uncomfortable silence. Moments passed until Sabinus stepped forward.

"Alright then, children. I'll look."

Clenching his teeth, fighting back the urge to retch at the coagulated blood on the smooth leather, he retrieved the pouch and began to work at the tiny string at one end. As he unknotted it and gently worked the aperture open, Fronto found he was holding his breath.

"Well?"

Sabinus held the pouch up, allowing the light to illuminate the opening. He stared into it for a moment.

"Sabinus…" Fronto prompted.

With a frown and a shrug, the staff officer tipped the pouch up, and its contents tumbled out onto his palm.

"It's a ring. And a note."

"A note?" Balbus frowned at it quizzically. "That's parchment! Where in the name of Jupiter did a barbarian druid get hold of good Egyptian parchment?"

Fronto stared.

"And that's a Roman ring. A good one, too."

He reached out and grasped the parchment, struggling one-handed to unroll the small sheet.

"It's in Latin. Well-written too."

"What does it say, though?" Priscus was tense and staring.

"Gods, I can hardly read it, it's so small." He held the document up to his face and squinted.

"It says…" he took a breath. "No matter how many tribes you make bend to your will, the Gods and their priests will never accept you. Savour your petty victory for, in time, all of Gaul will pucker to spit you back out."

He paused.

"Crap, who is this man? 'All Gaul will pucker'? He sounds like a slave in a Plautus comedy!"

Balbus nodded.

"May sound all very literate, but don't ignore what that message is actually saying. He's warning us... or possibly threatening us, I suppose... that the druids will continue to raise resistance to us. We can pacify all of Gallic and Belgic lands, but there's always the German tribes and even Britannia to the north that look to the druids. And, of course, we may have pacified places now, but what happens as soon as we withdraw the legions?"

Fronto nodded.

"Given the amount of influence these druids have over the barbarians, I think maybe if Caesar really does want Gaul, he's going to have to deal with the druids somehow."

"Fronto…"

The legate turned to Sabinus, who was staring at him and holding out the ring.

"What?"

The staff officer swallowed.

"This is Paetus' ring."

The four officers fell silent, staring at the small item of jewellery in Sabinus' hand.

"Then I suppose we know what became of our runaway" muttered Balbus.

Fronto nodded sadly.

"Poor bastard can't have got far. I hope they dealt with him quickly and not like this!"

Priscus cleared his throat.

"Gentlemen? Time to return to camp. I've got to deal with this."

Fronto was about to argue until his primus pilus wrenched the disembodied head from the spear tip with a crunch, a squelch, and a rush of dark blood.

"He's right. Let's go see if they've finished with my tent. I'll get some wine."

Sabinus and Balbus nodded emphatically, and the former straightened.

"I'll meet you there shortly." He closed his hand on the signet ring and reached out to take the parchment from Fronto. "I need to deliver this to Labienus, and Caesar ought to see the note."

Fronto relinquished the parchment and, with a last glimpse back at the grisly clearing, turned and made for light, warmth and civilisation.

* * * * *

Labienus shuddered. The vexillation he was taking from the legions had been prepared to move by first light and had been required to wait until the rest of the army was in order so they could take all the surplus gear on the carts. Caesar was travelling very light, with the legions and the cavalry and only two dozen wagons, leaving a half-mile train to head west with his lieutenant.

Three thousand men and a few cavalry. Enough of a force to deal with any small encounters, but Labienus repeatedly found his imagination playing out fantasies in which half a million Belgae, Britons, Gauls and Germans dropped from trees onto his slow-moving column.

And Gods, was it a slow-moving column. He had sent the couriers out in threes to deliver his message to the Belgic chieftains before they left, and then they'd started the long, mind-numbing journey to the oppidum of Nemetocenna. He had marched with the legions many times in his reasonably illustrious career, and they could move fast. It had sometimes been the major cause of victories that the legions moved so fast and efficiently, surprising the enemy by cutting them off.

But a long supply train slowed things down; and then there were the wounded. The worst of them were in wagons which had to be manoeuvred very slowly and carefully so as not to jar the occupants; and alongside them came the walking wounded, though such a description was being especially kind to some of them, men who Labienus expected to die on the journey. And if the carts and the wounded were not enough, there were the prisoners all roped together and being herded along at the back with an escort drawn mainly from the Ninth.

He would be lucky if they reached Nemetocenna before the place fell down from the ravages of time! Caesar and the chieftains would already be there waiting when he arrived at this rate. He grumbled and rolled his shoulders, allowing his cuirass to settle into a slightly less uncomfortable position.

And just to top it all off, the morning had been the first cold and grey one he could remember for months. His force had only been travelling for an hour when the clouds had broken, and the rain began to come down in diagonal rods. He was already soaked and chilled to the bone, and it was only mid morning… clearly Fortuna was shitting on him today. He could only hope that meant she was saving all her good stuff for Caesar against the Aduatuci.

He smiled grimly.

The general had, this morning, ordered the haruspices that travelled with the staff to gut a goat and read the omens for their next campaign. The strange thin and balding men in their white robes and shiny hats had carefully lifted out and examined each organ in order and had finally pronounced the omens to be good. Labienus had been standing next to Fronto when the legate had said quite loudly "but not for the goat."

In fact, Fronto had been very dour and quiet this morning. It was not the Fronto they all remembered, and this new facet of his personality, that kept reminding them of the perils they faced, was starting to infect the staff across the board.

On the bright side, Labienus had snatched the goat carcass when it was done with for the officers' dinner tonight.

He had to do something to ‘blow out the cobwebs’ as they said. Travelling at this slow walk was just killing his spirits ever further. He took a deep breath and leaned across to the tribune beside him, a man he did not know who had been drawn from the Eleventh.

“I’m riding on ahead to that rise; I need a little space for a moment.”

The tribune saluted, looking exceedingly unsure.

“Sir, you need to take a guard.”

Labienus laughed.

“I’ll not leave the sight of the column. I’m only going up the hill, not heading for Illyricum. Besides, no self respecting ambusher is going to be out in this. Even the druids will be inside by a fire. We’re the only idiots in this half of the world to be outside today.”

The tribune laughed.

“Apart from Caesar, sir!”

Labienus snorted.

“With the luck the general has, a small patch of cloudless blue sky’s probably following him. He is descended from Venus, after all.”

Another laugh from the tribune.

“Just be careful sir. There’s nobody here who can replace you.”

Labienus nodded darkly as he set off ahead at a canter. The man was right. There was not a soldier in the column above the rank of tribune. Oh, there were Procillus and Mettius, of course, who would be invaluable when it came to politics and treaties, but then they were spies and diplomats; no use if a million Celts fell out of the trees as they passed.

He kicked his horse into an extra turn of speed and rode up the slope. The rain was just as heavy, just as wet and just as cold but, for some reason, not half as depressing when you were racing through it at speed.

He was starting to feel a little lighter and easier as he reached the top of the hill and turned to view the long column snaking away behind him so far that it disappeared into the grey murk. Perhaps things would be a little easier if he continued to do this throughout the journey. Maybe Procillus and Mettius would appreciate the opportunity to leave the column... but probably not. The pair of them were travelling in a covered wagon and had made no attempt to venture out into the weather; not something a commanding officer could do, really.

He sighed and turned back to the view ahead.

“Juno, what happened here?”

Labienus stared at the dip beyond the ridge. To the left was the forest they'd been skirting for the last hour and which had given rise to his fantasies of tree-dwelling Belgae. To the right: a wide shallow bowl that had played host to a large camp; perhaps as large as the Belgae's camp where Rufus had massacred the warriors of the Atrebates.

Rough tents and shelters formed from logs, branches and ferns formed the bulk of the camp, with burned-out grey campfires dotted around, the whole thing arrayed around a central complex of buildings; presumably a local farm.

But the camp was not the issue.

The camp was not empty.

“Juno, Dis and Nemesis!”

The bodies lay so thick in places that they were piled on top of one another. For a moment, he worried for his safety, the words of the tribune echoing through his mind. No, he was in no danger. Nothing down there was alive. Taking a deep breath, preparing for whatever fresh horror lay ahead, he walked his horse down the slope and into the depression.

He had barely reached the edge of the distressing sight when he was forced to pull his tunic up over his nose to try and block out the smell. These bodies were fresh; fresher than those of the army back at the river yesterday. They'd died during the night.

In fact, as he walked his horse slowly and carefully in among the piles of the dead, he realised that some of the fires were still smouldering slightly. They had only been untended a few hours, but now the rain was finishing them off.

So many bodies. More than at the battlefield. Many more. So many dead. And…

He drew a deep breath and fought back a tear that threatened to run down his cheek. Not a single warrior among them. Not a man between the age of twelve and sixty. Mostly women and children. Girls of five or six years old, covered in their own blood. Gutted.

He became aware of shouting behind him. Turning, he realised the tribune had brought a dozen cavalry over the slope. Of course he had. His commander had gone off on his own.

"Sir!"

Labienus turned, his face ashen, and slowly walked his horse between the fires and the bodies, back to the riders who sat waiting for him, staring at the macabre array.

"What happened here sir? The Aduatuci you think? Did they come here and do this?"

Labienus shook his head.

"What is wrong with these people? With this world?"

"Sir?" The tribune looked genuinely confused.

"No one did this to them, tribune. They did it to themselves."

He stared at the piles again.

"Brother killing sister, father killing daughter. Must be well over a hundred thousand of them here. More…"

The tribune shook his head, his mouth open.

"Because of us?"

Labienus nodded.

"Us and stupidity. They heard they'd lost. And our reputation among the Celts is not the most savoury. They'd probably been told we would come and rape and murder them. This is defiance, after a fashion."

The tribune frowned.

"What do we do, sir?"

Labienus wiped the trickling rain from his brow.

"We're civilised men, tribune. What would you expect us to do?"

The man stared for a moment and then, nodding, turned to the trooper behind him.

"Get back to the column. Tell them to take an hour's rest and have the centurions form up three centuries for burial detail. These civilians need a proper tumulus."

The trooper saluted and turned to ride back over the crest to the army.

Labienus sighed and fished into the pocket of his breeches. His face taking on a slightly bleaker appearance still, he withdrew Paetus' signet ring.

"What a reputation we're building for ourselves, eh Lucius?"

With a deeper sigh, he looked down sadly at the item in his hand and dropped easily from his horse. A grim expression on his face, he strode over to the nearest pile of corpses and stared down at it.

Crouching, he located the body of a young girl and sadly, rolled her over on the pile of people; likely her family. Her throat had been cut. Possibly, looking at the jagged mess, she had even done it herself. The blood had soaked into the bodies beneath, and her face was now alabaster white.

Reaching out he stroked her hair. She would be about the same age as his own daughter. Ignoring the tear on his cheek and biting his lip, he reached for her hand unfolded the fingers, turned it palm-up and dropped Paetus' ring into it. Smiling sadly, he gently but firmly pushed the fingers closed on the ring and patted her on the cheek.

"We're not all monsters, girl. One day your people will realise that. If there are any of you left."

He stood, took a deep and heavy breath, and set his teeth together. Vaulting onto his horse, he walked it back up the slope.

"Come on. We have a job to do."

As he passed the centurions leading the burial parties back over the slope, he gritted his teeth and glared down at them.

"With respect. And no looting!"

The centurion, clearly surprised, saluted.

"Yessir!"

As Labienus rode back to the column, he finally felt a little peace descending on him. He had not had his heart in this particular task. He had envied those men riding off to chastise the Aduatuci, but not now. Now his purpose was really clear for the first time. Now he had a reason. He had to bring peace at whatever cost. He had to bring the Gauls and the Belgae into the fold. Not for Caesar; not even for Rome. For themselves. What happened here must never happen again.

"Never again."

He ignored the look of surprise his apropos-of-nothing comment raised from the tribunes.

No… never again.

Chapter 19

(On the plain before the oppidum of Aduatuca)

"Laqueus: a garrotte usually used by gladiators to restrain an opponent's arm, but also occasionally used to cause death by strangulation."

Crispus frowned.

"I cannot decide whether they have a very egocentric world-view or merely no imagination."

Fronto nodded.

"I see what you mean. The Aduatuci who live in Aduatuca."

Crispus laughed.

"No... they have no name for their town. I am informed by our Remi friends that they just call it 'home'. Aduatuca is a name others have given to it, for ease of description."

Fronto frowned.

"So they believe themselves to be the centre of the world? That's a little big-headed isn't it?"

Another light laugh from Crispus.

"Whereas our 'Mare Nostrum' shows no such weakness in character, eh?"

Fronto frowned blankly at him and then gave up, shrugged, and turned back to examine the oppidum they had travelled so many days to find.

Aduatuca, as the Belgae had named it, was a plateau with only one truly accessible side. The town stood atop cliffs and rocks that were jagged and uneven, and would make most siege techniques difficult. The remaining option would be to march directly up the one shallow slope, which was perhaps a hundred paces across, and assault the impressively-constructed double walls, crowned with piles of heavy stones with which to crush any attackers, and surrounded by sharpened stakes jutting from the ground and the walls like a bristling and deadly beard.

The legions had been hot on the trail of the Aduatuci ever since they'd left the Selle River and marched east but, no matter that the Romans had stripped out the slowest part of the army and travelled only with fast and healthy troops, the Aduatuci had simply travelled like the wind, managing to easily stay ahead of Caesar and almost taunting him. And now the Roman army assembled in units on the plain in sight of the oppidum but out of range.

Fronto sighed.

"Ah well. Best go see what the general has in mind."

Crispus nodded, and the two legates strode off to join the staff, who were gathering at the front with their commander. Caesar was rubbing his temples irritably.

"Alright, gentlemen. It's quite simple. I may have underestimated the time to get here and deal with the enemy, and so we need to deal with this fast. I want to be at Nemetocenna by the kalends of Septembris for the meeting of the tribes."

Sabinus shook his head.

"Sir, rushing these things is asking for trouble. Every time we've rushed a siege so far we've failed and taken heavy losses. Labienus can argue your position, especially with the diplomats you sent. You need to concentrate on this. Take Aduatuca with as few risks and losses as possible."

Fronto nodded. "The legions are severely depleted."

Behind him he heard the familiar nasal whine that announced Plancus was winding himself up to say something stupid.

"They're right, sir. Think of how expensive it will already be to restore the manpower of the legions. It will cost a fortune, sir."

Fronto frowned. To think of the men of the legions in terms of a mere commodity irritated him on both professional and personal levels. But the man had added to their point and any angle that might make Caesar careful should be attacked. The general frowned.

"So what do you all suggest? Talk to me."

Fronto cleared his throat.

"Can't assault that slope. Remember Noviodunum? I'll bet Plancus does. We could take the gates, but it would cost us a quarter of the army doing it, and that's too high a price to pay."

"So you expect our men to climb the cliffs, Fronto?"

The legate shrugged.

"I'm just warning you off a really dangerous attack. What you need is Tetricus. He'll have ideas."

"Then get him." Caesar continued to rub his temple, wincing.

As Fronto turned and strode back to the ranks of the Tenth, he pondered on his patron. The more time he spent with Caesar, the less he liked him. The man had always had his vicious side, certainly, which had shown on several occasions during the Hispanic campaign, but he seemed to be getting worse. Indeed, his mood, his health and his judgment all seemed to have declined over the last year or more.

Perhaps life would be easier if he left Caesar's clientele and found someone else? It was not like he needed the money or the political leg up. He served with Caesar, as he always had, because the general often left him alone to do his job and he could soldier on in his own way. Maybe Pompey would have use for him?

He shook his head. He was Caesar's man. So the general was going through a bad patch. A man who changed his allegiance for ease and comfort was… well wasn't Fronto. Besides, he knew he was a moderating influence on the general and, without him, how many good men would die in fruitless pursuit of glory?

Tetricus smiled as he approached.

"Had a feeling you might be sending for me, sir."

Fronto smiled.

"Get your thinking head on. Caesar's in a hurry as usual, but I don't want to lose too many men."

"Yes," the tribune smiled. "Already had some thoughts."

The two men turned and strode toward the command unit when a shout suddenly went up. Squinting into the distance, they began to run as they saw a flood of men pouring down the slope from the gate of the oppidum. Calls went up from the various cornicens, and the legions tightened formation into solid shield walls, waiting for the order to attack. Fronto and Tetricus veered off and made a beeline for the staff who were now pulling back between the legions to a position of safety at the rear.

As they reached the group of officers, Fronto frowned.

"There's only a few thousand of them. What can they possibly hope to achieve in open battle?"

Caesar smiled.

"It matters not. The legions will obliterate them and then we will besiege their town."

Fronto remained unconvinced and, as the command party reached a small rise where they could observe events, he studied the enemy warriors pouring across the turf towards them. This was no ordinary Belgic attack. These men were unarmoured and carried only spears; moreover, they were forming into what looked like a phalanx.

"General?"

"Hmm?" Caesar turned to look at him.

"Something's up. This is too stupid to be true, and I don't believe they're idiots."

The general sighed.

"Just for once, Fronto, have a little faith in your own eyes. The terms are definitely favourable to us."

They watched a moment longer until Caesar took a deep breath and bellowed out to the men "advance!"

Along the lines, centurions took up the call and their cornicens relayed the orders. Within moments, three legions: the Tenth, Eighth and Eleventh, began to march slowly, inexorably forwards with the crash of steel and the crunch of boots, closing on the relatively small phalanx of Belgae. Fronto watched with trepidation, his breath held. This was wrong.

The Roman lines rolled forward across the plain and, as he watched, suddenly the Belgae stopped in perfect order perhaps two hundred paces from the advancing legions. The front row with their spears went into a crouch as, behind them, two rows of men lifted bows, already strung and with arrows nocked. Calmly, smoothly, and with a discipline that would satisfy the strictest centurion, they drew back in unison and released. As the flight of perhaps two hundred arrows arced into the air and the Aduatuci fetched another arrow from their quiver, the next two rows behind them released another volley.

The legions, unprepared for missile attack, sustained dozens of casualties from the first assault. The lines faltered for only a moment before the centurions, ever professional, called for the testudo formation. The second flight of arrows struck home with brutal effect just as the legions reformed, a protective roof of shields going up just in time to save them from the third volley.

Caesar, satisfied that his legions were now protected, smiled as his men closed on the Belgae but once again, Fronto was startled to realise, the enemy were ahead of the game. They had stayed out of range of the Roman pila just long enough to launch a painful, stinging assault, and now that their edge was gone, the formation merely broke, and they ran back toward the oppidum, unencumbered and far faster than the pursuing legions.

"Cavalry to intercept!" Caesar shouted, but Fronto stepped in front and shook his head.

"Don't, general."

"What?"

"They'll never get there in time. The cavalry are marshalled behind the legions. If they do catch them it'll be right under the walls, and they'll drop boulders on us."

Caesar ground his teeth for a moment and then snarled.

"Belay that order" he barked, and then, turning to Fronto: "They rile me now."

The legate nodded.

"I suspect that's what they're trying to do. They're goading you into foolish actions. Don't fall for it. Just have the auxiliary archers posted to the front in case they try that again."

Caesar glared into the distance for a while and then growled.

"Alright. Give me ideas, then."

Beside Fronto, Tetricus shrugged. "How long do we have, Caesar?"

The general sighed, a harassed look crossing his face. He rubbed his forehead irritably and grumbled.

"Sabinus? Have a rider sent to Nemetocenna. Tell Labienus to start without me and that we'll be along in due course."

As the staff officer nodded and called over one of the clerks, the general turned to Tetricus.

"Very well. If time and manpower are no object, what is your best proposal?"

A gleam that Fronto knew very well came into the tribune's eye. The legate smiled as the tribune began to talk, illustrating all of his points with waving arms and pointing fingers.

"Firstly, circumvallation. I'd wall them in. The oppidum is in the 'v' shape between two rivers. We build a rampart and ditch that seals them off, and place redoubts at regular intervals along the far river banks to make sure they don't cross and, though I think the Meuse will be too deep and fast for that anyway, it's better to be safe than to be sorry."

Caesar blinked.

"That's a sizeable rampart?"

Tetricus nodded.

"I'd say for safety six miles from bank to bank. And around twelve miles of interspaced redoubts across the water."

Caesar frowned.

"How long?"

Tetricus shrugged.

"Given the manpower and peace in which to work, general, a day; maybe two. We'll need quiet and undisturbed time after that, protected by the rampart you see, while we build the tower."

"The tower?"

"Yes, sir. See, there's no way we're getting through those walls up the slope, so the only other way is up the rocks. Can't climb them, and there's no good materials for a ramp unless we quarry a few miles away and bring it here, which will take weeks and involve working within missile range of the top. So it's a job for a tower. We can build it out of range and then move it close."

Caesar frowned.

"Those cliffs are well over a hundred feet high, even in the easiest places. You're talking about building a hundred foot tower?"

Tetricus shrugged.

"It's been done before."

"It has?"

The tribune nodded.

"The siege of Rhodes over two centuries ago. Their tower was one hundred and thirty feet in height. And that was built by Greeks. Engineering has come a long way since then. I would say our issue is not the height, but the other dimensions."

"What?"

Fronto noted with a smile that Caesar's face had taken on the same frustrated incomprehension that all officers seemed to acquire when talking to a passionate engineer.

"Well" Tetricus went on, "it will need to be massive in all other proportions, partially to maintain stability with the enormous height, but also because we need to be able to flood them with troops from the top of it, and not just a gentle trickle of men. Also, the bridge across at the top will have to be pretty immense on its own."

Caesar boggled for a moment and then sighed.

"Do what you have to. Just get me in that city."

He turned to the rest of the officers.

"Have the legions construct a camp, then. Looks like we'll be here for a while."

* * * * *

Fronto stared at Tetricus.

"What the hell are you doing?"

The tribune turned back to see his legate and smiled, the moonlight picking out details on his man's frame, as he collected the massive, coiled rope from the ground beside him. Camp had been completed in mid afternoon and already the ditch and rampart had been begun, stretching half a mile with six feet of depth and height respectively. The finished product would be twice that.

"Measuring the height of the tower."

"What?"

Tetricus grinned.

"We need to know the height of the cliffs so we can work out what dimensions the tower must be. I estimated earlier on, but we need a more accurate measurement."

Fronto laughed. Only an engineer…

"So you're out in the no-mans-land in the dark with a rope. You are a madman, you know that?"

Tetricus shrugged.

"Safer at night. This is actually a lot easier in bright sun, but the Aduatuci would probably drop things on me."

Fronto blinked.

"You're actually going to climb that in the dark and measure it?"

"No, no, no. It's very simple. I know I'm five and a third feet tall, yes?"

"If you say so."

"And I've measured my shadow and cut a length of rope to fit."

"Err… alright" Fronto agreed hesitantly.

"So while the moon is at this height, that length of rope is equal to five and a third feet."

"Yes?" the legate said uncertainly.

"So now I just have to get to the base of the cliff and measure the shadow of the cliff, and I can work out how tall it is."

"If you say so."

Tetricus laughed.

"You're not a scientific man, are you, sir?"

"You have no idea, my friend. Come on. I'll be your bodyguard while you do your sums."

The two men strode off quickly and quietly into the moonlit night, leaving behind the lights and sounds of the camp. While they walked, Tetricus frowned as he regarded his superior officer.

"Would you be offended if I asked you a couple of personal questions, sir?"

Fronto laughed quietly.

"Gaius, I think we've known one another long enough by now you can stop calling me sir when there are none of the junior ranks around."

"Force of habit. Would you mind?"

"Go ahead."

The jagged rocks that formed the massive fortress of the Aduatuci loomed less than a quarter of a mile distant, and it occurred once again to Fronto that this could be a dangerous and even foolhardy little jaunt.

"Your arm's not getting any better, is it?"

Fronto shook his head. He had been trying not to think too hard about that. A future as a one-armed man was not a pretty picture.

"Perhaps not. I'm not sure. The medical staff say that since I can still feel the pain in it, then it's still alive. They think the…" he tried to think back to what he had been told. "Like in torsion artillery, where you wind ropes tight? Well that's sort of how the arm works. The doc said that some of the most important points in the workings have been badly damaged. He said that if it's still viable that it'll slowly heal and I'll start to get some movement back, though it'll take a long time and a lot of exercise."

He sighed.

"Or possibly there was too much damage, and it's severed inside. Then basically I have a decorative limb. I'm sort of hoping that's not the case."

Tetricus nodded.

"You're a very private person, I've noticed, legate? No one has dared ask you about your arm before now, I'll bet."

Fronto nodded.

"Stop looking into my mind… it's irritating."

Tetricus smiled.

"I think that a lot of people who think they know you don't know you half as well as they think they do."

Fronto gave him a warning glance.

"Anything else?"

Tetricus took a deep breath.

"The woman."

"What?"

"That native woman you left in Noviodunum?"

Fronto, unseen in the night, rolled his eyes.

"What about her?"

"Why look after her only to then leave her behind? You should by rights have thrown her in with the captives. She should be sold in Rome with the rest of them. Most officers would have done that… or killed her."

"I don't like killing girls."

"But to protect her from everyone and then just discard her among the Belgae?"

Fronto looked across at his companion. Tetricus was clearly weighing him up somehow.

"Go on…"

"Well." The tribune took a deep breath. "I hope you don't take offence at this, but… well, I saw the way you looked at her."

"What?"

"Like a hungry man staring at a cooked lamb. I know that look."

Fronto growled.

"I think this conversation is over."

"Fair enough. Any time you want to talk, though, I'll listen."

The tribune turned back to look at the looming cliff, missing the unpleasant glare that Fronto threw after him. Muttering things under his breath that he was not really sure even he believed, he hurried and caught up with the tribune, just as they passed into the shadow cast by the bright moon in the east.

"Not far now."

Fronto nodded.

"So what? We pin the rope and then walk back to camp?"

Tetricus nodded.

"I've got to…" he trailed off. "Did you see that?"

Fronto's face took on a sudden serious cast.

"What?"

He frowned and follows Tetricus' pointing finger.

"Shit!"

Shadowy shapes moved, silhouetted, across the ground between the oppidum and the partially-constructed siege works.

"These bastards are tricky. We'd best go warn the legions. Obviously they've not been seen, or we'd have heard the call go up."

Tetricus grasped his wrist as he turned.

"No point" he hissed. "Watch them…"

Fronto stopped and squinted into the moonlight at the black shapes. Tetricus was right; they were swarming back up the slope toward the oppidum's gate.

The tribune raised an eyebrow. Do we go check, or just back to camp?"

"We check. I don't like the look of this. The guards at the rampart should have raised the alarm. They must have seen them."

Tetricus dropped the length of rope and the two men jogged across the eerie moonlit landscape with its streaks of black, grey and white where poplars cast their shadows. They watched the last few shadowy shapes disappear among the defences on the slope as they came within clear view of the fortifications.

The torches and braziers of the guards still burned, but there was no polished reflection of helm or spear in the silvery glare.

"This is not good."

The two men skittered to a halt at the near end, where the ditch in front was only two feet deep, with the rampart of discarded earth the same height. Fronto strode purposefully across to the nearest brazier. Soldiers should have been sheltering over it, warming their hands in the night breeze, but no. No men here.

Scanning the area, he noted shapes on the floor nearby. With a sigh, he strode over, already sure of the guards' fate.

Sure enough, only a few paces from the brazier, a contubernium of eight men lay piled atop each other. Reaching down, he rolled the top man aside. Tetricus crouched next to him and examined the man.

"Strangled with a laqueus. From behind, clearly."

He examined the pile of men.

"Same for them all. They must have come out of nowhere and overwhelmed all the guards before they could raise an alarm."

"Shit," Fronto said again with great feeling. "There were an entire century of men guarding this work. All gone without a sound, and not a sword drawn. These Aduatuci are nasty. And clever."

Tetricus nodded.

"We'd best get back to camp and report this."

"What about your measurements?"

"I'll guess. Come on."

* * * * *

Paetus clenched his teeth. The first day of their journey he had spent tense, expecting at any moment to be hauled aside by the guards and accused of treason against Rome. The prisoners had been roped together in four lines hundreds of men long. There may have been some sort of order based on the tribe of the captive, but Paetus could not tell one man from another; with one exception.

That first day, as they had been roped together, he had noted that Boduognatus, chief of the Nervii, had been positioned through blind chance only three men ahead of him in the chain. The man had not cast a single glance at him throughout that long walk, but of all the barbarians in this motley collection, Boduognatus was the only one that definitely knew who and what Paetus was, and the only one who would likely turn him over to the Romans. Possibly he was keeping Paetus' identity as a piece in the game, to play at the last moment and save himself, but that seemed unlikely. The man who had initially wanted to skin him alive for merely being Roman was not the sort of man to play those games.

No. More likely the chieftain was waiting for an opportune moment during the night when the guards were not looking to quietly do away with him. The legionaries would not care too much. It would be a small financial loss for them in slave profits, but one barbarian was as good as the next to the average legionary. He probably would not even get buried, just thrown in a ditch when they moved on.

And so from that first agonising hour of expecting trouble, he had decided on a course of action. Boduognatus must die first, before he got the opportunity for which he was waiting. He had briefly worked on a plan to take the chieftain at night, but the man never seemed to sleep and, since Boduognatus was already looking for a way to deal with him, would be alert during that time. But during the day, all the prisoners experienced was hour after hour of painful shuffling and their minds drifted and switched off, especially if, like Boduognatus, they had slept little during the night.

So on the third morning, as the prisoners, bound by their wrists only during the night, were lined up for the rope to be passed along the rows, Paetus had positioned himself carefully. The chieftain may have noticed that Paetus was now in the line behind him but, if he cared, he showed no sign.

The column had started to move at sunrise and continued without a break, churning the mud of the track and eating away at the miles until the watery sun behind the thin clouds with their intermittent drizzle was high overhead. As noon came upon them, a rest was called, and the legions were allowed to sit and recover, while the prisoners remained roped and standing. Half a dozen soldiers came down the lines with jugs and baskets, dropping a chunk of bread into their greedy hands and tipping a ladle of water into every thirsty mouth. And everyone drank desperately, and tore into their bread; all except Paetus. The former prefect drank his water without comment as always, but the bread was tucked into his tunic, the pinion around which his plan revolved.

After perhaps three quarters of an hour's tense waiting, the column began to move off once again. Knowing your enemy and situation was important to a commander and Paetus was a planner by nature. Two more hours of interminable shuffling, as the rain began to fall heavier and heavier and the clouds became dark grey and pregnant with the promise of storms. Two more hours was Paetus' target. More, and he risked Labienus calling another halt; less, and the prisoners would be too rested and alert. Two more hours into the march and they were at their most docile, numbed by boredom and soreness and routine.

And now the time at last had come. His teeth clenched tightly, he fixed his eyes on the back of Boduognatus' head in front and slyly, as subtly as was humanly possible, he reached into his tunic and withdrew the bread he had secreted there.

Starving as he was, Paetus recognised the simple fact that the warriors around him were all equally hungry and desperate and would likely have less discipline than he.

Holding his breath, he waited until the nearest guard had looked away at another section of the line, and threw the torn loaf over the heads of the men in front. The item came down amongst the starving prisoners six or seven men ahead. He had meant to throw it further than that, but the ropes that held him restricted his movement too much for a good throw.

The effect was everything for which he had hoped. An explosion of activity followed, as half a dozen captives struggled and fought to obtain the precious food. The guards called the alarm and charged to intervene, but there were four roped lines of men and getting to the centre from the sides of the column was near impossible. As a soldier desperately jabbed lightly with a spear, trying to frighten them into submission, what was a small fracas expanded, almost turning into a somewhat restricted riot. The men nearest the soldier grasped his spear and tried to wrest it from him while, around the place the bread landed, men had now collapsed to the floor, fighting.

The ropes keeping them bound together lurched forward as the men fell and Boduognatus stumbled in surprise. Paetus, prepared and lithe as a cat, was on him the moment he fell. Leaping forward with the rope that connected them formed into a loop, he dropped it over the Nervian chief's head and had it round his throat before they hit the ground.

There was no time to slowly strangle the man. The guards were already beginning to get the minor riot under control; besides, ligature marks on the man's neck would be a give away and would bring Paetus to far too much attention.

With a move for which he was largely untrained, yet had thought out over and over for the last two days, he placed his knee on the Nervian's back between the shoulder blades and yanked hard on the rope. There was a clear snapping noise and the body beneath him went limp. Paetus grimaced as he loosed the rope and returned it to its correct position while he crouched there on the man. The entire attack had taken three heartbeats, as he was acutely aware. The guards had been too busy to see anything, and the prisoners around him were clearly more concerned with the bread and the fight than with this less interesting activity. The only possible problem would be the man behind him who, if he had been paying attention, would have likely seen what he had done. It was a risk he'd had to take.

As the soldiers moved up and down the rows, bringing the prisoners back into line with the occasional well-placed smack of a spear-butt, two legionaries reached down and hauled up the victorious captive, still chewing the last of his prize. The man grinned at them and they rewarded him with a hammerlike blow to the stomach before attempting to stand him upright.

"You! Up!"

The legionary gestured to Paetus and the corpse beneath him. As Paetus stood, he drew on every theatrical nuance in his being, feigning incomprehension and arrogant innocence as he stepped back as far as the ropes would allow spreading his hands as he crouched.

The legionary barely glanced at him, but smacked Boduognatus in the ribs hard with his spear. The body lay limp.

"Looks like we've got a dead one."

Another legionary came strolling over as the lines were being straightened to march once more. He crouched by the body and rolled it to the side as far as the ropes allowed.

"Broke his neck when this prick fell on him."

As he began to cut through the dead chief's bonds, the other soldier turned and delivered Paetus a crack on his shin with his spear, almost strong enough to break his leg. The former prefect staggered and gave the legionary a defiant stare.

"Hey" called the other man from beside the body. "Don't damage him. We've already lost one!"

"Screw 'em. Brainless pricks!"

"Your problem, Carus, is that you don't think ahead."

The two men dissolved into a friendly argument as the body was cut free and hauled away from the line. Paetus smiled to himself. The man behind him clearly either had not seen, or did not care, or he would have spoken up.

He straightened, ready to proceed. Now he was unknown. A miscellaneous Belgic prisoner as far as anyone was aware. All he had to do was keep quiet and unnoticed, and he would be taken in bondage all the way to Rome. Of course, when he got there, his life was effectively over, but he had bought himself weeks of thinking time; likely a month or more. And most importantly, he had be away from Belgica and Caesar's army.

He would survive. He had to.

* * * * *

Labienus stood at the gates of the camp. As Caesar had requested, he had made the fortress as impressive as possible and was pleased with the results. Fronto was right about his engineers; this Pomponius lad that was the chief engineer of the Tenth was really rather good at his job. Even Cornelius, the temporary camp prefect replacing Paetus, who had years of experience in fort construction from the Hispanic campaigns, had nodded in satisfaction at the work, clearly impressed.

In the half day since they had arrived at Nemetocenna, the vexillation of legionaries had been hard at work and had just now, as the sun set, put up the last of the tents, posted the night guards and set the watchwords. They had watched the large, low oppidum that was the home of the Atrebates since they arrived but had not entered yet. Labienus would give them tonight to think about the huge presence beyond their walls and to be impressed. It was vital to his plans that the chieftains were impressed not only with the power of the Roman military, as Caesar had intended, but also with their efficiency, patience and, later, when time allowed, their leniency and pragmatism.

He was determined, since the chances were low that Caesar would attend, to put this in the best possible light and to suggest to the Belgic leaders that the greatest future for them all was to be part of the great Roman confederacy.

And now, as his eyes left the oppidum with its twinkling lights and low air of suspicion, he glanced briefly at the impressive triple ditch to either side of the causeway, turned and strode through the gate. The legionaries on duty saluted and, as soon as he had entered, closed the portal and dropped the bar.

With a nod to the men, he strode up the via praetoria to his headquarters at the centre. As he passed the lines of tents, he mused on the tasks ahead of them. While the leaders of the Belgae gradually arrived for this council, he would create a permanent fortress here, setting the men to work in the morning constructing wooden buildings throughout.

He smiled. But where Caesar had told him to impress the Roman law on them and had meant him to frighten them into submission with his military power, Labienus had other ideas. The Belgae had to come to see Rome as a protective brother, advising and supporting them in their transition to a Romanised culture, rather than an oppressive victor. It would be tough, particularly given the reputation Rome seemed to have built in the north, but it needed to be done.

He smiled as the plans fell into place in his mind, and that smile broadened as he spotted Pomponius poring over some chart or other on a trestle by the lamplight from the windows of the headquarters, the only timber construction so far within the camp.

"Good evening centurion. May I borrow you for a few moments?"

Pomponius looked up from his work, blinking and, recognising the army's commanding officer, saluted urgently.

"No need for that right now, lad. I need your somewhat massive brain, rather than your obedience."

Pomponius grinned.

"With pleasure, sir. I've had just about all I can take of drainage diagrams for one evening."

"Drainage diagrams?" Labienus raised his eyebrows. "I wasn't even aware there was such a thing."

Pomponius laughed lightly.

"How else would we know where to put the pipes and what diameter of pipe to requisition from the smiths?"

"Pi…" Labienus shook his head. Time to give that up. Every question with this young man led to more and more unfathomable information.

"Walk with me."

He turned and strode down the via principalis toward the west gate, the engineer falling in alongside him.

"You've seen enough now of Belgic and Gallic oppida to have formed an opinion of their own construction techniques?"

"Yes, sir." The young man nodded.

"And?"

"Good grief, sir. How long have you got?"

"Just in brief, Pomponius."

"Well, sir… they're quite advanced for a so-called barbarian culture. They know about structural supports, drainage, load-bearing, and all sorts. Nowhere near our levels, but they have some intriguing ideas and certainly a grip on the basics."

Labienus nodded. They were approaching the gate now.

"If they were willing to do so, do you think it would be possible for you and some of the more engineering-oriented men to teach these barbarians more than the rudimentary basics; how to produce an aqueduct, for example?"

Pomponius laughed.

"If they're willing to learn, I see no reason why not, sir? May I ask why?"

Labienus smiled.

"Because it's time we stopped concentrating on destruction and began with construction. I have spoken to Mettius and Procillus, and Caesar has given them instructions as to certain specific demands and concessions he expects from this council, but our remit is surprisingly flexible. Caesar was intending to be here, but will likely not be, and so it'll come down to us to decide how we deal with the Belgae. And I intend to start something here."

"Sir?"

"A model community. I want to help the Belgae turn Nemetocenna into something resembling a Roman town; Belgic enough that it still feels like their own, but civilised enough to show them what peace with Rome has to offer. And the best way to do that is for Roman engineers to help, but for the Belgae to do much of the work themselves."

Pomponius nodded.

"A civil engineering project, sir. I look forward to it."

"Good," Labienus nodded. "Then we…"

He halted in mid conversation as there was a call to alarm from the nearby gate. With Pomponius on his heels, Labienus ran down the last few paces to the gate where the duty centurion came to attention and saluted.

"What's up?"

"Three riders sir. Romans, sir."

Labienus raised his eyebrows again.

"Word from Caesar. I wonder what? Open the gates."

The huge, wooden doors swung inwards, allowing the commander to see the three riders in the light cast by the torches around them. They were clearly regular Roman soldiers, and equally obviously exhausted. Their mounts steamed as they entered the fort.

Behind them, the gates were closed, and the riders dropped lightly and gratefully from their horses. One of them, wearing a harness that revealed him to be a centurion, strode forward, leaving the reins of his horse with his companions.

"Sir!"

He saluted smartly, his face running with sweat in the torchlight.

"Centurion? You come unexpected."

The man smiled.

"Begging your pardon, sir, but you have no idea. We're actually trying to find the general. Is he here? We've visited Noviodunum and Samarobriva. Wherever we go, Caesar has been and left."

Labienus frowned.

"Caesar is carrying out what is hopefully the last stage of the war, out to the east. He will be returning here when that is complete. I presumed you came from him. Who are you then, centurion?"

The man grinned and withdrew a small scroll from his tunic.

"Then, sir, as the senior officer here, I bring you greetings from legate Publius Licinius Crassus, quartered in the lands of Armorica." He glanced down and read aloud.

"I am pleased to report the conquest of northwestern Gaul and the tribes known as the Veneti, the Unelli, the Osismii, the Curiosolitae, the Sesuvii, the Aulerci, and the Rhedones all now bow to the power and might of Rome."

The centurion looked up from his note.

"Legate Crassus and the Seventh remain in situ awaiting the general's further orders."

Labienus blinked.

"He what?"

"He reports, sir, that…"

Labienus shook his head.

"Yes, centurion, I heard. Thank you. Go and find quarters and food for your men."

The officer saluted, looking slightly crestfallen at the unexpectedly low-key reception, and led his men up the street toward the quartermaster's tent close to the headquarters.

Labienus turned to Pomponius.

"One legion! The man had one legion! I can't even picture Caesar's face when he finds out!"

Chapter 20

(On the plain before the oppidum of Aduatuca)

"Civitas: Latin name given to a certain class of civil settlement, often the capital of a tribal group or a former military base."

The works of Tetricus stretched away out of sight in both directions. Caesar nodded appreciatively as he looked along the line. The ditch was more than two men deep and the rampart consequently more than two men high. Surmounted by a palisaded walkway, punctuated with gates, and peppered with lilia, it was everything a Roman defensive work should be.

"And this surrounds them?" The general asked, tapping his finger to his lip.

Tetricus nodded.

"From the River Meuse to the River Sambre is a solid line with three gates and four redoubts. We've got the Eighth, Tenth, Eleventh, and Thirteenth Legions and most of the support behind these."

He turned and pointed north. "The Sambre is crossable, though with some difficulty I'm told, so we've run another three miles of rampart and ditch along the shore there with one gate and four redoubts, though that's only at a height and depth of six feet. The Ninth Legion is stationed there and watching the river upstream. The Meuse is unfordable here, and there's no bridge for several miles in either direction, but I had redoubts set up there to watch just in case, manned by the Fourteenth, who crossed on rafts."

With a nod of satisfaction, he smiled.

"Basically, general, there's no way they can escape. We have them trapped like rats."

Caesar nodded and turned to Fronto, Balbus and Crispus who were standing together nearby.

"Have we heard anything from them today?"

Fronto shook his head. In fact the last eighteen hours since the rampart had gone up had been disturbingly quiet. The preceding two days had been painful. The Aduatuci had proved to be a cunning and subtle adversary; and dangerous. Since the initial archery assault that had surprised them all, and the night time attack at the rampart, the security around the camp had tightened. Pickets had been set, and watches kept, but the Aduatuci continually found new and fascinating ways to harass and wound Caesar's army.

The second morning, as the legions were going through the dawn rituals of washing and breakfasting before the day's backbreaking work, the Aduatuci had released one of their cattle pens, goaded, beaten and stabbed them into a frenzy, and then opened the gate, so that the stampede of angry and frightened beasts had run amok through the camp of the Ninth, causing massive destruction and a number of dreadful wounds.

Tetricus' workmen had also soon learned what could be considered a 'safe' distance from the oppidum, as the natives tested the range of arrow, slingshot, spear and boulder from the summit.

Then the next night, while the legions kept a careful watch on the slope in case of night assaults, camped out in the open before the works, the Aduatuci had climbed down the damn cliffs, presumably on great ropes, and had circled wide outside the guard posts to sabotage the works. The next morning Tetricus had surveyed the defences and noted with dismay the immense damage wreaked by so few saboteurs.

The third day since they arrived, the Aduatuci had discovered with glee that from the highest point of their defences, arrows had enough height and power to cross the river and just strike the redoubts on the far bank of the Meuse. That discovery had led to the use of fire arrows, two minor disasters, and finally the Fourteenth Legion pulling a hundred paces further back and constructing new redoubts.

Since then, with the completion of the system of defences, things had gone very, very quiet and the silence was beginning to unnerve the men.

Fronto sighed.

"There's been no sign of military activity. Actually no sign of life at all, sir."

Another nod from the general, who turned to Tetricus once again.

"So what is your progress with the next stage?"

The engineer smiled.

"We've constructed a whole load of new vineae, which should give us enough cover to get a great number of men close to the cliffs. The frame of the tower is ready, and so are the wheels and transport system. It still has to be armour plated and fitted with the bridge and ladders and so on, but that's less than a day's work. I would say that by tomorrow afternoon we'll be ready to move The morning after that, at the latest.

Caesar frowned.

"Have the enemy seen our works?"

"I couldn't say, sir. Perhaps, if they're very keen-eyed and observant, but we've not drawn attention to them and they're behind our defences."

The general tapped his finger to his lip.

"Is there any way we can keep the tower hidden until the last moment, or not raise it upright until then? If we can maintain the element of surprise, I'd very much like to do so."

Tetricus shook his head.

"I'm afraid not, sir. If they don't know what we're up to now, then they will within the hour. There's just nowhere on this plain that's out of sight of that oppidum, and we need to raise the tower onto the axles now while it's still a frame. Once we add all the plating, and the rest it'll just be too heavy to raise."

Caesar clicked his tongue irritably.

"Oh well. If it must be, it must be. But the Belgae tend to use their time and knowledge to great effect, I've noticed; far more so than the Gauls. I shouldn't be surprised if they haven't got a number of traps waiting for us when we get there."

Tetricus nodded. It was possible, but it would only delay the inevitable.

The bright mid morning sun shone down on the plain as Fronto and Crispus stood on their own, watching the engineering teams hard at work. Caesar had decided that, if the Aduatuci were to see the work of the Roman army, then the work should be spectacular. As such, three cohorts of legionaries had lined up in parade formation, gleaming and bright, around the engineers and the fruit of their labour.

Behind the legions, rows of vineae, mobile wooden frames with armoured roofs, stood waiting, alongside the onagers, ready to be moved into position.

And in the centre of this display lay the tower, a heavy wooden frame one hundred and twenty feet long. A wide trench had been excavated, and the base, with its axles, six great heavy wheels, and braking mechanism, had been rolled down the gentle slope into it until it was flush with the ground level. Following that, the tower itself had been brought from behind the walls, through a gateway and across the turf causeway, rolled along on thin, smooth logs until it reached the edge of the trench.

As Fronto watched, ropes were fed through rings and secured to the frame. At a call, four centuries of men strode out of the gate and past the frame to take positions on the ropes.

"It never fails to amaze me how engineers can construct such behemoths and make them mobile and flexible" Crispus wondered, staring at the massive construction.

Fronto shrugged and then stared at his dead arm for a moment. Recently, when he shrugged, he was not sure, but he got the impression there was a small amount of movement in the muscles. Hard to tell.

"Practice, I guess."

"Sorry?"

"Well," said Fronto frowning, "a soldier gets better with a sword by repeatedly hitting things with it and working out new and inventive ways to use it when he can't be doing it for real. A general gets better by studying other successes and failures when he's not actually involved in campaign and battle. And I've watched the engineers. They build things at every given opportunity, whether it's needed or not and, when they can't build things, they sit deep in thought and plan and invent things."

A commotion in the distance caught their attention, shouts from the walls of the oppidum. Ignoring what appeared to be jeering from the Aduatuci, Tetricus raised his hand and dropped it as a signal. A cornicen relayed the orders and the three hundred men took up the two ropes and leaned into the task. A second call and the men began, slowly and with a great deal of grunting and sweating, to grind forward, heaving on the ropes.

For moment, it looked like something had gone wrong. The huge bulk shuddered and groaned, but remained steadfastly grounded. The tiny movement among the legionaries that Fronto had noted was merely any give in the ropes and knots being taken up.

"It's too big. They should have tried building it already upright" Fronto grumbled, shaking his head.

Crispus smiled.

"They can't do it that way. Look!"

As Fronto watched, his breath held, he noticed the tiniest lift along the immense carcass of the tower. The far end came up by a foot, and then two. More and more and, the further it rose from the ground, the easier it became, moving faster and faster. Fronto watched with fascination as Tetricus and two of his engineers continually darted around the scene like flies around a horse's tail, making minor adjustments; slowing down one rope and then the other, issuing orders to the other engineering details to move a chock from beneath the corner. Gradually, as it lifted, it was manoeuvred carefully forward so that it rose square onto the wheeled platform.

Another call went up from a cornicen, and two more centuries of men marched from the gate and approached the rear of the tower, now straining at an impressive forty five degrees.

"Hell, I'm glad that's not my job" breathed Fronto as he watched the men pass under the looming bulk and grasp two more ropes that had been attached to the back.

Crispus nodded.

"Absolutely. Though without them, the tower would likely continue with its momentum, past the apex, and tip over onto the legionaries."

Fronto nodded and tried not to think what it would be like being one of those men at the back, with several tons of wood towering over you, only held up by your friends that you could not see on the other side of the structure. He swallowed.

"Sounds like the Aduatuci are enjoying the show."

Crispus laughed.

"They've probably never seen anything like it. They do construct their own ramparts and palisades, and they likely understand everything we've done so far, but this tower..."

He drew a deep breath as the tower reached its apex and wobbled perilously forward toward the men before settling with the men at the rear taking the strain on their own ropes.

"This tower is bigger than anything even we have used in war since at least the defeat of Hannibal. It has to be impressing them, and almost certainly confusing them too."

Fronto nodded. Not far away, Galronus of the Remi stood with his own officers. They seemed to be paying more attention to the oppidum than to the activity of the engineers.

"Come with me" Fronto nudged Crispus and the pair walked across to where the Belgic auxiliary officer stood. The man had a curious expression on his face; a mix of suspicion and humour.

"Galronus. Finding Tetricus' tower funny?"

The man, straight-backed and taller than Fronto and Crispus by a head, turned to look at them and harrumphed.

"I do not like this. Aduatuci too smug."

Fronto laughed.

"Your Latin is improving all the time. Why smug?"

The nobleman gestured to the oppidum and, squinting, Fronto followed his finger. The walls atop the great rock were lined with Aduatuci, and not just warriors, but women and children too, all making a great noise and gesturing.

"Aduatuci are clever" Galronus stated flatly. "They know what tower is for. They know they trapped and outnumbered. So why they make fun of you."

"Make fun?" Fronto stared.

"They ask how such small men push such a big thing and they laugh."

Fronto grumbled.

"They're entitled to their fun, I suppose. Bravery in the face of certain defeat is hardly unknown, and you Belgae are, if nothing else, a brave people."

Galronus nodded.

"Brave, true, but this stupid."

He turned suddenly and grasped Fronto by the upper arms.

"Do not trust Aduatuci. Something wrong."

Fronto stared at Galronus, but his mind was whirling and he barely heard what the man had said to him. Instinctively, as the man grasped his arms, Fronto had flinched; with both arms! His left arm had twitched. He stared down at the limb as the nobleman let go and he tried to move it. It hurt like hell and felt like trying to lift an ox with his finger, but there was definite movement.

His arm was alive. Damn it all, his arm was healing!

He grinned, first at Galronus, then at Crispus, and then back at the auxiliary officer again. Laughing, he slapped the man on the shoulder and grinned.

"Thank you, Galronus. Thank you very, very much!"

The man stared at him as though the legate had gone mad, and he opened his mouth to speak, but Fronto shook his head.

"If they're up to something we have to pre-empt them."

He grasped Crispus and marched with him back towards the command party, where Caesar stood, flanked by Sabinus and Varus on the walkway near the gate.

"What's happening?" Crispus asked as he rushed alongside his peer across the causeway and in through the gate. A short climb up the boarded steps and they reached the parapet of the rampart. Sabinus turned with a smile.

"What's got you so animated, Fronto?"

As the general and several of his staff officers turned to look at the two legates, Fronto pointed with his good arm, pausing only a moment to twitch his left, at the oppidum.

"The Aduatuci are up to something. We've been speaking to Galronus, and he's convinced of it. They're up there laughing at us while we work on the engines of their destruction. They're trapped and as good as dead, but they're in high spirits. Whatever they're planning we need to pre-empt it."

"And what do you suggest, Fronto?"

"They're laughing at us because they have a plan. We've already dealt with one almighty balls-up in this campaign because we underestimated them. Let's not do it again. Get the legions back from across the river. Have the plates and bridge attached to the tower as fast as they can be. Tetricus said it would all be ready to go by tomorrow afternoon. I'll bet if we pushed him, he could have it ready in the morning."

Caesar stared at him.

"Fronto, you are the man who keeps telling me to listen to the engineers and to slow down and not throw troops away. And now you want me to launch a massive barely-prepared attack ahead of schedule? Is this one of your 'bad feelings' again?"

Fronto glared at him.

"Don't make me sound like a superstitious lunatic, general. This is logical. Sensible even. Galronus knows these people better than all of us. He thinks they're up to something, and I think he's right. Hell, if there were plates on that tower, I'd launch the attack right now."

Caesar shook his head.

"Whether it be logic or the Gods you think are driving you, Fronto, we're not prepared for the attack. If it keeps you happy, treble the watch tonight and have everyone on standby, but we move when things are in position as planned."

Fronto's teeth ground together, but the general's face was set. He would not be persuaded. The legate turned and marched back down the slope and out of the gate, toward the First Cohort of the Tenth, standing in parade formation beside the tower, which was now upright and being secured onto its wheeled base. Locating the primus pilus at one end of the front line, he strode across, blinking as he passed suddenly from the sunlight into the deep shadow of the enormous tower, and then back out again.

"Priscus!"

The primus pilus of the Tenth, already at attention, saluted.

"Sir?"

"Come with me."

Priscus exchanged brief words with his signifer and then strode across to join the legate, who had walked back across the grass and was gesturing at Galronus. The three men converged at a spot not far from the impressive tower.

"Fronto?" A combined greeting and question from the Remi officer.

Fronto grinned at the two men with him.

"I have another suicidally reckless mission, and I'm looking for volunteers."

* * * * *

Labienus took a deep breath, acutely aware that he was, right now, not a staff officer, general, legate or any sort of soldier, but the very embodiment and representation of Rome herself. What happened at this council could shape the future of Gaul, the Belgae and Rome. And it was all down to him. Well, in truth there were others, but the responsibility rested in him. Procillus and Mettius would take on the minutia, dealing with the details, but it was up to him to make the impression.

And so, this morning, once he had been informed that the last of the chieftains had arrived, he had been to check over his preparations once again. In the six days since the fort was completed, all of the interior buildings had been replaced with permanent wooden structures. An aqueduct had been dug, lined and paved from a spring a quarter of a mile to the north, and even now a bathhouse was almost complete outside the walls.

But despite these great advances, there was a more important achievement.

He, Pomponius, and an Aedui auxiliary cavalry prefect by the name of Septimius had entered the oppidum of Nemetocenna that second morning, entirely alone; no honour guard or legionaries; on foot and unarmed. The surprise that registered on the faces of the Atrebates inhabitants had made him smile. The three men, in their best dress uniforms, had found their way to the centre of the oppidum and located the council hut, or chief's hut, or whatever they called it. Septimius, a Gaul who could speak their tongue, had accosted a frightened-looking fish seller and asked who was currently in charge. After much conversation, the man hurried off and brought back an old man; a nobleman presumably, who had been too old to go to war. He had limped into the square and stopped in front of the Romans. And so, Labienus had made contact with the Atrebates on a personal level.

They had asked permission, politely, of the old man, to use the long building for the upcoming council and the man had shrugged and, somewhat bitterly, told them to do whatever they wanted.

So, as Labienus had planned, he now walked in to a council chamber that was both Belgic and Roman. He had had two of the engineers manufacture close fitting shutters that let in the light and kept out the wind. Consequently the interior was light and warm, the fire pit in the centre blazing away.

By the door there were two tables on which stood flasks of beer and amphorae of good wine from the famous vineyards of Pompeii. Glasses and mugs rested there waiting to be filled. A trough of clean water for washing sat close by, and two more tables, awaiting food that would be provided by the soldiers later.

The most important change that he had wrung from this building, though, was the furniture. Previously the walls had been decorated with the standards and armaments of the Atrebates, while the floor was covered with skins and furs to sit on while looking up at the great wooden throne of the chief. These were gone. Well, not entirely; one wall retained the symbols of Belgic pride and power. The other held Roman standards and maps of both the Empire and of Gallic and Belgic territory. And between these two symbols stood a ring of seats, equal in size and quality; one for each of the chiefs that had been summoned and five for he, Procillus, Mettius, Pomponius and Septimius.

The door swung shut behind the Roman contingent, and Labienus cast his gaze around the room. The leaders of the tribes turned in their seats to look at him. He was saddened by the fact that several of them were either far too old to have fought in the battles, or much younger than one would expect. Several of these men had only ruled their people for a matter of weeks, and several had few people to rule.

"Good morning" he announced loudly. "I understand that many of you cannot speak my language, so prefect Septimius here will translate for those of you who cannot."

Next to him, the Aeduan auxiliary rattled off the translation in a passable Belgic dialect. Silence greeted both his words and their echo. Hoping this was not a sign of things to come, Labienus strode through the room and found a free seat. The other Romans also sat, flanking him.

"Two of my men at the back will be coming round as we converse, offering you local beer or wine brought from Italia. I urge you to try the wine, but will understand if you do not. Meats, cheese, and bread will be brought at noon."

Again, as Septimius' echo died away, the room remained stony silent.

"Very well, I can see that none of you is interested in entering into neighbourly negotiations. I can entirely understand that, but let me lay out a few truths for you…"

Next to him, Septimius continued to translate. The looks on several of the older chiefs hardened.

"You are a proud people and you see us as an occupying enemy. To a point, you are correct. However, I will point this out: Rome currently has treaties with most of the tribes of Gaul and legate Crassus has taken the eagle as far as the western sea. Caesar is, as we speak, completing his campaign. Rome is here, and no matter how much you may wish it or pray to your Gods for it, Rome is not going to go away."

He waited for Septimius to catch up.

"But there are benefits we bring. With Rome as your partner, you need never fear incursions from across the Rhine again. You will prosper. Our traders will bring exotic goods from desert lands further than any Celt has ever travelled, and in return will purchase your own wares."

Another pause.

"Rome brings peace and prosperity… but…" he smiled. "For those of you who just like to fight, we can use a good warrior!"

As Septimius translated that last, a laugh actually went up from a few of the chiefs, and low muttered conversation started here and there. Labienus waited for a moment. This was the breakthrough, but he mustn't waste it. He could lose them any moment.

"Quite seriously, my lords," he said, giving that last the most respect his could muster, "we are at a junction. We have warred against you and, without wanting to play any naming games, the Belgae initiated hostilities."

He noted the change in several of the chief's faces. He almost ruined it there, but it needed to be said. They must be aware of everything pertinent to this meeting.

"But that war is over. And while there will always be those who will seek confrontation, I myself have seen firsthand both the horrors and stupidity that go hand in hand with the glory and booty."

He took a deep breath. Here was the other point where he could lose them.

"Six miles north of where we fought a hard battle against worthy opponents, including your own warriors, we found the elderly, the women and the children of your people who live south of that field. Every single person there had taken their own life rather than co-exist with Rome, which is, frankly, idiotic."

The room had gone quiet once again.

"Traditionally, Rome has taken slaves after a campaign, yes. And yes, it still happens, but we do not rape and murder, nor do we enslave entire peoples. So, as I say, the war is over. As far as Rome is concerned, we have peace with you all. What you do with that peace is up to you, but I urge you to think on this: You have all lost greatly. What you need now is time to grow and heal once again, and Rome is willing to help you and support you in this."

There were gentle murmurings around the room.

"Rome is not a city; it is an idea. An idea that encompasses all who let it. The tribes of the Alps or the southern coast have considered themselves part of that idea for generations now and they have wine, and aqueducts and theatres and arenas and…" he gestured at the walls of the hut. “And windows… and most of all, they have peace.”

He leaned back in his seat.

“I have the authority to represent Caesar and Rome, and I am here to open negotiations with you. My proposal is this:”

He stood.

“Each tribe signs a treaty with Rome. Each tribe will donate money and goods to Caesar’s army, in quantities to be determined later, but that will not exceed what each tribe can easily spare. Each tribe will supply troops for the army, proportionate to both the size of the tribe and the current manpower available. Each tribe will open their gates to Rome and its couriers, soldiers and merchants.”

He noted the sourness to the silence now.

“In return, Rome will, as we are currently doing with a few of your tribes, train your warriors in the art of Roman warfare. We will give you engineers that will help you improve your lot. We will grant trade concessions such that you will pay no tax on imports from Roman merchants. You will receive the protection of our army and limited rights under Roman law. Once your levies and tithes are made there will be a consolidation period of three years during which you can heal your land and your people and return to strength before a standard provincial tax is levied, by which time you will be able to afford it.”

He smiled.

“Nemetocenna will become the focus of Roman influence here; a garrison town and a capital, but each of your civitas… your most important oppida will receive attention, to help them grow and become strong and important. In short, we need to take, but we also wish to give. Not a conquest, but a partnership.”

One of the older chieftains waved a hand at him and rattled something off in their own tongue. Septimius translated quickly.

“He says that what you offer is for them to stop being Belgae and become Romans, and that is no choice.”

Labienus shook his head.

“Rome is an embracing mother. Some of our peoples speak Greek rather than Latin. Some speak their own African languages. We do not stop them worshipping their own Gods… indeed, we take their Gods into our own pantheon. You have a sacred grove here in Nemetocenna. It may have escaped your notice, but if you watch, you will see our men going to pour libations and make offerings there. We do not seek to stamp out your culture, but to learn from it and embrace it."

He laughed.

"One of my good friends, a senior officer in our army, has lost his taste for good Campanian wine, favouring Gallic beer. This partnership I speak of can only succeed if we try to make it so, but it will also only fail if you make it. Now, the whole point of negotiation is that all points are flexible. I have made the opening offer. Tell me what it is that you seek, and we will find an arrangement that suits us all."

There was a long silence, during which two legionaries came round with drinks. Several chiefs waved them on and, as Labienus watched, a young chief of perhaps seventeen years, hovered for a moment over a mug of beer and then, with a smile, selected a glass of Pompeian. The young nobleman looked up at Labienus and spoke in his guttural language, the translation by Septimius almost instantaneous.

"There are eighteen tribes of the Belgae. Only seventeen are here. What news of the Aduatuci?"

Labienus stopped for a moment and selected a mug of beer. Time to build bridges, but... what news of the Aduatuci, indeed?

* * * * *

Fronto growled as he held the end of the rope to stop it flapping around. The others were absolutely right, of course. There was no way he could have climbed the cliffs with them, but he had been expecting to tie the rope around his waist and for them to haul him up afterwards. Priscus had told him in fairly blunt terms that they could not risk taking a one-armed man with them, and he had been left with the job of guarding the rope. Above him, the long cord wobbled as the four men climbed.

His plan for a few men dressed as Gauls to sneak into the oppidum and try to ascertain what it was the Aduatuci were up to appeared to proceeding adequately without him. Priscus and Galronus had each selected a man to take with them; Galronus had chosen a Remi warrior who had visited this place before, while Priscus selected a man called Mutiatus, renowned for his climbing ability.

Mutiatus had climbed the cliff in three stages, one stretch at a time, anchoring a rope and then returning for another coil to manage the next stretch. The whole process had taken well over an hour, but now there were three ropes that reached up the side of the oppidum, and Fronto's scouts were climbing them to the unknown dangers above. The legate grumbled again as the movement on the rope ceased. That meant that Galronus was over a third of the way up. Priscus must be at the top by now.

The edge of the oppidum was unwalled at this point. There was no real need for man-made defences here; no army could climb the cliff in sufficient numbers to pose a threat. Instead, the ground had been cleared of scrub and bushes so that, if the need arose, the defenders could gather at the edge and cast rocks and missiles at any attackers.

Priscus dropped into a crouch next to Mutiatus as the other two reached the cliff edge behind him. He felt distinctly uncomfortable. With no shield or armour, he was dressed like the other three: a bare minimum. Gallic clothes and boots, a sheathed Celtic sword and a helmet to hide his Roman features. Mutiatus wore the same, and the two Remi could manage without helmets.

He scanned the scene from where he crouched. There were a number of oak and ash trees scattered around that provided the only cover until they reached the first buildings. The construction here was much like the rest of the Gallic and Belgic settlements he had seen: stone courses at the bottom with timber construction above and thatched roofs. There seemed to be no plan to this part of the town, with houses scattered like the trees, each with its own little garden.

Off to the left, at the highest part, he could hear the lowing of cattle. So, the left would be rural woods and farmland, with the main centre of occupation down the slope toward the gates.

He suddenly became aware of the presence of others around him. The four men were all here and ready.

"Alright, Elitovius," he addressed his Remi guide. "Lead on. Let's see if we can find out what they're up to."

With the two Remi auxiliaries at the front, they moved out from the cliff edge at a crouch, slipping like ghosts between the tree trunks toward the edge of the settlement. Lamplight danced in the windows of some of the buildings, but what light there was out here came mainly from the silvery moon above.

Slowly, they picked their way through, moving lightly and making as little noise as possible, though there was no sign of movement nearby. As they reached the rear corner of the first building, Galronus drew them up in the lee of the walls.

"We go in front; you behind. You no speak. Walk like you live here."

Priscus nodded. He had no intention of standing out. Taking a deep breath, he fell in with Mutiatus behind the Remi, and the four men strode out into the moonlit streets of Aduatuca. The roads here seemed quiet; not deserted, for they could hear the sounds of life and movement here and there, and lights flickered in buildings. But then, they were still on the edge of the settlement yet.

The tension in the primus pilus grew with every step as the small group made their way down the gentle slope toward the centre. This was a sizeable oppidum; perhaps as large as Noviodunum, and remarkably civilised to Priscus' mind, with guttering in the gravelled streets to carry away the rainwater. As they descended, the buildings became more densely-packed and, after a few moments, there were signs that they were approaching the centre.

Rather than scattered houses with well-tended gardens, they were now passing buildings that directly fronted onto the street, and occasionally a shop or two. And then: the inevitable. Two Aduatuci, a young man and his girl, strolled up the street toward them. Priscus felt himself tense, and his teeth clenched as he tried with all his being to walk in as relaxed a fashion as possible. Next to him, he noted a stiffness to Mutiatus. They must be so plainly Roman. Priscus had been a soldier since he had been old enough to shave. He even slept at attention. How could then possibly pass as…

He realised, with a start that almost made him laugh out loud, that he had been so worried about ruining their ruse that he had not noticed the couple pass them and go on their way. Suddenly, he found himself relaxing. Good thing really, he thought to himself, as he saw another pair of people appear from the main square ahead and walk toward them.

Galronus elbowed him gently.

"You see that?"

Priscus frowned and squinted. The Remi officer could only be referring to the two men ahead. They looked like ordinary Belgic warriors, just carrying…

He blinked.

"What in the name of Mars and Bellona are they doing?"

He squinted again. The men were each carrying piles of weapons bound together with cord. As he watched, the warriors turned into a side street.

"That cannot be normal" Priscus demanded of his guides. Galronus shook his head.

"We follow. Find out."

Priscus nodded, and the four men picked up the pace. Moments later, they reached that side street and peered carefully down it. The two warriors, now not far ahead, had separated and were entering two buildings facing each other across the road.

"What the hell is going on?" Priscus asked in a whisper.

"Not know" replied Galronus. "But we find out. Us take left. You take right."

Priscus nodded, and he and Mutiatus veered off toward the right hand side of the road. Ahead, the door to the building stood open. With a quiet rasp, Priscus drew the unfamiliar Celtic blade and crept along the outside wall, Mutiatus following suit behind him. A few steps further and the primus pilus peered cautiously around the door frame. The building was a single room; a house by all appearances. And, inside, the warrior they had followed was fumbling at the far side of the room with a chest. Priscus frowned as he watched the man drop a bundle of weapons into the chest, close it up, and conceal it with a blanket, giving it the appearance of a seat.

"What is he doing, sir?" asked Mutiatus at his shoulder. "Why are they hiding weapons?"

Priscus clenched his teeth.

"Let's ask him, eh?"

Mutiatus nodded, and the two men crept as quietly as they could into the doorway. It was a novel experience for the primus pilus to be entering into a fight without several pounds of armour about his person, and he flexed his muscles, enjoying the freedom of movement. Mutiatus, with the physique of an acrobat, moved like a cat.

The two men crossed the threshold close together and then separated, each moving to the side like the horns of a bull. The warrior finished adjusting the blanket and stepped back to admire his handiwork. Looking up, he noticed a human shadow cast in the flickering lamp light and turned toward Priscus, opening his mouth to shout a warning, just as Mutiatus dived on him, his hand going over the warrior's mouth as he slammed him to the floor, driving the breath from his chest. Priscus grinned.

"Now let's go see Galronus and question this sack of crap."

As he turned, his companion bashed the Aduatuci warrior's head on the floor, knocking him unconscious, and heaved the limp form onto his muscular shoulders. Moments later, having checked the street was clear, the two men with their burden crossed the road and entered the building opposite. The Remi auxiliaries had the other Aduatuci warrior on the floor and were busy binding and gagging him.

"Galronus? Care to interrogate them?"

The man nodded.

"We interrogate, but not here. We go back. Safety. Take both."

Priscus nodded and turned to Mutiatus.

"We'll have to use the smallest backstreets we can to get back to the cliff, if we're taking these two with us."

Mutiatus nodded, the unconscious warrior still draped across his shoulder.

As Priscus helped the two Remi sling the other captive over Elitovius' shoulder, Mutiatus lifted the eyelid of his own burden.

"Flat out. He'll be gone for an hour or more, sir."

"Good. Then we can get them to the cliff and threaten to throw them off."

Mutiatus grinned at him.

"Let's see," Priscus said quietly, "exactly what sort of arms they're hiding here."

"We'll check the street, sir" the legionary said.

As Mutiatus and Elitovius moved toward the door with their unconscious and bound prisoners, Galronus and Priscus crouched over the hidden cache of arms behind the chair in the corner of the room. The bundle contained mostly swords and axes, with a number of slings and a bag of shot tied in along with them.

"Whatever they're planning, it's got to be in the oppidum." Priscus frowned. "No bows, so it's got to be close range, and no spears, so not in open ground. I really don't like the look of this. Let's..."

His head suddenly snapped round at a commotion. Their two companions, along with the prisoners, had stepped out into the street where clearly someone had seen them. A shout went up in the Belgic tongue, and the call went from voice to voice. Priscus stared through the door at the other two and Mutiatus made an urgent motion at him to run.

The primus pilus snarled and turned to Galronus.

"They've been seen. We've got to get away and warn the army."

Galronus nodded. The sound of running feet was getting close outside and, as he watched, Elitovius and Mutiatus dropped their burdens and drew their swords. The legionary turned his head and nodded; the least conspicuous salute he could manage, and then, roaring, he ran off down the street with the Remi auxiliary at his side.

"Shit!"

Priscus' head snapped back and forth as he tried to decide on a course of action.

"Can you find our way back?"

Galronus nodded.

"Think so."

Priscus took a deep breath, ran to the side wall, and threw himself unceremoniously through a window. Galronus was hot on his tail and, as the primus pilus picked himself up and disappeared toward the backs of the houses, his Remi companion hit the earth, rolled and came upright into a run.

At the rear of the building, Priscus looked around desperately. There were several other houses, some lit, some not, and he could see, not far away, the burning torches on the top of the oppidum's defensive wall. They were surprisingly close to the main gate.

"This way!"

He turned at Galronus' voice and raced away up the grass behind the houses. Behind them, close to the central square, the commotion was now audible over everything else. The Aduatuci were shouting; Guards were calling to each other. Briefly there was a scream; just the one, and Priscus found himself wondering which of their companions got the worst of it: the one that had just died, or the one that had not?

After a short run, Galronus slowed and came to a halt, breathing heavily. Priscus almost bumped into him.

"You lost?"

The Remi shook his head and pointed.

"Oh, shit."

They were now close to where they had entered the oppidum and, squinting, he could see through the trees to where they had reached the top of the roped climb. Torches danced through the velvet night over there, blinking between the tree trunks.

"No escape that way."

He frowned at Galronus.

"I take it you're not good enough to make the climb down elsewhere?"

Galronus shook his head.

"Not in dark. Not without rope."

Priscus nodded. It would be stupid to try.

"Then we're trapped in the oppidum. We're going to have to find a place to hide and work something out in the morning.

Down on the plain below, Fronto ran as though Pluto was breathing on his neck. His initial worry as he heard Belgic voices atop the cliff had become heart-stopping as the severed rope dropped to the ground by him. He had been wondering whether it was worth waiting there just in case when the Belgae had begun to drop rocks, speculatively, off the edge.

Now, he just had to get out of range of them and back to the Roman lines. Priscus and Galronus had gone with no results to show for it, and the whole thing had been his damn idea. He would look like such an idiot when he admitted this to Caesar.

He ran through his head how he would approach the subject and then jerked, fell, tumbled and rolled to a stop, unconscious and bleeding on the grass. The rock that had caught him a glancing blow rolled to a halt beside him, glinting burgundy in the moonlight.

Chapter 21

(Oppidum of Aduatuca)

"Mars Gravidus: an aspect of the Roman war god, 'he who precedes the army in battle', was the god prayed to when an army went to war."

"Ad aciem: military command essentially equivalent to 'Battle stations!'."

Caesar stood with Sabinus and Tetricus at the central gate in the defences and rubbed his hands in satisfaction. Though Fronto had been on edge and irritating as usual, there was something about his manner that had impressed itself on the general. Though the Tenth's legate had disappeared in a huff, probably to imbibe alcohol until he could no longer see straight, a sense of unease had settled on the general ever since, and he had paced uncomfortably in his tent for some time before sending for Tetricus and requesting that all efforts be made to speed up the progress on the tower.

Indeed, he'd had a night of fitful dreams; nightmares of betrayal and failure and, of all the dream fragments he remembered like polished shards this morning, the one that had left him with the deepest sense of grief was the tale his mind spun of Fronto dropping his sword to the ground and walking away, with Fortuna in all her glory at his shoulder.

But this morning, Tetricus had been the general's first visitor. The torches had still blazed around Caesar's tent where Ingenuus' men remained on guard, sizzling in the faint drizzle that had started some time in the early hours, when the tribune knocked politely on the doorframe.

The general, renowned for his wakefulness even in the dead of night, was already dressed and tapping irritably on a map of the oppidum and its surroundings when he invited Tetricus in and the man had entered, a satisfied smile on his face. The engineers had worked throughout the night, drawing support from the rest of the legions and had completed the bridge and enough armour plates to cover at least two sides of the tower.

And now, as the pale, watery sun rose over the horizon and the staff officers stood watching in the fine rain, the tower began to move. The plates had been affixed, and the bridge raised and attached in less than an hour, ladders being added for troop movement. The effect was truly monstrous. In the bright sunlight, the tower would be massive and powerful, but in this grey, misty drizzle, it also gained a glinting oppressiveness that added to the effect. Even Caesar, veteran of a great many campaigns and no stranger to the great works of military engineers, found himself drawing an awed breath.

Two cohorts, drawn from the Eighth and attached to the engineers for the night, hauled on the great ropes and slowly the tower rumbled forwards. The sheer size and weight of the machine shook the earth, and the ground vibrated beneath the officers' feet as they watched.

Sabinus tapped his finger to his lip, unable to tear his gaze from the great tower.

"Do we send a legion up the main slope as well, Caesar? Try to divide their forces?"

The general shook his head.

"No, but we do threaten to. We move the Thirteenth into position, below the walls but just out of range, and supply them with siege weaponry. As we move the tower and the vineae against the cliff, the Thirteenth put out calls and shuffle their men around as though they're preparing to attack. They may even have to take the occasional shot with the artillery and run up and down the slope as a testudo to keep the Aduatuci's attention. I need them to believe we're going to attack on that front too."

Sabinus nodded.

"Makes sense. Can I suggest that we have the Fourteenth begin to cross the Meuse on their rafts too? The enemy might not believe they're really going to do anything but, if the men are in full kit, they'll have to divide their forces just in case. They can't take the risk we're about to do something unexpected from across the river."

The general smiled.

"Yes, see to it. I..."

He stopped mid conversation as the sound of horns cut through the air.

"What's that?"

Sabinus shrugged.

"Whatever it is, it's coming from the oppidum. Do we go and find out?"

Caesar nodded and turned to the guards behind him, their commander present and stiffly at attention.

"Ingenuus? Have two turmae of the guard form up to escort us to the oppidum."

The young officer saluted and began to bark orders to his men. The bleating of the Belgic horns continued in the background, and there was clearly some activity on the walls. Sabinus sighed.

"Looks like a call to parlay. Maybe we can end this peacefully after all. Perhaps Fronto was wrong?"

Caesar frowned.

"Perhaps… perhaps not. I feel uneasy." He drew a deep breath and shrugged, as though shaking off a cloak of oppression. "Regardless, let us go and see what the Aduatuci want."

The two men turned to see that Ingenuus already had two turmae of cavalry lined up and ready to move, along with the two officers' horses ready to mount. Caesar swung himself into the saddle with practised ease as Sabinus climbed onto his own steed. Then, with a quick glance round to make sure all were present and correct, the general signalled with a dropped hand and the mounted column moved off, past the great, hulking tower and toward the slope of the oppidum.

The high walls of the Aduatuci were well constructed, heavy and strong, with an outer work of pointed stakes and pits. As they rode carefully between the obstacles, Sabinus found himself hoping that the enemy were about to cave in and that no assault would be required. The Thirteenth Legion would be thinned out like the culling of a herd if they had to march up this slope.

He looked up as they approached the first line of defensive works.

"I think we should stop here, Caesar. They have bows, slings, spears and rocks, so let's be sure we're out of range."

The general nodded and raised his hand to halt the column.

"Sound thinking, Sabinus. Now, what do we have?"

The defences of Aduatuca were punctuated with heavy, square towers, only a little taller than the walls themselves, but strong and projecting enough to make enfilade shots a possibility. The main gate of the oppidum was flanked by two such towers and surmounted by a walkway. The gates themselves were enormous, constructed apparently of shaped tree trunks bound with iron. Inordinately strong for a Celtic town, Sabinus considered, but then again, Aduatuca had walls on only one side, relying on cliffs elsewhere.

On the walkway above the gate standards waved with tapering streamers, and men with huge bronze horns shaped like wolf mouths blew tuneless tunes. Men in glinting armour and helms watched the officers and their guard approach and, as Caesar's column halted, one of their number stepped out forwards.

"You are Caesar, general of the Romans."

A statement, rather than a question. There was no uncertainty in his voice and no fear that Sabinus could detect. He sounded confident and strong.

"I am" called the general. "And this is Quintus Titurius Sabinus, my lieutenant, and the rest are my honour guard. To whom am I speaking?"

The man drew his great Celtic blade and dropped the tip to the floor.

"I am Damiacus, chieftain of this place and leader of the Aduatuci in time of war."

"You speak our language well" the general noted with interest.

The man shrugged.

"Rome seems to think we Celts are like hogs, floundering in our own swill and unable to read or learn. One would think that after two years of carving a path through our world that you, at least, would now know different. We are Belgae; proud and strong."

Caesar sighed.

"I had no idea this was just a meeting for you to posture. You waste my time."

Damiacus laughed.

"Were we to meet under different circumstances, Lord Caesar, I fear you would find we have much in common. Like you, I abhor unnecessary posturing. I wish to see the Aduatuci victorious and strong."

Caesar let out another sigh.

"Posturing, you see."

Damiacus laughed again.

"However, also like you, I detest waste. The Aduatuci are the last Belgic tribe to stand against you and, whatever may become of us, we will always have that. We were the last. But we can see clearly, and only a fool fights on when there is no hope. I would rather the Aduatuci lived to be proud that they were the last than they slip from history in one glorious fight to extinction. I have sons I wish to see grow."

Caesar nodded.

"An attitude that does you credit, Damiacus, but please come to the point."

The chieftain smiled.

"There are so many more of you than us. We have strong walls and high cliffs, but you have with you the means to destroy our walls and, in only a few days, you have constructed a machine of nightmare dimensions that can reach our town and deliver your troops. We have no hope of victory."

He drew a deep breath, and Caesar was about to comment, when the Aduatuci leader cast his great sword from the wall to the ground before them. As the general blinked in surprise, other warriors across the line of walls cast their weapons to the ground.

"We ask you to accept our surrender, general Caesar. We give you our oath, as your other Belgic allies have. We wish an end to hostilities and would ask that you treat with us as you have with others, as an ally. In return, our weapons are yours."

As he said this, bundles of swords, spears and bows were tipped from the walls and towers onto the grass below, gradually building a mound of discarded weaponry.

"Say the word and the gates of our oppidum will be thrown open to you. Will you accept peace with the Aduatuci?"

Caesar turned to Sabinus, whose look of relief was clear.

"You wanted peace, Quintus. It appears you have it."

He turned back to the wall.

"The word is given. We will ask for a small measure of booty, and in return we will accept you as an ally, Damiacus of the Aduatuci. I shall return with my men at noon."

The Aduatuci chief bowed from the wall.

Sabinus smiled as the Roman column turned and rode back toward the legions.

"Tetricus must be starting to feel very unfulfilled. Every time he builds something impressive for battle, the enemy surrenders as soon as they see it, and it never gets used."

Caesar sighed with relief.

"Frankly, I'm glad of it. We've lost so many men in these last few months it'll take a great deal of money and effort to refill the ranks."

The two men rode with their escort across the damp grass and past the great bulk of the glistening war tower. Ahead, the legions were being massed before the rampart. Clearly, in the general's absence, someone had decided that the enemy fanfares meant activity one way or the other and had put the legions on alert. Caesar smiled. That was why his army was more effective than that of Pompey or the elder Crassus. His unique approach to military command, associating set officers with particular legions on a semipermanent basis, meant that his army was capable of functioning well even without orders from the top. That was why men like Fronto and Balbus were worth a hundred Pompeys.

Cicero, in full dress armour and looking uncomfortable in the damp and drizzle, came striding out from the colour party of the Tenth Legion, their flags and standard flapping and waving in the wet breeze, the signifers weighted down with soggy wolf pelts over their helms.

"Caesar? What news? Tetricus informed us that you'd gone to parlay, so I put the legions on standby."

The general nodded.

"Perhaps a little premature, but a good decision nonetheless. The Aduatuci have surrendered and are discarding their weapons and opening their gates. We will wait the morning out and hope that the weather lifts. At noon, we will ride with the First Cohort of each legion and enter the oppidum. I want the place occupied. This Damiacus is far too sure of himself and Fronto's staunch belief that they're up to something has set my neck itching. I'll accept their surrender and oath, but only when we've got the town thoroughly under our control."

Cicero nodded.

"I was wondering whether perhaps legate Fronto was with you, sir?"

Caesar shook his head.

"I very much suspect the legate will have been practicing debauchery and drink last night. Check his tent."

The officer's face took on a worried look.

"Begging your pardon, Caesar, but we already have. I don't think he slept there last night. And the chief signifer for the Tenth,

Petrosidius, says they've not seen their primus pilus all morning either."

Caesar smiled.

"Fronto and Priscus? Find the empty amphora, Cicero, and follow the trail. Be sure they're at the end of it."

* * * * *

Priscus stretched his shoulders. The night had been surprisingly cold and with dawn had come a change in the weather. The cold drizzle would have been numbing had he and Galronus not located an apparently unused shed in a pig farm not far from the ropes but, even here, after waiting half the morning they were starting to feel chilled.

They had watched the area of cliff where they had arrived for an hour or more last night, waiting for the group of warriors to abandon the place. There was no doubt they'd take the rope with them anyway, but Priscus would have liked to check whether Fronto was still hidden near the bottom or had left. Unfortunately, the warriors had set up camp there and spent the night. Indeed, as the night progressed, the hidden investigators saw pairs of Aduatuci warriors taking up positions all along the cliff, presumably watching for any further intrepid Roman scouts.

The primus pilus crawled across the small hut and peered out through the cracks in the battered wooden door. Behind him, Galronus shivered.

"Warriors?"

Priscus nodded.

"They're still there. There's only two now, but I think that's because they're posting pairs of lookouts around the hill. We're not getting out that way."

Galronus hunched closer to ward off the chill.

"Then we die here. No way out."

Priscus shrugged.

"There's always a way. You'll learn this about Rome, my friend. We'll rule the world one day because we never give up; we just find the way that no one else has noticed."

Galronus looked unconvinced.

"But," the centurion said, squaring his shoulders once more, "we won't find a way out cowering in a pig-keeper's shit shed. We need to head down into the main town again."

The Remi officer blinked.

"Back? You mad. We die there!"

Priscus grinned.

"Look at it this way: they're watching the cliffs now. They know someone got in that way, so we won't get past them. But they won't be looking for anyone back in the town. Our friends must have gone to Elysium without mentioning us, or there'd have been more commotion. And they only noticed the other two 'cause they had bodies over their shoulder. We're inconspicuous, and you speak the language."

"But where we go when we get to centre?"

Priscus shrugged.

"Who knows, but we'll work that out when we get that far. It's easier breaking out of a place than breaking in."

Galronus rolled his eyes.

"You mad as Fronto."

"We've known each other a long time."

The primus pilus smiled and pulled his Celtic tunic up, allowing air to circulate round his armpits. There was an unpleasant waft of strong body odour.

"Come on."

Galronus scrabbled to his feet and Priscus shoved the partially-rotten door open as quietly as he could. Glancing between the tree trunks, he could see the pair of warriors at the point of ingress the night before. Taking a deep breath, he slipped out of the hovel and around the side, out of sight of the lookouts on the cliff edge. Galronus was out and at his heel mere moments later.

Taking a deep breath, Priscus strode from the shed, past the main farm building. There was little point in sneaking here. Two men running around the oppidum, crouched and ducking from alley to doorway would be far more likely to stand out than two men dressed as locals and strolling calmly along the street.

"Where we go then?"

Priscus shrugged.

"I'd like to get close to the walls. Let's try and skirt the very centre and make our way to the end of the defences."

Galronus nodded unhappily and fell into step beside him, glancing around nervously at the empty street as they left the farm yard.

"For the love of Venus, will you stop looking so bloody suspicious?"

* * * * *

Caesar frowned.

"What do you mean nowhere?"

Tetricus shrugged.

"Just that, sir. The whole camp's been searched, and everywhere along the ramparts. Varus has got scouts out now behind the camps, checking the woodlands, but I don't think they'll turn anything up. If Fronto and Priscus were in the woods getting drunk last night, I'm sure they'd have come back under cover once the rain began."

The general growled.

"Where are they, then? Fronto's nothing if not direct and he never misses the opportunity to say 'I told you so' to me. It's a vexing and worrying development."

Tetricus nodded.

"There is another possibility, of course" Sabinus interjected.

Caesar raised an eyebrow.

"That he and Priscus went to spy on the Aduatuci."

The general frowned.

"I know Fronto can be impulsive, but…"

He turned to Tetricus.

"Have Varus send out scouts toward the oppidum; right up to the cliff if necessary."

The tribune nodded and left the tent to find the cavalry commander and relay the orders. Once they were alone again, Caesar turned to Sabinus.

"Something is going on here. Fronto was right. Have the First Cohort from each legion assembled. I'm not waiting until noon. We're going now, and the rest of the army should stay on high alert."

Sabinus nodded.

"A sensible idea, if I may say, sir."

Fronto groaned and rolled over.

Grass. Confusion flooded his mind. Wet grass. And red. Lots of red. Sticky. Smelled like tin.

For a horrible moment, his memory took him back a year to that night when he had found the body of Cominius in his tent. But no. As his brain swam slowly into focus, he realised the thumping and pain in the back of his skull was from a wound. He prodded it tentatively, and something moved. 'Not good', he thought, as he almost blacked out from the pain.

He strained, thinking back to last night.

The cliff!

"Shit!"

Hurriedly, he began to push himself to his feet, but slipped in the blood and came down with a bang, almost knocking himself out again. He waited a moment for his head to clear and then, very slowly and carefully, he arched his back and began to pull himself into a seated position.

Yes, something was definitely wrong. Priscus and Galronus and their companions were gone. Were they dead? Did the Aduatuci hold them prisoner? Something had to be done.

Ignoring the warnings of his body, the legate pulled himself upright. Staggering slightly, he turned to take in his situation. He was only a hundred paces from the cliff… Within throwing range!

Suddenly, desperately, he began to run, floundering slightly, away from the oppidum. Behind him he heard shouting on the cliff edge in that guttural tongue. Uttering a prayer to Nemesis, he ran like the wind toward the ramparts.

And then he noticed all the activity. Legions were marching from the gate in the palisade toward the slope. What the in the name of Pluto were they doing? And small groups of horsemen were scattered across the plain, riding slowly.

His mind began to swim again. The activity and adrenaline, along with the pumping blood thumping through his brain, threatened to floor him once again. He stopped, woozily, and put his hands on his knees.

Just ahead, and as his legs gave out, he heard a comforting voice.

"Here he is! Tell the commander we've found one of them!"

Caesar gazed thoughtfully at the oppidum as the army approached the outer line of defences. The command party, led by the general himself, along with Sabinus and Cicero, was mounted, while their accompanying cohorts were afoot. Ingenuus' guards rode in a protective cordon around the officers, while Varus' regulars supplied extra support. In all, the general was as well protected as a man on a horse entering an enemy stronghold could be.

What in the name of the Magna Mater were the Aduatuci up to? Damiacus sounded so tremendously reasonable, and the Belgae were a proud people, so there was really no reason to suspect a problem. The tribes they had dealt with all summer had either submitted without the need for battle, or fought to the death.

He craned his neck to look up as the riders passed at a walk through the great open gate of the oppidum. Outside and in both directions along the wall, piles of weapons discarded in good faith told a story. Caesar's imagination told another.

Behind the gates was a square unlike those Caesar had seen in most Gaulish or Belgic oppida. The ground was paved with flush stones in a style more reminiscent of Latium than the barbarian north. The buildings around the edge of the square were of familiar style, with stone courses to shoulder height, surmounted by timber and either wooden or thatched roofs. Here, at the square, they were tightly packed, almost in a Roman style, fronting the street though, as he looked up the main thoroughfare, also paved, toward the centre of the town, the buildings seemed to become more randomly placed.

There were no warriors on the walls. Perhaps a show of peace and surrender there, since men folk, along with the women and children, stood beside the doors to their houses, proud and erect as their Roman conquerors marched past, through the square and up the sloping street.

Six cohorts of men, even depleted as they were, numbered almost two thousand men and made an impressive sound and sight as they tramped through the streets, crunching and clanking. This was Rome, as always, imposing itself on the barbarians.

Some of the men stared angrily at the officers as they passed. Good, the general decided. To be unhappy about the situation and angry at Rome and its commanders was normal; to be expected. It eased Caesar's tension a little. Fronto had been right; they had been a little too smug.

There was a clatter of hooves on the stone, and Varus reined in next to him.

"I don't wish to raise any further alarm, Caesar, but one of my men found Fronto."

Caesar raised an eyebrow.

"Alarm, Commander?"

"Well, general, he was only a couple of hundred paces from the cliff and had been wounded in the head. Raises some questions about the motives of the Aduatuci, I'd say."

"Wonderful. Just when I was starting to breathe a little easier."

The general leaned back to speak to Cicero, riding close behind.

"Quintus? As soon as we get into the square, have the cohorts form into a square; battle formation, but defensive rather than ready to attack. I want to be prepared."

Cicero nodded and turned to speak to the tribunes behind him as the army rode out of the street and into the main square. Aduatuci warriors and their families lined the edges, while at the far end, atop a low stair, stood Damiacus and his advisors and guards.

The general drew a deep breath.

This was it. The end of the Belgae.

Fronto staggered, his legs threatening to buckle beneath him once again. Two of the cavalrymen had dismounted and rushed over to support the wounded officer.

"Gerroff me!"

"Sir?" One of the troopers grasped him regardless. "We've got to get you to the medicus right away. You're pale as a Vestal's underwear; must have lost a lot of blood."

Fronto growled.

"I'm a little wobbly; that's all. Haven't got time for medici. Send for Florus from the Tenth; he can keep me going."

"Sir?" the man said urgently.

"More important things to do, soldier. Caesar's mobilised the army?"

The trooper nodded uncertainly.

"The general has taken six cohorts into the city to accept their full surrender and to occupy the oppidum, sir."

"Shit."

"Sir?"

Fronto tapped his head, trying to get his fuzz-filled brain to work faster. He seemed to decide something and then grasped the shoulders of the trooper for support as he looked at the second, so far silent, rider.

"This man and I are going to find Florus and my horse. You get your friends and go find every legionary legate and auxiliary prefect on the field and tell them to mobilise for action. Tell them to be ready to march on the oppidum as soon as they're in position."

The trooper blinked.

"Sir? They surrendered."

"Bollocks!"

"Sir, I don't have the authority…"

"I do!" interrupted Fronto. "Get the army mobilised now!"

As the man remounted his horse and rode off toward the lines, Fronto smiled shakily at the other trooper.

"That gives us a few moments to get my head seen to!"

* * * * *

Galronus peered through the crack in the door at the rear of the building and then stared down at the body at his feet.

"What's all the commotion?" he whispered.

Priscus, at the other side of the house, peered out between the mostly-closed wooden shutters. The central square was lined with people, even in front of this building, only a few feet from where he crouched.

"I think they're getting ready for a ceremony or something. That particular noise you're talking about, though, is legionaries. I know that sound anywhere. That's a hell of a lot of legionaries coming up the main street."

Galronus growled quietly and wiped his bloody knife on the body. They had sneaked in through the rear door of this building right in the centre of town around half an hour ago, hoping they would be safe from prying eyes, but moments later they'd had to hide as the front door opened and a man had entered and gone straight across to a cache of hidden weapons. Others stood in the portal and had weapons passed to them until the cache was empty. Then they left and closed the door, but the one man had stayed. Priscus had been impressed with how quickly and quietly the Remi officer had dealt with him.

"I can only see the Aduatuci near me, but they've got swords, axes and slings hidden behind them or leaning against the bases of the houses. I'll assume the same is true of everyone, wherever they are."

Galronus shook his head.

"Then we have to raise the alarm; warn the army."

Priscus held up a warning hand.

"Not yet. If an ambush was their only plan, they'd have carried it out in the narrow street. They're allowing the legions to get into the square, which is stupid. There the men can form squares, shield walls, testudos and so on. So why? Why let them have the room to manoeuvre?"

Galronus shrugged.

"Maybe…"

"Wait!" Priscus cut him off with a raised hand. He frowned and squinted across the square.

"Oh shit!"

"What's…" Galronus began, but he was too late. Priscus was already gone, flinging the door wide open, regardless of the Aduatuci waiting beyond, and running out into the square. Desperately, unsure of what was happening, the Remi officer rushed over to the window the centurion had just vacated and scanned the square outside.

Priscus had barged through the warriors outside, drawing his great Celtic blade. Confusion gripped the men lining the square as this apparent Belgae warrior had run out into the central square openly wielding one of the weapons they had gone to such great pains to hide. Those Roman Gods must be running at Priscus' shoulder indeed, he thought, for the confusion gripped the locals so strongly that the primus pilus was already across the centre of the square and accelerating before a shout went up outside the door.

Still unsure of what had caused Priscus' sudden panicked run, exposing them to the enemy, he followed the direction in which the man was running and squinted as he scanned the opposite edge of the open space.

Nothing unusual.

The warriors and their families lined the edge as they did on the other three sides, but there was nothing special about them. Behind them, the same single story buildings rose, stone based with wooden uppers and either wooden or thatched roofs…

Roofs.

The roof!

Galronus drew a nervous breath. Priscus must have sharp eyes; one building of the several opposite was undergoing extensive repair work, its roof only partially complete. The building stood open, with no door and no shutters on the windows. And the rafters were partially thatched, great sheaves standing tied and waiting to be attached.

But among the rafters stood two figures; two tall barbarians, barely visible, lurking among the debris. And one of them had a bow, already nocked and straining as the man gradually stepped back into the shadow, disappearing from sight.

Damn, that centurion really did have good eyes.

With absolutely no doubt for whom that arrow was destined, Galronus rushed out through the doorway, drawing his sword as he went. He had to buy Priscus time, which meant drawing as much attention as possible.

With a violent cry, he leapt out into the square, the sword raised above his head, and brought it down hard, almost cleaving the man before him in two. The viscera from the horrifying blow sprayed out, catching the men on either side and staining them crimson. With a grunt, Galronus heaved the heavy blade back out of the corpse as it crashed to the floor, spraying himself with gore in the process.

Heads all around the square turned at this commotion, just as the Remi officer swung the great blade sideways and bit deep into the midriff of the next man. Now the warriors around him were grasping their hidden weapons and struggling to fight back under this sudden and unexpected onslaught.

Between desperate, panicked blows, Galronus bellowed and cried, catching, as he did, the occasional glimpse across the square. Priscus had reached the far side and disappeared, though there was a commotion there too. Well, the auxiliary officer had done all he could now. The warriors outside the house had fallen like wheat to his blade as he surprised them, but now they were armed and beginning to block his blows. With half a dozen of them pressing on him, he would die here.

Swallowing, and hoping he had done enough to help Priscus, he suddenly dropped back through the doorway into the building once more, slamming and wedging shut the door as he did so.

Without pausing to take a breath, he ran through the house and out of the rear door into the well-tended garden. Should he run round to the square again and try to warn the Roman column? No. Pointless. They must be aware of the trouble after all his shouting.

It was all down to Priscus now.

Aulus Ingenuus, former cavalry prefect and, for the last year, commander of Caesar's praetorians, licked his dry lips nervously. To command the bodyguard of such an important man was always a great responsibility, but never more so than today. Ingenuus had done what he could. He had managed to get Varus, the cavalry commander, to supply extra troops, and the command party was surrounded by well trained and extremely alert troopers, all fully armed and armoured and on experienced war horses. And yet he was twitching.

He had actually requested of Caesar that the senior officers carry shields too. After all, they were in full armour and wore their swords, so it would only be reasonable, but the general had shaken his head. The commanders of the army had to look imposing, in control, and invincible.

But… in the name of Mars Gravidus, what were they thinking? As the column left the main thoroughfare and rode slowly out into the great open square at the centre of Aduatuca, Ingenuus became acutely aware that something was happening at the far end. There was a commotion that included sounds of fighting. As the command party and its guard made their way into the open area, Ingenuus, his eyes darting nervously from place to place, spotted two trouble spots immediately. A house on the far right, toward the top of the square, was the focus of attention for a small group of Aduatuci who were brandishing weapons and beating on the door and windows, and…

Brandishing weapons?

Even as the praetorian officer's eyes swept across the square to a similar scene on the left, he realised his voice had called the order without waiting for permission from his brain.

"Ad aciem!"

Caesar and the officers turned in surprise to stare at the young commander, but the order had been given. The praetorians closed up around the general as fast and as tightly as their horses would allow.

There was a thrumming noise that was all too familiar to Ingenuus, and he looked up and left. Something was happening in the eaves of that building off to the side that was a centre of activity. And, as he stared at the building, his eyes automatically refocused instead on the arrow whirring toward the general with alarming accuracy.

"Archer!"

He was too far away to help, but the trooper nearest the general heard his commander and noticed the arrow just in time to jump upwards, throwing his shield high. The arrow thudded into the wood and leather, and the praetorian fell to the floor, the momentum of his leap carrying him from his horse.

The general blinked as the threat to his life vanished with the guardsman to the ground.

"Form up!" a voice called from behind as the tribunes became aware of the sudden danger. The cohorts began to drive past the mounted officers and cavalry into the square, where they filtered out into lines and began to lock shields.

The Aduatuci, realising they had lost the element of surprise, let out a loud and violent roar and all around the square and back down the street, warriors lining the way drew their hidden weapons and lunged at the heavily-armoured and fully prepared legionaries. Ingenuus, however, was already driving his horse hard, several praetorians alongside him, as he made for the assassin's house. His guardsman had been lucky to catch the first shot, but they may not be so lucky again.

He looked up as they neared the building. Warriors were rushing out to stop them, but the legions were right behind him, filling the square. There was something happening on the roof.

Caesar shook his head.

"What?"

"Sir, you need to dismount, for safety!" Cicero sounded desperate.

"Unlikely" the general replied, drawing his sword. He turned to Sabinus, who had done the same.

"We may still be outnumbered!"

The officer grinned.

"I don't think so, sir."

He cupped his ear and pointed back down the main street. Above the din in the square, Caesar could clearly hear the cornicens of the legions calling out formation commands; and they were close. Maybe even outside the walls by now.

"Someone mobilised the legions without us" Sabinus grinned. "I wonder who would do something like that?"

Caesar nodded and turned once more to the areas of concentrated activity in the square. Something was happening on the partially dismantled roof of a building. That must be where the arrow came from. Ingenuus and his men, supported by heavy infantry, were now cleaving their way through the Aduatuci to reach the building, but someone was already there. The general squinted to try and see in more detail. There were three figures there, all apparently natives, and fighting a bitter struggle. As the general watched, the smaller and lighter of the three, clearly a man apart, thrust with a small blade and dispatched the archer, whose bow fell to the floor.

The man had no time to savour his kill though, for the other opponent, a great bearded brute of a fellow, leapt on him and began to pound and pummel. The two men vanished from sight among the stacks of thatch for long moments and the general frowned, turning his attention to ground level.

The Aduatuci had been well prepared, with hidden weapons and men in position throughout the line the Romans had taken. Had there not been a commotion in the square, the first thing they would have known of the barbarians' betrayal would have been the general being swept from his horse by an arrow through the chest. Then all hell would have broken loose as the armed warriors dived upon the unprepared legionaries.

But things had gone wrong for the Aduatuci.

Someone had given the game away too early.

The general smiled. Because of that, the archer had released his arrow too early, and the legions were already deploying as the warriors collected their weapons.

"Thank you Fortuna. Good to see Fronto doesn't have a monopoly on you."

The square was already coming under Roman control, and the sounds from back down toward the walls clearly indicated that the reserves that had been mysteriously mobilised were already engaging the Aduatuci that were trying to close the gates and trap their prey.

His eyes strayed once more to the roof of that building, just as the two figures, grappling and tearing at each other, punching and biting, battled their way out of the hidden stacks and to the edge of the roof where, with a last flurry of blows, both men tumbled from the parapet to the stone below with a crunch that was audible even over the dying sounds of battle.

Sabinus turned to Caesar.

"Do we give quarter, general?"

The general clenched his teeth.

"No quarter. Every last inhabitant of Aduatuca dies. Every last one."

Chapter 22

(Oppidum of Aduatuca)

"Subura: a lower-class area of ancient Rome, close to the forum, that was home to the red-light district'."

"Vindunum: later the Roman Civitas Cenomanorum, and now Le Mans in France."

"Octodurus: now Martigny in Switzerland, at the northern end of the Great Saint Bernard Pass."

Fronto sighed.

"But he's alive?"

The young capsarius, hunched over the figure of Priscus on the stone flags, nodded, though his face was bleak as he turned to look up at his legate.

"He's alive sir, but barely. He's broken so many bones I can't even think how we'll go about moving him. He's like a mosaic."

Fronto frowned.

"But will he be alright?"

Florus stood and met the gaze of his commander. Despite everything, it almost made Fronto smile. Over a year ago, this young man had sat on a hilltop near Bibracte as a green recruit panicking about the next day's battle. Now here he was, a professional soldier and medic, dealing with some of the nastiest aspects of war in a calm and collected manner.

"I really can't say at this point, sir. I'm not convinced he'll survive being moved, but we have to get him inside. The medicus wants us to clear out some of the buildings here for use as a hospital."

Fronto shook his head.

"Can't do that. Have to be back at the camp."

The capsarius' frown deepened.

"Then we'll have to carry him more than a mile, and I'm really not convinced he'll make it. Even if he does, he's going to need several operations and splints. And, to be honest, many men wouldn't make it though that either. And then if he does, he's still nowhere near out of the woods. If he's still alive tomorrow morning there's a chance. And every night he survives after that his chances improve."

Fronto's face was a picture of misery.

"Do what you have to. I've lost one of my best centurions and closest friends already this summer. I'm not going to lose another."

Florus shook his head.

"I'm afraid you are sir."

"What?"

The young capsarius sighed.

"Sir, the primus pilus shattered his left leg, including his knee, in the fall. Bones heal, but joints are a different matter. Whatever happens, even if he returns to robust health, he'll be lame the rest of his life, sir."

"Lame?" Fronto's face fell. "You're sure?"

Florus nodded.

"He may not even be able to walk. And I'm not sure about the damage to his arms yet either." He took a deep breath. "He may wish he'd not lived, sir."

The legate growled and took a step backwards, grinding his heel into the body of the man that had tumbled from the roof with Priscus, locked in a terminal embrace. He felt the man's bones crunch under his boot and clenched his teeth.

"Get him back and take care of him. Do whatever you have to."

Florus nodded and waved over a couple of legionaries who were leaning on their shields nearby and taking in the scene.

The oppidum of Aduatuca had fallen less than a quarter of an hour after the attack began. Caesar had called for no quarter to be given, and the troops had butchered every member of the Aduatuci they had come across for some time before Fronto had persuaded the general to call a halt to the murder. Even then, given the situation, he'd had to persuade himself that the halt should be called first. Caesar was, at times, harsh and even perhaps wicked in his dealings with his enemies and, while Fronto often stood in opposition to such measures, after betrayal, sneak attacks and the disappearance of Priscus and Galronus, he could see how people were tempted to such measures.

A centurion he did not recognise, and there seemed to be so many of them these days, approached him across the square. Fronto had been left in command of the oppidum by Caesar, with very specific instructions.

"Sir?"

"Centurion. Have you finished the count?"

The man nodded.

"Barring the farms and the woodland to the rear, all houses have been checked and cleared of booty and the Aduatuci dead stacked inside. We've counted just over four thousand enemy bodies. The optio who counted the prisoners out of the gate said there were over fifty thousand."

Fronto nodded.

"That's a good number for the slave markets in Rome."

"All of them, sir?"

Another nod.

"Caesar's orders. The Aduatuci are no more. Not a single one to be left free. Dead or enslaved."

"Now that the legionaries have been separated out and taken away, do we start the burials?"

Fronto shook his head.

"No burials. There's to be nothing left. Get everyone back to the camp barring one century and have them fire the oppidum, starting from the woods and working their way to the gates. Every building; every tree; everything. Use oil to make sure the place goes up like a torch. In a year's time no one will remember the tribe."

The centurion, startled by the decision, saluted.

"We'll get on it now, sir."

Fronto nodded and turned back to the three legionaries who had carefully shuffled the unconscious and broken form of Gnaeus Vinicius Priscus onto a blanket and were bearing him aloft toward the lower end of the square. Striding across and catching up with them, he fell in alongside the makeshift stretcher.

Trying not to look at the mess that was his old friend, he paid attention instead to the oppidum as he descended the street. The quality of the road itself and the houses that faced onto it was outstanding for Celtic tribes; almost Roman in its neatness and efficiency. Apparently the Aduatuci had been ahead of their peers. Was that what had made them so devious and calculating? Was this what Rome had become when viewed by an outsider?

He found himself once again thinking on the future of Gaul. The patricians of Rome saw themselves as a civilising force, offering culture and advancement to the barbarian world, through conquest if necessary. What the patrician class generally failed to realise was how much Rome itself could learn in return from those cultures. If only things would settle and stay settled, Gauls, Belgae and Romans could build something here.

He sighed. Such thoughts seemed so sensible and practical in his head, until his eyes strayed to the doorways of buildings as he passed and he saw the piled bodies within.

"Through conquest if necessary."

"Sorry sir?" the legionary beside him queried.

"Oh, nothing."

The small party continued down the main street where less than an hour ago Fronto had led the reserves into battle. Now, soldiers were carrying chests full of the booty they had stripped from the tribe, back down the paved avenue, across the square and through the gate to the camp.

At least they'd made something out of this. The campaign had been costly, with a chillingly high number of dead among the legions. Many of the centurionate, including some old friends, had gone to Elysium this year. But the Belgae were beaten. There would be peace, at least for a time and, after this, the Germans would be disinclined to cross the Rhine for a while. There would probably be trouble in the west of Gaul to deal with either in a month or so or, more likely, next year. But in all, things would be peaceful.

He looked up at the great wall, towers, and gate of the oppidum as he passed. He would have to speak to the artillery officers. No good burning all traces of the Aduatuci from the world but leaving their great fortification to be used again, particularly this close to Germanic territory. No, the walls would have to be completely destroyed. By the end of the week, the great oppidum of the Aduatuci would be nothing but a charred, denuded hill, and the process of wiping the tribe from history would begin. It was like Carthage again, though on a smaller scale.

He sighed as they strode out into the open and down the slope toward the hospital.

The camp of the Tenth Legion was sullen as Fronto left his tent and made his way to the headquarters of the general. It had been three hours since he had accompanied the stretcher-bearers back to the camp. Priscus had gone in to the medicus immediately, and the medicus had taken one look, sucked in air through his teeth in a timeless manner, and closed the door on Fronto. Since then he had sat in the doorway of his own tent, repeatedly filling and emptying a cup of wine as he watched the columns of smoke rise from the hill opposite, while the onagers were moved into position to flatten the walls. It had seemed wrong sitting there on his own, but for some reason, all he could think of was his primus pilus being opened up in the hospital, and he felt less than social. Galronus was the only other man he was inclined to talk to right now, but the Remi officer had suffered a minor head wound during the scuffle earlier and was in with the medics at the moment.

And now, as he left the lines of the Tenth and two morose-looking guards saluted, he glanced across to his right, behind the lines, where a large stockade contained thousand upon thousand of Aduatuci prisoners. They would have to be taken away before long, as feeding them on a daily basis while so far beyond Cita's supply lines was a difficult and costly business. But then, Caesar could not move just yet. They would have to stay a week or more to impose their presence on the surrounding tribes, to find the few pockets of Aduatuci who were not in the oppidum, and to deal with the wounded.

He heard the thunder of hooves as he strode toward his meeting with the general and turned to see a small group of riders slowing as they neared the command area. Ingenuus' men stood at attention by the entrance to the palisaded quarter as both riders and legate converged on the gateway.

Fronto frowned as the men arrived and the leader, a cavalry prefect by his armour, dropped from his saddle and saluted. The half dozen men looked tired and unshaven and had clearly been riding for days; their horses stamped and steamed.

"You looking for me or the general?"

The prefect wiped his brow.

"I have a message for Caesar, sir."

Fronto nodded.

"Come with me."

With the prefect at his heel, sweating and groaning after so long in the saddle, Fronto strode through the gateway to the large tent that was Caesar's headquarters. Two more of the praetorians stood beside the entrance, alongside the standards and the eagle. As the officers approached, one ducked inside for a moment and then returned.

"The general is ready to see you, legate."

Fronto nodded and he and his companion strode into the dim interior of the command tent. Caesar sat at his desk, carefully positioned so that a shaft of light fell across the tablets and parchments before him. He looked up.

"Ah, Marcus… good. I've been wanting to see you." As the second man entered, the general frowned. "And who is this?"

Fronto shrugged and stepped across to stand behind a chair opposite his commander. The prefect walked to the table and saluted.

"General Caesar… I bring greetings from commander Labienus at Nemetocenna."

Caesar looked momentarily surprised.

"Indeed? And news, I presume?"

The prefect smiled.

"News, indeed, sir."

"Well, go on..." the general prompted.

"Firstly, I bear tidings of legate Crassus and the Seventh in Armorica."

Fronto leaned on the seat back and turned with interest at this. Caesar's expression hardened, and the legate realised that he could not decide whether he hoped for success or failure on the part of the young nobleman.

"Legate Crassus wishes to inform Caesar that he has brought the seven maritime tribes of Armorica under the eagle, sir, and has settled into quarters in the territory of the Veneti on the north coast."

The general blinked in surprise as the prefect continued.

"Commander Labienus wishes also to inform you, sir, that he has concluded favourable terms with the Belgic tribes and that, assuming that the Aduatuci are no longer a threat to the pax Romana, all Gaul is now yours."

Fronto whistled through his teeth.

"That little bugger actually conquered the northwest. With one legion!"

Caesar nodded.

"A reminder from young Crassus, clearly, of his powerful lineage. Good. He has done me a service. Thank you, prefect. Is there anything else?"

The prefect fished a scroll from his tunic and placed it respectfully on the table.

"A full account from the commander, sir, but that's it."

Caesar nodded.

"Go and find yourself something to eat and rest for a while. Thank you, prefect."

As the cavalry officer bowed and exited, the general turned to Fronto.

"Well?"

Fronto sighed.

"Do I speak freely?"

A nod.

"He's trying to upstage you. Be sure he's already sent a message back to Rome informing the people that matter of his achievement. You can claim it as your victory, but certain factions will no doubt attribute all your success this year to the work of Crassus. I really don't have any great suggestion what to do about it, though. If you stamp on his achievement, it'll make you look petty and ungrateful. You may just have to cheer him on."

Caesar nodded sourly.

"This, Fronto, is why I sometimes envy your avoidance of politics."

* * * * *

Labienus smiled at the young chieftain.

"We will be pulling out in a few weeks and taking the army to winter quarters, once Caesar confirms where that will be, but I intend to leave a small garrison at the fort here."

The chieftain waited for Septimius to translate and then shrugged and said something in his guttural dialect.

The auxiliary officer smiled.

"The lord says that's not necessary. They have made an oath, and they will stand by it."

Labienus laughed.

"I have no doubt about that, my friend. The people I am leaving behind will be there for your aid and support, not to control you. They will be mostly engineers and scribes. What we have begun here should not be stopped just because we leave for winter quarters."

The translation seemed to make the chief happy, and he reached out and clasped Labienus' hand before turning and walking away toward the gates of Nemetocenna.

The commander turned to Septimius and Pomponius.

"I think, unless you have any objection, that I will leave one cohort here over winter, and I'd like you two to take command? I realise that you were expecting to return to 'civilised' lands, but you have been in at the top here on what I've tried to achieve, and I trust you will continue the good work?"

Pomponius nodded.

"Frankly, sir, with all the projects on the horizon here, I'm a happy as a pig in muck."

Labienus laughed. Engineers never changed.

"I too am happy to stay," Septimius agreed.

"Good."

Labienus glanced across the hillside to where teams of engineers were, even now, creating good solid stone flags to pave the roads of the oppidum.

"Not Gaulish; not Roman. Gallo-Roman perhaps?"

* * * * *

Fronto woke with a start. A medical orderly was shaking him as gently and respectfully as possible, and had been doing so for a while as Fronto snored like a sick bear.

"Whassup?"

The orderly looked visibly relieved.

"Sir, the primus pilus is awake."

Fronto, suddenly awake, scrambled madly out of the seat in the hospital that he had spent much of the last three days occupying. Three days of waiting, but he had been practicing stretching and flexing his left arm to keep himself entertained, and the muscle was clearly healing. There was less strength in it than he had ever felt, and he could not pick up even the smallest or lightest thing, but the arm worked, and every day brought some small improvement.

In the side room that had been sealed off from the main tent, the primus pilus of the Tenth lay flat on a table. Once again it struck him just how badly wounded the man truly was. Lying there in just a tunic, there was still hardly a morsel of flesh visible from the neck down, swaddled as he was in linen, splints, wraps and more. Where the skin was visible, around his neck and hands and one lower leg, it was largely purple and yellow.

"You've looked better."

Fronto forced himself to smile.

Priscus rolled his eyes and then shut them tightly for a moment.

"I… I can't move. Any of me!"

Fronto nodded.

"Don't try. You're being held together with sticks and ropes right now. But the medical staff tell me that most of it will heal nicely."

"Most?"

Priscus glared at his commander.

"Your arms should be fine, and your right leg will be alright, so long as your ankle heals properly. Your left leg… well…"

Priscus growled.

"What about it?"

"You're going to have trouble walking fast. Maybe even walking at all."

"Shit!"

Fronto nodded.

"They've done everything possible, Gnaeus. You know that."

Priscus' growl intensified.

"If I can't walk, they should have let me die. You know what a crippled soldier has to look forward to. I'm not a rich patrician; I came up through the ranks. When I get thrown out I'll end up begging in the subura and getting pissed on by people. You know how it goes."

Fronto shook his head.

"You saved Caesar's life, so you'll not be needy. Hell, it's possible you'll be able to stay with the legions. Just let it heal and then see."

Priscus sighed and let his head drop back.

"How are the lads?"

Fronto laughed.

"They'll be a sight happier when they hear you're awake. They've been moping like grounded children. I don't know how you do it. They're frightened to death of you, but they get all soppy about you when you're not there."

"Ha."

Priscus let out a low grumble.

"I can't even raise my arm to drink anything."

"Good. The medici don't want you to at the moment."

"So..." Priscus sighed, "you've not said anything, but I assume from the general tone and the fact that you're sat here that we won?"

Fronto nodded.

"The Aduatuci are no more. Aduatuca is no more. There are currently more prisoners in this camp than there are soldiers! The legions are stood down for now and will be going off to winter quarters shortly. Galronus apparently got smashed over the head and is somewhere in here too, but he's going to be alright."

The legate stood for a long moment and stared down at his old friend and finally Priscus sighed again.

"Look, I'm still very tired. Perhaps I should try and sleep."

Fronto nodded, noting with some distress the tear that rolled unbidden down the centurion's cheek and into his ear. Forcing himself to smile positively, he squared his shoulders.

"I've got my arm working a little again. Keep working on your legs, and I'll come back tomorrow when you're better rested."

With a final wave, he turned and, wrapped in sadness, strode from the tent.

* * * * *

Paetus sat in the stockade at the rear of the Nemetocenna fort, dirty and hairy. Every day that passed made him feel less and less human. But he had heard the guards talking. In a week or so the prisoners would be taken south under guard of a small force of provosts and Gallic auxiliaries. It was a long journey back to Rome, and he'd had plenty of time to devise plans.

Getting free would be easy. Even getting away from the guards without being noticed should not be too much trouble. The big problem was going to be getting away without the other prisoners either getting involved and interfering or drawing the attention of the provosts. But he had plenty of time for that. He could not escape until he was safely within reach of Rome, where he could go to ground, anyway.

Rome.

And Caesar and Clodius.

* * * * *

The weather, already on the turn when the legions had arrived at Aduatuca, set in for autumn over the next two weeks. The mornings were misty and cold and invariably gave way to overcast and damp days. Every day, Fronto noted the faces of the men who were looking forward to winter quarters and being settled somewhere. Even when winter quarters were deep in Gallic lands, six months or more of being stationary meant that local traders, bars and brothels would spring up to entertain them.

Even the senior officers generally wore faraway looks as they yearned for family estates in Italia and the south; of the waves of the Mare Nostrum, or sitting on a balcony on the Esquiline hill, looking out over the roofs of Rome with a glass of Falernian in hand. Fronto, unsure of what his plans were for the winter, strode across the ground toward Caesar's tent.

Despite the gloom, he was feeling unusually cheerful. He had called in this morning for his daily visit to Priscus to find him partially-raised up and practicing lifting things with his left arm. The medical staff had been impressed with his progress. Piously, they put it down to the offerings and libations that Fronto habitually poured on the altar of Aescapulus as he entered and left the hospital. Fronto, ever a man of the world, put it down to the sheer indomitable bloody-mindedness of the Tenth's primus pilus.

Ingenuus' guards saluted as he passed into the gloom once again. Inside, Sabinus sat with Balbus opposite the general, who smiled.

"Ah, Fronto, good."

The legate strode across the tent and dropped wearily into a spare seat. Caesar frowned momentarily at the impropriety and then brushed it aside.

"How is your chief centurion today?"

Fronto sat back and began to flex his arm as he habitually did these days.

"He seems to be healing. I think he aims on being able to resume his post next year."

Caesar raised his eyebrows.

"The medical staff told me his military career was over."

Fronto laughed.

"Priscus? You know the centurionate, Caesar. They're a hardy breed. Look at Balventius; or Baculus. Baculus suffered over a dozen wounds at the Selle, but refused to go in a cart when he left with Labienus. The man actually marched off. You can't keep them down." The smile faded slightly.

"But I think you're right about Gnaeus; his combat days are over. Can't have a centurion limping at the front of the lines with a gammy leg."

Caesar nodded sagely.

"But we must do something for him. The man deserves to be recognised for what he did. He effectively saved both the army and my own life."

Fronto smiled.

"He shouldn't end up as a beggar in the streets of Rome, certainly. Perhaps a sizeable pension, like you offered Balventius? An estate in Cisalpine Gaul or Illyricum? A villa by the Adriatic?"

Caesar grinned; a cheeky and unexpected look that made Fronto frown suspiciously.

"What?"

"I have a better suggestion, I believe. Priscus, like Balventius, would not take to the life of a country gentleman."

"Ye-e-e-s" Fronto said slowly and uncertainly. "So?"

"I need a new camp prefect. A primus pilus needs to be fit and active, but I think you'll agree that previous evidence suggests the camp prefect can be a fairly sedentary person."

Fronto frowned.

"He won't like the idea. He'll hate the idea."

"More than retirement?"

Slowly, like a sunrise, the smile spread across Fronto's face.

"D'you know, general? You might be onto something there."

Caesar nodded.

"There will, of course, have to be a great deal of reorganisation this winter. We may even need to delay our campaigns next year."

"Next year?"

"Of course," Caesar smiled. "The lands of the Gauls and the Belgae are ours, but there's bound to be trouble with the Germans; or the Britons, or even the Aquitanii. We've stamped our presence here, but we're far from done."

Fronto nodded.

"Then the legions will be wintering in Gaul?"

Caesar turned to the great map of the northern lands on the wall of the tent behind him.

"Given the flighty nature of tribal politics and the newness of accords between us, I intend to keep the army close to the areas of activity this year. Labienus has concluded some solid treaties. I, myself, would have given less on our side of the treaty and taken more from theirs, but the result is not unsatisfactory. As part of his work, he intends to leave a caretaker garrison of one cohort at Nemetocenna."

His hand strayed west across the map.

"Crassus claims to have pacified the northwest. Hopefully he has been thorough and things are settled, but there is always the possibility of reprisal attacks and uprisings, and I don't like not leaving Crassus entirely unmanaged. So, most of the army will be picking up the stray cohorts at Nemetocenna and heading to the west, to Vindunum in the land of the Carnutes, where Crassus' force will rejoin them."

Fronto nodded, frowning.

"So you're leaving only Labienus' one cohort among the Belgae?"

Caesar sighed and an irritated look passed across his face.

"One of the things Labienus has agreed with the Belgae is that we will not station a large military force within their lands, only the caretaker garrison there. However, a force at Vindunum can be anywhere in northern or western Gaul, or in Belgae territory, in a matter of weeks."

He pinched the bridge of his nose.

"He has also arranged for a number of fairly beneficial trade agreements with the Belgae but, if I am to make the best of this, I will need to open a major trade route from Cisalpine Gaul across the mountains and down to Vesontio. The current route that runs up the Rhone is too slow and long."

He tapped at the southern edge of the map, where a deep pass was marked across the Alps between Lake Geneva and Cisalpine Gaul.

"The straightest route for trade would be through this pass, starting at the oppidum of Octodurus, capital of the Veragri tribe."

Balbus frowned.

"That's a bad area, general. Some of the braver merchants already use that pass, but it's rife with bandits and the Veragri levy unreasonable tolls to cross through their lands. That's why everyone goes along the coast into Narbonensis and up the Rhone."

"Indeed," the general nodded. "That's why I'm going to install a garrison at Octodurus. I thought the Twelfth. They distinguished themselves in battle this year."

Fronto shook his head.

"General, there's hardly anything left of the Twelfth!"

"Yes," the general agreed, "but they should only have to keep down banditry along the pass, and I'm intending to levy new troops in Cisalpine Gaul as time and money allow. The Twelfth will be close, so the reinforcements can join them in short order."

Fronto continued to shake his head.

"I don't like it, Caesar. It's dangerous. If anything goes wrong and trouble flares up, the Twelfth will be undermanned and on their own. The rest of the army will be several hundred miles away."

The general smiled.

"Fortunately, Fronto, I do not require your permission to do these things. That is the disposition of the legions then: the Twelfth at Octodurus, one cohort at Nemetocenna, and the rest in the west at Vindunum. As new troops are levied, they will be sent to the legions, starting with the Twelfth, to bring the numbers back up, hopefully to full strength, though I will set one of my lieutenants to the task, for I shall be needed in Rome."

Fronto caught the look on Sabinus' face. The staff officer clearly knew the task was destined for him. He suddenly realised Caesar was watching him intently.

"General?"

"Are you bound for Rome for the winter, Fronto, or to some drinking and whoring pit on the edge of the civilised world?"

Fronto grinned. "There are plenty of uncivilised drinking and whoring pits in Rome, general. Yes, I think it's time to visit the family."

"Good. Then we shall travel together."

Fronto continued to look at the general, the smile plastered across his face, nodding jovially while, inside, the prospect of travelling the best part of a thousand miles with the general and his entourage made his very soul cry out.

"That would be nice, sir."

Willing his smile to stay there, he turned to Balbus and Sabinus, both straight faced and avoiding his gaze.

"I take it we're not leaving immediately?"

Caesar shook his head. "A few days. Very well, gentlemen. I think we're done here."

The three officers stood, saluted, and left the tent, heaving sighs of relief as they stepped out into the air. Fronto stretched.

"You two coming for a drink? I need a drink."

"I'll bet you do. Get the amphora open. I'll be along very shortly." Balbus laughed.

Sabinus nodded."Since we're going to be departing shortly, perhaps we ought to get all the officers together for a send-off?"

Fronto grinned.

"I'll get the wine. You get the company."

As Balbus and Sabinus strode off about their business, Fronto called in quickly to see Cita. He could not be bothered to argue with the quartermaster and simply paid him above the odds for a large quantity of wine to be delivered to the legate's tent.

"You know you never invite me to these sessions, Fronto?"

The legate grinned.

"Maybe if you stopped complaining at me…Half an hour. My tent. Bring money and be prepared to lose it."

Leaving the man with his wagons, he strode across to his own encampment, the guards saluting him as he passed through the gateway. More salutes and polite greetings met him as he walked up the decumana to his tent. The atmosphere in the camp had improved no end since news had spread of Priscus' rapid recovery.

Smiling at the guards around the principia of the Tenth as he approached, Fronto frowned. A centurion he vaguely recognised was standing by the tent flap.

"Can I help you, centurion?"

The man, middle aged and surprisingly rosy and large for a combat officer, saluted. "May I speak to you, legate?"

Fronto shrugged and, throwing aside the tent flap, made his way inside. The centurion waited for a moment for a command and, receiving none, also shrugged and made his own way in. Fronto, in no mood to stand on ceremony, collapsed to his bunk, where he sat, removing his boots and sighing with relief.

"So. I know your face, centurion. First Cohort, yes?"

The man grinned. His smile was infectious, like a happy puppy, and Fronto realised that he was smiling himself without intending to. Idiot. He forced a straight face. In front of him, the centurion unbuckled his helmet and placed it beneath his arm. Removing the padded cap that protected him from chafing exposed his pink, shiny head; not a hair to be seen. Fronto struggled to keep his face straight.

"I am Servius Fabricius Carbo, centurion of the First Cohort, Second Century."

Fronto sighed and fell back on his bunk.

"Ah… this is about promotion. I see."

Carbo smiled. It was, Fronto noted, a confident and knowing smile. There was apparently more to this shiny, pink, chubby officer than at first there seemed.

"In a manner of speaking, sir. Essentially, I have taken the liberty of promoting myself."

"What?" Fronto gripped the bunk and turned his head.

"Sir, the primus pilus has been out of action for a long time now. The legion has to have a chief centurion. I am the second most senior man in the legion and the obvious choice for the position. I am quite capable of the job and, frankly, since you and Priscus were such good friends, it's going to be very unpleasant for you trying to organise his replacement, which is, I assume, why it's taking so long."

Fronto stared at the man. "What if Priscus can retain his position?"

Carbo shook his head. "You know that's not going to happen, sir. You're in denial. That's why I have to take charge."

"What?"

Fronto's voice had gone up an octave and yet, inside, he realised this was not so much through anger, but more a mixture of shock and regret.

"Legate, you've lost two senior centurions this year. More than that, I'm very well aware that they were two of your best friends. The reason the Tenth works so well and functions beyond all expectations is that the officers know each other well and work well together. You need people like Priscus and Velius who will talk straight to you…" he smiled that infectious smile again "… and even down to you, when necessary. You need that as much as the Tenth needs you."

As Fronto watched, his mouth hanging open, Carbo jabbed his vine staff into the ground, hung his helmet on it, strolled over to the cabinet where the last of Fronto's current wine store was, and poured two cups.

"Drink."

Fronto stared at the cup and then took it, dumfounded.

"You presume a great deal, Centurion Carbo."

The shiny pink face split into that wide grin again. "Servius if you prefer sir, when we're alone, but Carbo's fine if you're uncomfortable with it."

Fronto took a deep quaff from the cup and stared over the rim at this incredibly insolent man. His face split into a smile. "I think we'll get on just fine, Servius. But there's a condition attached to the position."

Carbo nodded professionally. "And that would be?"

"Finding an excuse for me not to travel back to Rome with the general."

Carbo smiled and refilled his commander's cup.

"Rome? Now? Not a hope, Marcus. You'll be busy here for a while. I have some new schedules, promotions, budgets and so on. And we have to select a new training officer. And of course, you need to be here during the hand-over between Priscus and myself. Oh, no. You could be here for weeks."

Fronto grinned. "I was hoping you'd say that. A lot of the senior officers will be here shortly, with enough wine to float a trireme. I think it's time they met you."

He raised an eyebrow humorously. "Can you play dice?"

* * * * *

The light of the oil lamps and the fire in the hearth cast dancing golden waves around the shadowy interior of the room. Crimson drapes covered the leaded windows and one had to squint to pick out even the most basic detail on the intricate wall paintings. From the corner of the room in deep shadow, a strong hand reached out, a gold signet ring on the little finger, and collected the jewelled glass from the small table.

Publius Clodius Pulcher raised his own glass in salute to his shadowy companion and took a quick drink, frowning at the taste.

"I distinctly remember telling Appio to get the best Falernian. I suspect he bought a cheap substitute and pocketed the change. I shall have him flogged until he is unrecognisable."

The hidden figure rumbled and chuckled in a deep voice.

"You will set a dangerous precedent by punishing a man with vision and a taste for profit. Most governors and senators are no better."

Clodius smiled; a crocodile smile. "Perhaps. You've heard that, despite my best efforts, Cicero has returned from exile?"

"Yes. He will likely pick up where he left off in his attempts to prosecute you."

Clodius laughed. "I have taken the first step there. I had him attacked and beaten on the Clivus Scauri yesterday. We also wrecked his house and burned down that of his brother. I trust now that he will think twice before bringing up old cases."

There was another deep laugh from the shadows.

"Burning down his brother's house may have been a mistake. The younger Cicero commands one of Caesar's legions and the man has already set his sight on you."

Clodius shook his head dismissively.

"Caesar is a jumped up little fish trying to command a pond full of pike. He seems to think he's invincible, but I assure you he's not. I have several people quite close the general, some of whom are somewhat disaffected with him. I am aware of every move he makes, often before he's made it. No; Caesar's not a worry to me. My sister… now she's a worry. I have to find a way to contain her and dampen down her more excessive desires."

The shadowy figure laughed once more and replaced the glass on the table.

"I had best leave. Terentius' play will finish presently, and there will be comment if I am not seen to stand and applaud at the end."

As Clodius nodded respectfully, the figure stood in the shadowy corner and wrapped the toga more tightly about himself.

"As always, this conversation never took place. I was never here."

Clodius nodded again, leaning back on his couch.

"Enjoy the post-theatre party."

"I shall," the visitor yawned, "as much as possible. Remember: be careful. And, regardless of what you say, watch Caesar. He may yet surprise you."

Clodius took another sip of wine as the figure left the room. Moments later he heard the door open and close, and he was alone once more. Grinding his teeth, he flung the glass at the fire.

"To Hades with Caesar. Damn the man."

END

Author's Note

The Belgae are noted by Caesar to be the fiercest of all the Gaulish peoples. The divisions of Gaul in this period are somewhat complex, at least from a Roman point of view. Rome neatly divides the lands that are modern France and Belgium into three parts: the lands of the Gauls, the Belgae, and the Aquitanian tribes. These are treated as being subdivisions of the whole and yet, from the natives' point of view (which is not truly recorded for posterity) there was likely no division beyond their own tribes in their minds.

I have attempted in this work to define a certain something among the Belgic tribes that separated them from the rest of Gaul, while keeping them within a 'racial umbrella'.

One of my main focuses in this book has been to take a slight move away from the straightforward military campaign that was the first book, placing Fronto in charge of smaller missions where possible and tying a little more 'adventure' into the war. This was a deliberate attempt to shift the direction of the Marius' Mules series away from being a fictionalised account of Caesar's war diary and more towards being a new set of tales based upon the events told therein - a move that will become more apparent in the following stories.

Perhaps the main facet of the book that could do with a little explanation is the new legions. These two were, according to Caesar, raised in Cisalpine Gaul, which would make them Romans, in essence. I have taken the liberty of twisting this and having them raised in the new lands of Transalpine Gaul, partially to give the army a little extra tension and some new fascinating characters, but partially also to explain why the Thirteenth and Fourteenth were assigned unique badges rather than the standard bull emblem adopted by the rest of Caesar's legions. The Fourteenth were also often-overlooked and left to guard the baggage train.

The location of Bibrax (site of my favourite siege) is debated, and so the terrain is largely fictionalised, though it is based on several sites in the area.

Once again, this is a work of fiction and not a direct copy of the accepted history and therefore the reader can account for any changes or mistakes from the canon as my own invention to excite and entertain.

Simon Turney - Feb 2013

Full Glossary of Terms

Ad aciem: military command essentially equivalent to 'Battle stations!'.
Amphora (pl. Amphorae): A large pottery storage container, generally used for wine or olive oil.
Aquilifer: a specialised standard bearer that carried a legion's eagle standard.
Aurora: Roman Goddess of the dawn, sister of Sol and Luna.
Bacchanalia: the wild and often drunken festival of Bacchus.
Buccina: A curved horn-like musical instrument used primarily by the military for relaying signals, along with the cornu.
Capsarius: Legionary soldiers trained as combat medics, whose job was to patch men up in the field until they could reach a hospital.
Civitas: Latin name given to a certain class of civil settlement, often the capital of a tribal group or a former military base.
Cloaca Maxima: The great sewer of republican Rome that drained the forum into the Tiber.
Contubernium (pl. Contubernia): the smallest division of unit in the Roman legion, numbering eight men who shared a tent.
Cornu: A G-shaped horn-like musical instrument used primarily by the military for relaying signals, along with the buccina. A trumpeter was called a cornicen.
Corona: Lit: 'Crowns'. Awards given to military officers. The Corona Muralis and Castrensis were awards for storming enemy walls, while the Aurea was for an outstanding single combat.
Curia: the meeting place of the senate in the forum of Rome.
Cursus Honorum: The ladder of political and military positions a noble Roman is expected to ascend.
Decurion: 1) The civil council of a Roman town. 2) Lesser cavalry officer, serving under a cavalry prefect, with command of thirty two men.
Dolabra: entrenching tool, carried by a legionary, which served as a shovel, pick and axe combined.
Duplicarius: A soldier on double the basic pay.
Equestrian: The often wealthier, though less noble mercantile class, known as knights.
Foederati: non-Roman states who held treaties with Rome and gained some rights under Roman law.
Gaesatus: a spearman, usually a mercenary of Gallic origin.

Gladius: the Roman army's standard short, stabbing sword, originally based on a Spanish sword design.
Groma: the chief surveying instrument of a Roman military engineer, used for marking out straight lines and calculating angles.
Haruspex (pl. Haruspices): A religious official who confirms the will of the Gods through signs and by inspecting the entrails of animals.
Immunes: legionary soldiers who possessed specialist skills and were consequently excused the more onerous duties.
Kalends: the first day of the Roman month, based on the new moon with the 'nones' being the half moon around the 5th-7th of the month and the 'ides' being the full moon around the 13th-15th.
Labrum: Large dish on a pedestal filled with fresh water in the hot room of a bath house.
Laconicum: the steam room or sauna in a Roman bath house.
Laqueus: a garrotte usually used by gladiators to restrain an opponent's arm, but also occasionally used to cause death by strangulation.
Legatus: Commander of a Roman legion
Lilia (Lit. 'Lilies'): defensive pits three feet deep with a sharpened stake at the bottom, disguised with undergrowth, to hamper attackers.
Mansio and **mutatio**: stopping places on the Roman road network for officials, military staff and couriers to stay or exchange horses if necessary.
Mare Nostrum: Latin name for the Mediterranean Sea (literally 'Our Sea')
Mars Gravidus: an aspect of the Roman war god, 'he who precedes the army in battle', was the God prayed to when an army went to war.
Miles: the Roman name for a soldier, from which we derive the words military and militia among others.
Octodurus: now Martigny in Switzerland, at the Northern end of the Great Saint Bernard Pass.
Optio: A legionary centurion's second in command.
Pilum (p: Pila) : the army's standard javelin, with a wooden stock and a long, heavy lead point.
Pilus Prior: The most senior centurion of a cohort and one of the more senior in a legion.
Praetor: a title granted to the commander of an army. cf the Praetorian Cohort.

Praetorian Cohort: personal bodyguard of a General.
Primus Pilus: The chief centurion of a legion. Essentially the second in command of a legion.
Pugio: the standard broad bladed dagger of the Roman military.
Quadriga: a chariot drawn by four horses, such as seen at the great races in the circus of Rome.
Samarobriva: oppidum on the Somme River, now called Amiens.
Scorpion, Ballista & Onager: Siege engines. The Scorpion was a large crossbow on a stand, the Ballista a giant missile throwing crossbow, and the Onager a stone hurling catapult.
Signifer: A century's standard bearer, also responsible for dealing with pay, burial club and much of a unit's bureaucracy.
Subura: a lower-class area of ancient Rome, close to the forum, that was home to the red-light district'.
Testudo: Lit- Tortoise. Military formation in which a century of men closes up in a rectangle and creates four walls and a roof for the unit with their shields.
Triclinium: The dining room of a Roman house or villa
Trierarch: Commander of a Trireme or other Roman military ship.
Turma: A small detachment of a cavalry ala consisting of thirty two men led by a decurion.
Vexillum (Pl. Vexilli): The standard or flag of a legion.
Vindunum: later the Roman Civitas Cenomanorum, and now Le Mans in France.
Vineae: moveable wattle and leather wheeled shelters that covered siege works and attacking soldiers from enemy missiles.

If you enjoyed the Marius' Mules series why not also try:

The Thief's Tale by S.J.A. Turney

Istanbul, 1481. The once great city of Constantine that now forms the heart of the Ottoman empire is a strange mix of Christian, Turk and Jew. Despite the benevolent reign of the Sultan Bayezid II, the conquest is still a recent memory, and emotions run high among the inhabitants, with danger never far beneath the surface. Skiouros and Lykaion, the sons of a Greek country farmer, are conscripted into the ranks of the famous Janissary guards and taken to Istanbul where they will play a pivotal, if unsung, role in the history of the new regime. As Skiouros escapes into the Greek quarter and vanishes among its streets to survive on his wits alone, Lykaion remains with the slave chain to fulfill his destiny and become an Islamic convert and a guard of the Imperial palace. Brothers they remain, though standing to either side of an unimaginable divide. On a fateful day in late autumn 1490, Skiouros picks the wrong pocket and begins to unravel a plot that reaches to the very highest peaks of Imperial power. He and his brother are about to be left with the most difficult decision faced by a conquered Greek: whether the rule of the Ottoman Sultan is worth saving.

Legionary by Gordon Doherty

The Roman Empire is crumbling, and a shadow looms in the east. 376 AD: the Eastern Roman Empire is alone against the tide of barbarians swelling on her borders. Emperor Valens juggles the paltry border defences to stave off invasion from the Goths north of the Danube. Meanwhile, in Constantinople, a pact between faith and politics spawns a lethal plot that will bring the dark and massive hordes from the east crashing down on these struggling borders. The fates conspire to see Numerius Vitellius Pavo, enslaved as a boy after the death of his legionary father, thrust into the limitanei, the border legions, just before they are sent to recapture the long-lost eastern Kingdom of Bosporus. He is cast into the jaws of this plot, so twisted that the survival of the entire Roman world hangs in the balance.

CPSIA information can be obtained
at www.ICGtesting.com
Printed in the USA
LVOW04s1051140316
479059LV00033B/914/P

9 781484 968970